TWILIGHT

Also by Markus Heitz

THE DWARVES

The War of the Dwarves
The Revenge of the Dwarves
The Fate of the Dwarves
The Triumph of the Dwarves

LEGENDS OF THE ÄLFAR

Righteous Fury
Devastating Hate
Dark Paths
Raging Storm

DOORS

Doors ? Colony
Doors ! Field of Blood

Oneiros
AERA: The Return of the Ancient Gods

Some say history is made by the victors.
Sometimes it's rewritten by an author.

MARKUS HEITZ

DO✖RS

TWILIGHT

Jo Fletcher
BOOKS

First published as *Doors X Dämmerung* by Verlagsgruppe Droemer Knaur,
Germany, in 2018
First published in Great Britain in 2021 by

Jo Fletcher Books, an imprint of
Quercus Editions Ltd,
Carmelite House
50 Victoria Embankment
London EC4Y 0DZ

An Hachette UK company

A CIP catalogue record for this book is available
from the British Library

PB ISBN 978 1 52940 235 3
EB ISBN 978 152940 236 0

10 9 8 7 6 5 4 3 2 1

Typeset by CC Book Production
Printed and bound in Great Britain by Clays Ltd, Elcograf S.p.A.

Papers used by Jo Fletcher Books are from well-managed forests
and other responsible sources.

If you would like to know how Viktor von Troneg and his team of experts came to be tasked with rescuing Anna-Lena van Dam and how they managed to enter the cave system beneath the van Dam estate, read from the beginning.

If you would like to go straight to the door marked with the X, please start with Chapter IV on page 97.

INTRODUCTION

FIRST DEAD END

Trepidation.

Trepidation and a sinking sense of hopelessness were all she could feel in the darkness as she wandered endlessly through the stone labyrinth, refusing to succumb to fear.

The smell was one known only to ancient buildings, of cold stone, damp dust and the millennia of abandonment. The leather soles of her high-heeled shoes scraped over rocky ground and slipped on the loose stones rattling around her, but there was no chance of her giving up.

She knew this place; she had heard plenty about it and now she had to find a way to leave – or remain there for ever. Death was coming for her more quickly than she could have imagined: she understood that now.

She tried to keep her breathing as quiet as possible as the LED light on her mobile phone glimmered into life for a promising second, before immediately switching off again, as if out of spite. It continued to flicker on and off, emanating a frantic, cold glow like a stroboscope.

The young woman swiped and tapped the display with her broken fingers again and again, but to no avail. The indifferent message remained: No Service.

If she had been less afraid, she might have felt the

energy all around her, as pervasive as the air she was breathing. It was not electrical, nuclear or even thermal, but rather the sort of energy that might accumulate at a spiritual site: churches, monasteries and sacred places in the middle of forests were full of this kind of energy.

As her phone continued to flash on and off, the young woman swore quietly to herself. 'Stay on!' she whispered, infuriated.

Then the little light lit up and illuminated her face, tearing it out of the darkness. Her features were striking: pure, bright, freckled skin with a light layer of make-up, her coppery hair artfully arranged in a weather-beaten up-do. She wore a small stud in her left nostril and a pair of expensive diamond earrings that glittered in the light as if she were seeking to impress a congregation of the great and the good.

But there was no one around to be impressed by her distinctive appearance.

Dazzled by the light, the young woman screwed her eyes shut and her phone slipped out of her usually well-manicured fingers: the last few hours had clearly taken their toll.

As the mobile fell to the ground, the beam of light passed down her body, briefly illuminating her dark green silk dress, now torn and flecked with mud. It revealed scratched and filthy forearms, the shattered glass of her eye-wateringly expensive watch, a small handbag clutched under her right arm and, finally, the black evening courts, the soles and uppers now covered with scratches. There was nothing practical about this attire for such an environment: her visit here was entirely unplanned.

The phone skipped across the floor and the cold white LED beam brought the stony, dusty ground out of the darkness and illuminated several empty cartridge cases, for use in a modern military weapon. The sound of the impact echoed around the room, the full size of which was beyond the reach of the small light.

After one final rattle, the phone settled on the ground with its light facing downwards. Blackness descended.

'Kcuf.' The young woman quickly bent down and picked up the device. 'Gnikcuf lleh!'

She was fully aware that words were coming out of her mouth backwards: she'd discovered it was just one of the many idiosyncrasies of this place. At first she had doubted her own sanity, then gradually she'd managed to suppress that fear. There were worse things down here.

She picked up the mobile and flashed the light all around her, illuminating walls made of grey concrete and reddish-brown brick that receded into the distance. Eddies of whirling dust danced their way through the artificial brightness like tiny moths attracted to the glow.

Then the beam passed over a series of doors made of stone and weathered wood. Three of them bore wrought-iron knockers and two were bare. The ring that should have been held in the mouth of the beautifully crafted creature adorning the second door was missing. The doors were embedded in the rocky wall as if their existence in this godforsaken place was entirely natural.

'On erom,' she whispered in frustration. 'Please, no more doors!' Her prayer was purely rhetorical.

She walked forwards slowly and cast her light over the

five doors. She had realised long ago that she was not the first visitor to try to unlock the secrets of this mysterious place. There was more than a kernel of truth to her mother's stories after all.

That knowledge was of no help whatsoever.

Markings both old and new were carved into the stone and wood; some had been scratched in, others added in pen, and they were mostly written in languages the young woman did not understand. Some of the characters might have been decipherable by archaeologists or experts in ancient and pre-history; some might even have been of interest to cryptologists or etymologists or those with knowledge of Eastern studies.

What stood out. however, were the thick red question marks on the first three doors, drawn on in lipstick and clearly new.

'Pull yourself together,' she whispered to herself, wiping a dirty strand of hair from her green eyes. Her forehead glistened with sweat and her deodorant had long since given up on her. It was not at all cold in the maze and running had become increasingly more of an ordeal with each futile escape attempt. She was ravaged by hunger and thirst and she could feel the blisters on her feet rubbing with every step she took, but she dared not walk around barefoot. 'Come on now!'

She tried to slow her breathing as she stepped up once more and withdrew a red lipstick from her handbag.

As she walked off the step, the now familiar feeling of a world being turned upside down grabbed her from behind her navel and flipped her over. The first time it had happened, she'd panicked and injured herself on the wall next to her. The second time the world turned on its axis, she found herself half drifting and had managed to manoeuvre herself so she was half pressed up against the wall in an attempt to offset the worst of the damage when gravity reasserted itself. This time she carefully raised her arms in order to remain upright.

She floated, waiting for her inevitable painful return to the stone floor.

Everything loose on the ground started to rattle and clatter around; fine particles of dust swam through the lamplight, accompanied by pebbles, bones and pieces of metal and fabric that had belonged to previous visitors.

After ten seconds, everything crashed to the ground.

She scrambled to her feet and took a few steps, stopping in front of the furthermost of the five doors: the one made from weathered oak. Instead of a knocker, it had a sliding bolt and a box lock. Her grandmother had once told her a story about this door, but she couldn't remember any of the details. The metal was thin, with inlays of gold, tarnished silver and some sort of copper alloy. Using her mobile light as a guide, she pulled out her lipstick and painted a large exclamation mark on it.

A noise suddenly erupted from the surrounding darkness. All she could hear was the pounding of heavy paws and the grinding of claws. She didn't even notice smearing lipstick on her palm as she instinctively covered the light with her hand. The beam scattered through her fingers, framing her face and eyes as if she were in a silent film.

She didn't dare turn off the light, in case she couldn't make it turn back on again.

Listen. Hold your breath. Just one more time.

She hadn't yet caught sight of her pursuer, but she knew this creature was on her tail. Perhaps it was there to guard this place? Or perhaps it was just a being who had heard her moving around and wanted to put a stop to it.

She inched towards the fourth door, which was made of stone with a knocker in the centre, the only one without a marking, and stood silently with her back against the wall, so as not to be ambushed in the darkness.

The quiet scuttling stopped abruptly.

Almost there, she thought as she placed her hand carefully on the latch and tried to push it down. Nothing happened.

She tried the door again while she carried on looking around her, before stopping to listen once more.

All was quiet.

'Kniht,' she muttered, taking a chance and illuminating the door knocker. 'Emoc on, think!'

A heavy silver ring with a bulge at the bottom could be seen in the elaborately carved ebony wolf's mouth resting imposingly on the metal plate in the centre of the door. The stone was dark grey with black grain, with inlays of white marble and onyx forming incomprehensible symmetrical symbols.

She hesitantly stretched out a hand, grabbed the ring and knocked hard against the stone, leaving behind some of the red lipstick that had stuck to her hand.

The noise was metallic, hollow and far too loud, filling the entire room with a deafening *boom*, as if someone had simultaneously played all the notes on an organ in a cathedral. An iridescent flickering accompanied the eerie yet welcoming clamour above the door. All the worlds and planets and creatures of the known and unknown universe now seemed to gather to witness her arrival.

The flickering light leaped to the other doors, illuminating them briefly, the markings on the walls gleaming as if they'd been written in gold and giving off a warm light that betrayed the presence of a fine vein in the rock. It was visible for no more than the duration of a heartbeat. A crackle and a crunch flew through the room before mutating into a whisper and a rustle.

The young woman suddenly felt as if a giant were pressing down hard on her shoulders, the gravity in the room becoming overwhelming, forcing her to her knees and compressing her vertebrae and joints so hard that she cried out in agony – but it stopped as suddenly as it had started.

The darkness returned; the weight was lifted.

'What on earth . . . ?' she muttered, rising to her feet.

She put her hand gently back on the latch, which this time offered no resistance.

Relieved, she slowly opened the door.

She was met with the presence of a soft, silvery light, accompanied by the sound of owls hooting and foxes barking, intermingled with the peaceful whoosh of falling leaves. A fresh, cleansing wind began to dance through her coppery hair. It felt as if she were being offered the freedom she had been hoping for the whole time she had been wandering through the maze.

She wanted nothing more than to step across the threshold into a world that could soothe her ills – then the growl of a predator cut through the idyll like a knife, stopping her in her tracks. It was followed by the lingering, mournful howling of a wolf: a pack was being summoned for the hunt. She drew her foot back carefully: this was a freedom she would pay for with her life. She knew she wouldn't stand a chance against such skilled hunters.

The silvery light lit up the area behind her, revealing an empty cavernously high room with only one entrance: the one she had come through. As well as the scribbled inscriptions, notes and memos from previous visitors, the brick and concrete walls were also decorated with rusty brown splodges and ancient flecks of spilled blood. Some had used it to write a final message or curse before succumbing to their anonymous deaths.

The broken ring of the destroyed door knocker lay on the ground, alongside all manner of broken grey bones and the scattered remains of skeletons.

The light also revealed something else.

A man – a *dead* man – could be seen just at the edge of the light's reach, through the haze, where silver became ghostly grey, crouching in an unnatural position. He was wearing grey-white camouflage gear with a Kevlar vest over the top; in his right hand he clutched a sub-machine gun. Empty magazines and dozens of bullet casings littered the floor around him. His throat had been slit and the blood that had poured out of it had dried and plastered his body.

Panting, the young woman quickly shut the door and using her phone, once again the only source of light, saw a large red X marked on it. 'Not there,' she whispered. 'I can't . . .'

The sound of heavy paws could be heard again, coming ever closer, accompanied by a scratching noise, as if there were several beasts approaching, all manner of beings who, in her imagination at least, would do all manner of terrible things to her if she ever found herself in their clutches.

'Go away!' The young woman shone the light all around her as if its weak glow suddenly had the lethal cutting power of an industrial laser. 'Evael em enola! I've got a gun!' she lied. 'Stay yawa morf em!'

For an instant, an enormous shadow could be seen in the trembling cone of light – then everything went dark.

'Kcuf! *Fuck!*' She frantically pulled on the door knocker and the gleam of the wood lit up the room. With a cry of anguish, she yanked the door open again.

The silvery light struck her once more as the wind blew through her hair as if to welcome her in.

The young woman hurriedly crossed the threshold and entered a world she knew would not offer her the freedom she desired. Perhaps she had merely exchanged a quick death for a slow one.

Giving up was out of the question, however.

She armed herself with a branch from the ground and ran off into the unknown.

CHAPTER I

Germany, Frankfurt am Main

Viktor headed straight through the 'Nothing to Declare' doors. The white duffle bag slung over his right shoulder and his casual sporty attire rendered him utterly inconspicuous amid the throng in the arrivals hall.

The plane had been stacked for more than an hour as a result of bad weather, turning what ought to have been a forty-minute flight into a two-hour débâcle as they waited for a runway to become available. It had made Viktor's mood somewhat sub-optimal, and it was only exacerbated by the rumblings in his stomach.

He looked at his phone and read the message from his prospective client once more:

DEAR MR VON TRONEG
LOOKING FORWARD TO MEETING YOU AND GLAD TO HEAR YOU'RE
WILLING TO START SOON. MY CHAUFFEUR MATTHIAS WILL PICK YOU
UP FROM ARRIVALS. KEEP AN EYE OUT FOR HIM THERE.
REGARDS
WALTER VAN DAM

Viktor looked around.

There were several people milling around at the exit holding pieces of cardboard, mini whiteboards or tablets bearing the names of the passengers they were waiting for, although his name was nowhere to be seen.

He decided to carry on through the hall to track the man down. His blue eyes were concealed behind a pair of sunglasses and on his head he wore a white baseball cap. He was in his mid-twenties, in excellent shape, and hardly seemed to notice the weight of his waterproof bag; one of the reasons it had taken him very little time since leaving his previous job to become one of the finest potholers in the world.

'Where is this chap?' Viktor muttered, pulling out his phone again to give his client a ring, when he spied a man in a dark blue suit with a cap and black leather gloves. He was holding a printed card that read 'Cave Tours' and carried himself in a manner reminiscent of a gentleman's valet.

Van Dam should have called him Jeeves as his work pseudonym, Viktor thought. He turned around and waded through the crowd towards Matthias; as he did so, he thought about Walter van Dam, about whom there was disconcertingly little information to be found online.

He'd been born in the Netherlands and was the head of a global import/export company founded for overseas trade in the eighteenth century. Very little was known about the man himself; he shied away from the public gaze and for the most part sent proxies to his official engagements. The van Dam family had allegedly branched out further, but Viktor had not been able to find out much beyond that. That was understandable, as there was quite a trade in kidnapping and ransoming the very rich. The less the public knew about you, the better.

It was ultimately irrelevant to Viktor, as long as the Dutchman did not attempt to drag him into any criminal activity. The first payment had already landed in his account and was substantially higher than anything the German state had paid him for far more dangerous jobs.

Next to the chauffeur stood a gaunt man about fifty years old, wearing a bespoke checked suit and highly polished brown shoes that made him look a bit like an Oxford professor. His foot was resting on an expensive-looking aluminium case, as if he were trying to stop it escaping, and he was reading a newspaper. The designer glasses gave him an arrogant demeanour.

'Good afternoon, gentlemen.' Viktor removed his own sunglasses, catching a glimpse of his three-day-old beard in the reflection as he did so. 'Mr van Dam is expecting me. My name is Viktor Troneg.'

'Welcome to Frankfurt.' The chauffeur inclined his head in greeting. 'My name is Matthias. The rest haven't arrived yet.' He gestured towards the other man, who was still absorbed in his reading and did not react. 'May I take this opportunity to introduce you to Professor Friedemann, renowned speleologist and geologist.'

Viktor inclined his head and Friedemann, whose long grey hair was drawn up in a ponytail, nodded in reply without looking up from his newspaper; Viktor thought his angular face had more than a passing resemblance to a skull.

'This is Mr von Troneg, a potholer and free-climber,' Matthias said. 'From what I gather, he's got quite the international reputation.'

'Very good.' Friedemann turned the page and busied himself in the next article.

Viktor already knew which one he liked the least. 'Were we all on the same flight?' he asked.

'You were indeed, Mr von Troneg.'

'No need to keep the *von*. I'm not overly keen on my ancestral name.' Then he broke into a grin. 'Whatever would you have done if it had crashed?' he asked.

'The plane? Highly unlikely,' replied Matthias. 'In any case the clairvoyant wouldn't have boarded.' He laughed drily.

'Clairvoyant? Well, that's something, I suppose.' Viktor lifted up his baseball cap and slicked his long black hair back before replacing it. 'And what if she *had* got on?'

'She'd have suffered a tragic death, and rightly so,' commented Friedemann, without looking up. He carefully adjusted his glasses.

Viktor grinned and was about to respond when he noticed a particular woman out of the corner of his eye – and he clearly wasn't the only one: practically all the passengers appeared to have turned their gaze in her direction.

She was dressed in a tight-fitting, cream-coloured designer dress and pushing a large, outrageously expensive designer suitcase in front her. With a fashionable handbag hanging artfully from her right arm and large sunglasses hiding her eyes, she had the aura of an haute couture model. She held a vanity case in her left hand. Her curly long blonde hair had a theatrically black strand at the front.

Viktor stood there, admiring her. 'Impressive entrance.'

'I hope you're being ironic.' Friedemann finally looked up from his paper and turned his eyes towards her. 'Dreadful person. Sat behind me on the flight and kept ordering champagne. They must have wanted to drown her in it by the end.'

'That is Ms Coco Fendi,' the chauffeur clarified, raising his arm to catch her attention. 'Our clairvoyant, gentlemen.'

'Really? *Coco Fendi*?' Viktor had to laugh. 'Perfect name for a performer.'

'Coco Fendi: a cross between a handbag and a fashion brand. I'm assuming she's really called Sabine Müller or something,' Friedemann added. 'A double fraud, if you ask me. Only frauds need to dress up like that much of a cliché to be able to perform.'

As Ms Fendi was walking through the hall in search of her welcoming party, the lock on her vanity case snapped open, scattering the contents all over the floor. Pendulums, crystals, tarot cards, bone cubes and runestones rattled and rolled around as if a magician's box had exploded. All that appeared to be missing was a white rabbit, a black candle and a painted skull.

'She didn't see that coming.' Friedemann looked back down at his newspaper. 'Not a good sign at all, gents.' The lenses of his glasses flashed in the light, as if to underscore his statement.

Coco Fendi swore so loudly that she could be heard from the other side of the hall: not the sort of attitude her initial appearance suggested. She let go of her suitcase and bent down to pick up her paraphernalia, which was made all the more difficult by her tight dress.

Viktor was about to walk over and help her when a thickset man in a tight jacket, baggy jeans and crumpled shirt approached from the magazine stand. He acknowledged her briefly before putting his own bag down and lowering himself to his knees to assist in the clean-up operation.

'The white knight has come to rescue his fair medium,' observed Friedemann, who had become a rather acerbic commentator.

'By your leave, that's Doctor Ingo Theobald,' explained Matthias. 'He's part of the team as well.'

'Ah, a doctor? Good.' Viktor folded his arms, happy not to intervene now that Fendi and Theobald were doing such a good job of clearing up. 'Still a shame, though. I'd hoped we'd have another young woman in the group.'

'I bet you'd regret that almost immediately,' barked Friedemann with the pomposity of a snobbish fifty-year-old. 'There's not much that can beat the wisdom that comes with age. Knowledge is power and this woman has neither years nor knowledge on her side.'

Viktor wondered how the man was able to see what was going on around him without moving his eyes. *A master of peripheral vision*, he thought.

Coco Fendi was so engrossed in the recovery of her belongings that she only belatedly noticed the helper kneeling beside her.

'Thank you – that's most kind of you.' Her tight dress

was hindering her movements somewhat, but that was the price one paid for beautiful, expensive clothing, which she could well afford. Her bright hair obscured her vision, the curls hanging like a curtain in front of her eyes. 'A true gentleman.'

She positioned her enormous suitcase as a shield, preventing anyone from absconding with her possessions. The small group of people around the chauffeur disappeared behind it.

Coco turned towards her saviour, stroked her hair out of her face and recognised Ingo Theobald, a man in his early forties with greying blond hair falling down to his neck. A pair of youthfully nerdy nickel glasses perched on his unshaven face.

'You?' she laughed, kissing him on the mouth.

Ingo let it happen more out of surprise than anything else. 'What are you doing here?' he asked in astonishment.

'Working,' she responded curtly, bridling at his obvious discomfort at meeting her here. She picked up the tarot cards. 'And you? Investigating a case?'

'Working.' He examined her, then looked over her suitcase at the uniformed chauffeur waving at them. 'Don't tell me . . .'

Coco raised her eyes and understood. 'No! You as well?'

Ingo sighed and took her free hand in his. 'Don't do this, Beate. It's going to be incredibly dangerous!'

'It's well paid,' she retorted. 'And don't call me that. I am Coco Fendi, the acclaimed clairvoyant and medium, known for my work on the radio, television and online. Do you know how many followers I've got?'

She stuffed her scattered belongings back into the case; there would be time to sort everything out later.

Ingo had not expected to see Beate again, and certainly not to learn that they had been commissioned by the same company. He looked at her reproachfully, wanting to say something back – something cruel, like, being a clairvoyant, she must have known they were going to meet again at the airport. Instead, he said, 'That outfit's a bit much, isn't it? You're pretty much confirming every prejudice under the sun about people in your line of work.'

'It's all part of my brand. I'm like Elvira, Mistress of the Dark. Only more stylish.'

'You do realise that Elvira was satirising the whole gothic horror genre?'

'I don't care. I'm giving people what they expect, and that makes them happy – people love clichés. You know I tried doing it differently before and how much of a failure that was. So now they're getting the mother of all extravagant psychics.' Coco kissed him again behind the suitcase and caressed his cheek. 'Play along. Please. Once we're upstairs you can fuck me like it's going out of fashion, I promise.' She looked at him intensely. 'Please, Ingo – it was only your expertise that got me this job.'

'We're not talking about one of your shows where all you've got to do is entertain your followers,' he responded, concerned.

'Just let me do me, okay?' she asked, her voice noticeably cooler. Her kisses had failed to win him around, which annoyed her greatly. She slammed the case closed and snapped the locks shut. 'Just one more time. Then I'll have got enough money together.'

Ingo frowned, remaining silent as they stood up. Thanks to her love of the high life, Beate was always in dire financial straits. She viewed herself as being from the tradition of divas in the Roaring Twenties, although there weren't many men nowadays willing to bankroll a spiritualist. The fact that she looked like a garish walking cliché didn't bother her in the slightest. He found her explanation plausible, but she was giving little away. Beate was old enough to decide how she wanted to come across.

'Wrong bag?' came a stern female voice from behind them.

Ingo and Coco turned around to see a woman in her mid-thirties standing two feet away. She was dressed in city camouflage trousers and a fine rib vest with a brown, scuffed leather jacket over it and holding a steaming coffee cup in her right hand.

The words were not intended for them, but rather for a young man wearing a wide-brimmed fishing hat, who frowned guiltily. She had stopped his bag with her right foot – which was in fact Ingo's bag.

'Hey! That's mine,' protested Ingo.

'It's so easy to pick up the wrong bag at the airport,' said the stranger. With her mid-length blonde hair tied up in a braid, her appearance was the absolute opposite of Coco's: one could win wars, while the other was only good for entertaining the troops.

'Let go of me!' exclaimed the thief as he tried to escape her clutches and make off with his stolen goods. Greed had clearly overridden sanity.

The woman stepped back, then struck him in the

solar plexus. He crumpled to the floor and remained there, panting and clutching his stomach.

She grinned down at him and took a sip of her coffee. Not a single drop had been spilled. 'It's pretty slippery here, so be careful not to lose your footing. Good job you haven't broken anything.' She raised her hand. 'My fist is harder than your sternum. Shall we find out together what that means?'

Two security guards approached with caution. 'Can we help you?' announced one of them, withdrawing his radio to call the security post.

The unknown woman turned to face Ingo with a wicked grin on her face. 'This is a security announcement. Please do not leave your luggage unattended.'

He smiled and extended his hand. 'Thank you! I'd have been lost without you.'

'Lucky you were here.' Coco explained what had happened to the security officers, while they picked up the thief and secured his hands with cable ties.

'Ah, it would appear everyone from the Cave Tours group has managed to find one another,' said the chauffeur, who had appeared alongside the two guards without either of them noticing him. 'My name is Matthias. Mr van Dam has sent me to pick you all up.' He gestured around him and started to introduce everyone. The militant coffee drinker was apparently one of them.

'And this most attentive lady here is Dana Rentski, a renowned free-climber,' Matthias said, concluding the introductions. A flurry of handshakes followed.

'But we're not at full capacity yet,' he continued. 'There's still one missing. Then we can make a move. Mr van Dam will explain the rest to you.' Matthias turned to the two airport officials and handed them a business card, in case there were any further questions that weren't covered by their statements and the security cameras, then the men took the captured thief away.

'Quite the show,' said Viktor to Dana. He couldn't help but notice both her firm handshake and athletic physique.

'Thank you.' She drained the last of her coffee and tossed the cup confidently into the nearby paper recycling bin. 'I like to be of use when I can.'

A silence fell upon the disparate group; apparently nobody wanted to be the first to start a conversation. Friedemann returned to his newspaper.

Meanwhile, an overweight man in a pair of bright jersey trousers and a garish shirt hurried across from the check-in desks. He had clearly tried to emulate the beard and haircut of the comic superhero Tony Stark, but the rest of his look and his physical appearance were utterly unsuitable for the role, making him look more like a caricature of Magnum, PI, than Ironman.

Viktor guessed this was the final person hired by van Dam. The man cut rather a ludicrous figure at first glance, even more so than Friedemann.

The fag-packet Magnum caught sight of the group, raised his arm in greeting and clumped his way over to them.

'Watch where you're going,' he snarled at a little boy walking hand-in-hand with his mother, ruthlessly carving his way towards the people awaiting him. 'Sorry. There was some old biddy taking an age to get her bag off the luggage belt.

I had to wait yonks for mine. She didn't want to let go of her Zimmer frame and took for ever to hobble off with the ancient piece of crap that passed for her suitcase.' He nodded to those around him. 'Pleased to meet you. Carsten Spanger's the name, but you can call me Tony.'

'Helping her might have speeded things up,' remarked Dana coolly.

Carsten scratched his head. 'And then who would have helped me?' he added, before laughing to show that he had clearly misunderstood her. 'Well? Am I the last one here?'

'Yes, you're the last,' replied Dana.

'Don't bite my head off,' Spanger retorted. 'Next time I'll be a very good little Boy Scout and help every old lady I come across.'

'Right, that's everyone then.' Matthias took control of the situation before this minor tussle could go any further. 'If you'd all like to follow me?'

They left the hall together and were soon standing in front of a black Mercedes people carrier. They got in, with Viktor and Dana stopping to help the chauffeur load the cases into the storage area.

'Thanks, that's very kind of you. More than can be said for the other lot,' said Matthias, reaching up to shut the boot.

'The other lot?'

Matthias realised that he'd been blabbing. 'The others, Mr Troneg.' He closed the boot, smiled and gestured to him that he should get in as well, before hurrying over to the driver's seat.

'After you, Ms Fendi.' Carsten allowed her to get on

ahead of him and immediately stood to admire her backside as she bent over, then wiggled his eyebrows like a sleazy ventriloquist's dummy. 'I'm already your biggest fan.'

Viktor ruminated over what Matthias had said. 'The other lot,' he repeated to himself softly. So they weren't the first group van Dam had hired.

Unknown to Viktor and the rest of the so-called Cave Tours group, an inconspicuously dressed man in his mid-forties was sitting on a bench not far from where the incident with the vanity case had taken place. He had a small laptop resting on his knee, but there was nothing to distinguish him from the dozens of other people milling around, apart from the unusually concerned expression on his face – as if he had just learned about an event that would change the course of history for ever.

The man occasionally looked over the screen to check the arrivals board, then turned his piercing gaze to the right again and looked at the people who were introducing themselves to one another. Frown lines began to form on his forehead.

In the open chat window could be seen the message he had written:

ARRIVED WITH TRONEG AT FFM.

HAS BEEN MET AT ARRIVALS.

PART OF A TEAM. WILL SEND PHOTOS OF THE GROUP SHORTLY.

INSTRUCTIONS?

The man reached for his paper cup and tasted the drink that had ostensibly been sold to him as an espresso. It looked more like a brown slurry that had been forgotten about and simply heated up again because someone had neglected to throw it away.

The answer arrived with a beep:

FOLLOW THEM.
KILL TRONEG IF YOU CAN.
COLLATERAL DAMAGE ACCEPTABLE.

Next to the chat window, the man had opened a photograph showing Viktor in front of a tumbledown shack, holding a fully-equipped G36 rifle. It was not clear where and when it had been taken, but the colour of his camouflage suggested it was in Iraq or Afghanistan, or another desert country. He had been there with a German unit that had no official reason to be there.

But this was not the reason why Viktor von Troneg was on the hit list. German Special Forces were constantly moving through forbidden terrain without governments or any other regulatory bodies being aware of them.

There was a second photograph underneath, far grainier, that had clearly been enlarged, showing an antique-looking stone door with a door-knocker made from black metal, shaped like a lion's mouth and bearing a golden ring between its white teeth. The signs and symbols carved into it were too pixelated for them to be deciphered. The door belonged to the hut Viktor had been kneeling in front of in the first photo, casting his eyes around for enemies without once looking behind him ... which might have been a lethal error with a door of this kind.

The man responded in acknowledgement and, as the chauffeur led the sextet across the hall, lifted up his smartphone to take photos of the group and send them off.

Calmly, the middle-aged man stood up and slinging a rucksack over his shoulder and carrying his laptop under his arm, began to follow them, just one of countless anonymous business travellers making their way through the terminal. No one could possibly guess what he was up to or what organisation he worked for.

The man left the building and leaned against a pillar a few yards back from the black Mercedes people carrier, looking around for a taxi. There was only one car in the rank.

The group had finished getting in; the vehicle's indicators blinked and it drove off.

The man strode purposefully towards the last taxi. 'Hello. I'd like to go to—'

'Sorry. I've just had another booking come through on the radio,' replied the driver through the window with a regretful gesture. 'One of my colleagues will be with you shortly.' He turned on the ignition and drove off.

Shortly wasn't soon enough. There were no other taxis as far as the eye could see.

Cursing, he turned around and took out his phone, keeping his eye on the Mercedes as it faded into the distance. 'It's me,' he said to the gruff voice at the other end. 'I need to find the owner of a black Merc people carrier.' He recited the model and registration number.

In a matter of seconds he knew where he had to go to find Viktor von Troneg.

Instead of waiting for the next taxi to come along, the man walked over to the closest car hire kiosk. His orders were clear and had to be carried out to the letter.

SECOND DEAD END

After her courageous step across the threshold, the young woman in the dark green evening dress wandered a few yards forwards before stopping and gazing around at the dark forest; it was disconcertingly peaceful.

She was surrounded by ferns and the ethereal glow of the silvery moonlight dappling through the giant trees. The earthy cry of a screech owl rang in her ears, accompanied by the barking of a fox. The wind coursed playfully through the branches and foliage, creating a rustling sound all around her.

The young woman was not going to be fooled again, not when everything she had read about in the stories had been proved right. She stood still, casting her eyes all around and listening out for signs of danger while clasping the branch ever more tightly in her right hand.

The ominous rumbling of the predators inhabiting this world had died away for now. She hoped that the creatures had found other prey, preferably this invisible creature from the labyrinth.

It was only when she was certain that there was nothing moving near her that she decided to press on slowly. She looked down at her smartphone.

No Signal.

'For fuck's sake,' she muttered, looking back at the door she had just come through.

On this side, the passage belonged to the remains of an old bunker which had become embedded into the landscape and overgrown with greenery. The markings on the door were illegible and the signs themselves gave away no clues as to their meaning. It was clear, however, that this was not a place that had anything to do with the world she knew. There was nothing reminiscent of the cavernous hall with its five enigmatic doors.

She'd known that would be the case, though.

The sound of an electronic beep suddenly rang out and she looked at the display.

The signal bar started to flit rapidly between showing one and two bars.

'Yes! Please!' she cried out in relief. 'That must mean . . .' She stretched her arm upwards in an attempt to find more reception and strode cautiously forwards.

She had been wrong after all. *Thankfully!* This wood was part of good old Planet Earth, with its mobile phone masts and boosters that would help her to escape. Perhaps she had opened a door to a nature reserve or a wolf enclosure. That would explain the howling.

She slipped through a dense field of lush green ferns, constantly looking for an even better signal. She caught her high heels repeatedly on the soft ground and kept having to avoid unhelpfully located boulders, but finally she emerged in a clearing bathed in moonlight. The celestial body looked considerably larger and closer than normal.

She made her way cautiously into the centre of the clearing and held her phone up as high as she could. 'Come on,' she whispered imploringly. 'Take me home.'

A faint crackling could suddenly be heard and the ferns swirled all around her.

The young woman remained stationary but looked around, listening attentively, her branch thrust out in front of her to ward off any potential attack. Her nose-stud and one of her earrings glimmered icily in the starlight. The other one must have fallen off at some point; she certainly wouldn't be going back to look for it.

At that moment, the display on her phone showed a full bar of signal as her reward. 'Yes!' she screamed with joy.

Her scratched fingers flitted over the device to start dialling.

She kept looking around, trying to avoid becoming something's dinner just before being rescued. She looked at the ferns suspiciously as they swayed in the breeze. A distant howling erupted once more, far enough away for her to not have to fear it, but close enough to remind her that the animals had not altogether gone.

She ducked down reflexively so as not to be discovered; she would have preferred to crawl out of the exposed area and head towards a tree in order to wait for the park ranger or official to rescue her from the compound.

As if to punish her, the signal bar went back to how it had been before.

She stood up again and pressed the phone to her cheek. After what felt like an eternity, it started to ring.

Three, four rings.

A click. Someone had answered.

'Papa – can you hear me, Papa?' she exclaimed joyfully. 'Listen to me! I was at Great-grandad's house—'

A distorted, unhuman voice emanated from the speaker, nothing but unintelligible babbling.

She looked at the display. She had definitely dialled the right number. 'What on earth—?'

She hung up and dialled the emergency services.

Her phone tried to get through again.

The howling returned, much closer than it had been a few seconds earlier, while the ferns suddenly moved in the opposite direction to the wind. Something was running directly towards her, protected under the cover of the green canopy.

'Fuck!' The young woman ran back towards the door through which she had just come. Her prospects of survival felt greater on the other side of this forest, even if there was something else waiting for her in the chamber. At least now she was armed with a branch.

The bar had returned to zero. No Service.

The ruined bunker appeared between the tree trunks; the door was now wide open.

Moonlight shone into the room beyond, illuminating the markings on the concrete and brick walls; it was the closest thing to temporary safety she was likely to get. She could see the broken door knocker on the floor, as well as the skeletal remains and the dead man in his camouflage gear. The sub-machine gun in his hand looked tempting, though she had no idea how to use it. It would at least give her something more robust than the branch to defend herself with.

She'd started panting with exertion but still managed to keep her speed up. She stumbled on the steep ground but just about stayed on her feet.

The rumbling approach of the beasts came ever closer.

I'm going to make it, she kept thinking. She wasn't even ten yards away now. *I'm going to make it!*

A man in a pin-striped suit, his white shirt and black tie arranged immaculately, emerged from inside the bunker and stood in the entrance. His abrupt arrival had something of the surreal about it. His face wore a curious expression as he watched the young woman running for her life.

Then he raised his right arm, revealing a ring on his finger that shimmered in the moonlight. He placed his hand on the door and pushed it shut before she was able to make it to the passage.

'No!' exclaimed the young woman angrily, '*No* – I've got to get in! Listen to me – I've got to—' She threw herself against the door at full speed and reached it while it was still slightly ajar; in her attempt to jam the stick into the crack to keep the door open, it split in two and the wood shattered in her hand. 'No! No, open the door!' She rammed her shoulder against the door repeatedly, tearing her skin and green dress in the process. 'You prick!' Warm blood began to seep from the fresh cuts and scratches she had just acquired.

A deep laugh erupted from the other side of the door and the unknown man pushed back. He was too strong for her. The door closed. The lock clicked into place and at the same time a terrible whirring sound could be heard.

The young woman kicked it miserably. She knew what that noise meant: there was no way back.

Now it was just her, the forest and the monsters.

CHAPTER II

Germany, Near Frankfurt

The journey was made in silence at first, the Mercedes cruising along the motorway, taking them further and further away from the airport. Matthias was a cautious but skilled driver, nipping from lane to lane to make decent progress.

Coco Fendi rummaged in her box of tricks and began to rearrange the stones, runes and other odds and ends that had fallen out so ignominiously earlier, then she opened the case completely, spreading it out on the seat next to her so that the other passengers all had to shuffle up, but nobody complained.

Viktor examined Dana Rentski's face in the reflection in the tinted window. She looked vaguely familiar, but he couldn't think where from. He had taken part in numerous climbing competitions over the years and it was not at all out of the question that they had come across each other at one time or another. As soon as he tried to talk to her, however, she made it perfectly clear from her body language that she had no interest whatsoever in having a discussion. She was reading a book on her smartphone and did not wish to be disturbed.

If his feeling of having met her before had anything to do with his old job, then it probably was not going to be a happy story. It would mean they were not on the same page whatsoever.

Spanger dozed, snorting and grunting every time they went over a bump.

'Now then.' Friedemann was the first to speak. The man folded up his newspaper and placed it in his lap before allowing his mocking gaze to pass over the group. 'What have we here?' He pointed to his chest. 'Rüdiger Friedemann: geologist and speleologist.' Then he pointed to Dana and Viktor. 'Two free-climbers.' He inclined his finger towards Coco. 'And a medium.' His brown eyes turned to Ingo. 'You are our doctor, and you' – he looked towards Spanger, who had opened his eyes at the sound of his voice – 'are our technical support, if I had to guess.' He looked smugly at the man with his curious beard. 'You're a bit too tubby for caving, though. We can't have you getting stuck down there.'

Spanger rubbed his eyelids and cleared his throat to reply, but before he could muster a response, Ingo said, 'I'm not a medical doctor. I'm a doctor of physics and parapsychology, from the Freiburg Parapsychological Institute.'

Friedemann laughed. 'A ghost-hunter? Sweet Jesus, what a team we've got here!'

'I'm not just a climber,' said Dana. 'I also do a bit of martial arts on the side. Just about enough to give thieves a good hiding. Or arrogant tossers. Age makes no difference to me whatsoever.'

'Touché,' replied Friedemann, amused. 'How refreshing it is to see someone with a bit of courage about them.'

'Don't be a dick, Friedemann. Just because you're a professor, it doesn't mean you have to get off on your title,' replied Spanger sourly. 'You look like you'd fall over if someone blew on you. Or—'

'With all due respect, *this* is the strangest group I've ever had to lead.' Friedemann looked around the interior of the vehicle.

'*You?*' exclaimed Dana with disbelief. The look she gave him made it perfectly clear that she did not believe he would last an hour in a climbing harness. '*You're* going to be leading our team?'

Friedemann smiled. He appeared to be enjoying this. 'That's what it says in my contract.'

The surroundings they were whizzing past had started to change dramatically. The Mercedes was now driving through an affluent suburb of old mansions and enormous gardens.

By now, Viktor was certain that Dana's face was not familiar from any climbing exploits. 'Help me out here,' he said to her. 'We know each other from somewhere. But it's not from anything involving caves or climbing, is it?'

She shrugged and carried on reading.

Viktor could not fathom Dana's behaviour. He continued to rack his brains but the story of where or how they'd met was lost in the fog somewhere. Or had he become a victim of his own imagination because she resembled someone he knew?

'Why don't you ask our clairvoyant, Mr von Troneg?' Friedemann smiled at Coco, who was still engrossed in her triage. The car slowed down and stopped with a gentle sway.

'She'll definitely be able to tell you where you've met before. Or in what life.' He rolled up his newspaper and thumped it down on her open suitcase. 'Ms Fendi, give this gentleman a hand. Spiritually, that is. Impress us.'

'I don't provide those sorts of services for free. Nor good impressions, for that matter,' she said coolly before closing the case. 'We've all got bills to pay.' She snapped the locks back into place with a flourish and tossed her blonde curls with that unusual black streak in a well-rehearsed, suitably melodramatic gesture.

Spanger laughed bitterly. 'There's something to be said for that. By the way, I'm not an IT geek, Professor Friedemann. I'm a bodyguard.'

The old geologist's smile turned into a vicious grin. He could think of a million jokes to make about the man's corpulence, but he chose to keep the ones about being a cushion for bullets to himself for the time being. 'I'm sure you're the very best.'

The team climbed out, Friedemann leading.

The Mercedes had stopped in the drive of an imposing Art Nouveau mansion in the middle of carefully curated parkland. The sun was warm on their backs and shone welcomingly through the trees; it smelled of the last days of summer, though autumn was well underway.

Matthias walked around them and opened the boot. 'Don't worry, I'll take care of your luggage.'

'As you did for the others?' replied Dana. Clearly she had also noticed his slip of the tongue earlier.

'Please make sure nothing falls open,' Coco reminded him. 'And don't scratch them! Bags can feel pain too – especially when they're as expensive as mine are.' Keeping hold of the case containing all her paraphernalia, she pulled a golden pendulum hanging from a silver chain out of her coat and pointed it at the mansion. 'There's sorrow in this house,' she muttered darkly.

Ingo looked at her in warning, but she smiled dismissively. She was perfectly happy being a walking cliché.

'Sorrow, yes. And even more money,' added Spanger. 'Good for us – means we'll definitely get paid.'

'Go on in,' Matthias implored with a friendly smile. 'Mr van Dam is keen to meet you all.'

At that moment, the front door opened. The servant who appeared in the doorway, dressed in a uniform similar to the chauffeur's, invited them inside. 'Follow me, please. Everything's ready for you.'

The group passed through an imposing entrance hall, glimpsing a series of elegantly furnished rooms on the ground floor, before heading up the stairs. Viktor looked around in amazement; he felt as if he were in a museum. He was not particularly well versed in art, but the paintings looked as if they might have been from the eighteenth century and would certainly have been worth a small fortune, just like the rest of the treasures adorning every room they passed.

Spanger was mimicking the brisk pace set by the staff, his substantial posterior wiggling left and right as he moved. Coco was holding her pendulum out the entire time, her face set in a mask of concern. Ingo, meanwhile, was walking with his hands behind his back as if he were a philosopher.

'We're here.' The woman knocked on the door and,

upon hearing a voice from inside, ushered them through the impressive set of double doors into their client's office. 'If any of you have got any dietary requirements or allergies, please let me know. I'm here to serve.' After making sure no one needed anything right then, she gestured inside. 'I'll be back soon, ladies and gentlemen.'

They were hit by a smell of a fresh aftershave that somehow complemented the room perfectly. The dark interior was a daring mixture of old and new, Bauhaus and baroque, combining steel, leather and wood to give the impression of having been put together at the whim of some progressive designer. Thick, dusty tomes and antique-looking folders stood on sober, functional shelves, while one corner was taken up by a large, elaborately crafted wardrobe that looked as if it might lead straight to Narnia.

Walter van Dam was seated behind his desk, hunched over a laptop. He was about Friedemann's age, mid-fifties, with greying hair and similarly coloured moustache and sideburns, and was dressed in an expensive-looking dark brown suit. He glanced up and gestured to the six chairs in front of his desk. 'Welcome, ladies and gentlemen.'

They offered their greetings and sat down. The woman who'd met them at the door returned, pushing a trolley on which an assortment of coffee, tea, mineral water and biscuits was laid out, before retiring again.

'I must apologise in advance for the urgency of this matter. I'm running out of time, you see, so please don't be offended if I come across as rude,' van Dam explained. 'Do I need to introduce you to one another, or did you get that out of the way on the journey here?'

'Already done,' Friedemann announced. 'They all know I'm in charge, at any rate.'

'Then I'm sure you also understand that you're a rather special group,' said van Dam, his tones clipped. 'Including a medium.'

'Indeed.' Viktor cocked his head to one side, looking at Mr van Dam, who seemed to be more of a grounded businessman than a fringe lunatic. 'For which I'm sure there's a reason?'

'Desperation, I imagine,' muttered Spanger.

Van Dam's business-like manner faded and he appeared to sink a little behind his computer. 'You're right, Mr Spanger, I am desperate,' he admitted quietly. 'Beyond desperate.'

The group exchanged glances.

Coco looked as if she wanted to say something and began to point the pendulum at him, but Ingo gently touched her arm to stop her. Now really wasn't the time. She relented.

Van Dam cleared his throat and took a sip of water from the glass next to him. A few droplets got caught on his beard, making his face glimmer for a moment. 'My daughter has been missing for a week.' He turned a picture frame around to show them the face of a freckled, red-haired young woman, no older than twenty, with a cheeky smile playing on her lips. 'I suspect she's in an unexplored cave system. Alone.'

'I'm so sorry,' replied Viktor spontaneously. He knew all too well what it felt like to be worried about a loved one. He just about managed to stop himself from asking where she had gone missing.

'The police and fire service would be your best bet, then,' Spanger said, making no attempt to conceal his disappointment. He had been counting on something exciting. 'The emergency services, at any rate.'

'I've got nothing against the authorities,' van Dam said, having regained his business-like demeanour, 'but there are some matters that do not concern the government. The last thing I want is to have hordes of curious firefighters or police officers swarming all over my property.'

'I'll track down your daughter, no matter where she is,' Coco assured him in a theatrical voice, as if she were trying to entertain an audience. She couldn't turn it off, no matter how hard she tried. 'That I promise you, Mr van Dam.'

'I have every faith in you, Ms Fendi. Given that you have passed Doctor Theobald's parapsychological tests, you are clearly predestined to do so.' He clasped his hands together. 'As I've said, I'm running out of time. My daughter . . .' He paused, taking a deep breath as he struggled to maintain his composure.

'How could she get lost when she was on your property?' ventured Viktor.

'And what's our resident ghostbuster here for?' Dana enquired, her voice sounding matter-of-fact. 'Do you really expect we'll have to contend with ghosts?'

'There's no such thing as ghosts,' added Ingo. 'I should know, after more than two hundred investigations.'

'My reason for inviting Doctor Theobald is because . . . because he *is* scientifically very well versed. I need the six of you to be prepared for *anything* on this expedition, ready to deal with any situation that might arise,' said van

Dam quickly. 'It is your job to find out how precisely she disappeared, Mr von Troneg. You'll have state-of-the-art caving equipment, ample provisions, as well as helmet cameras and signal-boosters to make sure images are fed back up to me. I'm afraid my claustrophobia will prevent me from accompanying you, otherwise I would have gone to rescue my daughter myself. But even if I can't be there in person, I'd like to know what's going on underground.' He hesitated briefly, then added, 'Firearms and light body armour will also be provided.'

Spanger laughed, his mood improving. 'Whoa – because?'

'As you may be aware, I am a wealthy man. My daughter is usually protected by bodyguards from the moment she steps foot outside the house. But this was not the case on her last outing.' He glanced down at his laptop. 'There's a very good chance that criminals took this opportunity and are holding my daughter captive down there. That's why Mr Spanger is with you. As a firearms expert.' He stood up and smoothed out his waistcoat and tie. 'As I said, you must be ready for anything.'

Viktor found his explanation rather odd. 'Has anyone sent a ransom note?'

'No. The kidnapping idea is just a guess.' Van Dam pointed at the door. 'Please excuse my lack of manners. And I beg you not to consider me unprofessional because I didn't brief you in advance, but the nature of this matter required the utmost discretion, not least because of my daughter's profile. Your contracts have all been signed and the first instalments have been paid. Feel free to check your accounts.' He walked around the desk, clearly heading for the door. 'Time is pressing, ladies and gentlemen – time my daughter doesn't have. Everything you need to know about the caves and your fellow teammates can be found in the files Matthias has given you. You are to leave immediately. As the most experienced speleologist and geologist, Professor Friedemann will lead the group, as per his request. If you'd be so kind . . .'

Viktor raised his hand, which van Dam deliberately ignored, but Viktor continued regardless, 'Sorry, just a quick question. Have you already sent another team out?'

'No.'

His reply was firm and abrupt, but after the chauffeur's slip-up earlier, everyone now knew that they were the second group to have been despatched and that the first had not returned. Van Dam's unconvincing denial served only to suppress any further enquiries.

Everyone stood up.

Friedemann was looking closely at the cabinet behind van Dam's desk. 'These carvings are exquisite.' His face had acquired an expression that was typical of an expert spotting an anomaly or making a spectacular discovery. 'I've never seen such a specimen before. It must be priceless.'

'Not this one. I got it from a flea market. It's just my cocktail cabinet.' Van Dam pointed emphatically to the exit once again. 'Bring me back my child – alive – and I'll make you all rich beyond measure. The hundred thousand euros each of you has received is just a fraction of what you'll get if you return my Anna-Lena safely to me.'

*

The team got back into the same black Mercedes that had collected them from the airport. They began to drive through a wilderness of sorts, passing increasingly fewer houses and ever-deeper woodland, until Matthias announced that they would arrive in a few minutes. 'Don't worry about how remote it is,' he added. 'It'll make your task a lot easier.'

The ragtag bunch read their dossiers in silence.

They were all wearing dark military clothing, climbing gear and light Kevlar vests and were armed with pistols, holstered on thighs or underarm. The semi-automatic she'd been issued looked like an alien life form to Coco, but Friedemann had insisted that she take something other than clairvoyant trinkets to protect herself. Two light rucksacks were resting in front of him and Spanger.

Viktor considered it rather a bold move to arm people with weapons when they no experience in handling them, nor any legal authorisation to do so. He also doubted whether a civvy with a gun would actually be able to hold their own against potential kidnappers.

Friedemann put his folder to one side and fumbled around as if looking for something, before pulling out a well-thumbed notebook from his right trouser pocket. It looked old, both in terms of style and wear and tear. Clearly relieved, Friedemann looked at it briefly, then stuffed it under his Kevlar vest, something Viktor didn't fail to notice.

'Not much information in here,' Spanger grumbled. 'Just a load of stuff about van Dam's daughter.'

'What were you expecting?' Dana put a piece of chewing gum in her mouth. 'He said the cave system hadn't been explored before.'

Viktor and Coco both gave a quiet laugh, which somehow reinforced his suspicion that the clairvoyant could do more than just predict the future. He had been trying to talk to her about the official investigation by the Parapsychological Institute, as he had never heard of a real, verified psychic before, but she was having none of it, claiming she needed to concentrate as she shuffled her deck of cards. She said she'd be happy to tell him all about it after their assignment, by way of consolation.

'I'm curious to find out more about these caves,' Ingo said as he put his folder to one side. 'I've never come across someone who considers a cavern to be his own private property.'

'I don't like caves,' came Spanger's irritable reply.

'I'd have put money on that. You look like the sort of chap who needs a lot of room. I can't imagine narrow spaces are your thing.' Friedemann looked around intently. 'I don't believe this young lady has been kidnapped.'

'Neither do I,' agreed Viktor, who already knew the information in the file off by heart. 'Otherwise van Dam would have hired people with experience in hostage negotiation. Anyone else would put his daughter in danger. Though I suppose it could be the case that the first team was just that but they weren't able to manage it.'

'I'm so pleased I've got your approval,' said Friedemann, his voice laced with mockery. 'I don't foresee any problems. We'll follow the safety rope mentioned in the handout. Anna-Lena is almost certainly just lying around somewhere, waiting for help.'

'What's so special about you that he's put a geologist

in charge?' Dana had doubted his leadership credentials from the start. 'Just curious,' she added. She smiled coolly.

Friedemann looked at her calmly. 'I suppose you think you should be leading us, just because you can climb like a mountain goat?' He rubbed his thumbs over the tips of his index and middle fingers. 'I can see where the rock is fragile and where it's dangerous; where there are cracks and what you need to look out for. And what routes we shouldn't take. I've led dozens of expeditions to the furthest reaches of the Earth. And everyone has returned safely.' He returned her cold smile. 'Just for your information.'

Dana's smile faded; she was clearly still not convinced.

'What about the first team?' Spanger interjected. 'What do you think happened to them that van Dam doesn't want us to know?'

Coco finished her shuffling. 'They might have had a fall, or just given up, or . . .' She pulled out the ace of spades. 'Oh.'

'Oh?' echoed Spanger.

'This is the death card,' she breathed, giving the bodyguard a long, meaningful look.

Dana snorted contemptuously and pulled her ponytail tighter. 'Good job it wasn't me who picked it then.' She looked out the window. 'What's that? It doesn't look like a cave.'

The Mercedes was stopping in front of an enormous dilapidated house. There was something classical about the façade, which looked like the end of the nineteenth century in style, complete with resplendent turrets and oriels.

The windows were stained glass and would certainly provide a fascinating mixture of colours inside during the day. Despite its shabby condition, the house looked far too magnificent to be haunted.

The remains of what appeared to be a small factory could be seen next it; what was left of the collapsed building suggested it had fallen victim to fire.

Viktor picked up his file and skimmed it to check he had not missed anything about this place, but there was nothing to be found. It concerned itself only with the unknown Anna-Lena, a girl of barely twenty years. One week was enough for a person to die of thirst; it could take maybe three times that to die of hunger – less for a skinny girl. Van Dam was right: there was no time to lose.

A black Black Badge Wraith was parked at an angle in front of the building; judging by the layers of dust, it had been there for rather a long time. The Rolls-Royce, which, according to their dossiers, belonged to Anna-Lena van Dam, was a clear sign that she had been here.

Viktor quickly checked his phone to see if he could find anything about Friedemann online, as Dana's scepticism was proving contagious. This gaunt professor truly was a luminary, though he looked rather different in the photographs – more like a distant relative. *Mind you, these photos are probably ancient*, thought Viktor.

'We're here,' Matthias announced redundantly, before getting out. He had a tablet clutched in his left hand. 'It's up to you now.'

The team climbed out the car. Viktor and Spanger grabbed the backpacks and strapped them on as Dana said, 'Let's go.' She checked her pistol, took out the magazine and pushed the slide back and forth, then secured the trigger and loaded the semi-automatic.

Coco was watching her closely. 'That looked ... well-practised.'

'Gun club,' replied the woman with a grin.

'I'll accompany you as far as the entrance.' Matthias strode towards the door of the building, pulling out a large bunch of keys.

'So the entrance to the cave is in the basement.' Ingo pointed at the Rolls-Royce. 'Why is that still here?'

'Mr van Dam wanted it left in case his daughter managed to find her way out on her own. That way she could just set off straight away or ring for help. It's equipped with a VPN.' Matthias walked up the steps to the door. 'Oh, and don't forget the rifles. They're in the boot.'

Spanger hurried back to the car, removed the parcel shelf and had a look at the G36 automatic rifles, complete with several spare magazines and retractable shoulder supports. 'That's more like it!' He picked one of them up and loaded two magazines. 'We could put these to good use.' He began fiddling with it, looking for the magazine ejector, then pulled on the breech block to no effect. Nothing about the way in which he was handling the weapon gave the impression that he had a clue what he was doing.

Coco and Ingo caught each other's eye, silently agreeing that they wouldn't be taking one. There was no way they'd be able to handle them.

Viktor and Dana were looking at the automatic weapons as if they were souvenirs in a gift shop.

'These are good if you're dealing with terrorists, but they're not going to be much use in a cave system.' Viktor tapped the pistol resting in his shoulder holster. 'These are perfect at short range, though.'

To his surprise, Dana took one of the G36s out of its case. She examined it briefly, swivelled around and adjusted the sight. Then she loaded a full magazine, attached it and checked the safety was on before slinging the rifle over her shoulder. She put two cartridges into the holders on her vest, then still without a word, she turned around and followed Friedemann, Ingo and Coco.

Spanger and Viktor looked on in amazement.

'You can find all sorts of dangerous animals in caves,' she called back over her shoulder. She was fully aware that the two men were looking at her. 'Cave bears, for example.'

Viktor hesitated. No one truly believed this was a kidnapping; rather, that some sort of accident had befallen Anna-Lena. Despite not wishing to come across as paranoid, he nevertheless decided he too would bring one of the automatic weapons with him. He went through the checking and loading process with the same ease as Dana.

'She's right,' he said out loud, before setting off.

Spanger looked even more confused. then began to run, his gait making him look like a clumsy bear. 'Hey, Rentski! Can you show me how to use one of these guns?'

'You're better off not using it at all,' came her spare reply.

The rest of the group laughed. They put on the radio headsets and fastened their helmets, which were all equipped with cameras in special holders that would transmit pictures back to the surface from the cave using a series of signal-boosters. Their backpacks contained all the necessary electronic equipment to operate such a system.

'Can you tell us what sort of magic is going on here?' Coco asked Matthias. Her pendulum had been swinging incessantly. She kept all the other items she intended using for detection in a pouch on her belt. 'I'm getting some very strange energy. Something terrible has happened here.' She came across as far less artificial than she had at the airport or in van Dam's office.

'We can all see the burnt-down shed next to it as well,' Spanger muttered.

'Yes, but you're only looking. I'm listening to the full story.'

'The fire on the woodwork has been there for ever.' Matthias opened the double doors, which were studded with bronze inlay and set in a heavy frame adorned with intricately carved floral patterns. 'This is a very old property; it has belonged to the van Dam family for years. Once the fire destroyed the factory and Mr van Dam's grandfather retired from the board, there's been no use for it. The surrounding woods have been leased to a hunting club,' he added, pushing open the heavy doors. 'You'll need to turn on your helmet lights. There's no electricity down here.'

Using his tablet to create a small pool of light, the chauffeur led the group through the abandoned house.

White sheets had been laid over the furniture and thick cobwebs had formed in the corners, in one of which could be seen the skeletal remains of a dog.

'Hmm, that's not what I'm getting.' Coco pulled out a bottle of fragrant water, which she began to spray around her. 'It hasn't got anything to do with the fire. It's ... something far worse.'

'Oooooh,' replied Spanger, giggling like a schoolboy.

'Pull yourself together, man,' Friedemann snapped. 'Whatever our talented Ms Fendi is sensing might well be of help to us. It certainly can't hurt to pay attention to the unusual things going on around us.'

The only tracks through the dust and dirt were the lonely footprints made by what Coco identified as a pair of lady's high-heeled shoes, which gave the rest of the group food for thought.

'Tell me, did the first team not come through this house on their way to look for Miss van Dam?' enquired Viktor, ignoring the denial that another group had already been despatched. 'I can't see anything here apart from this pair of size 38 high heels.'

'Forgive me, but that's not something I have any knowledge of,' Matthias responded. He opened another door, revealing a steep stone staircase beyond. 'This is as far as I can go.'

He turned on a monitor, where Messenger was open. Van Dam's moustachioed face appeared on the screen: he looked exhausted but excited at the same time. 'Your mission will begin down there,' came his voice tinnily through the speaker. 'Please get a move on – follow the rope! It's the best way down. And make sure to use the signal-boosters for your helmet cameras so I can see what you see.'

'We will, Mr van Dam. No problem,' Friedemann promised.

Coco took a crystal necklace out of the pouch on her

belt and put it on. 'We'll find Anna-Lena: the cosmic forces are with us.'

'Sure they are. And firepower as well.' Spanger was fiddling in vain with his G36, until Dana snatched it out of his hands and armed it for him.

'For a bodyguard you seem to know very little.' She pointed at the safety catch and raised her index finger to show him he needed to make sure he knew what position it was in.

'I wish you every success. Find my daughter.' Van Dam nodded and the signal switched to stand-by mode.

'Let's be off then.' Friedemann pointed to Spanger, indicating he should start, and he began to move, Dana and Friedemann following, with Viktor and Coco next. Ingo took up the rear.

They made their way down, step after worn step. The beams of light cast by the helmet lamps spun around the room, flitting over old brick walls like the confused rays of tiny lighthouses. It smelled neither musty nor stale, only of cold rock and dust. Carved pillars of the same rock held up the vaulted brick ceiling.

Spanger held his G36 at an angle, his index finger twitching nervously on the trigger as if he were already fearing an attack at this stage of the mission. The light from his helmet fell abruptly on a rust-flecked steel cable stretched horizontally across. 'I've found the rope!'

He looked back along it: the end of the steel cable was wrapped several times around a pillar and held in place by a carabiner that looked disconcertingly old.

Spanger turned his head the other way, the light following.

The finger-thick cable passed horizontally through an inwards-opening door and into the darkness beyond. The beam from his helmet was mostly lost in the darkness, only occasionally illuminating the taut, steel cord in the distance when he twisted his head. There were no walls, no floor and no ceiling to be seen on the other side of the door.

'Holy shit—!' Spanger exclaimed in disbelief. 'Come on – you've got to see this!'

One by one, the others arrived at the bottom. They all looked in astonishment at the open door as they shuffled their way slowly towards it. Coco started to lift up her crystal pendant, but Ingo grabbed her hand and pulled it down.

'Now that's what I call a cave.' Friedemann pressed forward and shone his light into the blackness. Like Spanger's, the beam met no resistance other than the rope. He ran his hand over the door frame and smiled, as if he had found something unspeakably valuable and remarkable.

'I can't hear an echo.' Ingo picked up a stone from the floor and threw it into the void. 'Let's see how deep it is.'

They waited for several seconds, but no sound was forthcoming.

'That's . . . not good,' whispered Coco.

'No it's not,' Viktor agreed. The hairs on the back of his neck were standing to attention. 'I've never seen anything like this before. This cave has got to be . . . enormous.' He looked at Friedemann. 'What do you reckon? Have you ever come across anything like this?'

'No. I fully agree with your assessment.' Friedemann peered uncertainly into the blackness beyond.

Dana took a step past the men, clipped a safety carabiner and a low-friction roller onto the old steel rope and slipped into her harness. 'Van Dam told us to follow the rope.' She took a run-up, leaped through the door and went shooting along the steel cable into the darkness.

'Off you go, Spanger, follow her,' Friedemann ordered.

Spanger swore and hooked himself up to the rope. As Friedemann fiddled laboriously with his own climbing harness, struggling to secure the carabiners to the cable, Spanger too jumped and set off after Dana. Meanwhile, ignoring her complaints, Ingo was helping Coco to lash the last of the straps around her body.

Viktor watched Friedemann's awkward attempts to fasten himself in, which he considered rather peculiar; a speleologist of his renown really ought to be able to do that in his sleep. 'Is this the first time you've used this equipment?' he asked.

'Yes. I haven't needed harnesses on any of my other expeditions,' explained the scrawny geologist between curses. 'Not this sort, anyway. I used to be able to do it, Mr Troneg.'

Viktor bent down to help him. His eyes betrayed his doubts about this statement, but all he said was, 'It could happen to anyone, Professor.'

'Then let's go and save the girl. You bring up the rear.' Friedemann chased after Dana and Spanger, closely followed by the parapsychologist and the clairvoyant.

Viktor could hear the whirring of the rollers through the darkness and caught glimpses of the five lances of light as they flew through the gloom. Instead of setting off straight away, he thought to test the fastening of the rope to the column. Although there were five adults hanging from it, the cable appeared to be completely untroubled by the load.

'There's something very off about this,' he said to himself, screwing up his face. A young woman driving a luxury car to an abandoned house, wandering around with high heels on her feet and sliding down a steel cable? In a cave without a floor or ceiling? Not on your life. A search party who had left no trace of their presence? The dossiers they had been given were useless; there was no map and their client had hidden the fact that he had already sent out a team before them.

But orders were orders – and a hundred thousand euros, increasing to one million if they succeeded, was not something to be scoffed at. He could put that to very good use indeed. He was familiar with the G36, although he had hoped to never have to lay eyes on one again, let alone use one. It appeared he could not shake off his old life that easily.

Viktor examined the carved doorframe in the helmet light. An inlaid stone that reminded him a little of fool's gold reflected the beam.

A door to a cave system, he thought. Who would build such nonsense? He closed the door gently until the edge hit the cable, then spotted a rather puzzling door knocker on the inside: a grotesque face was holding a rusty metal ring between its fangs.

What on earth is this? Viktor touched the skull of this fantastical beast and ran his fingers over its rough teeth. He had seen something like this before, at an old job. Scenes appeared in his mind: the rattle of gunfire, burning wind, blood and screaming.

He quickly started to look for something to focus on to stop him from falling back into the past, back into trauma that could never be defeated. *What would it sound like if I were to use the knocker?* His fingers lifted the ring up carefully.

The hairs on the back of his neck began to stand on end again. Through his gloves he could feel an invisible stream of energy flowing through the metal. *Probably not a good idea.*

'Troneg? Where have you got to?' Friedemann's voice was far away but there was no echo at all. 'Everything all right?'

Viktor slowly lowered the heavy ring, causing it to squeak eerily. He had a bad feeling about what would happen if he brought it down with force – he might not have Coco's abilities, but a quiet little voice at the back of his head was warning him of highly unpredictable consequences if he did so.

'Coming. Just wanted to test the anchoring.' Viktor clicked himself on and took himself as far back as the pillar in order to work up as much of a head of steam as possible. He was breathing very deeply. 'Whatever this is, it's not just a cave,' he muttered, before running forward.

He threw himself onto the rope through the door.

At the same time, Spanger's scream could be heard a long way away. 'Shit, no – *no—!*'

A G36 roared and a bright muzzle flash tore through the darkness.

And the light reflected onto rock.

CHAPTER III

Germany, Near Frankfurt

The man who had secretly followed Viktor von Troneg from the arrivals hall and had photographed the team was sitting in the driver's seat of the BMW X5. He had parked his rental car less than a hundred yards from the dilapidated house, outside which stood the black Mercedes people carrier and the ostentatious Rolls-Royce.

The mini laptop was resting on his lap while he looked over at the estate through his binoculars, which were equipped with night vision. No one from the group had reappeared yet; they were either in the house or in the vault beneath it. Frank Sinatra's 'Strangers in the Night' was coming gently through the car speakers, providing a melancholic accompaniment to the scene playing out before him.

New photographs of the group had come in from headquarters via the car's internal Wi-Fi system. It was impossible these days to keep things secret; nothing was difficult to find if you knew where to look. Thanks to the wonder of the internet and its myriad possibilities, it had been easy enough to track down the sextet and trawl

DOORS X TWILIGHT | 60

through their backgrounds. And there were several things that did not match what they had told van Dam.

'Those little liars.' His mouth twisting in amusement, he read the most recent report about Coco Fendi, whose real name was Beate Schüpfer. Van Dam had been unimpressed by the tragic past of his psychic, which included a disastrous stage show.

Then he typed into the open chat window:

NEW INSTRUCTIONS?

After a brief delay, the reply appeared:

WAIT.

He gave a short growl of irritation and cast his eyes back onto the estate. It looked as if he would be here for a while.

The beam of his helmet lamp was lost in the darkness. Viktor dragged himself along the rope with his hands, the low-friction roller making it a virtually effortless task. Every now and again he knocked off flakes of rust that were coming loose from the wire.

He could see four beams of light in the distance.

A long muzzle flash emanated from the barrel of one of the G36s as it tapped out a staccato rhythm. Then the shooting ended abruptly.

'Spanger? Spanger, what's happening?' Viktor enquired nervously, preparing himself to intervene if necessary.

'Shit, I'm . . .' came Spanger's incoherent reply.

Viktor slid forwards along the cable towards the group, who had assembled on a plateau several yards wide. Stone walls towered above them all around; there was only rock below.

He landed, scattering the empty ammunition cases at his feet. 'What have I missed?'

Coco held the pendulum in her hand; Dana had her rifle in position, while Ingo was shining his light into the dark corridor opening out next to the ledge.

Friedemann had secured himself to the rope with two carabiners; he and Spanger were standing at the edge, their helmet lamps pointing down into the depths below.

'You won't be getting it back,' said the geologist rather spitefully.

'Shit,' was all Spanger could say in response.

Viktor detached himself and moved over to stand with them. 'What's going on?' he repeated. He stole a glance at the ancient twisted-steel cord that was fastened to a rust-brown bolt that ended at the cliff-face.

Spanger sighed. Staring over the edge, he admitted, 'Utter carelessness.'

'Utter stupidity,' Dana said. 'I told him he should have put the safety on, but he didn't. It's gone – he's dropped it.'

'It happened while we were moving, okay?' Spanger grunted. 'It went *click* and the damned thing moved. My finger slipped on the trigger and—'

Friedemann pulled him back from the edge by his shoulders. 'Now you've just got your pistol to protect us with.'

'We'd better get going,' Ingo shouted, shining his lamp into the passage.

'What's to say that our little van Dam hasn't fallen in?' Dana looked at Viktor. 'We'd never find her body. God knows how long the rope would need to be for us to reach the bottom of this cave.'

Coco held her pendulum out towards the dark passageway and gave a meaningful nod. 'No, she's alive – she's down here!'

'Then let's go and look for her.' Ingo stepped forwards.

'Hey, stop – not without me.' Spanger hurried alongside them as if the incident with the G36 had had nothing to do with him.

Coco followed them.

Meanwhile, Friedemann was struggling with his climbing harness, unable to remove the carabiners from the steel rope.

Viktor walked over to him and released the catch. 'Like this, Professor.'

'I know – I know. I'm just out of practice, Mr Troneg. Too much time sitting at a desk. You get rusty.' Friedemann ignored his suspicious look and followed Ingo. 'Come on, then. If our clairvoyant is saying this young lady is still alive, we need to get her out of danger as quickly as possible.'

'The others are in rather a hurry – and they are surprisingly optimistic. Perhaps Ms Fendi and her superpowers have given them a sense of security.' Dana gestured to Viktor to take the lead, but he refused. 'Fine then.' She took a few steps to the side and shone her light down once more over the sprawling ledge. 'Sure you haven't forgotten anything?'

The beam of her lamp fell upon a black military-style boot poking out from behind a shelf of rock. The foot was trembling slightly.

'What's that . . . ?' As quick as a flash, Dana armed the G36. 'Troneg, can you see that?'

'I can see it. Let's have a proper look.' Viktor moved to join her, his own rifle lowered, the cones of light from their helmet lamps illuminating the ground in front of them.

Someone was lying next to an overhang on a narrow ledge with a vertical drop right alongside. Apart from his boots, he was wearing nothing but a pair of plain grey underpants. He had been shot several times – the state of his chest left little hope for his survival. His body was also covered with scratches and open wounds probably caused by the fall, and there was a hunting knife lodged in his right shoulder. His blood had spread out in a pool all around him, with rivulets running across the stone and dripping over the edge into the black depths.

'Holy shit,' exclaimed Dana.

The mortally wounded man stared blindly into the light, his face etched with pain and horror. He groaned and tried to say something, but all he could manage was to spit out red droplets.

'Van Dam, are you seeing this?' Viktor said over the radio.

'Yeah, I can see it.' The voice through his earpiece sounded agitated.

Dana approached cautiously, knelt beside the dying man and examined his wounds. 'There's nothing we can do for him. It was a nine-millimetre, I reckon. Probably a sub-machine gun.'

The injured man relaxed, as if he were ready to finally move into the light. With a clink, a long tool was released from his slackening right hand, which was lying just outside the illuminated area.

'Do you know him, van Dam?' Viktor asked.

Dana was balancing fearlessly on the ledge. She took off the dead man's boots and searched them, but was unable to find anything inside them that might cast any light on the matter. She walked through his blood and lifted up the object that he had been carrying; the light from her helmet revealed it to be a bolt cutter.

'I've never seen him before in my life,' came their client's curt reply.

Dana and Viktor exchanged glances.

'What was he doing with that?' The blonde woman stood up and examined the steel cable more closely in her lamplight. She ran her fingers along it, then pointed to some furrows she could feel: the spot where the blades of the cutter had been attached. 'Trying to remove all contact from the outside world? Why, though?'

'And an armed stranger prevented him from doing so.' Viktor looked around, wondering if perhaps Dana was wrong in her assessment of it being a nine-millimetre and the man had accidentally been on the wrong end of Spanger's volley. 'Or did he take the bolt cutter off someone to stop them from cutting the rope?' His concern for Anna-Lena grew. 'What's going on here?'

'*Could* it be a kidnapping?' Dana pointed to the coiled

strands. 'Working hypothesis: they follow her for a little while, or even lure her down here under some false pretence or other. Then they bag her up, carry her through another exit and cut the cable – making it impossible for anyone to follow them.'

'But who shot this bloke if we're certain he didn't get in the way of Spanger's salvo? And why?'

Dana put her hand over her microphone and gestured to Viktor to do the same. 'From one of the members of the first team van Dam isn't telling us about,' she said quietly. 'For whatever reason. And it was definitely a nine-millimetre.'

Spanger's head appeared in the passageway, dazzling both of them with his light. 'Where have you two got to, then?'

'We're coming,' called Viktor. 'We were just having a look around.'

'Come on.' Mini van Dam wants to be rescued and I want to be above ground.' Spanger disappeared again.

They both moved off.

'Do you not want to tell Friedemann?' Dana guessed.

'No, only once we've found something that leads to a definitive conclusion.'

'That's a bit risky. We've already got at least one armed stranger on the loose down here.'

'Who could be miles away from here by now. And it's not a good idea to scare the shit out of the others for no reason.' Viktor studied her. 'By the way, you've really got a very good eye for ammunition and bullet holes.'

'I told you all: gun club.' Dana swivelled the muzzle

of her G36 to point at Viktor as if he were her prisoner, gesturing at him to walk ahead of her. 'What do you think of Friedemann?'

'Not all that much. But he's our leader.' Viktor sloped off. The soft click behind him indicated that Dana had carefully switched the gun's safety catch. To *live*.

'That makes two of us.'

It didn't take them long to catch up with the rest of the group and slide into place. Ingo and Spanger were at the front, followed by Coco and Friedemann, then Viktor and finally Dana.

The passage they were hurrying through had been carved out by hand, supported in some places by brick or concrete with rusty iron wires protruding from where the material had been chipped off. The reinforced concrete looked as if the expansion had been undertaken at the end of the nineteenth century – at the earliest.

'This won't have been a mine.' Viktor occasionally stooped to place a signal-booster on the ground, checking each to ensure its diodes were blinking obediently and that he could still hear van Dam. 'Any ideas, Professor?'

'It's not built on any sort of mining structure, not even a mediaeval one. I don't even know what you'd be able to mine here anyway. I'm guessing it used to be some sort of hiding place for smugglers,' Friedemann explained. 'Or perhaps an attempt at a home-made bunker system in the event of Germany being overrun during a war – a precursor to the survivalist movement, if you will.'

Their march was taking them ever deeper into the system. They occasionally came across forks in the tunnel, where they left it up to Coco to decide which path they should take. All the while there were no clear signs or marks on the wall, they were happy to follow the medium's expertise.

'I'm receiving Anna-Lena's signal loud and clear,' she whispered, running forward purposefully, clutching her pendulum in an outstretched hand. 'She's still alive. Yes, I can definitely sense it.'

Ingo threw her the occasional sceptical glance, but she ignored him and he stayed silent. He didn't have the heart to crush her spirits.

Viktor could not help but notice when Friedemann briefly switched off his helmet camera and furtively pulled out his worn notebook from under his Kevlar vest. He was about to start leafing through it when Ingo suddenly stopped in his tracks. Friedemann hastily put it back. 'What is it?'

'Just a sec. I need to get a few things out of my rucksack.' The parapsychologist moved towards Viktor, rummaged around in his backpack and pulled out a tablet and what looked like some gauges. He connected a few wires, then plugged them into the tablet in order. 'This way I can read the results in real time.' With the press of a button he turned on the entire contraption. 'Just in case we need a bit of science.' He studied the display closely.

Spanger watched him, holding his pistol in his right hand. 'What are you measuring?'

'Spanger, keep moving forward,' Dana was hissing when a loud crash erupted, like a heavy door being slammed, or maybe something ramming into a steel bulkhead. The threatening rumble that rolled through the passage and echoed all around them was closely followed by a strong breeze.

Dana immediately dropped to one knee and spun around, ready to fire, while Viktor readied his own G36.

The gauges emitted a series of warning beeps, then fell silent a few seconds later. Ingo stared at the display, babbling something about 'an anomaly' and 'physically impossible', neither of which statements Viktor liked one little bit. It was a fact that 'impossibilities' always spelled trouble. A great deal of trouble.

'A rockslide?' Spanger's face was creased in puzzlement.

'No, it sounded more like . . . a door,' said Friedemann in alarm. 'Or like the sort of large gate you'd find at the entrance to a city. Most unusual.'

'Unusual indeed,' added Ingo distractedly, his gaze still fixed on his readouts.

'There,' whispered Coco. 'Look at that!' She looked at her hand in amazement: the pendulum was floating horizontally in the air, pulling against the chain in an apparent attempt to drag the woman further along the passage.

'How are you doing that?' Ingo lowered his voice so only she could hear him and added, 'Is this some new trick of yours?'

Coco shook her head, her eyes wide with wonder and amazement, as if this were the first time she had truly believed that she actually had clairvoyant abilities.

Friedemann gave a satisfied smile. One hand was resting on the Kevlar vest with his notebook underneath. 'We're spot on,' he whispered delightedly. 'Onwards!'

Walter van Dam sat in front of a triptych of monitors, looking over the various helmet-camera feeds. The booming crash that sounded as if someone were banging down the gates of the underworld had made him sit up and take notice.

'Professor Friedemann, what was that?' he asked anxiously. 'What's going on down there?'

'We don't know yet,' he replied, his voice distorted, 'but we've picked up a clear trace of your daughter, thanks to Ms Fendi.'

'If that was a gate or something,' Spanger called out from the background, 'it must be enormous. Why on earth would there be something like that down here?'

'Ingo, have you seen this? The pendulum! It's standing . . . horizontally!' Coco was wittering away, still acting as if this were the first time her gift had ever actually worked.

Van Dam poured himself a drink. 'Well, get on with it then,' he demanded. 'Don't just stand there. Find my daughter.'

'We're going, we're going,' announced Viktor.

'Good – now hurry up.' Van Dam sounded anything but reassured.

Viktor was at the front, his rifle locked and loaded, while Dana stalked along beside him, their helmet lamps lurching from side to side. They could not see anything dangerous in the passageway and the commotion surrounding the loud rumbling had abated.

But they had not forgotten about it.

Ingo, Coco and Friedemann followed, with Spanger

bringing up the rear. The doctor was carrying his gauges, occasionally stealing a quick glance at them. The pace of the group had increased as they trudged along in silence, the only sounds coming from the stamping of their boots and the jingling of Ingo's equipment.

'You're a free-climber then?' Viktor muttered to Dana, who was advancing in the manner of a well-trained soldier. Catching a glimpse of her beside him, he was struck by an image from a very long time ago – and it was at that moment that he remembered where they had met before. 'And a martial arts expert to boot. And a gun-club member. What kind of gun club? It must have been where you—?'

'Not the time,' she growled without looking at him.

'On the contrary.'

She looked at him closely. 'What's with all the questions?'

'As I said, I've seen you before somewhere.' Viktor returned her gaze. 'In Darfur. A report on military reconnaissance that had nothing whatsoever to do with free-climbing. Tell me I'm wrong.'

Dana narrowed her eyes. 'What were you doing in Darfur?'

'I didn't say I was there.'

'But you had access to reports – so you're not just a free-climber either, then, are you?' Dana did not like where this conversation was heading. 'I've got a twin sister who's a mercenary. Not that we get confused for each other much, though.'

Viktor was not prepared to be shaken off that easily. 'I don't know what kind of game you're—'

They both stopped abruptly, their faces wide with amazement at the scene before them.

'What it is?' Friedemann asked from behind them.

'Stop! I'll get some more light.' Viktor removed a flare from his belt, lit it and threw it into the enormous chamber opening out in front of them at the end of the passage. 'I want to have a better look before we go in.'

Dana hurled a second from behind him.

A barren, cavernous room with markings scrawled all over the walls was illuminated in deep red by the hissing, smoking light emanating from the flares. All manner of inscriptions, scribbled notes, arrows, signs and scratched messages could just about be made out, as well as broken pieces of iron and the destroyed remnants of at least one skeleton.

Viktor could see a dead man on the ground. In contrast to the man on the ledge earlier, he was wearing camouflage gear and armour and had a sub-machine gun lying next to him.

Behind him stood five doors embedded into the rock face. They were made of wood and stone, with both old and new markings alike etched onto them. The three doors in the middle had door knockers in the shape of a ring, the second one of which was broken. The two outermost doors were equipped with large box locks. A thickly drawn question mark could be seen on each of the first three doors; the fourth door had an X on it and the last bore an exclamation mark. They were all painted on with red lipstick, and when Viktor touched one of the symbols, he found the lines were fresh and still a little moist.

'What's all *this*?' Spanger exclaimed in disbelief. '*Doors?*'

'Looks like it,' replied Viktor. 'So what's the plan, Professor?'

'We should probably ask our medium.' Friedemann joined them at the front. 'It's beautiful, isn't it? They really are fine specimens.' His gaze drifted to the door in the centre, the one which bore a red question mark. 'That's where the vandals were holing up.' He pointed to the door on the left. 'What a pity the ring has been destroyed – it can't be used any more.'

Dana and Viktor exchanged glances once more. The fact that a geologist was looking at doors as if he had just discovered an extra-terrestrial stalagmite seemed more than a little peculiar to them.

'Doors? In a cave?' Ingo squeezed his way between them into the entrance and was babbling away as if the dead man were not there at all. 'How fantastic! A mystery – I love mysteries. Let's have a closer look.'

'Definitely,' said Coco, exhilaration filling her voice, holding the chain with the energised pendulum firmly between her fingers. 'Anna-Lena is very close by!' She took a step inside the chamber.

Ingo held tightly to her harness.

Only then did Coco spot the dead man with his torn throat. She uttered a low cry. 'By the spirits of the beyond!' She almost let go of the chain. 'Why didn't any of you warn me?' She could not take her eyes off the corpse. Her enthusiasm for their task and this place was fading more and more with every heartbeat. 'I . . . I think I'd rather go back up.'

The flares suddenly rose into the air, along with everything else in the chamber. The sextet looked on in silence: for reasons beyond them all, it looked like gravity had suddenly stopped. Ingo's equipment once again began to emit loud warning sounds.

A young woman entered the foreground, floating up from behind the upside-down armoured corpse; she had apparently been lying against the wall in the man's shadow. Her long red hair enveloped her like a gently blazing flame; her nose piercing and a single earring sparkled in the red glow. She was wearing a badly torn ball gown and high-heeled shoes. Her eyes were closed and her arms and legs were relaxed as if she were underwater.

'There,' Dana shouted, 'that's her – Anna-Lena!'

'Should we go in and get her?' Viktor looked at Friedemann. 'What do you think, Professor?'

The flares, corpse, Anna-Lena and everything else fell back to the ground.

'What ... what was that?' Viktor turned to face the parapsychologist in amazement.

'Not ghosts, that's for sure.' Ingo swiped the display of his tablet. 'That was a—'

Friedemann interrupted him. 'Well, it's stopped now, so we can go and investigate,' he announced, as if this were the sort of thing he encountered all the time on his field trips. 'If your little gadgets pick up anything dangerous again, let us know, Doctor. Let's go and get Miss van Dam out of there.'

The group advanced slowly, plunging into the flickering red light and smoke cast by the flares. Friedemann instructed Viktor and Dana to tend to the young woman lying on the ground next to the dead body; her limbs were somewhat contorted after the fall. 'Doctor, keep an eye on everything else. Make a record of what we've found here. *Everything.* I want to have a look around in peace.'

'Really? Why?' Spanger took a step back towards the passage.

'Because it's all rather exciting.' The professor sidled up next to Dana and Viktor as they were examining Anna-Lena. Looking at Spanger, he muttered, 'You wouldn't understand anyway.'

'Nothing looks to be broken at first glance, nor are there any external injuries,' Dana announced as she lifted the young woman's eyelids and shone a light into her eyes. 'Pulse normal, but no pupil reaction.'

'God, Anna-Lena!' They could hear van Dam's relieved voice. 'Come on, get up – now!'

'Just a moment. We've got to make sure she's physically capable of surviving the journey back,' Dana replied resolutely as she carried on checking the girl over.

Ingo turned off his gauges and pulled out a camera. 'I've never seen anything like this before – not during any of my investigations! Gravity reversal? That's impossible – well, usually.' He began to take endless photographs of the doors, the inscriptions and the symbols. 'You can clearly see magical formulae in the graffiti – some look as if they're hundreds of years old,' he continued enthusiastically. 'Look: there's cuneiform, hieroglyphics, ancient Greek, Persian . . .' He could hardly contain his excitement. 'It's quite possible that our little anomaly had something to do with these.'

Viktor saw Friedemann pulling out his notebook and caught a glimpse of his first entry: *Arc Project // Arkus // Arcus.*

The professor started leafing through it, comparing the markings on the pages with the inscriptions on the doors. Some of them matched.

'I'm here if anyone needs me.' Spanger remained near the entrance, strapped into his harness.

Viktor decided to confront Friedemann about his book later, instead choosing to have a look around. 'Who the hell would build doors in a place like this?'

'What I find far more impressive is their condition and distinctiveness,' Ingo added happily. 'These doors are all from different centuries. The symbols on them . . . are . . . I mean, some of them, well, I don't even know what they're supposed to be. I'm not talking about all the scribbling that's been added later, but what the creators of these doors actually inscribed themselves.'

Spanger had changed his mind. He walked over to the armoured dead man, took his gun from him and began to search his body. 'Sub-machine gun. H&K, MP5, nine millimetre,' he shouted over to the group, adding, 'See? I'm not completely useless.'

'You could learn that just by playing a first-person shooter.' Dana looked at Viktor and raised her eyebrows in triumph. It was this weapon that had most likely done for Underpants Man. The boots belonging to the two dead men were identical in design and tread pattern.

'But he's got nothing on him – no badges or papers or anything. Looks like he could be part of some sort of special unit.' Spanger bent down to examine the wound on the man's neck more carefully. 'Throat slit.' He pointed to the empty sheath. 'And his knife's missing.'

'These your people, van Dam?' radioed Dana after finishing her examination of the unconscious woman.

'I'll tell you again, I haven't sent out another team. Now bring me back my little girl,' he ordered, putting down his glass. 'Tell me, Mr Troneg, have you made sure to put all the boosters down? The picture has suddenly gone all fuzzy and I can barely hear you at all.'

'I have, Mr van Dam,' Viktor replied.

'That sort of thing can be triggered by magnetic fields and radiation,' said Ingo, who was standing next to his equipment and looking at the display on his tablet. 'Oh my God – my devices are going haywire again. I can see . . . measurable differences in the magnetic field and so forth. The gravitational pull is slowly decreasing. A little more and we'll start to feel it.'

'Or it could be a jammer,' said Dana. 'Or someone's found one of our boosters and switched it off. We need to get a move-on. Van Dam, your daughter is in a good enough state for us to bring her out.' She looked at Viktor. 'You can carry her.'

Viktor handed his rucksack to Coco, who in turn handed it to Ingo, and picked up the young woman. He could not believe how light she was – surely no more than seven and a half stone. He laid her gently over his shoulder.

'Pack up your stuff, Doctor,' Friedemann ordered. 'We're leaving.'

Coco looked at her golden pendulum, which was

showing no inclination towards the younger van Dam but was instead pointing at the doors. 'That's . . . odd.'

'Your pendulum must be wrong,' said Ingo, giving her a look to suggest the show was over before he turned back to his gauges and stuffed them into his backpack.

'It can't be.' Coco looked at the doors. 'There are more secrets through there.' She looked at the corpse and shuddered. 'Probably for the best that we're not going to be the ones to investigate them.' She put her pendulum away.

'Right, let's go.' Friedemann shooed Spanger forwards with a wave of his hand. 'We've found what we were looking for.' He gave the doors a curious look.

Viktor thought it was almost as if he had really been there for them and not for the young woman.

The group made their way back through the passages by the light of their helmet lamps. The place was silent, making it feel all the more depressing.

Where are you going? said a voice that appeared to be inside Coco's head. *Stay a while longer.*

She slowed down, prompting Ingo to give her a nudge. She began to shiver all over. 'Can you hear that too?'

He can't hear me. I thought I was talking to you. You're rather special, you know, said the sombre voice. *What if I were to kill the others? Would you stay then?*

Coco felt her throat tightening. 'No,' she whispered.

'No?' Ingo looked at her, confused.

We could have ever so much fun, Beate. That is your name, after all. Or would you rather I called you Coco?

She didn't know what she could say that the unknown voice would not consider as a challenge.

Suddenly her mind was flooded with images: a dog-like beast pouncing on and slaughtering the group; an armed unit that wanted to attack and kill them; a monster made of smoke stabbing them with burning blades. A mounted unit riding into a mediaeval battle, followed by drones chasing their group through an unknown city, and finally a man in an American Second World War uniform with his gun raised, aiming the barrel at her face – and pulling the trigger.

Coco's mouth opened into a scream – and everything around her disappeared.

She found herself standing back in front of the five doors.

They were opening and closing, opening and closing, opening and closing, incessantly. They roared and rattled, creating a loud rumble that shook the walls. Scree and stones tumbled down, crashing onto the ground. Blood poured out of the first door, hissing with steam, while liquid fire rushed out of another, with the one next to it producing some sort of acid that mixed with the scattered pieces of bone that came coursing out of the door alongside it; from the final door came piles of putrid entrails. The hellish conglomeration seized Coco and dragged her below the surface.

The decaying corpses of Ingo, Friedemann, Spanger, Viktor and Dana danced around her, their clawed hands striking her. Their shrill, screeching laughter shook her to her core.

'We're dying in this cave,' they sang. 'We're dying! And you didn't warn us – that's why we're going to kill you!

We're going to kill you!' The five of them then threw themselves onto the clairvoyant and opened their jaws as wide as possible.

Coco began to burn, her body dissolved by the acid as she suffocated, while the drifting bones crushed her. As the group feasted upon her flesh and tore her to pieces, she somehow found the strength to utter the loud cry of anguish that had been stuck in her lungs.

The illusion was shattered immediately.

Panting, she stumbled through the passage in front of Ingo, barely able to stay upright on her trembling legs. Fear constricted her heart as the beams from the helmet lights danced in front of her eyes in double vision.

'Everything all right?' Ingo had spotted that something was amiss. 'What's wrong? Pins and needles?'

Coco didn't dare to speak. Horror had paralysed her voice. She was certain that death would fall upon her the moment she made a peep. How was she suddenly able to see these visions? Should she ever manage to escape from this place, she would never step foot in it again.

'Well, that was easy.' Spanger felt heroic when he held the sub-machine gun, just as he had always wanted – maybe not exactly like Tony Stark, but like a man who had done a good deed. It did not concern him in the slightest that their task had been so easy, or that they had found a dead body. If they should happen to stumble upon any enemies, he was ready: ready to pull the trigger and become even more of a hero. 'What was it killed the other bloke?'

'Let's hope we don't have to find out.' Dana was keeping a close eye on their surroundings. The cones of light rendered them easy targets, which was making her rather uneasy. A decent marksman would simply have to aim just beneath the light and it would all be over.

'Oh, I'm sure we can handle it.' Spanger fiddled with the safety catch. 'We're pros.'

'You certainly are,' remarked Friedemann.

'Didn't we say you were going to be a bit nicer to me?'

'Calm down,' Viktor urged them. 'Even if every man and his dog can see us, that doesn't mean we have make a racket the entire way back.'

His reminder had the desired effect: silence descended upon the team.

Ingo kept looking at the recordings from his measurements, trusting that they were all correct. What other experiments could he do in the hall with the doors? Where did the volatile gravity come from? The dead body made him uneasy, but scientific curiosity pushed those doubts to one side. He had already made up his mind that with another, more appropriate team and van Dam's permission, he would return and astonish mankind with what he had discovered.

Ingo didn't know he wasn't the only one with that idea, though.

'Don't dawdle,' Dana hissed at him. 'You can marvel over your findings once we've reached the surface.'

After a short while they arrived back at the platform.

'Good,' came Friedemann's voice. 'We're nearly there – now we just need to cross.'

They secured the helpless Anna-Lena to the rusty cable and began to make their way back through the darkness, moving forwards in silence until they could see the entrance in the glow of their helmet lamps. One after the other, they arrived in the basement.

As easy as their task had been, and as pleased as he was to have found the missing woman so quickly, Viktor thought their mission had been entirely surreal. If you ignored the abnormalities such as the sudden changes of gravity and the two dead bodies, it had been a walk in the park. It wasn't that he had been looking forward to a shoot-out, but he thought it curious that they hadn't encountered a single serious problem. A bunch of Boy Scouts could have saved the young woman, as indeed could the first military unit who had been sent out. Or was this all some kind of a test?

Viktor carried the unconscious woman up the stone steps and onto the ground floor of the villa, where the chauffeur was waiting for them. They assumed van Dam had informed Matthias of their return.

'I've already re-configured the seating in the car,' Matthias explained, adjusting his cap. 'We can get going straight away.' They hurried through the rooms towards the exit. The chauffeur handed Spanger the spare key for the Rolls-Royce. 'I don't suppose you'd be able to take this back?'

'You're kidding!' Spanger grinned. This was the first time he had ever been allowed to drive a luxury car like this.

'Don't you want to call an ambulance?' Dana said over the radio to her employer. 'I don't know whether she's got any internal injuries tha—'

'No publicity,' van Dam interrupted. 'I've arranged for

a team of specialists to come to my house and examine my daughter thoroughly. Then we can decide what to do next.'

When they reached the exit, Coco wanted to weep with happiness. The black Mercedes was parked with its side door open; as Matthias had said, the seats had been joined together to create a large flat surface in the middle.

'Thank you all once again,' said van Dam through their earpieces. 'You will of course each receive your rewards, as promised. Ms Rentski and Mr von Troneg, you'll go with Matthias, while the rest of you can take the Rolls.'

Not a test, then, Viktor thought with a shrug, his mood improving. He laid Anna-Lena onto the seats and shuffled back to allow Matthias to fasten her seatbelt. Relief suddenly washed over him. 'Good job we managed to find her so quickly.' Saving a human life was a wonderful feeling. He could not resist shaking hands with everyone in the group and congratulating them on a job well done. 'I think you'll find we've done rather well here.'

That same joy was clear onto the faces of his comrades too.

'Easy money, that.' Spanger said callously as he fiddled with the key to the Rolls-Royce. 'A million, right? All for just under three hours' work.'

Coco was standing next to Ingo, who was busy checking the measurements on his displays. 'Yes, but what's the explanation for all this?' She felt liberated; the tremor in her hands had abated.

'There isn't one.' Ingo looked excited. 'Mr van Dam, may

I go back down and have a look around? These physical phenomena are crying out for proper, in-depth research.'

'No way. Nothing can make me go back down that hole again,' Coco said quickly, putting down the equipment. 'It's not a good aura at all. Whoever it was who built that place and those doors – they did *not* have good intentions.' She left out telling them about the voice, her vision and her terror.

'I'd like to join Doctor Theobald,' Friedemann interjected. 'These geological structures are quite unique. As my colleague has said, they absolutely *must* be explored further.'

'Unfortunately, I cannot allow that,' replied their client. 'Let's all just be happy that you've returned to the surface unscathed.'

Dana had also detached herself from the harness. She was trying not to catch Viktor's eye, so as not to jog his memory any more. 'We will need to talk to you about a few things once we're back at your house, Mr van Dam,' she said. 'About what we saw down there.'

'That can be dealt with once you're back with me,' he said. 'What goes on in the caves, stays in the caves. That would be my suggestion. Leave everything else to me and don't allow yourselves to be burdened by it.'

Friedemann glanced back through the front door. Who would try to stop him if he went back down? The chauffeur? He could easily bribe the other five to either go with him or leave him alone. With a bit of cunning he was sure he could convince Theobald to make a second descent. By the time van Dam had found another team to get them back out, he could have explored everything he wanted to. He *had* to. He ventured a first, discreet step back towards the verandah.

'What do you mean by that?' Spanger scratched his back. 'What we saw down there? Do you mean the doors?'

'Mr van Dam!' Matthias picked up his tablet nervously. 'I . . . I don't think this is your daughter.'

The group turned to face the chauffeur, who was sitting next to the supine woman.

'What nonsense is this?' snapped the businessman.

'Her eyes, Mr van Dam.' Matthias turned the tablet around and filmed the sleeping woman with its camera. He carefully opened her eyelids with his thumb and fore-finger. 'Can you see that?'

The team all huddled around the car.

'I told you so,' muttered Coco. 'The pendulum – it knew we hadn't found Anna-Lena.' The consequences of this realisation made her heart sink like a stone. They would have to go back.

'Ridiculous,' Ingo whispered to her.

'What about her eyes?' Dana enquired.

'They're blue,' replied Matthias, his face growing pale. 'But Miss van Dam's eyes are . . .'

'Green. She's got green eyes.' Van Dam sounded both startled and anxious at the same time. 'Have you checked she's not wearing contacts?'

'Yes. No lenses.' The chauffeur was continuing to film the girl. 'Even if everything else is identical, Mr van Dam – her figure, her hair, even her jewellery – her eyes tell a different story.'

'Is there anything that could have changed her eye colour?' Spanger threw the keys to the Rolls in the air and caught them. 'Bright light or something?'

'Don't talk rubbish,' Friedemann scolded him. 'You can't change eye colour unless you tattoo the vitreous, but in any case, they wouldn't look like this.' He pushed his way forwards and pulled up the sleeping woman's eyelids to double-check. 'See this, Matthias?'

The chauffeur leaned forwards and swore, then checked the other eye himself. 'Green – they're green again! But I swear they were blue before.'

'This is insane.' Dana looked around at her colleagues.

'Beyond insane.' Coco leaned against Ingo, feeling like she needed human warmth and closeness to ease the ominous feeling inside her. Someone she trusted.

'There's only one thing for it.' Van Dam's voice over the radio sounded agitated. 'You'll have to go back down and look for her. Your job is not complete. I need to know for certain.'

'What are we going to do with ... this person?' Dana looked at the sleeping woman. It could still be van Dam's daughter, or someone else altogether.

'Matthias will bring her to me,' the businessman decided. 'I'll have her examined and looked after. In the meantime please find Anna-Lena – *my* Anna-Lena, not this copy or whatever she is.'

'You could always try a DNA test.' Viktor recognised the feeling that had crept up on him. In a matter of seconds his feeling of safety had turned into the very opposite. 'It could still be that this is your daughter,' he pointed out.

'Who knows what happened to her in those caves? There were all sorts of strange things going on down there.'

But Matthias was already reaching out to reclaim the key from Spanger. 'Understood, Mr van Dam. I'll bring the woman to you in the Rolls. The Mercedes will have to stay here because it's got the internet connection.'

'I've got a question.' Spanger handed him the key. 'We will get a million for this one? *Another* million, that is? I mean, technically, we've already got your daughter so—'

'Come on, let's go,' the professor interrupted. 'You're an embarrassment to even ask that.' Friedemann was secretly cheering to himself. He now had a legitimate excuse to descend into the cave again.

'Quite right,' Dana confirmed, putting her own gear back on.

'I don't want to go back down there.' Coco looked at Ingo. 'I'm serious. There's something waiting for us.'

'No, no, it's just a bit of wonky physics.' He patted his instruments. 'And we'll find the real missing girl in no time at all. Just like before. Your pendulum seems to know where she is.'

Coco couldn't detect any mockery in his voice. 'But there's still the small matter of the dead man with his throat torn out. And whoever it was who killed him.' She climbed into her harness as if in slow motion. She still couldn't bring herself to talk about that voice, or her vision. 'It's waiting for us.'

'Nothing's going to happen to us.' Ingo too was looking forward to another opportunity to take some measurements. 'I'm absolutely certain of it. We've just got to be careful, that's all.'

'Departure, take two.' Friedemann sounded like he was in a good mood. 'We've already been successful once. Now let's go and rescue the real Anna-Lena van Dam. Green eyes, everyone: make sure you remember that.'

Viktor and Dana, communicating with their eyes, checked their weapons. They had still not told anyone about the half-naked dying man with the bolt cutter and bullet wounds they had discovered and they wouldn't, not yet, so as not to put a downer on proceedings.

The group set off again immediately, passing through the estate and back into the cellar, readying themselves to slide along the steel cable to the platform once more.

Coco was close to tears.

The unknown man watched the entire scene outside the villa in peace, reporting every detail to headquarters, along with photographs. He had even been able to follow about half of their conversation by lip-reading.

The group surrounding the professor disappeared back into the house; the chauffeur once again opened the side door of the people carrier and lifted the comatose doppelgänger, carried her over to the Rolls-Royce and laid her down on the back seat.

This time, along with acknowledgement of receipt of his report, he received an order:

IMMEDIATE ELIMINATION OF ALL PARTICIPANTS.
EVEN THE UNCONSCIOUS ONE.

The man closed his laptop and placed it on the passenger seat. He started the BMW and drove along the approach road to the abandoned house, then intentionally stalled. He wanted his arrival noticed.

The chauffeur promptly stepped back from the Rolls and closed the door. He looked at the BMW curiously as it rolled across the fine gravel with a soft crunch.

The unknown man took out a slim boning knife from the glove box. The price tag was still on it – he had bought it after he'd arrived, knowing he would have no chance of getting his own weapons through airport security. With a practised movement he slid it inside his sleeve, then got out of the car and walked towards the dilapidated mansion.

'This is private property,' Matthias called out to him, pointing back down the drive. 'You need to leave immediately.'

'Please excuse me. I've just had a technology omni-fuck-up. First my satnav sent me the wrong way and now my rental car has given out on me. It's a good job there's someone here.' The man approached, smiling. 'I don't suppose you could lend me your phone so I can call for breakdown assistance?'

'Ah, understood.' Matthias sighed and briefly looked over at the Rolls to check the woman, but she was still unconscious. Then he removed a packet of cigarettes from his dark blue uniform. 'What's up with your car? Might be quicker if I just help you.' He lit a cigarette and proffered the pack to him. 'I know what I'm doing.'

The man took a step closer. 'I'm afraid with this kind you need a diagnostic computer to make any headway. The curse of the modern world.' He refused the cigarette. 'Bit of an odd set-up for such a deserted place. Nothing illegal, I'm sure?' He grinned to show Matthias he was joking.

'We're in the process of selling the house. Someone's having a viewing.'

'Luckily for me.'

'You could say that.' Matthias felt for his phone inside his pocket. 'Here, go ahead. But I can still try to have a look under the bonnet for you.'

'By all means.' The man's movements suddenly became clumsy as he took the phone. It slipped out of his fingers and landed on the gravel. 'Oh – forgive me! I'm so sorry. I hope your phone's not broken.'

Matthias didn't allow his irritation to show, instead flicking away his half-finished cigarette and bending to pick up the phone.

The man drew the knife out of his sleeve and held it over the chauffeur's exposed neck.

Matthias saw his attacker's shadow with a blade in his hand and quickly turned, his arm raised to defend himself.

Contrary to what Coco had feared, the group travelled the same way through the labyrinth without incident, arriving unmolested at the cavernous chamber with the five doors. Her pulse was racing and she was sweating with fear.

Dana and Viktor once again lit two flares to give them some light, then began to discuss the plan with Friedemann.

'I'm an idiot. I should have brought another G36 with me.' Spanger looked at the sub-machine gun next to the dead man. 'Now I've got to make do with this child's toy.'

Ingo had unpacked his instruments again and was paying close attention to their displays. 'There it is again,' he said with fascination. 'The first tiny deviations.'

Coco walked slowly past the doors, the golden pendulum in her hand. She felt sick. This whole place was dripping with danger. She would not be staying a second longer than necessary, that was for sure. With each passing moment she expected to hear the voice, to see the visions – to be exposed to that same mental torture again.

And that was not forgetting Anna-Lena's doppelgänger with the wrong eyes. Who knew what sort of being they had brought to the surface?

'It's getting stronger,' she announced with simultaneous awe and anxiety. She could hardly stand it; her skin was itchy and prickly. 'You can do the rest yourselves. I've got to get out of this godforsaken hole!'

'Sorry?' Friedemann gave her a look of consternation. 'And how exactly do you propose to do that?' He was holding his notebook in his hand again, consulting it from time to time as he examined the door frames.

'Ms Fendi,' came van Dam's voice in her ear, 'only you can hear me now. I beg you, please stay with the group. I have confidence in your powers. It may well be that the team will find itself in a situation where only your abilities can help them! You saw what happened to the torches before.'

Coco placed her hand over the microphone so that the only sound was the one transmitted through the helmet speakers. 'There's a dead man down here, Mr van Dam. A dead man and something that . . . that wants to kill us. That was not part of the agreement.'

'I'll pay you two hundred thousand euros extra,' he replied. 'The others are watching you, Ms Fendi.'

Coco cleared her throat. 'Mr van Dam, I . . .'

'Nothing's going to happen to you. Think about my daughter, please!'

His heartbroken appeal softened her slightly and she was about to agree when she remembered the cruel voice in the passage. 'You don't understand – you couldn't, not without feeling what I felt.'

'I'm begging you. Without you, my daughter doesn't stand a chance!'

Her sense of duty calmed her fears and drowned out the voices imploring her to turn back. 'All right. I will.' She turned to face the doors so as not to have to look at the man's remains. 'I'll take you at your word, Mr van Dam.'

'Right, we're all here. What are you picking up, Ms Fendi?' Viktor turned to look at the medium. 'Where's our missing girl?'

Coco paused in front of the fourth door, the one bearing the red cross marked in lipstick. The pendulum was standing out from the chain, facing forwards like a pointer. 'Behind this one.' She placed a hand on the enormous handle and tried to pull it, but nothing happened. Shaking didn't help either, nor did leaning on it with all her strength. She took a deep breath. 'By the grandfathers of the four elements . . .' she said, starting an incantation.

'Slow down,' called out Spanger in alarm. 'Who knows what's behind—?'

'*She's*. Behind. It!' Coco's face bore a strange expression.

'By the grandfathers of the four elements ...' she began again, her voice drifting away into a quiet invocation.

Friedemann put his notebook away, this time stuffing it into a trouser pocket in order to retrieve it more quickly next time. 'No. She's not.' He walked purposefully towards the door on the far left, which also had its knocker intact. 'We'll find her here. There's an arrow on the ground I recognise—'

'Hang on.' Spanger was shining his light at a glimmering spot on the floor that was reflecting the light. 'There: a diamond earring!' The piece of jewellery was lying in front of the furthest door, which had a heavy mediaeval drawbar and a thick box lock. It was this door that had the exclamation mark painted on it. 'Our little van Dam was wearing a pair just like this in the photo in our files.' He looked from Friedemann to Coco and back again. 'What if you're both wrong and she's behind this one?'

Walter van Dam sat enthralled in front of the triptych of monitors, watching what was happening underground with increasing agitation.

Then he noticed that one of the split screens on the right-hand display was black; he frowned with concern. This was not linked to one of the team's helmet cameras, but rather to Matthias' tablet.

He picked up his phone and called his chauffeur, who was supposed to be on his way with Anna-Lena's double.

It rang.

And rang.

And rang.

The fact that Matthias was not answering made him nervous. He poured himself another drink. His nerves shot to pieces by this rollercoaster ride, he had long since replaced water with whisky. Earlier, when they'd announced they'd found Anna-Lena, he had been so happy, but now his anxiety was increasing with every breath. 'Where is my daughter?' he asked again.

'We need to clarify what's going on first, Mr van Dam,' said Viktor. His words were all distorted.

'Unfortunately, there are three possibilities for where your Anna-Lena might be,' radioed Friedemann, who sounded no less distorted than Viktor. The transmission from the cave system must be more or less at its limit. 'Any decision we make could be the wrong one – or the right one.'

'What about the other two?' Van Dam rubbed his moustache frantically.

'We'll check those once we've ruled out the others,' said the professor.

'Show me these doors, Mr von Troneg,' van Dam asked. He would have liked to send Matthias to check the Wi-Fi connection and the Mercedes' built-in modem.

Viktor filmed the doors, which van Dam enlarged on the second screen, and explained the three clues to him. 'Have you seen this before?' he asked. The connection was becoming worse with every word he spoke. 'Anything that could help us?'

Van Dam did not answer but clicked and zoomed in on the feed, took snapshots of all the details and fanned them out on the third monitor to get a better overview.

Then he stared closely at the symbols.

Looking at them caused vivid memories to flood into his mind: memories he would have sooner never returned to. He could still recall his mother's words – and what she had begged of him in her declining years. He had never had the opportunity to carry out her final wishes, and after her death – until this moment – he had all but forgotten about them. He had added Theobald to the group without really believing that his parapsychological knowledge would ever be required – like a parachute you hoped never to have to use. It had come from just a feeling, nothing more, one whose origins lay in the past, indefinable, yet compelling.

'Van Dam?' Viktor's voice was now almost entirely drowned out by a loud humming noise.

Then van Dam heard him say, 'Professor, the signal's gone. He can't hear me any more. What shall we do? Which door do you think we should take?'

Van Dam rose unsteadily and hurried to his shelves. He searched through the books until he finally found the old tome he was looking for, along with the collection of loose papers that had belonged to his grandfather. He removed it and returned to his desk, then put it down and opened it.

Dozens of old drawings of doors were depicted on the fragile, stained pages, and they all had dates and cryptic markings drawn alongside them. He flicked through the sheaf until he found exactly the five doors he had seen on the third screen. The year '1921' was written next to it.

'It cannot be!' he exclaimed.

'Mr van Dam? What did you say?' he could hear Viktor asking. 'If there's anything you know that could help us, please tell us. We need to decide which door to go through first to find your daughter. We can't agree. Do you understand? Any clue you could give us will allow us to find your daughter faster.'

'One moment, Mr von Troneg.' He wanted to make absolutely certain. In a matter of seconds he had compared the symbols on the monitor with the sketches and illustrations in the book and there was little doubt that he was on the right page. Then he noticed a door knocker missing on one of the doors that he had filmed. If his daughter had gone through that one, the consequences would be devastating.

A notification popped up on his computer alerting him to a new email from Professor Friedemann. In the subject line he was asking precisely what time he would be picked up from Frankfurt Airport.

At first van Dam thought it was a delayed message, for the geologist was now roaming around underground looking for Anna-Lena, then he saw the time at which the email had been sent: two minutes ago.

That was surely impossible. But he'd deal with that later; right now he had more urgent matters to attend to.

'Listen to me, Mr von Troneg.' Van Dam propped his head on his hands and fixed his eyes on the descriptions written underneath each door. 'I—'

With a crack the connection died. The monitors went blank and the sound cut out.

'No!' Van Dam stared at the black displays.

Viktor looked at the third, fourth and fifth doors, each representing one of the three most likely possibilities for where to find Anna-Lena, knowing they were running out of time.

Ingo was calibrating his devices in an attempt to update his measurements. He raised his eyebrows as he read the latest results. 'Unbelievable. This . . . this trumps everything else I've seen so far. As we speak, the gravitational values are changing – they're already slightly above the norm. There are enough physical anomalies down here to keep an entire institute busy!'

'We could split up,' Viktor suggested, 'into two teams.'

'No,' said Dana, pointing to the dead man with his slit throat. 'It's far too dangerous for that. We've got to stay together.' She looked at Friedemann. 'You're leading this mission. Make a decision.'

All of Friedemann's earlier certainty suddenly vanished. He stood stock-still in front of the door he had chosen before – the one with the barely visible arrow drawn in the dust – while Spanger bent down to pick up the diamond earring and Coco, muttering incessantly to herself, struggled to control the pendulum tugging on her chain.

'Professor?' Viktor's anxiety was growing. Should they go through the door with the X, or the door with the question mark and the knocker, or the door with the exclamation mark and the antique box lock?

'Tell us where to go, Professor.'

CHAPTER IV

Dana took a few steps away from the group as they stood there considering which door to go through to search for Anna-Lena. It concerned her that no one had been watching out for what might be going on behind them. After all, they could not rule out the possibility that there were more gunmen lurking around. They had already found two dead bodies: one shot and the other with his throat cut open.

She peered back down the passage; the dim, red glow from the smoking magnesium torch gave them about twenty yards' worth of light, after which the brightness vanished into the gloom like dying embers. Dana had turned off the lamps on her helmet and gun so as not to give potential pursuers any indication as to where she was. She was annoyed that van Dam had not given them any night-vision equipment. She could have brought some from her private stash, although that might have raised some questions – especially from Viktor.

She'd have to make do with the torches, even though the smell carried through the passages, betraying her presence even without the light. She had always hated those things, on all of her jobs.

Apart from the voices of Friedemann, Ingo, Viktor and

Coco, whose heated conversation echoed through the red-illuminated cathedral-like hall, Dana could hear whispering and muttering, as if the spirits of those who had died in this place were trying to contact her. They spoke to Dana using her name, sounding friendly and engaging, like someone asking for the best table at a restaurant instead of the one next to the lavatory.

Dana dismissed it as just interference over the radio. It was bad enough that the parapsychologist was practically wetting himself with excitement – something in these caves was both measurable yet inexplicable, and that worried Dana.

She kept her eyes fixed defiantly on the passage.

As much as she considered Viktor to be the only dependable man down here, Dana was annoyed by his constant interrogation of her as to how and when they had met. She was certainly not going to help him with that – because she knew.

The quintet behind her was still debating which door to open. Dana left the decision to Friedemann. He was their leader, so by all rights he should take responsibility for it.

She spotted a movement in the corridor at the point where the dying red glow transitioned into darkness. A dog-like shadow was brushing carelessly back and forth, protected by the blackness. The beast appeared to be undecided as to what to do, but Dana felt as if hunger, bloodlust, curiosity and a desire to defend its territory were mixing together to create some overriding impulse, although what that was going be to, she could only guess . . .

She looked through her visor and adjusted the zoom. It

was too gloomy to see what was going on with the four-legged creature. 'At least it's not a cave bear,' she said quietly, trying to get a better look at it. 'How did you get down here, you little stray?'

This opened up the possibility that the chamber system had more than one entrance and exit, which was good news for van Dam, but bad for her rescuers. The clues on the doors might prove to be wrong and lead them to search in completely the wrong direction.

The dog-sized quadruped clearly knew he was being watched. He made clever use of the shadows, moving purposefully forward through the passageway.

Through her optical sight, Dana caught the occasional glimpse of magnified long fangs flashing menacingly. Her pulse quickened. The creature baring its teeth was coiled, ready to attack.

She would have to risk turning on her gun's tactical light.

The focused blue-white beam flitted across the walls in search of a target.

She was just about to call a warning to the group, who were still busy arguing, when the outline of the creature blurred, just as if it had activated a cloaking device before the cone of light could strike it – and it reappeared moments later next to Dana in the passage, its jaws wide open, revealing a forked tongue that bounced over its rows of fearsome teeth.

Dana instinctively squeezed the trigger.

Her G36 obediently spat out a long burst of fire as the muzzle flash glared, temporarily blinding her.

Dana continued to hold down the trigger, feeling the rhythmical recoil on her shoulder and imagining the creature twitching under the impact of the bullets.

The racket of the assault rifle suddenly dropped in pitch and the head of flame in front of the barrel blazed away in slow motion, while each of the ejected bullet cases took an age to hit the ground.

Dana was still wondering about the sudden slow-motion phenomenon she was caught in when the G36 struck up its initial tone once more and after a final crackle, it clicked off.

She took her finger off the trigger and crouched next to the entrance to the cave, her heart pounding. Still panting, she switched off the lamp. Sweat was running down her spine as she took in the empty cartridges scattered all around her.

In her panic she had emptied the magazine, so she quickly set about swapping it over, angry with herself for behaving like a complete novice.

'Ms Rentski?' Friedemann called out in alarm. Even cowering, he towered over her. Ingo was still looking at his equipment with fascination, as if he hadn't noticed the gunfire at all.

'I swear there was something there,' Dana said, letting the breech block snap forwards before looking back over her shoulder at Spanger and Viktor, who were crouching nearby, both locked and loaded. 'We desperately need to find out where this girl is, and fast!'

'Well, "there was something there" is a bit vague,' Spanger complained, although he was looking a bit too keen to join in with the shooting. 'That was quite the racket you were making.'

'It was a shadow – as large as a big dog. It came out of the passage and as soon as I opened fire it disappeared.' Dana recalled the forked tongue, the vicious teeth and indefinable whine which, combined with the voices whispering her name, were causing her nerves to become increasingly frayed.

'Spanger, have a look around,' Friedemann ordered.

Viktor thought he was obviously enjoying his role as group leader, and he was trying not to make his excitement about the doors too obvious.

'*Me?* It's Troneg and Rentski who are carrying on as if they're fresh out of Special Branch. They should be the ones to go.' He tapped the pistol in his holster. 'This is all I've got – the MP5 is as good as empty. I'm completely ill-equipped for this job.'

'You're not wrong there.' Friedemann smiled and placed his hand on the second door from the left – the one with the knocker removed – as if he were greeting a long-lost friend. 'But you're here to protect us, aren't you? You said so yourself.'

Spanger glared at the professor in disbelief. He had nothing against a shoot-out, but alone in the dark? He thought feverishly of ways he could get out of it without being considered a coward.

Ingo looked at Coco, who shrugged her shoulders to suggest she did not care in the slightest whose job it should be to investigate the movement in the passage. She tugged on the taut chain of her golden pendulum, which was pointing unerringly at the door with the X marked on it.

'My gauges are proving to be rather enigmatic, but . . . there's nothing down here that would be strong enough to have an effect on precious metals in this way.' Ingo tapped the pendulum, causing it to quiver slightly in the air before it returned to its former position like a stubborn tracker dog. 'Where did you get this from?'

'Found it.'

'Found it? Where?'

Coco pressed her lips together. She didn't want to reveal the truth of the matter. 'At a flea market. It had a . . . a *presence*. I could feel it.'

In fact it had been a present, arriving in a unsecure tatty parcel which looked as if it had already been sent all over the world.

Sender: illegible.

Enclosed was a handwritten note, stating that this was an artefact used by a number of renowned clairvoyants to help them to make their prophecies.

Coco had almost thrown it away, but after speaking to a jeweller who had assured her it was real gold, she'd decided to keep it. And today it was revealing its power for the very first time.

'We both know you're not a proper medium. You didn't feel a thing.' Ingo stole a quick glance at the others, who were still deep in discussion after Spanger's refusal to comply with Friedemann's order. 'You're a terrible liar. Who was it who sold it to you?'

Coco cleared her throat and took a couple of steps away

from him. She had ruled out the notion that the present was a coincidence. The pendulum was *meant* to find its way to her. It was Providence.

'Professor, why do you think this isn't the right way to find her?' Ingo tried to hold Coco back, but she skilfully evaded his fingers.

'I've got an idea.' Spanger raised his sub-machine by way of explanation. '*I'll* secure the area. *Rentski* was the one who started shooting, so she can come with me. It's only fair.'

Dana rolled her eyes. 'In my next life I can only hope to be as wonderful a person as you. And don't point that thing at me!'

'We'll do it our way,' Viktor said, signalling to Dana to move forwards. 'Spanger, you keep an eye on the five doors. I'll cover Rentski.' He lifted the holster for the G36 onto his shoulder. 'Ready?'

'Ready.' Dana stalked forwards, rifle in hand. The helmet lamp and the tactical light shone ahead, illuminating her path. This time she felt fearless.

She proceeded by advancing in military fashion, her knees bent and body inclined slightly forwards, taking two or three steps at a time, then stopping and listening before carrying on again. She shone her light up and down as she crept her way yard by yard back down the passageway and away from the hall – and from the rest of the group.

She could find no evidence of the beast.

She came across bullet fragments from the G36, compressed and splintered, but without any blood or tissue fragments on them. Yet she was certain she had hit the monstrous four-legged creature. Fear crept through her once more, raising the hairs on her neck and paralysing her thoughts. She had not been counting on there being bulletproof beasts down here.

'Well?' Spanger bleated behind her, his voice echoing down the passage. 'Have you found anything?'

'Fucking idiot,' Dana muttered, turning on her radio. 'We've got radios, Spanger. But if you want to tell everyone else down here where we are, you feel free to carry on yelling.'

'Sorry,' he shouted back, 'after your trigger-happy incident I imagine we're already lit up like a Christmas tree, though, right?'

Dana rolled her eyes.

'Wait there. I'll make it brighter for you.' Spanger threw a flare inches past her face before she could stop him; it came to rest a couple of feet beyond her.

'If he does something like that again I swear I'll stick it up his arse,' she swore, kicking the flare and causing it to strike the wall and disappear around a bend in the passage.

With a light crackle the reddish flame began to emerge; first it smoked, then it rushed out of its casing as the mixture of chemicals caught fire, burning unquenchably.

She could see a crossroads in front of her which appeared to be just as empty as the passage she had just crept through: no beast; no blood; no foes.

'There's nothing there. Come back, Rentski – we've got to investigate those doors,' she heard Viktor saying over the radio. 'Anna-Lena is our priority.'

The familiar sound of soft footsteps and the clinking

of combat gear suddenly emanated from the surrounding passages. Dana knew those noises very well. She swore and switched off her lights, then shifted position. She lay down flat on the floor and raised her rifle. 'I can hear footsteps,' she whispered. 'It sounds like some sort of commando unit.'

'What are you going to do?' Viktor asked anxiously.

'Wait. There are too many of them. If I stand up I'll be a sitting duck. Cover me, Troneg, and watch your back, at least while Spanger hasn't learned the difference between *safety on* and *safety off*.'

In the red glow of the torch, human shadows danced along the walls, then abruptly stopped. A murmur set in and the name 'Anna-Lena' was combined with the name 'Ritter' on several occasions. Or was it someone's name? A radio beeped softly; a call was coming through to the other team.

'I count at least four people, presumably men,' Dana said quietly. Anything was better than the bullet-proof beast. She would gladly back herself against human opponents. 'I don't recognise their weapons, though. They've definitely been kitted out differently from us.'

The flare began to lose its luminosity, burning lower and lower until the glow went out completely.

Dana lay in the pitch-blackness, keeping her breathing as quiet as possible so as not to reveal herself. She found herself wondering if the unknown group had been using the beast as a bloodhound and whether they were about to set it loose once more. She promptly broke into a sweat.

The sound of careful footsteps echoed towards her as they moved forwards. They paused again – then abruptly withdrew.

All was quiet in the passage.

'Troneg, I think they know where she is. And these aren't the goodies.' Dana stood up and switched the tactical light at the bottom of her G36 back on, narrowing the beam with her hand to create a slit. 'I'll follow them and come back once I know who we're dealing with.'

'No, Rentski – don't,' she could hear him saying, but she paid no attention.

The noises from the unknown troops were unmistakeable: boots and the clanking of military equipment served as her guide. Cones of light flitted across the walls a long way in front of her; several times the team went around corners. The smell of burning flares occasionally reached her nostrils, but for the most part she was surrounded solely by bare, cold rock.

Dana left small markings on the stone walls to help her to find her way back. She had moved beyond the range of the signal-boosters, so she could hear neither van Dam nor the other members of her team.

She stole through the burrowed, brick-reinforced corridors until she suddenly stopped being able to hear the group in front. It looked like they had completely disappeared.

'Shit.' Dana removed her hand from the lamp and shone it all around her.

The bright light flashed over an old enamel sign with white writing on a black background. The ancient lettering revealed the presence of a headquarters, with an arrow underneath pointing to the left.

Was that where these strangers were staying?

Dana followed the arrow, which led her around a sweeping turn in the passage and left her standing in front of an open steel door covered in rust and dirt; thick spiders' webs were stretched across the gap where it had been left ajar. It was clear no one had entered the room from this side for a very long time indeed – either that, or this underground world was host to the fastest-spinning spiders known to man. Nevertheless, her curiosity impelled Dana to step through both the cobwebs and the unlocked door. The threads crackled softly and left silvery patterns on her black clothing and helmet.

She found herself in an ante-chamber with thick iron doors leading off on all sides. They had signs on them – telephone room, map room, meeting rooms I to IV, armoury – and there were also rooms she thought were meant to be relaxation areas.

Dana switched on her helmet lamp. 'Must be from the Nazis,' she said, grinning. 'As always.'

But there were neither swastikas nor military insignias on the walls.

Dana paused, reflecting. Perhaps there were maps and other documents down in this underground facility that they could use to help them find Anna-Lena? Who knew how large this labyrinth might be?

She entered each room expectantly, only to discover they had all been cleared out, stripped bare, except for the dusty furniture and occasional yellowing scraps of paper hanging from rusty nails on the walls; it looked as if all the documents and maps had been torn down in a hurry. A forgotten typewriter, two telephones and an instruction booklet for using the power system made her search feel like something more akin to walking through a recently looted museum.

'Not Nazis then,' Dana muttered as she walked into Meeting Room IV. The rays of light from her lamp illuminated poorly erased blackboards; she could make out the remnants of formulae surrounding a drawn-on door. 'And no Amber Room.'

The abbreviations and symbols meant nothing to Dana, although she didn't think they looked like the sort of formulae commonly used in maths, physics or chemistry.

'A door and some calculations.' Since she could not send photographs with her camera, van Dam would not be able to view them on the surface. Instead, she pulled her phone from her pocket and took a few snapshots of the blackboard. She hoped the parapsychologist would be able to find some use for them.

Before she returned, she inspected the slate surfaces and the little notes that had been inscribed into them. In one corner, the panels were more than one hundred years old, so this headquarters almost certainly predated the Nazis. But there were still no clues as to when and why the place had been abandoned, nor who had used it.

When Dana turned back to the exit, she glimpsed a pile of scorched pages in the corner behind the door that had not been completely burned.

She bent down and skimmed the handwritten reports, which all bore different dates, from the previous century.

At first glance there didn't appear to be anything of use for her or her team.

The text was handwritten, clearly scrawled down in a panic and it was written in the old German *Sütterlin* handwriting script, which made it even more difficult to read. It took a considerable amount of effort for Dana to decipher the note at all.

... the whole time!

But no one believed me.

I've now provided evidence that the Particulae are becoming unstable – and not just since yesterday. The fluctuations are only a small part of the phenomena, as there are numerous physical effects as well.

It is far too dangerous to remain in the immediate vicinity of the doors. The defects in the fragments are such that we cannot guarantee the proper function of the passages. Everything we have established for regular service no longer applies, as the anomalies now extend to possible temporal shifts and the creation of random realities.

It appears we have needlessly sent several good men and women to their deaths, which we will have to write off as losses resulting from arguments. We absolutely cannot do any more experiments with our best people.

In addition, my calculations have shown that with the increasing decay in the fragments, not just the function of the doors in this locale is affected, leading to defective results, but also violent exothermic reactions occur as soon as the metal parts start to dissolve as a result of their instability.

Records from the 18th century suggest that all manner of disasters can ...

Here the message ended.

Dana slipped the sheet under her bullet-proof vest to show to the parapsychologist. He'd have a better chance of figuring it out than she would.

'Fluctuations,' she whispered to herself pensively as she left the headquarters.

Fluctuations and phenomena.

She remembered the way her G36 had suddenly begun to fire in slow motion and how gravity had ceased to exist in the hall. These things had not been merely figments of their imagination – so was that what the author of this note was talking about? And were the dog-sized shadow and Anna-Lena's replica part of it as well? If that was the case, what else could they expect?

Dana returned to the labyrinth of corridors and looked for her markings on the wall. She couldn't return to the group quickly enough.

'Rentski?' Viktor called over the radio, his voice concerned. 'Rentski, come back.'

She did not answer.

'Mr van Dam?'

But their employer was silent as well.

Viktor turned to the group. 'Is anyone still able to make contact with the surface?'

Friedemann, Coco and Ingo, standing in front of the doors, were talking quietly together, ignoring his question.

'He's gone for me as well.' Spanger looked at Viktor and scratched his Tony Stark beard. He was about to add something when he suddenly gave an involuntary shudder. The hairs on the back of his neck were standing to attention, as if they could feel a ghost standing next to him.

Don't move a muscle, Carsten, came a voice in his ear, a whisper that was neither male nor female. *I've come to save you. If I don't save you, you'll die. Along with the others. All the others who have been underground with me for decades.*

Spanger froze. He managed to stop himself from spinning on his heels to look for the origin of the voice. Spirits. Demons. Something he could not explain and the reason behind the parapsychologist's excitement. Van Dam must have known from the start – and yet he had sent them into this nightmare regardless!

I'll always be with you from now on. To give you a helping hand whenever you need it. The voice spoke softly in his ear, enveloping him with warm breath that smelled of dust, dry skin and oil. *If you don't do it, you'll lose your mind. You'll find out what I mean by that soon. I am the only force who recognises you for what you are – for how* strong *you are. For what a wonderful nature you have. You deserve to be saved. We'll talk soon!*

Spanger swallowed hard as he felt the presence dissipate. The spirit, or whatever it was haunting him, had completely dissolved away. 'Hey, Doctor Theobald. What's going on with your gadgets?' he asked. 'Anything special?'

'No, Mr Spanger – well, yes, but nothing has changed, if that's what you mean.' Ingo blinked at him through his glasses. He had attached the gauges to form a relatively wieldable block, meaning he would not have to keep rebuilding them every time they moved on.

'Why do you ask? Have you seen something or . . . ?'

'Oh nothing.' Spanger rubbed his neck to feel whether

the area felt colder. He had imagined it. 'Just wondering. What's the plan then? For the doors?'

'I'm absolutely certain it's this one.' Coco was looking at her hovering pendulum, which was now lightly vibrating and trying to force itself closer to the penultimate door.

'Just because the door is the only one marked with an X? Is that not a bit too obvious?' Friedemann pointed to the middle door, in front of where he was standing. 'We've got to go through this one.'

'How have you come to that conclusion? Since when did geologists know anything about mysticism?' Ingo said, taking Coco's side. After all, there had to be a very good reason why her pendulum was acting like that.

The professor barked a laugh. 'Oh, you'd be surprised.'

'What do you mean?' Coco drew her perfectly plucked eyebrows together.

'Surprised at how many places of worship are underground. There are more than just crypts and sepulchres to be found in caves.' Friedemann gestured around the enormous chamber, the reddish light making him look like a self-satisfied demon who had lured them all into his trap. 'What do you think we've got here? It's certainly not a collection of doors made by an elderly hobbyist looking for an excuse to get away from his wife. Someone knew exactly what they were doing.'

Ingo loosened the chin-strap of his helmet and rubbed his cheeks where the material was starting to cut into his flesh. 'So this isn't the first time you've seen something like this.'

Friedemann smiled and laid a hand on the broken knocker.

'No, it's not. I once stumbled upon a mysterious door while exploring a cave system.' He pointed to the symbols, which looked as if they had been added by a set designer: they were mystical and attractive, and at first glance, both familiar yet incomprehensible. 'It had the same markings.'

Coco stared at her twitching gold pendulum, spellbound. 'But . . . we can all see it reacting to *this* door. The door with the X. Well, as soon as I think about the missing woman, that is.' She looked uncertainly at Ingo, who smiled back at her. 'What happened with the door you came across last time, Professor?' she asked.

'It brought us back to the surface.'

'What a surprise,' Spanger remarked. He'd slung his sub-machine gun over his shoulder as if he were an action hero.

Viktor was following their discussion attentively. He had not expected the geologist to be a connoisseur of these sorts of situations, but this did explain why he had been assigned as their leader.

'You're quite right it was a surprise,' Friedemann said, ignoring Spanger's sarcasm. 'We were about a mile below the surface at the time. And here' – he tenderly stroked the lion's face, wiping the dust off it – 'the miracle is repeating itself. I'm sure of it.'

'How?' Spanger enquired, speaking for everyone. 'Was there a lift behind it?'

Friedemann shook his head. 'I've . . . heard of those. Doors that . . . lead to nothing. The Topos door is very old. It's always been an inspiration for fairy-tales, scary stories and all manner of myths and legends.'

Ingo was sorely tempted to start giving them a little talk about the cultural history of doors, but thought he'd rein himself in a little under the circumstances. He said, 'For as long as men have been building doors, gates and portals, they have been combined with something special: protection; defence; the next level. This is not specific to any one culture. I'm talking about doors to the heavens, Open Sesame; Narnia. The monster that lives in your wardrobe.'

'Narnia wouldn't be too bad,' Spanger commented with a smirk. 'Paradise? Would that do?'

Ingo looked at his gauges and their displays. 'But to date, I haven't been able to verify any of these stories. Every investigation I've ever undertaken as a parapsychologist has drawn a blank – nothing, nada, zilch. Just as with ghosts.' He pressed the buttons on his paired-up instruments, his tongue protruding a little from the right-hand corner of his mouth as if he were a child deep in concentration. 'Now I've finally found some proof.'

'Doors that lead to nothing. Or to the surface.' Friedemann was still convinced he had chosen the correct passage. 'Or to wherever else.'

Coco remained stubbornly in front of the door she had chosen, the one with the X on it. 'I still don't understand, Professor, why you think we'll find the girl through there. My pendulum and the energy it's harnessing are all speaking with one voice.' She pointed to the cross drawn on in lipstick. 'The supernatural and the laws of physics are in unison here.'

Friedemann shone his lamp onto the floor. A barely discernible arrow had been drawn in the dust, and there was a scrap of dark green cloth lying next to it. 'That's why. Miss van Dam has left us a clue. I think that trumps both your pendulum and the earring Spanger found in front of the other door.' He placed his hand on the door handle. 'Speaking of which, Mr Spanger, get ready. Reckon you'll be able to keep us safe? Or have you got other ideas again?'

'Wait a minute – don't be so hasty. We've lost Rentski,' the stocky man responded, running the muzzle of his sub-machine gun nervously over his beard. 'Don't you think we should wait for her to come back?'

Viktor approved of the suggestion, even if it had come from Spanger. He directed his own light into the dark passageway, but there was still no sign of the woman. A slow realisation was beginning to dawn on him, about where he knew her face from. Of course there was no twin sister, as Dana had asserted.

Friedemann shook his grey head, his glasses reflecting the light in such a way that it looked as if there were nothing behind them. 'I'm the leader here. And our orders are clear.'

He walked forward and opened the door with the broken knocker.

It swung wide without offering any resistance.

The only thing that was revealed by the light of the torches and lamps was a wall of bare rock.

Spanger laughed out loud. 'Oh yes! *Much* better than a pendulum and an earring – I can see that now!' His laughter bounced off the rocky walls, the echo fluttering around them like an excitable bat.

'I don't understand!' Friedemann closed the door, then

opened it again. It weighed much less than he had expected, as if its hinges had an invisible supply of air supporting the door. He repeated the process several times, but still the bare stone remained. 'It was different before,' he said angrily.

In a rage, he slammed the door shut and walked over to the one Coco had chosen, the one with the red lipstick X. He pushed the medium roughly aside and grasping the handle, turned it – but even after violently shaking it, it made no difference.

The X door was locked.

'This *cannot* be happening!' The professor stalked back and forth in front of the doors several times, his thin frame making him look like an angry black flamingo. He eventually stopped in front of the one on the far right, the door with the box lock and an exclamation mark drawn on it, where Spanger had found the earring.

'Then it's got to be this one!' He jerked it open.

Instead of rocks, the light from Friedemann's helmet lamp cut into a deep blackness. He quickly moved in front of the others to have a closer look. He wanted to be the first, like Roald Amundsen or Neil Armstrong or Howard Carter.

'Finally!' he exclaimed jubilantly. 'I might have been wrong about my initial decision, but we're making some progress now.'

'Careful! You can't just open *my* door like that.' Spanger dropped his heavy rucksack and set off at a shambling run, his sub-machine gun at the ready. 'I told you this was the right one. Weren't you listening? I said so straight away.'

'Professor, we really need to talk about your previous experiences with these doors,' said Ingo. He picked up his instruments and followed Spanger. The weight of the block he had fashioned was cumbersome, but there was no other way: he was making discovery after discovery down here and they all had to be properly documented. 'We must, you hear me? It's vital for our mission.' And for his own research. A Nobel Prize was suddenly within his grasp.

Coco fell in behind them, the pendulum still twisting in her hand to show that the door with the X was the right one to find the missing girl. The idea of going through a different door felt utterly perverse to her, not to mention dangerous.

Spanger's laughter could still be heard bouncing back and forth between the walls, the sound soft but reflected in such a way that it sounded backwards, which made the noise all the more sinister.

'*Your* door, Mr Spanger? Hardly.' The professor stepped fearlessly across the threshold of the furthest right-hand passage. 'Let's go – everyone follow me! Look, there's a passage here. We can talk later but right now there's no time to lose. Our young woman is in grave danger.' He looked over his shoulder at Viktor, an excited glow glimmering in his brown eyes. 'Troneg, you wait here and keep an eye out for Rentski. Once you've found her, come and join us. Can you do that?'

'Of course, Professor.' There was no point in trying to hold Friedemann back, even if his impetuous actions were the complete antithesis of appropriate behaviour. The fact that the professor had already had some contact with these doors that had such an inexplicable effect on their surroundings had apparently made him entirely blind to the dangers they were facing, such was his enthusiasm.

'Very good. Best of luck.' Friedemann strode into the darkness and the diminished group stepped through the doorway one after the other.

Ingo, at the rear, looked back at Viktor once more. 'I hope it won't take you too long. You're a better bodyguard than Spanger.' He put down his instruments for a few seconds and placed a stone in one corner of the frame to stop the door with the red exclamation mark from slamming shut. 'I'd feel much more comfortable if I had you two with me.'

Viktor acknowledged him with a wave, then returned his attention to the passage.

Ingo took a deep breath and re-tightened his chin-strap. 'What an adventure. Such possibilities!'

He disappeared into the darkness.

The hall was quieter now, the soft conversations of the quartet from the chamber and the adjoining passageway becoming a distant murmur until even the last of the echoing laughter had died away.

Viktor cursed Dana silently for pursuing the unknown intruders on her own. The group had become separated, all because of this so-called free-climber.

The pressure on the stone Ingo had placed in the door frame was so great that a small piece of it came loose. With its altered shape, the wedge could no longer withstand the force of the heavy door and it slid free. The door gradually started to close, clicking shut with a curious, barely perceptible sound.

Viktor, crouching impatiently at the entrance to the hall with its towering walls, did not notice it. His imagination was racing, creating scenarios in which Dana was in danger and needed his help. He had severe doubts about Spanger being the bodyguard for a group that was not exactly combat-ready. The man was far more likely to shoot one of them by accident. All this waiting around was making Viktor nervous, one useless thought following another.

He had to do something.

'Kcuf!' Viktor drew out another flare – then stopped short.

The word had come out wrong.

He repeated it slowly: 'Fuck.'

It was fine this time. He must have misheard himself.

He rose and threw the lit flare, which hissed and sparked its way into the passage, emitting a bright red glow. Crystalline stone walls, ageing brick edifices and rust-flecked concrete pillars loomed over him.

When nothing happened, he sprinted off, holding his rifle lightly, looking for the spot where he had seen Dana earlier. But even when he got there, it cast no light on the matter; she was obstinately refusing to reappear.

Several questions arose: should he advance or not? And what if he got lost while looking for Dana? What if somebody grabbed him – or if he fell into a chasm in the ground?

'Can anyone hear me?' Viktor suddenly heard van Dam's voice in his headset and gave an involuntary wince.

'Mr van Dam!' He breathed out, relieved. 'We lost reception. Are you still in contact with Rentski?'

'No – not with her, nor with Friedemann or the others. You're the only one I've been able to talk to.'

'Right you are.' Viktor gave the businessman a brief summary of what had happened in the intervening period. 'Friedemann hasn't taken any boosters with him. That'll be why.' Viktor trotted back into the hall, crouched down beside the entrance and took up a position to guard the passage where the flare was burning. It would be a particularly stupid idea to do the very thing for which he had just chided Friedemann as being unprofessional, which was to simply head off. He had to overcome his impatience.

'Tell me, did Anna-Lena know these doors were down here?'

'Well . . .' Van Dam hesitated.

Viktor sighed. 'Right. Another question then. Why did you choose to keep this from us?'

'It's irrelevant to your mission. I never believed in their existence – neither did my daughter.'

'*Believed?* Whatever's going on down here has nothing to do with *belief*. Doctor Theobald can measure it: *physically*.'

'It was a story my mother told me, and when I stopped wanting to hear it, she talked to Anna-Lena instead – and from an early age.' Van Dam tapped something on his keyboard. 'The house you walked through belonged to my grandmother. She was a talented storyteller and she loved telling tales about magical doors. But my grandfather forbade her to ever go into the cellar, because of the monsters that might come out of the doors.'

'That's why you gave us a parapsychologist,' Viktor said. 'And Professor Friedemann.'

'Sorry? Why should the geologist have anything to do with that?' the businessman asked in astonishment.

'Because he was already familiar with the doors.' Viktor was irritated. 'Was that not the reason for his involvement?'

'Mr Troneg, I had no idea that those doors even existed! I thought it was merely something she had invented. But my daughter always wanted to pursue the matter further. Ever since she was a little girl she's been fascinated by the house, the cellar and the factory. How many times have I had to go looking for her ...' Van Dam sighed. 'It doesn't matter. You know what I expect of you, whether or not any of those doors lead you directly to Hell.'

Maybe we're already there, Viktor thought. 'Mr van Dam, we'll need to—'

'Troneg?' Dana suddenly broke into the middle of their conversation.

Viktor breathed a sigh of relief. 'Oh thank God! You had us all worried. Do you have any idea where you are?'

'I tried to follow the other group but they lost me. I should be with you any minute now.'

'Have you seen any sign of my daughter yet?' van Dam asked hastily.

'No, I'm afraid not. Does the name *Ritter* mean anything to you, Mr van Dam?'

'Ritter ... ? No. Why do you ask?'

'Those guys mentioned it. Could be that ... Well, don't worry. I came across some sort of headquarters that looked as if it had been abandoned a long time – maybe early 1900s, or a bit after. I'm no historian,' Dana said. 'Other things as well, but first I need to find my way back to the hall.'

Viktor stood with his back to the door, his eyes fixed on the corridor. Cones of light were scurrying around one another. 'Have you turned your lamps on, Ms Rentski?'

'Yes! Can you see the beam?'

'Wiggle it twice horizontally, then once vertically. I don't want to get you mixed up with an enemy and shoot you by accident.'

The light immediately moved as instructed. 'Best leave that to Tony Stark. Spanger can do that for us without needing a misunderstanding.'

'Right you are. Come on then.'

Unnoticed by Viktor and Dana, who was approaching cautiously, the latch of the door with the broken knocker slowly opened. The entrance swung open by an inch, tentatively and hesitantly, as if someone were considering whether it would be a good idea to step out into the open and reveal themselves.

The gap was tiny ... but sufficient.

Blackness trickled out of the gap like a flow of ink, crawling exploratorily into the red-lit hall.

A few seconds later, the door behind Viktor flew open.

BEHIND DOOR !

Professor Friedemann, Coco, Spanger and Ingo entered a dark, twisting passage. The beams from their helmet lamps flitted around them, striking nothing but dry rock and what looked like hastily constructed brick walls. The floor was covered in debris – dirt, the occasional chunk of stone and what looked like bone fragments. The air smelled stale, with a disconcerting note of strong electrical discharge and fried electronic devices. The smell was not a pleasant accompaniment.

'Let me go in front,' said Spanger, holding his MP5 carelessly in one hand as he tried to take the lead, but Friedemann refused to allow him past.

'I'll tell you if I need you to shoot anything,' he said shortly.

The group moved carefully forwards. After a few yards, what they had thought was a corridor turned out to be a room with no other exits. The only door available to them was the one they had just come through.

'Damn it! I thought ...' Friedemann looked around angrily. 'I thought we were on the final stretch.'

'No missing daughter then,' Coco noted with satisfaction. Her pendulum was still standing horizontally in the air, held in place by the silver chain, with its golden tip pointing back at the exit. 'I told you before: it's the door with the red X.'

'No other passage . . .' Ingo examined the rough brick wall to his left. 'There could well be something behind here.'

His fingers brushed over the ridges caused by the bricks having been so roughly laid while he peered closely at them over the rim of his glasses. 'This wall looks as if it was built in a hurry. Someone wanted to get out of here fast.'

'Better off getting out of this hole,' Spanger breathed out reproachfully, once again denied his opportunity for heroism and a safe shoot-out. 'What's this all about then? Who built—' He looked past Ingo and back at the exit. 'Shit! The door—'

It closed softly, a metallic sound mingling with the light click, as if a thousand needles had fallen onto a glass shelf.

The quartet remained rooted to the spot, as much from the eerie sound as the shock. The hairs on the back of their necks were standing to attention.

'Don't panic,' said Friedemann unnecessarily. 'We've managed to open the door once before and we'll do it again.' He moved towards the exit. 'And then we'll go through your door, Ms Fendi. I promise.'

Coco was staring at her pendulum, which was suddenly just dangling from the chain, devoid of any tension. 'What . . . what's happening?' she whispered. 'This room – it's suppressing my . . . my abilities.' The fear in her voice was palpable. She was locked in, cut off, isolated – surrounded by kryptonite.

'One moment.' Ingo picked up his instrument pack and moved it back and forth, looking for anything unusual, but the numbers and curves on the small displays remained within their regular parameters. 'At least we haven't got any weird physics to worry about.' He put his hand on Coco's back, feeling the heat emanating from her.

The adrenalin was making her sweat. 'Nothing's going to happen to us,' he said quietly.

She looked at the pendulum again, her face drained of colour. She should never have come back down here, not for van Dam's entire fortune. 'This can't be good news.'

'Stop being a prophet of doom and let me handle it.' Spanger pushed past the professor and tried to open the door.

The latch refused to give way.

'Shit, really? If this is Troneg's idea of a joke, he'll be getting a bloody nose from me.' Spanger examined the ancient box lock, trying to see the lock's mechanism, then shook the handle and started pounding on the wooden door. 'Troneg – hey, Troneg! Can you hear me?'

'Van Dam? Are you with us?' said Ingo, trying the radio again but getting only silence in response. The chamber was absorbing any signal there might have been. Since the lock had clicked shut, nothing could enter or leave the area, be it electronic or metaphysical. With a quick glance he checked to see that his instruments hadn't broken. 'It must be the walls. They're too thick, I think.'

Coco glared at Friedemann. 'You've got us all trapped in here!' She pointed her finger at him threateningly, her pendulum swinging lightly back and forth on the chain as if to identify the man as the guilty party. 'I said right from the start we ought to trust my pendulum, Professor – trust *me*. That was the whole point of bringing a medium along.'

'I don't understand.' Feeling rather sorry for himself, he raised his arms helplessly. There were clearly gaps in the knowledge he had been able to glean from the markings.

'Neither do I. But what I do understand is that we're fucked if Troneg and Rentski bugger off somewhere else. We'll run out of air before we've even had time to die of thirst.' Spanger's gaze shifted to the bone remnants. 'Or does anyone doubt my assessment?' He picked up a flare from his belt. 'I'll search the room more thoroughly.' He lit it, muttering, 'I won't be able to see a thing without this.'

The chamber was filled immediately with red light and acrid smoke.

'Oh, so you'd rather suffocate us before we die of thirst?' Coco, inhaling grey-white plumes of smoke, started to cough. 'Put that thing out!'

Spanger hadn't thought of that in his zeal to help. 'No can do. They'll even burn under water – and we haven't got any sand to put them out.' He kicked the torch into a corner of the small room. Coughing, he blustered, 'We . . . need the smoke . . . to look for cracks and air pockets in the wall. I'll watch out for turbulence.'

'You fat idiot,' hissed Friedemann. 'You are the very essence of incompetence. What on earth could have possibly made van Dam hire you?'

Spanger had nothing to say in his defence. The professor's words stung him more than he cared to admit. He stood in the red glow like a guilty schoolboy, surrounded by smoke and the reproachful looks of three pairs of eyes.

Ingo, Friedemann and Coco began to debate how to proceed, deliberately excluding him. He had only wanted to help – to be cool, for once. To be *liked*.

Spanger suddenly felt that presence again: the spirit, the being who'd offered to protect him. It was strangely comforting to find somebody who did not hate him.

It appears your situation is somewhat awkward, said the voice to him alone. *As awkward as before, Carsten. Am I right? They all want to be rid of you now. They'll never be your friends. But I will.*

Spanger could see the trio glaring at him occasionally, their eyes full of contempt, anger and disgust as they spoke quietly to one another. It reminded him precisely of how he'd felt before – of the situation that had torn his life into pieces.

It's bad, isn't it? whispered the voice. *Bad how much it still hurts. But I can help you. Just say the word and I'll arrange an . . . accident for them.*

Images from the past rose up in his mind, leaving him feeling degraded, a helpless spectator of his own memories. He didn't want to see that day again, feel it again, go through it all again – but there was no antidote for the poisons of the past, for the trauma.

In the discount shop's barren office he sat at a table under a neon light, wearing his staff uniform. In front of him was an old laptop with a pile of lists lying next to it. There was a half-eaten sandwich by his right hand and a packet of digestives, although most of the biscuits had gone.

An annoyed voice could be heard on the Tannoy outside the room barking, 'Staff to till number two, please. Staff to till number two!'

Carsten looked at the monitor and remained at his seat.

His hand was resting on a book entitled *How to be a Bodyguard*. 'I can do it,' he muttered. 'I can do it this time!'

The door to the staff room swung open.

Svetlana Schiffner, his manager, a very young woman wearing a tight-fitting smock, entered and looked first at him, then ostentatiously at the clock. She represented competence, ambition and diligence, all in a very attractive package – the complete opposite of him. 'Mr Spanger, did you not hear me?'

'I'm on a break. I've still got three minutes.' He pointed to the computer in front of him. 'I'm in the middle of some work.'

'Still pursuing your bodyguard pipe-dream?' She laughed at him contemptuously. 'Have a look at yourself, Mr Spanger. No offence, but there's a good reason why you keep failing.'

Carsten slowly raised his grey-blue eyes. 'I'm afraid I'm going to have to take offence.'

'No, I just mean ... they're *fit*.' She grabbed the book and flipped through it. 'Look at all these training drills. Dear God, they make my gym sessions look like a day at the beach. Have you actually tried any of these?' She didn't wait for him to answer, instead looking at the monitor. 'You're actually signing up for a boot camp? To become a bodyguard in two weeks?' She laughed loudly again, sneering.

'I can do it.' Carsten felt a paralysing weight inside his mind and body. It had taken him a long time to build up his confidence, but his manager was easily tearing it down with her laughter and questions.

'Yes, in precisely the same way you passed your exam to become a branch manager. In that you didn't.'

'I was too nervous.'

'You didn't work hard enough. You had me to speak up for you that time, but it won't happen again, Mr Spanger.' Svetlana was not someone who believed in second chances. She looked back at the clock. 'Your three minutes are up. Till two, please.' Then she left.

Carsten decided to fill in the rest of his information anyway. In his hurry to click through to where he needed to be, he accidentally opened his inbox and immediately saw an old email that he had already read far too often.

IT'S OVER, CARSTEN.
I NEED TO DO WHAT'S BEST FOR ME.
I HAVE NO PROSPECTS IF I STAY WITH YOU,
AND WITH MARIO I GET ...

Carsten deleted it, stony-faced. It had been a mistake to open it again. So many things in his life had happened by mistake and those sorts of events had failed to improve his life. Everything had been a struggle but he wanted nothing more than to find his place in the world: a better place.

'I *can* do it,' he shouted at the computer. 'I'll show everyone.' His fingers curled into a fist. '*Everyone!*'

The door opened again and a trainee called Tilo entered. He was sixteen, dynamic and optimistic. He threw Carsten a pissy look. 'Hey, Chuck Norris' flabby younger brother! Are you going to open till two or—'

'You prick!' Carsten leaped to his feet. He had warned

Tilo a hundred times to give it a rest. He gave the younger man a well-timed blow to the forehead with the heel of his hand. 'You fucking prick!'

Tilo fell to the floor without a sound.

And stayed there.

His blow had had the precise effect described in the handbook. He had knocked his assailant unconscious.

'Mr Spanger,' came Svetlana's icy voice through the speaker, 'please restack the cereal aisle. I'll do the till myself.'

'You're such an arsehole.' Carsten stepped over Tilo, who was groaning on the floor, and left the room. This particular arsehole could get to his feet by himself. He knew he would go running after Svetlana to whine about him, but he was fed up with being constantly insulted. A warning, the sack – it was all the same to him.

Carsten turned away from the checkout tills and headed towards the cereal shelves. He stood there for what felt like an age, staring at the boxes. His mind was racing. He tried to control his rage but he could feel himself slipping inexorably away.

An elderly customer clutching a full shopping bag approached him. 'Excuse me. I'm looking for the special offers shelf. Could you tell me where I can find the organic—?'

'No,' he interrupted absent-mindedly, closing his eyes.

'But you don't even know what I was about to—'

'I said no!'

The woman looked at him indignantly. 'Looks like I'll be spending my money somewhere else.'

Carsten turned his head slowly to face her. There she stood, in her designer clothes and expensive perfume, dripping with arrogance, dressed up to the nines but still rummaging around discount supermarkets looking for bargains. 'Oh, piss off.'

'*What?*'

Carsten marched down the aisle, pursued by the outraged woman. This had really been a shitty day from start to finish and he was fed up with it. He was definitely in the wrong job. For once in his life, he wanted to do something *good* – something *meaningful* –rather than always being an eternal loser.

'You'll regret this,' the woman shouted after him, before turning to address the manager.

Svetlana was immediately on his case. 'Mr Spanger—?'

He stopped and turned around. The look in his eyes seemed to give Svetlana pause; she looked as if she were facing an aggressive dog.

'I've been working here for ten years, every day, for shit pay.'

'Mr Spanger—'

'My wife has left me and I've got an apprentice taking the piss out of me. In fact, they're all taking the piss out of me.' He walked slowly towards her. 'You've been here for six months. I know you put yourself forward for it – but only because you hoped it'd mean I'd move to another branch.'

Svetlana backed away, not daring to contradict him.

Carsten casually took a packet of cereal off the shelf. 'I wanted to put the entire place to the torch. Or blackmail the company. And every time I thought, *No. Don't do it. You'll ruin your life.*'

'Mr Spanger, calm down. Go home, then tomorrow . . .' Svetlana's voice had for once lost its sneering, conde-scending tone.

'Yes, yes, I'll be given my notice. I know.' He glanced at the customer, still seething, as she stopped playing with her pearl necklace and dialled a number on her mobile phone. 'All I've ever wanted is to become something – to *be* someone. What gives you the right to constantly humiliate me?' He walked past her, placed the packet back on the shelf, then paused for several seconds.

He had managed to conquer his inner turmoil, the wild storm raging within him. He didn't want to ruin this moment – he had said it himself. So he followed his own advice. 'It's busy, Ms Schiffner. I'll open the checkout – there's enough change in it, I assume?'

He went to till number two and sat down. At the push of a button and a swipe of his magnetic ID card, the green light above his head was illuminated. Nobody from the long queue at checkout number one switched to Carsten's, where he was sitting behind the till and smiling tensely.

Svetlana and the organic-sale-items lady looked at him with irritation, weighing him up.

'The man's gone insane,' said the well-dressed woman, as if she were an expert. 'I would like an apology. And for him to receive a warning.'

'Mr Spanger – Mr Spanger, just leave it,' Svetlana called from across the shop. 'Go home.'

Then Christel, the cleaner, rushed out of the staff room.

She was waving a cloth in the air, her hands clad in yellow gloves so bright you'd be able to see them through a dense fog. 'Our apprentice – Tilo – he's dead!'

Thirty minutes later, Carsten Spanger found himself once again in the barren office, sitting at the table beneath the neon ceiling light, but this time with two policemen opposite him. He had put his things together in a pile and closed his laptop and the bodyguard manual.

'Mr Spanger, please will you tell us what happened?'

He squinted at the inspector's upper body. Leather jacket, service shirt, black tie. He could not bring himself to look at the man's face because he knew what he would see: indifference. Or disgust.

'Are you refusing to make a statement?'

Carsten shook his head slowly.

'Well then?'

'I just wanted to finally become something. To do something with my life.'

'Mr Spanger, this Mr . . . ?'

'Jungsen. Tilo Jungsen.'

'Mr Jungsen entered the room and . . . ?'

'And called me "Chuck Norris' flabby younger brother". He used to say that to me all the time – and far worse shit than that as well. Constantly.' He studied his powerful fingers. 'How easy it is. They didn't say that in the training manual.'

'You felt provoked and you lashed out.'

'I didn't hit him hard at all. And then – bang, the little twat's dead.' He glanced at the table top, which was still covered in crumbs, with grubby finger marks all over it.

Christel must have stopped working the moment she discovered the dead man. 'He made my life a misery. Truly. I was going to become a bodyguard, you know. I'd've been a damn good one at that. I've already lost twenty pounds. And now this arsehole's dead.'

'Mr Spanger, I'm going to take you for a medical examination first. You're sounding a little confused to me. It is my assessment that you should remain in custody for the time being, until we've clarified the matter.'

Carsten looked at his hands again, as if he could not believe what had happened.

Humiliated.

A convicted murderer.

Completely lost.

A total loser – then, and now . . .

Do you understand? If you ever need me, Carsten, came the androgynous voice in his ear, *I'll always be here for you. I can save you and show you the way out. I'm your friend: your only friend when the dead rise up and come to seek their revenge.*

Spanger rubbed his eyes and beard, then looked at his watch. It appeared that no time at all had passed while his mind had thrown him back to his darkest hour. The dead. The dead are coming for revenge, that's what the voice said. And in a place like this he had no doubt whatsoever that it was speaking the truth.

'What now?' Spanger asked, hoping the others would think the scratching was coming from the smoke, which was becoming gradually thicker.

'As I said, Troneg and Rentski will come and get us out.' Ingo gave Coco's shoulder an encouraging squeeze. The red light of the flare was dancing on his and Friedemann's glasses. 'The young man knows we're in here.'

'Good. But to be on the safe side we need to look out for ourselves as well.' The professor gestured to the walls. 'Start tapping – let's hope we find something that'll help us. As long as the chamber is blocking our medium's abilities, we're going to have to resort to a manual search.'

The quartet started thumping their way along the walls, working inch by inch. There was nothing to differentiate them from the walls in the hall outside other than a few scratched-on words, some chipped edges and crumbling corners – nothing that was of any help to the four of them.

'I can't stop wondering about how the hook found its way into the rock,' said Coco, more to herself than anything else.

Spanger, lost in his thoughts, was using the handle of his sub-machine gun as a hammer. 'What hook?'

'For Christ's sake, Spanger,' Ingo shouted, pointing at the sub-machine gun, 'if you're going to mess around with that fucking thing, make sure the safety's on!'

'It's fine.' Spanger hated Ingo for revealing yet another act of negligence on his part, right in front of Friedemann.

'In the wall where that rusty old steel cable was fastened. When we passed through that enormous cave without any ceiling, floor or side walls,' Coco explained. 'Who was the first person to venture into the cave and install a hook? How did they get there?'

'With some sort of launcher, perhaps,' suggested Friedemann. 'And who's to say they were the first?'

'But then they'd have to have known there was something

to anchor it into at the other end,' Coco countered. 'This person knew precisely what they needed to do. And it was a long time ago.' Someone had clearly tried to get to the bottom of the mystery of the doors long before them – but who? And for what purpose?

They continued to search the place in silence as more and more smoke billowed around them, making them cough.

Shall I help you, Carsten? whispered the voice. *It would be ever so easy for me. And the dead are approaching. Believe me, none of the mortals in your group can protect you. They'll laugh at you, jeer at you and leave you behind. One favour for another. That's all it is.*

'This whole job is a load of shit,' Spanger burst out. 'Nothing fits together at all down here: dead bodies; doors that lead to nowhere; this . . . whole nightmare; soldiers who—'

'Oh, don't start complaining, Mr Spanger,' Friedemann snapped, suppressing a cough. 'It's far too early for that. And thanks to your . . . your limited mental capacity, we're about to be smoked out. Then *we'd* have to start moaning and you'd have to keep apologising to us.'

Ingo took a step backwards, away from the brick wall they had just examined. 'Okay, we can stop. These walls are massive. Let's put our faith in Mr Troneg and save our energy in the meantime. And take shallow breaths.' He removed a handkerchief from his pocket and held it over his nose and mouth.

Coco did not want to wait. She was already finding breathing hard enough and her fear was not dissipating at all. She turned to the professor. 'Does your notebook have anything to say about this, Mr Friedemann?'

He whirled around and placed a protective hand over the bag, as if to conceal something. 'What kind of—?'

'I saw you with it earlier. You were leafing through it, with a curious little smile on your face. Is there anything in it that could help us to get out of here?' Coco should have phrased it less like a question and more like a medium would, as someone who knew precisely how to build up tension. 'Now would be a good time for it.'

Spanger turned to look at Friedemann, while Ingo gave him an encouraging look.

'Umm, I don't think so,' he replied.

'Show it to us, Professor,' Ingo demanded.

Friedemann refused him with a cold stare. 'This is my business alone, colleagues.'

'I think it's time for you to open up about your previous experience with these doors,' Ingo insisted. 'It's your duty to us as our leader.'

Spanger raised the sub-machine gun slowly. Sometimes you could become a hero by standing up to the boss to save the rest: a well-intentioned mutiny. 'I also think it would be a good idea.'

'Really? Well, I think it would be far better if you were to shoot the door with your little gun there. The wood looks pretty old.' Friedemann was using the weakest member of the group to divert attention away from himself. 'I can't believe we haven't already tried that.'

Spanger turned and examined the entrance. 'I could – then Troneg will also realise we need his help.' His mutiny was on hold for now because Friedemann's suggestion appealed to him far more.

'If he's still alive,' Coco added.

'Professor.' Ingo held out his hand, not prepared to let it go. 'Show me the book. From one academic to another, as you said earlier.'

'What would you allow yourself to do, Doctor?' Behind his glasses, Friedemann's eyes flashed with fury. 'I have no interest in seeing any of your records, so leave me to my business and I'll leave you to yours. As befits "academic colleagues".'

He thrust Ingo's hand away so violently that the parapsychologist lost his balance and stumbled into Spanger, who promptly staggered away, shocked by the impact. And because, against all advice, he had still not secured the safety catch on his fully automatic weapon, the MP5 roared uncontrollably and spat its bullets out violently in all directions.

Coco screamed and crumpled to the floor.

CHAPTER V

Viktor was crouching at the entrance to the hall, looking over at Dana, when the door, which had previously been shut, flew open. With a crack, it struck the wall and bounced back.

Viktor whirled around, lifting his rifle above his head but could see nothing to shoot at. 'Rentski – come here!' He swung the cone of light all around him as he was searching, trying to make sure he had not overlooked anything – unless there was someone hiding behind the door.

Dana ran into the room, her G36 also at the ready. 'What is it?' She knelt down beside him. 'Where are the others?'

Viktor pointed at the half-open door, fixing his gaze on it. 'The one with the broken door knocker has just sprung open – for no reason at all – at least, so I assume.'

'And?'

'And . . . I don't know. Friedemann and the others went through the one on the far right – the one with the lock and the exclamation mark on it. I think.'

'You *assume* and you *think*?' Dana frowned. 'I'd have thought you'd be more professional than that.'

'I was giving you some light and securing the corridor

because you said you had seen some attackers – or have you already forgotten that?' Viktor replied, feeling insulted.

Dana shone her own light at the half-open door. She somehow felt like the enormous dog-like creature was about to jump out and attack her.

The passage was quiet and peaceful, but what looked like liquid black paint had stuck to the threshold.

'Did you see that?' Dana was gradually becoming used to these strange occurrences underground.

'Yes.'

'And the door simply opened?'

Viktor nodded. 'Tsuj ekil taht ...' He bit his lip and tried again. 'Just like that,' he repeated as Dana look at him with astonishment.

'Did you just say that backwards?'

'I ... no.' He had thought and said the words correctly, but somehow the hall had flipped them around. 'This place is insane. What's next, I wonder?'

Dana contemplated telling him about her slow-motion experience with the rifle, but decided to postpone that. 'Yes, it really is.'

Together they aimed at the gap. From their positions it was impossible to see the other side. There could be anything there: thick rock, a passageway, a chamber – or something altogether different.

And of course, *anything* could be lurking there, such as a dog-like monster that moved so fast you couldn't even properly discern its outline.

'What are you waiting for?' van Dam suddenly urged them over the radio. 'Go and have a look!'

'Very well.' Viktor signalled to Dana to cover him, then hurried forwards. As he did so, he felt as if he had suddenly lost a lot of weight – the abruptly diminished gravity in the room was making him take giant steps, as if he were walking on the moon.

Viktor moved towards the door, behind which could be seen only darkness, until his beams of light revealed walls carved from rock with traces of the cutting work still clearly visible.

'There's something to explore through there.' He stepped forwards. 'It doesn't look like a dead end.'

'Okay.' Dana changed her position and took turns aiming at the passage behind her and the door in front of her. She too had been taking enormous hops before gravity finally pushed her back to the ground. For a brief moment she even thought she could see light bending under this invisible force. 'All safe,' she said tensely.

'Ms Rentski, did you find anything in those passages?' van Dam enquired. 'Any clues about—?'

'Yes, some sort of abandoned headquarters that—'

'Not now,' Viktor hissed from the doorway. The smell had given it away first and now his helmet light illuminated the battered bodies of five men lying on the floor of the small room. 'Ms Rentski, I need you here.'

Their limbs were hanging off them, partly torn and partly bitten off. Their blood was forming a red mirror on the floor that reflected the beams of Viktor's lamp. The wounds did not appear to come from a chainsaw, but he knew of no animal capable of inflicting such injuries, not unless you included the velociraptors from *Jurassic Park*.

The liquid blackness they had spotted at the threshold had vanished.

Dana pressed forward. 'I'll be right there.'

'Dear God—' exclaimed van Dam in horror, seeing the images via Viktor's helmet camera.

'Is that your first team?' Viktor shone his light down and filmed everything around him.

'Yes,' choked the businessman. 'Yes, I . . . That's them.'

'So we were right! It's going to cost you a lot of money, van Dam, for me to stay down here for a liar,' Dana growled as she stopped next to Viktor. She studied the corpses closely, thinking about the creature she had seen in the passage. With the dead bodies in front of the chamber and on the ledge, that made seven. There was still one missing. 'What else are you hiding from us? What's all this shit with the doors? You clearly know far more than you're letting on.'

'I . . . I'm just trying to get more information. *Please*, just look for my daughter – my *real* daughter. I'll give you each an extra million euros!'

Their earpieces suddenly began to crackle.

'Van Dam?' Viktor thumped the uncompliant radio. 'Van Dam?'

Silence.

Dana swore and tried to shut the door, but Viktor stopped her.

'What are you doing?' she snapped. 'Are you seriously planning to spend another second in this tomb? We know who they are and it's not as if we can give them a burial in the cave.'

'We'll leave the door open.'

'Why?'

'So we can find out what's going on in there.'

'What should be going on in there?' Dana laughed in disbelief. 'Do you think the dead are going to rise? Do you believe in zombies? Or ghosts? I thought Doctor Theobald was our resident Ghostbuster.' She was trying to cover up her unease, when what she really wanted to do was to shut the door, lock it, then weld and seal it shut for all eternity.

Viktor's face remained serious. 'The door didn't open by itself. Something pushed it open from the inside. Now, either there's a secret passage in there that someone can creep through, just as this killer has done. Or . . .'

'Great, so you *are* saying you believe in ghosts.' Dana took a few steps back and looked at him in astonishment. She had to admit, secretly though, that it might not be completely out of the question. Not in this place, at any rate. 'Okay. Let's just leave it open, then.'

Viktor tried the remaining doors as a precaution. They were all still shut, apart from the one that had only a large wall of rock behind it. 'I do hope we'll see the others again.'

'Definitely.' Dana had decided to use mockery as a defence mechanism. 'They've got the medium with them so the power of the supernatural will show them the way. The pendulum of doom!'

'Quite the Vincent Price impression, Ms Rentski.'

They returned to the hall entrance and took up positions facing both the room itself and the corridor, with their backs leaning up against the wall as their flares began to spit out their final embers.

Viktor lit two new ones and threw one each into the cathedral-like hall and the corridor. 'Before you tell us what happened in those passages, I'd like to know what you were doing in Darfur back then,' he said, trying once more.

'My twin sister—'

'You haven't got a twin sister. It was you I saw there.'

Dana was about to give a fierce reply, then stopped. 'Hang on a minute. You said *there*. You were talking about photos before, but this time you said "*there*".' Her eyes narrowed. 'You were in Jebel Amir! What's going on?'

'You're right. I was in Jebel Amir.' Viktor lowered his head slowly. 'Unofficially, that is. And not on eht emas edis sa uoy.'

'Shit – you know that came out backwards? This can't be happening again.' Dana was more than happy to let the topic of Dafur drop. In any case, the past was unimportant. She had to tell Viktor about her G36 slowing down earlier. 'This backwards-talking thing is insane, but it's not the strangest thing to happen down here.' She could feel herself becoming lighter again, pulling away from the ground like an astronaut. Her weightlessness caused her to start rising before she could find a ledge to hang on to. 'What the—?'

But this time the no-gravity effect did not end immediately.

'Hold on – to anything!' Viktor cried as he also began to hover uncontrollably. His panicked arm movements caused him to spin around and around.

Everything else on the ground began to rise at the same time. The hissing, smoking torch drifted around, making the shadows waver in harmony with the swirling flames.

'It's because of those bloody doors – I read all about it back at the headquarters.' Dana pointed down at the five doorframes. 'Something about splinters, partic-somethings and anomalies. And about not approaching the doors. You'd have thought Friedemann or Theobald would be educated enough to have understood that.'

'The professor has a little book with him that's got something about this place or the doors written down. I saw it earlier. We'll have to ask him about it when he shows up again.'

'He had a book?' came van Dam's voice in their ears all of a sudden. They had no idea how long he had been listening . 'Why didn't he say so straight away, instead of playing dumb about it?'

'Quiet,' Dana hissed, pushing her foot gently against the wall. 'I can see something.' She lifted her G36 and directed the two beams of light into the passageway. 'Oh shit – it's the beast!' As she had feared, the creature was coming to take a bite out of her.

Viktor, although completely unable to control his flight path, managed to steal a glance back into the corridor while he was spinning.

In the reddish glow of the floating torches and the white light of the concentrated lamps, he could see the same thing as Dana: a creature the size of a large dog – but it was more of a cross between a crocodile and a dog. Its mouth was slightly open and it looked ready to attack.

It ran along the side wall, evidently completely unaffected by the weightlessness. Its muscular body was covered partly with armour and partly with fur, while its eyes glowed like the flames of candles.

'Troneg! Troneg, you've got to find a way to turn back towards me and kill that thing, otherwise we'll end up as dead as those poor bastards in the chamber,' Dana called.

Viktor manoeuvred himself as best he could. It felt odd, trying to handle his automatic rifle in the position he was in, and it was anyone's guess what would happen once he pulled the trigger. The recoil would probably catapult him straight across the hall.

But he had the enemy in his sights and his index finger curled around the trigger to take a shot. 'Now?'

'On three,' Dana replied. 'We've only gone one—'

Gravity returned seamlessly to their lives and things went downhill in a hurry for Viktor. He instinctively rolled over his shoulder but lost the G36 in the process. At least, he thought, he hadn't broken his neck, or any other bones.

Dana landed deftly on her feet and dropped to one knee. Her rifle swung to aim at the beast, who'd leapt from the wall to the floor without breaking stride. It was crucial not to panic again, no matter what tricks her opponent might play. She had to remain calm. 'Troneg, pay attention to where the beast reappears.' She fired off a series of rapid shots.

'Sraeppaer?' Viktor grabbed his own weapon and raised it. He could clearly see the bullets shattering two of its teeth as a hole gaped open at the back of its mouth – but instead of collapsing under the impact, the creature's outline blurred. In a heartbeat it appeared just in front of Dana, hissing angrily.

It teleported – moved across dimensions – too fast for the human eye.

'Oh fuck!' Viktor switched into automatic mode and emptied his entire magazine into the creature's flank and skull. He ignored the recoil jolting his shoulder and kept his aim firmly on the target.

Nevertheless, the finger-long gleaming white fangs tore the G36 from Dana's grasp.

She leaped backwards, pulling her fingers away just in time. 'Finish it off!' she cried out, ripping her Walther P99 from its holster.

To Viktor's relief, the projectiles carved their way through the layers of skin and fur. One of the beast's eyes exploded under the force of the blast, sending white-green blood splattering all over the hall, striking the doors and the floor and causing acrid smoke to rise from the doorframes.

Screaming, the creature spun back around, its outline becoming fuzzy once more, which made it harder to target.

It threw the captured rifle aside.

And sprinted straight at Viktor.

BEHIND DOOR !

A metallic click heralded the end of the MP5's magazine.

The projectiles had been expelled uncontrollably, scattering around the entire chamber, and Spanger had wanted nothing more than for the ground to swallow him whole. Not a single mark or hole had been left in the door at all, but instead, the faintest of glows shimmered over the wood, oscillating up and down as if it were suddenly playing host to the Northern Lights. The crackle accompanying it was reminiscent of a high-voltage current.

Ingo and Friedemann were still crouching on the ground, where they had sought refuge from the flying bullets. Coco was sitting in a corner, whimpering and holding her arm. She'd been struck by a ricochet and blood was seeping out from between her fingers.

'Why is it glowing?' Spanger shouted, the first one to notice the light phenomenon on the door. 'Doctor, why is the door suddenly lit up like that?'

The pendulum on Coco's chain suddenly moved and pointed towards the exit, distracting her momentarily from her pain. 'Quickly – try to open the door,' she cried. The pendulum remained hovering in the air and she gave silent thanks to the mystical powers in whom she had not even believed at the start of the assignment. So far that was the only good thing about this place: it had turned her into a real medium.

Spanger hurried to the door, grabbed the handle and pushed it down. 'Ha – I've got us out!' He pushed the door open. 'There's nothing like escaping a trap.'

'And managing to injure one of us in the process.' Ingo stood up and looked at Coco. 'I'm hoping Troneg or Rentski will have some bandages with them.' He helped Coco to her feet, letting her lean on him.

Fresh air streamed into the chamber, drawing away the smoke from the torch and making it easier for them to breathe. The reddish light grew smaller as the chemical fuel started running out.

When he reached the door, Ingo stopped, staying inside the room, and passed Coco to Friedemann. 'I want to make a record of what these lights mean.' He pulled out his gauges and pointed the block at the door. 'Something must have triggered this process – perhaps one of the bullets? But what exactly did they hit?' There were clear curves shown on the display; the values for electricity and magnetic field were astronomical.

'Get out of there, Nerd Boy,' Spanger urged.

'Coming,' said Ingo, gazing in fascination at the instruments. 'Coming. I . . .' He began to tap the devices, flicking switches on and off and frowning. Then he had an idea for a small, harmless experiment. 'Leave the room and shut the door, please.'

'What?'

'I want to test something – it might give us a better idea about what these doors are all about. And that'll give us a massive advantage when it comes to finding Anna-Lena. Maybe she's in the same situation we were in, only in a different chamber?'

'He's right,' the professor agreed, standing in front of the door as he supported Coco. 'If it could save our lives we mustn't leave anything to chance.'

'Umm . . . and what if we can't get it back open?' Spanger was unconvinced. 'Do you know what you're doing, Doctor?'

'I'm touched by your concern.' Ingo grinned and removed his glasses to wipe the dust off them. 'If I don't come back out, open it from the outside. That worked perfectly fine last time.'

'Be careful,' Coco said. 'No more than a few seconds, do you hear me?'

'Best of luck, then.' Spanger gave Ingo a look that hopefully expressed just how insane he thought this idea was, before shutting the door again.'

A faint crackling echoed around from all sides of the brick chamber, as if ice were slowly cracking under an invisible weight. Then all was silent again. The flare was barely glowing at all now.

'Right. Let's have a look and see what this is all about.' Ingo looked at his measuring devices gleefully.

No sooner had the door closed and the lock snapped shut than the spikes on his gauges flattened out. All the displays were showing zero.

'Mm. That was unexpected.' Disappointment coursed through his body as he turned on his voice recorder.

'Day one. For several seconds the door was surrounded by a force field that collapses as soon as the door closes,' he dictated. He studied the wood, placing his hand on it. 'But what caused it to build up? The impact of the bullets? Our body heat? The light or smoke from the flare?'

Ingo switched off the recorder and pushed the door latch down.

Nothing happened. The door refused to release him from the chamber, which had once again started to fill up with the smoke from the flare.

'Shit.' He tapped on the wood and waited. 'Mr Spanger – open the door, please. The door's locked again.'

Nothing.

His tapping became firmer.

Nothing.

'Spanger? Spanger, open up!' Ingo angrily kicked the door several times. 'If this is some sort of joke at my expense, it's not funny in the slightest.'

'Right, let's leave the ghost-hunter to his little measurements.' Spanger turned to Friedemann and Coco, who was now wearing an improvised bandage, thanks to the professor's handiwork. 'Where's our special ops unit, then?' He looked around.

The light in the corridor they had originally come through was lit up as brightly as if they were underneath a giant floodlight. The dead man in camouflage had disappeared and the skeletal remains lying on the ground had instead been replaced by empty packets of crisps, rubbish and leaves piled up in a corner. Instead of the hieroglyphs and hastily written notes and incantations, there was just graffiti; the whole place reeked of exhaust fumes and damp air, like the petrichor smell after a long rainstorm.

Viktor and Dana were missing. There was neither a trace of blood, nor any missing shells that suggested a fight had taken place.

The scene was wholly wrong.

Coco and the professor looked past him towards the rock face.

'We must have missed something?' Spanger turned around.

There was only one door in the wall – the one through which they had just stepped.

What they had first assumed was going to be the cathedral-like hall, in fact turned out to be a meagre structure, no more than ten feet high, with rust-brown water dripping from a grey concrete ceiling. There was no floodlight, either, but instead a dim natural light that was eking its way through the exit on one side. The wall that had the door embedded in it was also made of concrete.

'We've got this completely wrong,' Friedemann said firmly. 'The force field has taken us to a different place.'

Coco held the pendulum by the chain, but it was behaving like a normal pendant, dangling down and showing not even the merest hint of any extrasensory activity. 'We noticed it too late,' she said apologetically, as if it were her fault for not preventing Spanger from closing the door and shutting out the chamber's former energy.

'No, no, it was my own negligence. I was paying more attention to Ms Fendi's injury than to our surroundings,' Friedemann insisted. 'And by the time we noticed our mistake, it was too late.'

'What is all this shit?' Spanger looked over his shoulder, read the 'Staff Only' sign on the door and pushed the handle down. 'Let's get back to Doctor Theobald, then.'

Behind it lay an untidy room with a burnt-out generator, torched filing cabinets and charred monitors.

Spanger slammed the door shut again. 'Okay, how about this? I'll shoot the door to get the force field to flare up again. Agreed?' He swapped the empty magazine for a full one. 'That's how we did it last time, at least.'

'Wait,' Friedemann ordered. 'First of all, we're on the other side – we have no idea whether it'll work that way around. And you could very easily find yourself shooting Doctor Theobald by accident in the process.'

'There's no one in the generator room,' Spanger replied defensively. He was not about to about to allow his role to be diminished that easily. 'What do you think? How many bullets do we need? I'd like to be a bit more economical with them this time.'

'Why would Theobald be in the generator room? As long as there's no force field around it, the door remains a normal door, my trigger-happy friend. Did you not realise that? So I repeat: *wait*,' the professor ordered snippily. This corpulent health and safety disaster was increasingly getting on his nerves. 'I cannot have you doing us any more harm.' He looked at Coco and forced himself to be kind. 'Can you feel anything, Madame?'

She narrowed her eyes and raised the golden pendulum, which quivered slightly, but that was only because her hand was trembling from cold and fear and uncertainty. She hated this place beyond belief. 'No.'

'The pendulum is refusing to serve us. Perhaps you could see if there's something else in your repertoire that we might try?' Friedemann tapped her bag of utensils encouragingly. 'What else have you got in here that could be of use?'

'No, nothing. Except for my gift.' Coco placed two fingers of her right hand against her temple and closed her eyelids. 'I'm probing. Mentally.' She sent off a prayer to her hidden forces and concentrated hard.

Feeling thwarted, Spanger shouldered the MP5 and, keen to occupy himself with another task, announced,

'In the meantime I'll have a look around to see where this door has spat us out. If you want me to wait, I'm sure you won't mind me doing so outside. That way you won't have to worry about me endangering anyone else.' He gave Friedemann a defiant look. 'Well? What do you suggest?'

'What do you mean?' Friedemann looked at him. At least their talented bodyguard would not be able to shoot him or the medium while he was outside.

'There must be something in your little book about what these doors can do.' Spanger walked past the entrance, in front of which stood a broken chain-link fence.

'Well, it certainly didn't intend to bring us down to the Morlocks.' The professor stayed close to Coco, the P99 in his left hand in case a sudden threat emerged.

'The Morlocks! Wow, I'd completely forgotten about that band.'

'I'm talking about H.G. Wells' classic. *The Time Machine*,' Friedemann replied. He could not believe the man's ignorance – but then, what else had he really expected from Spanger?

Coco opened her eyes and shook her head. 'I'm not getting anything.' In fact she felt no connection to higher forces at all. Walking through that door had apparently made her entirely normal again.

'Fine.' Friedemann cleared his throat and turned his body slightly to retrieve his notebook. No one else was allowed to know what was written in it. 'I'll have a look to see if there's anything in here about it. Sit tight for now.'

'Agreed. As soon as the whole group is back together, we're going to need some explanations from you, Professor.'

Coco picked up her pendulum and strode through the concrete room. 'Meanwhile, I'll keep trying.' Perhaps her gift just needed time to get used to the new environment.

'Lots of explanations.' Spanger glanced outside. 'Fuck academics,' he muttered – and stopped and stared.

The skyline of an enormous city dotted with skyscrapers was stretching out over the horizon. The tallest of the buildings, gleaming in the midday sun and reflecting light for miles all around it, towered over twelve hundred feet high.

Spanger emerged onto a hill. From his elevated position he could make out the furthest foothills of the city. Helicopter-like vehicles of various sizes were buzzing over what must be the suburbs and industrial complexes, sometimes strung out like a string of pearls, at other times roaming in packs like a swarm of insects. Their rapidly spinning rotors reminded him of unmanned drones. Banks of lasers were projecting colourful images onto the façades looming over the streets, but from where he was, he couldn't discern what was written on them, or what was being advertised.

High-banked paved roads and enclosed tubes led to the metropolis from all directions. The capricious door that had spat Spanger, Friedemann and Coco out in this place could be seen within a titanic strut that was supporting a road. They were, in the broadest sense imaginable, beneath a motorway bridge.

'Ms Fendi, Professor – come out here. You've got to see this!' Spanger had never seen a city like this in his entire life, not in terms of architecture, or in terms of transport. 'I don't even know if we're still on Earth.'

Less than ten yards down the hill stood a concrete area piled high with what looked like scrap metal and plastic. Blinking rotor drones whirred all around it, balancing enormous crates while cranes hoisted steel cargo containers into the air, which the flying machines deftly avoided.

'A load of discarded shit,' Spanger muttered to himself. He removed his helmet, looked both ways and left the protection of the pillar to approach the recycling centre. He was definitely going to bring back a souvenir from this particular trip – a souvenir of the impossible, and proof that he hadn't imagined the entire thing.

'What are you doing up there?' came Friedemann's voice from the rear. 'Come back!'

Spanger made a reassuring gesture behind him. Holding his MP5 in such a way that it could not immediately be seen from the front, he announced, 'I'll handle this.' The professor did not need to play at being the boss now; it was his turn. 'Use your radio – that way you won't have to bellow.' He had finally managed to get the right words out!

The drones passed overhead, camera lenses peering indifferently down at him to identify him as an obstacle and allow the cargo units to fly in an arc above his head.

Spanger stepped between the mountains of plastic to his right, which had been neatly pressed and stacked together, and a massive wall made of compacted metal cubes that bore no trace of what they might have been in their previous incarnation. The place stank of oil and chemicals stewing somewhere deep within the scrap heaps.

If he wanted a souvenir, he'd have to force it out from one of those cubes. He drew his knife and hung the sub-machine gun over his shoulder to enable him to use both hands.

'You will come back immediately,' ordered the professor over the radio. 'Mr Spanger, you moron – and by the way, this isn't some foreign planet. It's Frankfurt.'

'How could you possibly know that?' His eyes darted over the blocks, searching for an appropriate keepsake that was without a doubt not from the same year as the one in which he had entered the caves. Anything technical – something unknown and a bit unusual. 'The aliens could have copied it.'

'For Christ's sake, Mr Spanger, why would they do that?'

'For laughs. Because they felt like it.' He pushed further on, still searching. 'A bit like how the Chinese rebuild entire villages based on ones from the Black Forest. Or the way Americans erect Scottish castles in the middle of the desert.' He caught a glimpse of a flashing object embedded in one of the metal cubes. Flashing was good. That meant it was still working.

'Mr Spanger, I'm starting to think I should just leave you behind.'

'You don't even know what century we're in – or what universe.' He did not care what the professor thought of him and he was not about to forget all the insults any time soon. He and the medium could very well wait.

Spanger tried to slip his hand through the crack to retrieve the object, which was glowing rhythmically. When this failed, he put the blade of his knife on it and started to use it as a lever until the brittle material gave way, sending splinters everywhere.

He groped around inside until he managed to get his fingers around the device, which was about the size of a smartphone. The flashing was coming from a symbol on the display, with a counter showing 4.2 million.

4.2 million: what a jackpot!

This wealth, however, only existed in this universe. And who could say whether 4.2 million in contemporary currency was a large amount of money anyway?

He resolved to find out, so he began to press buttons and swipe his finger over the small screen.

If it were anything like the fortune it would represent in his era, it would be a good idea to not go back through the door but to stay here instead, as a millionaire.

The team had made it clear that they could do perfectly well without him. And he had no desire whatsoever to return to the dead bodies. Rich and safe – that was the sort of future that appealed to him.

'Leave that where it is,' Friedemann instructed him over the radio. 'Mr Spanger, come back. I've found a way for us to—'

A dialogue window appeared on the display, revealing the face of a woman with a slightly Native American look. She smiled at first, then groaned. She had clearly been expecting someone else. The time and date were superimposed over the image: 13.21 CoTi // 02.12.2049.

'One second, Professor. Something's happening.' Spanger had no idea how he had made the call, or what CoTi was. He tried to find the camera with his fingers, but there appeared to be no lens. 'Hola. No hablo español,' he said with a very bad accent.

'Who are you?' the puzzled woman asked him in German. 'Where did you get this Dig-Y? It doesn't belong to you.' She looked at her own device. 'Why is your DNA not in the database? Or your retinas? Are you one of *them*?'

Spanger swore. He'd only wanted a souvenir, not more problems. And he certainly objected to any database acquiring his retinal scans and DNA.

On the other hand, he had someone from this world in front of him. Perhaps he could find out whether 4.2 million was worth anything. He lifted the device closer to him. 'What do you want my DNA for?'

The expression on the unknown woman's face shifted to one of perplexity. 'You've got several relatives in Germany, I can see that. But . . . they're all registered. And you're not.'

Spanger looked at his fingers, then back at the surface of the device. This thing was capable of detecting his DNA, presumably via sweat or dandruff, and scanning his eyes. 'Tell me,' he asked, 'how much is 4.2 million . . . ?' Without knowing what the symbol meant, he drew it in the air with his finger.

'Spanger! Throw that thing away and come back immediately,' Friedemann raged.

'They've got my DNA, a scan of my retinas and samples of everything stuck to my fingertips,' he responded. 'I can't just leave it here.'

'It's been in the system for ages,' said the woman, irritated. 'Have you spent your entire life in the arse-end of nowhere?' She looked to her right. 'Stay where you are.

The Dig-Y will be picked up by our courier in a minute. Then you'll forget everything you've seen and heard.'

'Is there a finder's fee?' Spanger asked. This must be how the heroes in thrillers felt. 'Fifty per cent?'

'Of what?'

'Well, of the 4.2 million.'

The Native American woman blinked. 'You're really following this through?'

'Sure,' he said emphatically.

'What do you want with the votes? Who do you work for?'

'The *votes*?' Spanger felt himself making a rather stupid face that even his superhero-trimmed beard could not rescue him from.

'No more games. The 2.1 million votes you're after are a hell of a lot, Mystery Man. And yes, they could be enormously valuable in the coming election. So I'm assuming you've been sent by some corporation as an unregistered individual in order to buy a proportion of our well-earned quota.' Her face grew larger on the display. 'Tell me who you're voting for – *what* you're voting for. And for what polls: there are seventy-four in the city alone today, plus some more at national and state level, for everything from mergers, the death penalty and taxes through to food prices, terms of dismissal and sales practices.' She looked at him expectantly. 'Or is there something else going on here?'

'Well,' said Spanger, trying to buy himself some time. He had not understood a word, other than the fact that this had *nothing* to do with money. Moving to the future had suddenly become rather less attractive.

A man emerged from the labyrinth of rubbish, visibly out of breath and with a harried look on his face. His clothes were a mixture of fantasy apparel and a black leather kilt, with high white boots with red laces. He looked at Spanger and clearly recognised the Dig-Y in his hands. His reached into his open jacket to reveal the handle of a pistol.

Spanger raised the MP5 and aimed at him. 'Put the gun away,' he shouted. '*Now!*'

'Quiet – be *quiet* – that's our courier,' the woman said loudly through the device. 'Hand the Dig-Y over to him and don't cause any more trouble.'

'Agreed. But he needs to give me something in return. As . . . a souvenir,' Spanger said. 'Hey, come over here, comrade,' he shouted over to the courier. 'Do you smoke?'

The man put the pistol away and approached cautiously, his hands slightly raised as a gesture of peacefulness. 'Smoke? You mean . . . ?'

'Cigarettes.'

He frowned. 'Cigarettes? As in tobacco?'

'Spanger, give the gentleman his gizmo and come back here,' Friedemann announced over the radio again. 'This is my final warning. Otherwise Madame Fendi and I will leave you in the future that you're about to change.'

'Shit. Really? I can alter time?' Spanger grinned and lifted the sub-machine gun level with his head. Friedemann was bluffing, that was certain. They wouldn't leave without him. As the leader, the professor couldn't afford to leave anyone behind. An unusual feeling of power started to flow through Spanger. Each of his actions could potentially have serious consequences for history from 13.29 CoTi on 02.12.2049. 'Could this be a parallel universe?'

'No, I don't think so. My notes say otherwise.'

The courier looked around him hastily. 'Who are you talking to? The cops? Or those PrimeCon soldiers?'

'Just a couple of friends.' Spanger liked the idea of being in the future, but it was unfortunate that he didn't have enough time to gather the information he would need to make him rich in the present. Like the football results or something. He could have won every bet he placed. But he still wanted to take something back with him. 'So, have you got any tabs on you, pal?'

'No. Only old farts smoke tobacco.' The courier kept his hands up. 'I've got an Eesha on me.' He slowly reached into his jacket pocket and took out a small ballpoint pen.

'Aha: a bit like an E-cigarette?' Spanger suggested. 'Okay, that's a good souvenir. Hand it over.' He threw the Dig-Y down without lowering the sub-machine gun and held his free hand open. 'Then you can scarper, pal.'

'Give it to him,' said the Native American woman.

The courier laughed with relief. 'Okay, that was easy.' He handed Spanger the electronic pipe and bent down to pick up the device. 'Are your friends you're talking to also not registered either?' he enquired casually. 'I might have a job for you.' His fingers closed around the Dig-Y. 'Very lucrative.'

'We're not from around here.' Spanger wiped the mouth-piece clean on his sleeve. 'Let's see what smoke from the future tastes like, eh?'

He placed it between his lips and sucked on it. A thick,

heavy smoke with a hint of vanilla began to drift through his mouth. Then the strength of the nicotine struck him like a hammer – if it was nicotine; it was apparent that this Eesha contained some rather unconventional substances. Clearly they smoked much harder drugs in the future.

'Fuck,' said Spanger, coughing. His legs lost all strength and he had to lean against one of the metal cubes before finding himself slowly sliding down it. The arm holding the MP5 lowered against his will; the weapon suddenly weighed a ton. 'What's in that thing?'

Images began to shift in front of his eyes; the two halves of his brain could no longer parse information properly. He tasted warm caramel and the smell of fresh oranges and wood drifted into his nose. The drones above his head turned into birds and the whirring of the rotors became a pleasant chirping sound.

'Otherland,' said the courier, who had suddenly turned into two, three, four people, spinning around him like in a kaleidoscope. All four of them were holding the Dig-Y in their hands and wiping it clean. 'Don't you know it?'

'No.' Spanger chuckled at the whirling images before him. They were too funny not to laugh at. He waited for the kilt to fly up as the man went spinning around him, but nothing of the sort happened.

'It turns your surroundings into something completely new and peaceful. As if you're in another country.'

The four couriers looked at him. 'What do you want me to do with him?' they asked the woman on the display.

'Take care of him. The idiot could identify us both,' she instructed him.

'Nnn . . .' Spanger tried to raise the sub-machine gun. He wanted to shoot the couriers who had calmly drawn their pistols and aimed them at him – or at least have another hit of the Eesha. Death would certainly hurt less in Otherland.

Spanger could do nothing but watch as the four unknown men released the safety catch on their pistols. The chemicals were coursing through his bloodstream, blocking receptors at random and turning him into a cross between an empty puppet and a spineless fish. A hysterical giggle tumbled out of his mouth.

The shot rang out, bright and soft, like a whip at a great distance. *Rawhide.* The whip in the country song that the Blues Brothers played in Bob's Country Bunker, that's what it sounded like.

The couriers were all hit at the same time.

They cried out and threw their shoulders back, while their hands opened and let the pistols fall to the ground. After taking several deep breaths, all the colour drained from their faces and they fell unconscious.

'Now it looks like I've got to save our bodyguard,' came an accusatory voice through Spanger's radio. 'Can you walk, Mr Spanger?'

'Crawl. Crawl like a snake.' He chuckled and slumped onto the metal cube. Just as he had suspected, Friedemann's threat to leave him behind had been a bluff. 'You're a good boss, Professor.' He slid his way towards the motionless couriers, his limbs slowly regaining their feeling. 'This thing can come with me. As a memento. In revenge for what these wankers have done. And for you as well, Professor.'

Spanger's eyes finally focused again. He shoved the Dig-Y

MARKUS HEITZ | 165

into his pocket and a heartbeat later felt inexplicably tired. He could have fallen asleep there and then.

'I'm coming.' He pulled himself up using one of the cubes and shuffled his way along the wall of scrap metal, clutching onto it for support.

The chirping changed back into electrical whirring as the shapeshifters turned from birds back into flying drones in the blink of an eye. His surroundings appeared entirely normal again. Boring, really. His brain still felt as if it were swimming like a wet compass that had lost its bearing. The world bucked and swayed.

'Hurry up,' he heard Coco saying worriedly. 'I can feel . . . strong vibrations. Disaster is approaching.'

He considered that to be rather funny. 'That's me. I am the disaster,' he chuckled, before stopping and bending over, wheezing, from the exertion. 'No. I'm Batman.' He thought it would be a good idea to have another toke on the Eesha. 'I. Am. Batman!'

Once more the drug shot through his mind and jumbled up his perceptions. His ailing synapses were unable to defend themselves from this renewed chemical assault. Spanger's sluggishness increased immeasurably and weighed him down completely the next time he breathed out.

'I. Am. Batman. And I could. Fall asleep. Standing up,' he announced slowly, grinning moronically. He looked over at the pillar, where a host of Professors and Coco Fendis were waving at him encouragingly. 'Batman is . . .'

Spanger's hand suddenly found nothing to hold onto; flailing, he fell head-over-heels into the window-like gap, straight into a cavity in the cube of scrap metal.

CHAPTER VI

Frankfurt, Lerchesberg

Walter van Dam stared at the triptych of screens in front of him, his hands balled into fists and his teeth firmly clenched, causing his head to pound and his joints to ache. He had long since taken off his jacket, undone the top two buttons of his shirt and loosened his tie, but could not bring himself to stay in his chair any more. He was desperate for fresh air, air to breathe.

On the monitors, images of Dana and Viktor flickered, the lousy connection revealing only a series of half-moving images as the transmission frequently kept freezing, blurring and pixelating the feed.

'What a . . . !' He ran his fingers through his grey hair, not knowing what to do with himself. It was impossible to follow how the two of them were faring in their fight against this creature that had suddenly emerged from nowhere. The poor sound quality was not much use either.

The signal-boosters were not doing what they were supposed to – was it sabotage, he wondered? They clearly had an unexpected foe. Why had he never taken seriously the stories his grandparents and his mother had told him?

It looked like everything he had ridiculed, dismissed or ignored as a young man, all the descriptions, tales and requests, was now coming back to haunt him.

Next to the monitors was the book from 1921 containing descriptions of the various doors, as well as a collection of loose sheets of paper that his grandfather had compiled. Alongside this were piles of notes he had made over the last few hours before finally succumbing to fatigue, depression and the effects of alcohol and medication and falling asleep while the team was searching for his daughter – his *real* daughter.

Now he wondered where Matthias had got to. His chauffeur really ought to have arrived by now with the woman who apparently resembled Anna-Lena in every way other than eye colour. Van Dam believed Matthias, who had known his daughter for several years, when he said that this was not *his* Anna-Lena.

But who or what was this other person?

Or had the daughter of his flesh and blood been changed irrevocably by the doors?

Had the doors created an identical copy of her?

Did this person know where his daughter was?

He smoothed his bushy grey sideburns and moustache, telling himself he had to concentrate – he had to do everything possible to shake off this dizziness that had overcome him. Coffee would be just the ticket. Running companies, doing business, arguing with the authorities, preparing IPOs and intimidating stubborn competitors were naught but a minor nuisance compared to what he was undergoing now.

If he had had any idea about what was still awaiting him, he would have returned immediately to alcohol and strong medication.

The images on the displays froze again, and this time they were overlaid with a pattern of black and white lines and dots.

Van Dam closed his eyes. He felt as if he were about to have a heart attack. If his daughter had encountered this beast, she would be gone for ever – but he could not allow himself to believe that was the case!

Instead, his eyes fell on his findings.

He had been looking for blueprints of his ancestral estate in Bavaria, as well as all the old boundary records, which he had heaped up into these untidy piles. He'd hoped to find something there, but hadn't managed to unearth anything whatsoever about how the labyrinth underneath the estate and the former sawmill and joinery had been built.

He knew his grandmother had set fire to the workshop one day, allegedly in the wake of one of the fits of madness that had plagued her throughout her life. During those dark hours she had spoken of beasts and ghost-like human forms – of doors that led to everywhere and nowhere. Of slaves and sacrifices, of murders and shameful crimes. And of a group of conspirators who ruled the world.

Later, when she was still a young girl, his mother had made her own attempt. She'd been cleverer: they hadn't been able to save the workshop, and after that, no one went near the old estate.

Van Dam recalled the arguments between his

grandparents, his father's stony silence and his mother's mysterious tales every time she visited her granddaughter. No one had believed her, apart from Anna-Lena.

And it was that belief that had killed her.

His phone suddenly rang. The chauffeur's name was illuminated on the display.

Relieved, van Dam answered the call. 'Matthias, finally! Where the hell are you?'

There was no response.

'Matthias? Can you hear me?'

'Van Dam, if you want to see your daughter again, alive and intact,' an unfamiliar voice whispered, 'you'd better recall the second team you sent underground.'

'What?'

'Sending the first team was a mistake – and you've gone and made it worse, van Dam.'

'But ... who are you? How do you know ... ? Is this about a ransom? I'll pay you whatever you want – just bring me back my child!'

'Understand this: call off the second rescue team immediately and await further instructions, or your daughter will die – your *real* daughter, not the doppelgänger. And believe me, I'm serious.'

The connection broke off.

Van Dam stared at the frozen screens, utterly baffled, feeling at a loss for what to do. He had no idea where Viktor and Dana were, nor what had happened to the other half of the squad. His hopes were crumbling more and more with each passing second.

The whispered threat had turned his fears into reality:

MARKUS HEITZ | 171

someone had kidnapped Anna-Lena – *his* Anna-Lena – and the first one they'd brought back really was a copy.

His phone beeped. Someone had sent him a picture from Matthias' phone.

Van Dam opened the message with foreboding.

It showed Matthias, lying on the steps of the verandah, a slim knife buried in his neck up to the hilt. Underneath was written:

Think of your daughter!

Frankfurt am Main: 02.12.2049. 13.49 COTI

Friedemann was standing next to Coco, watching as a visibly drugged Spanger fell head-first into a large recess in a cube of scrap metal. And did not reappear.

'All for the best,' he said. 'And hardly a surprise.'

'We'd better go down there and fish him out.' Coco hurriedly stuffed the pendulum away. She hadn't been lying when she'd said she'd felt an imminent disaster coming on – she could sense things again, as clear as day. Her gift had apparently become accustomed to the new environment. 'Come on!'

Friedemann held her back by the shoulder. 'No.' They had already wasted enough time. 'Our incompetent bodyguard had his chance to return to us. And because of him I had to shoot someone.' He pointed to the door. 'I know how to get us back and it's going to happen any minute now. After all, you yourself warned us of disaster.'

Coco did not want to leave Spanger behind. His presence in this place would certainly cause a catalogue of errors – the world might change for ever because of his ignorance. And that gadget still belonged to the courier.

She looked over at the scrapheap where the flying drones were hard at work while the cranes, probably AI-controlled, lifted the enormous containers effortlessly through the air. The ominous feeling in her bones was not receding. 'We can't just give up on him.'

Friedemann eyed her. 'We're not here to save the life of a simpleton, but to rescue a young woman from a dangerous situation.' He pointed to the cube into which Spanger had disappeared. 'This device is surely being tracked. Someone will find him – Spanger will just have to get by in the future.'

'But what if he changes the entire timeline?'

'We won't know that until we're back in this period, will we? I'd be far more concerned if this idiot were stuck in the past. Come on.' Friedemann released Coco's arm and turned back towards the door that led to the burnt-out generator room. He picked up the notebook. 'I need you for our real mission.'

The extent of his coldness, lack of empathy and indifference frightened Coco. Before Friedemann could react, she wrested the valuable notebook from him, spun around vigorously and ran towards the scrapheap, removing the helmet and releasing her long blonde hair with its black strand as she did so. 'Spanger is important – I just know it. My gift is telling me so,' she shouted as she raced on. 'Come on! If you help me I promise I won't tell him you wanted to leave him behind.'

'You— How dare you!' Friedemann also took off his helmet so as not to draw any more attention to himself, then tore after her angrily. He was not about to let his plans be thwarted by some two-bit medium. 'Give me—'

Three large black motorcycles bearing white badges showing the German Federal Eagle suddenly appeared, electric motors humming quietly as the light from their headlights shone blue and cold onto their surroundings.

'Take cover,' Friedemann hissed, squeezing himself into a gap between the towering metal cubes.

Coco stood still, looking around frantically, then walked backwards and secreted herself beside one of the containers.

The riders, all wearing closed helmets obscuring their faces, were armoured men who looked like some sort of special unit. The same emblem was printed on their chests and on the number plates. The trio dismounted and the engines shut down. One after the other, they each drew a sub-machine gun from the holsters around their waists and started to walk around the junkyard. One secured the area while the second looked at a display embedded in the armour covering his forearm. The third one made his way to the wounded courier and looked down at him.

'He's still alive,' he announced, his voice distorted electronically by the invisible speakers in his helmet.

'The Dig-Y must be nearby,' said the person with the display, turning in various directions to try to locate it. 'Fuck all this metal. It's breaking up my reception.'

Coco was closer to them than Friedemann was and she could hear the soft radio traffic being transmitted from the display on the man's forearm. Someone – their central controller, maybe – was enquiring about the theft of recycling materials.

None of the policemen responded.

'I'll wake him up.' The armoured man next to the courier lowered the barrel and squeezed. With a dull thump, the bullet struck him in the arm right next to where Friedemann had shot him earlier.

With a long wail, the man opened his eyes and immediately lifted his upper body, only to find himself staring down the barrel of a sub-machine gun. Groaning, he held his hand over the fresh wound, which had blood running from it. 'Wow, Percutors – and three of you at that. Who called you?'

'Good day, citizen,' the policeman greeted him, not removing his mirrored visor. 'We have received notification of the attempted theft of recycled material. May I ask what you're doing on this private property? And your Dig-Y, please.'

'Control, Percutor One here. We've got him,' radioed the officer.

The third man was tracking the signal from the missing Dig-Y and had started to approach the cube containing Spanger.

'The thief is resisting heavily. Use of firearms,' the policeman next to the injured man reported.

'What?' The seated courier groaned. 'Oh fuck. You've been bribed by PrimeCon. You total wankers!'

'Do you need back-up, Percutor One? I can send a drone for air support if you need.'

'No.' The policeman nodded to his two companions. 'We'll take care of it.'

Coco began to tremble with fear at her poor choice of hiding place. Nothing more than a metal corner of the container was preventing her from being discovered.

Friedemann remained in the gap, pressed tightly against the sides as he kept an eye on the action unfolding. He felt tense, but he was not afraid. It was just a question of not being seen so they could return to the door still alive and escape to their own time.

The professor's obvious composure surprised Coco, who would have expected a geologist to act somewhat differently – to panic, perhaps, or even try to strike up conversation with the Percutors – something like that. She, on the other hand, didn't have the faintest idea how to go about rescuing Spanger or returning to safety.

'Okay, they're off our cases. Let the games begin.' The policeman next to the courier raised his visor, revealing the face of a woman who was probably in her fifties. With the amplifier module switched off, Coco and Friedemann could hear her normal voice, which sounded soft and smoky. 'Where's the Dig-Y with the votes?'

'Fuck you, corporate cunt!' The courier spat on her boots and started to get up.

'Stay down.' She kicked the man's injured shoulder. 'Who was it who put the first hole in your arm?'

The courier cried out as blood started gushing from the wound. 'That's none of your concern.'

'It appears you've been careless. Someone's stolen your Dig-Y.'

'Fuck you, and fuck PrimeCon!' The courier leaned forward, writhing in agony, but no matter how hard he pressed down on the wound, the bleeding refused to stop. 'They can get their support from somewhere else.'

'Who says we're with PrimeCon?' The Percutor grinned coldly. 'Don't assume things, citizen; they might not be true.' She took his Dig-Y from him, switched it on and checked the data. 'Mr Tim Hauser, by all accounts a respectable Frankfurt resident with a clean track record.' She swiped the display. 'Ben, how much are you willing to bet that the Dig-Y belonging to this young man at my feet has been tampered with?'

'Ten, Madam Director.'

'Frederic?'

'Twenty, Madam Director.'

'Boys, boys. Have some courage. I'll bet my entire annual salary.' She let the barrel of her sub-machine gun slide down onto the courier's legs. 'Well, we can find that out later. But first I'd like to know what happened here, citizen. Otherwise I fear you're in for a rather unpleasant time. Who took it off you?'

'You're going to shoot me anyway,' the courier replied. 'I know your names and faces and I know you're looking for the Dig-Y.' He spat down at her shoes again. 'If I could get my cock out right now, I'd piss you right off your feet.'

'Oh I believe you.' The director looked at the Percutor called Frederic, who had approached the cube. 'Well?' she asked.

'Can't be far.' He lowered his arm and leaned forward

to slide himself carefully into the recess. 'I'm assuming he threw it in there before—'

The shot rang out loudly.

The Percutor's head snapped back like a footballer being taken out by a defender. The visor prevented the bullet from striking his face, but the force of it caused the policeman to stagger backwards and fall limply to his knees.

The director spun around, stepping on the courier's wounded shoulder and pushing him to the ground as she did so, and aimed her weapon at the cube, ignoring the man moaning in agony.

'Come out, citizen,' she ordered in a loud voice. 'You are guilty of resisting the power of the state. This attack on a Percutor will be punished unless you surrender immediately and hand over the stolen Dig-Y. You are in possession of stolen goods and an illegal electronic device.'

Ben, the second Percutor, raised his sub-machine gun and pointed it at the cube. Red laser dots indicated precisely where he and his supervisor were aiming.

Coco looked at Friedemann. Tremors had taken over her entire body and her mind felt completely paralysed. The disaster she'd been sensing had arrived.

From his hiding place, the professor made no attempt to intervene on behalf of Spanger. He simply watched coldly and waited.

'Ben, advance,' the director ordered. 'Frederic, are you all right?'

Still on his knees, the man raised one of his hands weakly to show he had survived the blow. 'Professor,' Coco whispered on the radio, 'they're going to shoot Spanger.'

'Which will be our fate in a minute unless you stay quiet,' he replied, placing his index finger to his lips.

'But—'

'Not another word, Madame. No more radio contact!'

With her heart pounding painfully, Coco watched the action as Ben worked his way step by step towards the recess. The director was covering him, although she kept her boot still firmly on the shoulder of the bleeding courier.

The Percutor reached the cube, picked up a handful of dirt and threw it into the hole.

A second shot sounded, the muzzle-flash flaring up briefly.

'One person with an old sub-machine gun,' Ben said to his supervisor. 'I'll get him out.' Without hesitation he jumped through the gap.

Several shots rang out, then Spanger screamed and the next second flew out of the cube. His face was covered in blood and he was no longer in possession of his weapon. He spat out a tooth, coughing, while blood streamed from his nose and mouth, staining his beard.

Ben followed him out, holding the Dig-Y with its 4.2 million votes. 'There he is.'

The director looked at Spanger in amazement. 'Some fat bloke in combat gear from about thirty years ago, plus a gun that looks just as old,' she remarked. 'What's gone wrong with your life? Is this some form of cosplay?' She turned to look at the courier beneath her boot. 'Was that the one, citizen? The one who attacked you?'

'Yes,' the man on the ground gurgled back.

Ben grabbed Spanger by the neck and yanked him to his

feet. He pulled the P99 and knife from their holsters and dropped them; they landed on the ground with a clatter. He also tossed away the Eesha and patted him down. 'No personal Dig-Y.' Then he took off Spanger's radio. 'He's a walking museum-piece, Madam Director.' He held it out to her. 'The channel's open. Looks like someone's overhead what's been going on.'

'For fuck's sake.' She looked at it. 'Low-frequency, so they must be nearby.'

Spanger smirked. The Eesha had not just made him insensitive to pain but appeared to have robbed him of his faculties. 'I love what you're wearing. Can we swap?'

'Should I call it in?' Ben continued to hold Spanger firmly by the neck.

'No, that'll be recorded, which might raise some questions.' The director brought the confiscated radio to her lips. 'Citizens, we've got the stolen Dig-Y in our possession. Pull back and nobody needs to die.'

Coco and Friedemann heard the announcement twice: once in their ears and once directly in front of them.

The medium's eyes grew large. Perhaps they should have left without Spanger after all – he really was disaster in human form. How could one person contrive to cause so much trouble?

The professor gestured to her to remain silent.

Frederic had pulled himself together after the attack and now stood up slowly. 'Shit.' He straightened up and aimed a kick at Spanger's stomach with all his might, then bent down to vomit. 'You fucking prick – you tried to kill me!'

'What shall we do with them?' Ben looked coldly at the

prisoners, then handed the illegal Dig-Y over to his colleague. 'Here. You're better at this sort of thing than I am.'

'What are you going to do?' the courier replied in disgust. 'You're the ones who'll—'

The three Percutors all shot him in the head at the same time and his skull burst into countless pieces. A pattern of red droplets spattered everywhere, plastering the plastic and scrap iron cubes.

Coco screamed loudly in shock and the Percutors instantly swung their weapons in her direction.

'Right then, come out, citizen,' the director ordered. 'Show yourself.'

Coco wanted to reach for her P99 and surrender it immediately – she couldn't handle it in any case. In a desperate bid for help, she looked over at Friedemann, who pointed up with a trace of a smile on his lips.

The next second, one of the enormous thirty-ton containers landed in the middle of the policemen, burying Ben and crushing his motorcycle – which made the fuel cell detonate with a dull explosion.

The director just managed to jump back to safety, but Frederic, struck by the edge of the falling container, was cut deeply down one side – not that he had time to notice, for seconds later he was engulfed by the flames from the exploding fuel cell. He disappeared in the blaze, screaming.

'You fucking pigs!'

It looked like Spanger had been feigning his delirium, for he moved swiftly enough now, grabbing up his gear before snatching the Dig-Y from the dying man and hurrying between the metal cubes, somehow dodging the furious hail of bullets the director sent in his direction; they buzzed wildly around, sending sparks flying everywhere and punching holes in the cubes.

More boxes and containers rumbled down from the sky as the drones and cranes unloaded their cargo, ignorant of the living people below them.

'Madame – get away!'

Hearing the professor's voice sounding in her ear, Coco tilted her head back and saw a box falling straight towards her, but she was still paralysed with fear. Instead of running, she just stared at the tumbling container, unable to move. This was her foreseen disaster: and her end.

Then she felt a strong hand yanking her out of the way and the box crashed onto the concrete floor behind her, sending scrap metal flying off in all directions around her feet.

'I told you to get out of there,' Friedemann snapped at her.

'Don't move!' The director appeared in front of them, covered with the blood of her crew. She brandished her weapon. 'Who are you bunch of jokers? Who hacked the drones?'

'Madame Fendi, put your head down and turn right,' the professor said quickly. 'Spanger's somewhere around there. Go!' Then he ran off – just as another iron container fell to the ground, giving them some cover.

This time Coco nodded mechanically and did as she was told, hurrying after him while the director's lethal bullets clattered harmlessly against the metal. She was not going to let the Percutor eliminate her that easily.

THIRD DEAD END

Anna-Lena sat with her back against a tree, breathing rapidly, trying to make herself as small as possible. Her expensive dress and elaborate coiffure had suffered greatly from the hunt; her red curls were tangled and full of twigs, while nothing but rags remained of the glamourous attire she had put on for her evening at the opera. Mist rolled over the ground, almost as if it were afraid of being inhaled by her.

After the door had shut, Anna-Lena had run and run, eventually succeeding in shaking off whatever it was that had been following her, at least for the time being. A wolf howled in the distance and its pack answered in kind: the beasts could smell blood and they were on her trail.

Anna-Lena winced at the noises, then scolded herself. 'Pull yourself together,' she ordered. 'If you want to live, just, pull yourself together. Don't forget you were the one who wanted to solve this mystery in the first place.'

She swore a cold, heartless revenge on the man in the pin-striped suit – the man who had closed the door of the bunker and left her stranded in this dangerous jungle. She didn't know who this man was, but she had come across him before and managed to escape him then. This time it was obvious he wanted to ensure she would not be able to evade him again. He evidently knew all the secrets of the labyrinth underneath the old mansion – and he intended her to die, just because she was trying to solve the family mystery her father had never wanted to know about, not even when he'd heard about it from his own mother.

Anna-Lena would have liked to see the look on her father's face when she told him about what she had found in the basement. She had taken dozens of photos: of the old headquarters, of the clues on the walls, of everything she had discovered in the passages and corridors. Her grandmother's stories had become reality.

But for the time being there were a few things contriving to prevent Anna-Lena from making it back to her father. For one, she didn't even know how many routes there were out of the world in which the man in the suit had locked her.

'Prick.' Anna-Lena picked up a stick from the ground. It felt heavier in her hand than the previous one, and she imagined knocking the man in the suit to the ground with it. As she swiped it through the air, feeling the heft, she got a burst of renewed courage.

There was a quiet crackling nearby: the beeping of a modern radio. Listening carefully, Anna-Lena could make out a muted conversation between two men, one of whom was looking for her, while the other was talking to him over the radio.

'The tracks lead in this direction, sir,' said her pursuer in English.

'Olkin believes otherwise.'

'I can see her footprints, sir. Belief doesn't come into it.'

'Fine. Just be careful, Krinsler. We'll need every inch of her body,' came the instruction.

'And if the beasts have eaten her?'

Anna-Lena could see Krinsler through the ferns: he was a man of about forty, with an angular face, and he was clutching a large, futuristic-looking weapon. He wore olive-coloured body armour with no insignia and he had a helmet secured to his utility belt. In the moonlight he looked like a character from an action film waiting on the eve of an encounter with the monsters. He was talking to his supervisor over a throat microphone.

'If the redhead's been eaten, bring me the beast that did for her – the whole damn pack of them if necessary.'

'Understood, Mr Ritter.' Krinsler looked down at floor. 'I'll keep going, but I don't like it here. I've never been in such foreign territory before.'

'If it were up to me, you'd be in a bar, sipping a cold lager . . .'

'The cinema, if it's all the same to you, sir.' Krinsler raised his rifle. 'Salted caramel popcorn.'

'You can do that once this is over. Bring me the woman and I'll pay for a year's supply of tickets and popcorn.'

'Understood, sir.' Krinsler signed off and advanced slowly forwards.

Anna-Lena was flummoxed: what was so special about her that she needed to be captured fully intact? But she was relatively certain that the voice on the other end of the radio belonged to the man in the pin-striped suit who had locked her in this world and had then sent his people after her. She would remember the name Ritter. She had unfinished business with him.

Krinsler moved through the forest at the edge of the clearing. He wasn't using any other light to guide him; she guessed the moonlight was enough, as he wouldn't want to attract the attention of either the beasts or the woman he was hunting.

He surely has a map of the area, Anna-Lena thought, *and he'll know where the exits are.* He was her ticket out of here.

She breathed even more quietly, holding her stout stick at the ready. She would only have one chance to down the gunman, but at least he wasn't wearing a helmet; that made her task slightly easier.

She stole occasional glances at the man as he unwittingly passed her hiding place, still searching for fresh prints. He was taller and broader than she was, so she was certain to fit into his gear, and once she had, she would be able to fool his cronies, at least at a distance, ensuring she could escape from this world and its maze of passages. And in any case, the armour would be far more useful than the tattered remains of her evening dress.

Anna-Lena stood up quietly and barefoot, she stalked Krinsler, her pulse quickening to an unhealthy degree.

Four yards. Three yards. Two . . . one . . .

Out of the undergrowth beside the man came a rustling sound.

Krinsler raised his rifle, shining its bright tactical light straight into the bushes – which illuminated a mouse, its tiny fangs gnawing nervously on a dead cat.

'Oh, you little fucker,' Krinsler muttered, lowering his

weapon. 'What sort of . . . ?' Then he spotted her shadow out of the corner of his eye and leaped backwards, the barrel of his gun pointing to the heavens, crying, 'Stop!'

But Anna-Lena was already hurtling forwards and she could hear herself screaming like a banshee. With all her might she brought the wooden branch down onto her opponent's head, hitting him in the face. The skin underneath his eye split open and blood immediately began to pour from the wound.

Krinsler grunted and collapsed to the ground, where he lay motionless at her feet. He was no longer gripping the gun. The spotlight coming from underneath the barrel went out.

'Shit,' Anna-Lena whispered with relief and excitement. 'Shit a brick.' She peered nervously down at him: he'd been knocked unconscious, but she could see his carotid artery pulsing vigorously, so he was still alive. To ensure Krinsler wouldn't come round any time soon she struck him a second time, a little less violently, to make sure he really was out of the picture.

She hastily stripped the man of his clothes. The tight-fitting under-garment he had on underneath reminded her of a wetsuit. It was far too large for her, but still way better than the rags she was wearing. Anna-Lena felt like she needed at several hours to get herself fully equipped, but this would have to do. Finally she pulled off her remaining earring and tossed it aside, then placed the helmet on her head and shut the visor. To her relief, she found a map of the area in her right trouser pocket – with another exit marked.

The radio squawked suddenly, and she heard, '... you, Krinsler? For God's sake, say something!' Ritter was raging, but she didn't know why. 'What's going on?' the leader demanded.

Lowering her voice as far as she could, she whispered, 'Sir, I can't talk now. I'll report back soon.' She broke off radio contact, then, panting with the exertion, dragged the heavy man deeper into the undergrowth. She bound his arms and legs together with his own cable ties, then she stuffed a generous handful of grass into his mouth.

Her eyes swept across the clearing, then she searched for her location on the map.

The silvery moonlight gave the billowing ferns a haunted appearance; the wind felt warm against her skin. Under different circumstances it would have been a perfect night – and the perfect place for a date. Under very different circumstances indeed.

The ferns bent even further in the wind and now a low rumble could be heard – followed by a loud yelp.

'Shit!' Anna-Lena reached for the man's rifle. She had no idea how precisely to handle it, but thought that aiming the muzzle at her target and pulling the trigger would probably be enough to defend herself for now.

Krinsler groaned through the improvised gag, then his eyes fluttered open. He immediately grasped the situation he was in – and who was wearing his gear. With a great deal of effort he managed to spit out the clump of grass and demanded hoarsely, 'Get me out of this!'

'Certainly not.'

'Those things will kill you – both of us!' He nodded at the gun. 'You're not—'

A shadow the size of a wolf leaped out of the long leaves and sank its teeth into Krinsler's bare shoulder. Growling, the animal shook its prey around as a shark would a seal, throwing the wailing man back and forth like a rag doll. Flesh and sinew tore audibly and his agonised screams became a wet gurgling. Then the beast dragged its prey into the undergrowth and disappeared until all Anna-Lena could hear was the sound of snapping jaws, breaking bones and the greedy noises of feasting.

Anna-Lena was frozen in shock, her rifle still pointing to the ground. The expression in the man's dilated pupils and the fear and pain etched onto his blood-spattered features would haunt her dreams for ever.

And if she were not very lucky, she would be next on the menu.

At last Anna-Lena managed to unfreeze herself and, spinning around, went running off without looking back. 'You're not going to get me that easily!' she vowed – but shadows appeared to her right and left, flanking her as she went rushing through the rustling ferns. Howling and whining, the pack were regrouping.

One of the creatures appeared out of nowhere, its jaws wide open, and stood in front of her. Judging by the earlier attack, she knew she would have little time to react – but instead of using the rifle, she suddenly slowed right down – then threw herself into a slide across the ground, shooting underneath the creature before it could react.

She stumbled back to her feet and carried on running, shaking as she heard a howl of disappointment.

But the pack was already closing ranks again.

Her quick look at the map had suggested that she was approaching the second exit. She had no intention whatsoever of giving up, so all she allowed herself to think about was staying alive and not being eaten – that, and overcoming the man in the pin-striped suit. Then she could tell her father about what she had discovered and they could investigate this place together. So she had a lot to achieve, but first she needed to find the exit, which hadn't looked far off at all.

Anna-Lena risked a quick glance back over her shoulder and noticed a shadow ploughing a straight line towards her. She couldn't risk repeating her trick; she didn't think diving to the floor would work a second time, so this time she stopped, released the safety catch on her weapon and turned to face her assailant.

The rifle released its payload with a loud *boom* and its recoil kicked like a mule, slamming backwards against the padded shoulder rest, but she hardly moved an inch in response.

The ferns in front of her were mown down as if by an invisible scythe, sending fronds, plants and tree bark spraying across her path like biological confetti. Before she could take her finger off the trigger, the rifle fired twice more, its muzzle drifting skywards, and this time the shock of the repeated recoil made her almost drop the weapon.

The tiny missiles struck the approaching outline and

atomised it. Black blood spurted out in long streaks, soaking the surrounding plant life.

Anna-Lena felt ill, but she had managed to kill her first enemy, one of the many who were prowling around her, and she was determined not to let go of the rifle all the time she was still stuck here, especially now she knew it was capable of killing the beasts which were stalking her.

The howling and whining increased, but now it sounded further away: the creatures were withdrawing – although she did wonder if they might be calling for support from other packs.

'Stay where you are,' she ordered, and started walking forwards again. Her feet were sliding around in the over-sized boots she was wearing; they had had already started to blister, but she gritted her teeth, ignored the pain and plodded on, ducking under branches and pushing her way through bushes – until she bumped into an object that appeared to be made of solid steel.

Anna-Lena fell onto her back among the ferns, and this time she did lose her grip on the rifle. Her helmet came loose, sending her red curls falling treacherously around her head. Her disguise had been rumbled.

Anna-Lena stared up through the long leaves at the human silhouette.

CHAPTER VII

Frankfurt am Main: 02.12.2049. 18.56 COTI

Friedemann and Coco stood in the pouring rain opposite the Working Class Diner at the edge of the recycling centre and stared through the glass. They had stolen two yellow hard hats and orange jackets with the inscription DelEv from a service hut they'd found, which meant they were now part of a logistics company. So far they had managed to get by with their rudimentary camouflage.

'Are you seeing the same thing as I am, Professor?' The pendulum Coco held in her hand was once again doing its job to perfection, for the heavy end was pointing inside. They had found their target destination, which evidently had not wanted to be found.

'Are you surprised?' he snapped back at her, adjusting his dripping wet glasses on the bridge of his nose. At least he had managed to retrieve his book from her, having promised to look for the missing man.

'No.' Coco fought her desire to say something else.

Underneath their jackets they were completely soaked. They had searched the junkyard for hours, all the while dodging the police investigating the death of the

Percutors, and the downpour had taken them completely by surprise.

The news ticker running over the façades was reporting a cowardly ambush on a Percutor unit that had been despatched to investigate a known hiding place of the FreedomLovers. Coco and the professor, who knew the truth – or at least parts of it – didn't understand all of it, obviously not being exactly overly familiar with the state of affairs in 2049.

Through the diner's large barred windows, the professor and the medium were observing Spanger, who was sitting with a bottle of beer and a row of shot glasses in front of him. Empty shot glasses.

Although the Working Class Diner looked relatively full, he was sitting alone at a table with the captured Dig-Y lying in plain sight in front of him. The other patrons were keeping their distance from him. Occasionally he leaned over and spoke softly into the device.

'What an idiot,' Friedemann growled. He wanted nothing more than to give the man the dressing-down of his life – in the old-fashioned way. 'It's a miracle they haven't caught him yet.'

Coco considered it to be less of a miracle. 'He's not engaging in a monologue. He's negotiating.'

'To stay in this world? Fine, for all I care. I'll just tell Mr van Dam that unfortunately he hired an utter clot.' Friedemann looked at her. 'You're my witness. I'm going to go into this dive and I will make precisely one attempt at bringing this idiot man to his senses, as I promised you

I would. Then we'll disappear through our door – for good.' He pushed his glasses back again. 'I have no intention of getting stuck in this era.'

'Fine.' Coco was still watching the news on the façades without understanding anything about the election results being reported. All she had managed to grasp so far was that a lot of stuff, matters great and small, was apparently decided by referendum. Every voter aged sixteen or over cast their vote on every ballot – it was done electronically; there was no direct participation – and that was what made Spanger's little gizmo with its 4.2 million votes a very valuable commodity indeed. *Lethally* valuable.

Swarms of rotorcraft of all sizes traced their way through the sky, from small drones making deliveries to larger ones bearing people trying to avoid the nightmare that was Frankfurt's traffic. Their engines must all be electric, for the air was surprisingly clean for a metropolis, especially an industrial area such as the one Coco and Friedemann were currently visiting.

Heavy transporters bearing containers rumbled their way along the street where the two of them were standing, but they couldn't see any drivers: cameras, radars and other sensors appeared to be keeping the tons of rolling cargo in their correct lane, and probably far better than any human could have done.

'Would you rather wait outside or come in with me?' The professor looked like an old-fashioned maintenance worker with his equipment and harness underneath the high-vis jacket. 'I can't say whether it'll be more dangerous inside or out.'

'I'll come with you.' Coco linked arms with him. 'You'll need my powers.'

'You reckon?'

'I know.'

When a gap in the traffic appeared, they crossed the road together, then entered the Working Class Diner.

Almost all the seats were occupied, the 6 o'clock crowd merrily enjoying the end of a working day with a chat over coffee and beers, burgers and chips. Still none of them were venturing near Spanger, but nor was anyone taking any notice of his outfit or the weapon he'd tucked away in its holster.

Friedemann and Coco walked down and sat opposite Spanger. He looked at them with a glazed expression, appearing to take a while to recognise them. Then he grinned and the moustache underneath his nose jerked upwards. He was nothing like how he'd been a few hours ago at the recycling centre.

'You're off your face,' Friedemann hissed at him, removing his dripping glasses and wiping them dry with a napkin. 'What the hell are you thinking?'

'Not drunk. Well, not *just* drunk.' Spanger took the Eesha out of his pocket and waved it in front of his face. 'This stuff is the best!'

'Leave the Diggi—'

'Dig-Y. Digital You,' Spanger corrected, imitating the patter of a television salesperson. 'It's ID, wallet, social media and a whole lot more, all in one device, unlocked by retinal scan and DNA recognition.' He gave it a short tap. 'Except for this one. This one has been hacked into. And votes is what votes . . .'

'Your speech is declining rather badly.' Coco looked at the display, which was still showing the Native American woman's face. 'Excuse me,' she said, turning the device over. 'Our friend is rather upset.'

'I know. He's quite the storyteller,' the stranger replied. 'Not to worry – we've sent some more couriers to pick up the Dig-Y. Our hackers saved your lives by manipulating the container drones, so you owe us something in return.'

'You wanted to kill Spanger yourself – I could hear you giving instructions to the courier,' Friedemann said to the back of her head. 'We owe you nothing. You're one of the FreedomLovers – and you need those 4.2 million votes to manipulate the upcoming elections.'

'We're not manipulating them,' she hissed, 'we're fighting back – against the lies being told to us every day by the big corporations and the crooked government.'

'For God's sake, keep your voice down,' Coco urged both the professor and the Native American woman. 'We don't want to attract the attention of the police.'

'They won't be able to locate the Dig-Y. Our people have blocked the registration signal. It's using the diner's Wi-Fi to send out its signals,' said the unknown woman calmly.

'Have we got a deal or not?' Spanger babbled, grabbing an empty glass, putting it to his lips and trying to drink deeply. 'Otherwise I'll stand up and smash your little Dinghy Ditsy thing to bits, sweetheart.' He slammed his glass down and fumbled around with the electronic ordering card to request replenishment. 'Shit, I'm wankered.'

'We're going – and the device will stay here,' Friedemann snapped. 'You know we've still got a job to do, Spanger.'

'Ah yes, saving some redheaded woman,' the FreedomLover interjected. 'Nice story. The one thing I didn't understand is where the maze with all those doors is supposed to be. It sounds as if it would make quite a good film. Or a television series.'

Coco laughed tensely. 'Yes, Carsten is . . . entertaining.'

'I want my gold.' The stocky man folded his arms like a stubborn child. 'As agreed. Two pounds' worth. Plus another two for trying to kill me.'

'The courier will bring it with him. Just stay there' – the Native American woman looked to her right – 'for another ten minutes. Then everyone's happy.'

From the look on Friedemann's face, Coco highly doubted that.

'I'm not going to wait for these people for one more second.' The professor grabbed Spanger under his armpit. 'Up you get. That Eesha thing must be reward enough.'

'No, please,' the Native American woman pleaded, 'we really need those votes!'

'Why?' Coco asked.

'Some clairvoyant you are. You don't know anything,' Spanger chuckled. 'You're an imposter, aren't you?' He raised his finger, his arm shaking. 'You had something going on with our doctor – did he give you a certificate in return for a bit of how's your father?' He made a number of offensive gestures and chuckled again.

Coco's face felt hot, his accusation stinging her to her core.

'Please accept my sincere apologies for trying to kill your friend. We had no idea who we were dealing with.' The Native American woman clasped her hands, pleading with them. 'Please wait – let me try to explain. PrimeCon wants to strengthen its hold in the upcoming General Election: it's trying to gain far-reaching powers.' Her gaze became penetrating. 'Then they'll have a monopoly of the entire instant online supplier market, which means they'll have access to knowledge they can use for any purpose they want. But people don't understand what's really going on.'

'If they don't understand, it's their own fault,' Friedemann replied. 'Humankind's ability to abandon its self-inflicted immaturity was lost years ago.'

'What did the Percutors want with the Dig-Y?' Coco interjected, trying to distract herself from Spanger's allegation. She could still feel her face blushing.

'At first we thought PrimeCon had hired them,' said the Native American woman candidly, maybe trying to win herself the time she needed. 'The director probably works for hardliners within the government who could well be interested in having some so-called terrorists executed. Or corrupt politicians. There have been a few on the public prosecution list recently, for whatever reason.'

'Capital punishment?' That realisation was the final straw for Coco. She looked at Friedemann in disbelief. 'Since when has Germany had the death penalty?' she whispered.

'It's rather macabre that the German people are able to vote on whether or not to convict and execute someone,' he replied. 'The Constitution seems not to apply any more.'

The need to leave this point in the future was becoming increasingly urgent.

A police car painted dark green and white was lowering itself to the ground outside the Working Class Diner. When Coco stared at it, she realised it had been held in the air by four rotors at its sides, but now those power units had flicked up, allowing the car to land on conventional wheels.

Four uniformed men in light green-white armour reminiscent of that of the Percutors got out and put on black berets. They all bore pistols at their hip and one of them was holding a shotgun in his gloved hands.

'Out,' Friedemann ordered, pulling Spanger to his feet. When he reached for the Dig-Y, the professor pushed it away from him. 'That thing stays here.'

'But my gold—!' Spanger complained, but he was caught in Friedemann's surprisingly strong grip and the professor started dragging him relentlessly towards the lavatories in a bid to evade the police officers. 'My gold!'

Coco looked down at the display. 'Sorry.'

'Take it with you,' the Native American woman begged. 'Please!'

'The police . . .'

'I can't hear any sirens. They're just on a break from patrol,' she interrupted frantically. 'You can't leave 4.2 million votes in the hands of the enemies of freedom! Please! Put it in your pocket and wait for the couriers on the other side of the road.'

Coco looked at the officers entering the diner, quietly laughing and joking as they sat down at the counter. The atmosphere among the workers wasn't changing as a result of their presence, however – in fact, seeing the way some of the patrons were greeting the uniformed men, they did appear to be regular customers.

'They'll find the Dig-Y and destroy it – it's illegal,' Coco said. 'That's got to be better than—'

'No, it's not – we need the votes!' The woman stretched out her hands. 'Our couriers are less than two minutes away. Please!'

'Fendi,' Friedemann called through the babble of voices and the quiet background music.

'Good luck.' Coco gave the unknown woman a nod. 'I wish you all the best.' She rose and crossed the room, heading for the second exit next to the lavatories.

'Hey! Hey, DelEv lady!' The youngest of the police officers had been following her progress and now he moved to block her path. 'You've left your Dig-Y behind.' He smiled at her. 'Imagine if I had to check your ID and you had nothing to produce.'

'It's not mine. But thank you,' Coco replied nonchalantly, giving him a friendly look. Her pulse quickened.

'She's right,' said the waitress. 'It belongs to the fat bloke.'

'Not him either. He just found it.' Coco nodded to the policeman. 'Have a good day.'

She pushed her way past him and forced herself to maintain a slow pace on her route through the diner towards the professor, who was pushing Spanger outside despite the rain that was still cascading down. Once out in the open, she pulled her hood over her blonde hair.

'Don't run, Madame Fendi,' Friedemann said to her

sharply as they walked past the brightly lit window. He had Spanger's right arm draped uncomfortably over his neck and was more dragging him along than merely propping him up. The cold raindrops were having no effect on Spanger's spirits. 'Remember, we're just workers going home after a long day. With our drunk mate.' He would have gladly drowned Spanger in the next puddle they passed.

Coco's pulse slowed down with every step she took. She saw the young policeman acknowledging her through the glass, tipping his beret while one of his colleagues inspected the abandoned Dig-Y; the other two officers had disappeared, presumably to the lavatory.

A shabby dark red Dodge Ram pulled up in front of the Working Class Diner and a man and a woman hurried out. They gave Coco, Friedemann and Spanger a look of recognition, but the FreedomLovers' couriers had arrived too late.

They went in regardless, bravely and somewhat cockily, headed straight for the policewoman at the table and demanded the Dig-Y back, obviously not realising that it would be two-on-four, not two-on-two, in the event of an altercation.

Then Coco and Friedemann were beyond the window.

'Have we done the right thing, Professor?' She walked faster, helping him to keep Spanger upright.

'You're asking me?' He gave her an enigmatic look. 'Or was Spanger right, Madame Fendi?'

'About waiting?'

'About his accusation that you're a fraud.' The professor quickened his pace as the first shots rang out behind them.

The door of the diner flew open and the customers fled from the shoot-out between the state and the terrorists.

Then the glass shattered with tremendous force, sending a torrent of splinters everywhere. The policewoman fell back against the thin bars in the window frame, breaking through them, and landed on the pavement. She lay there motionless, her arms outstretched, bleeding from a fist-sized hole in her throat.

'Let's get out of here!' Friedemann lost his patience with the drunk man. He drew his knife and poked Spanger's buttocks lightly to wake him up and spur him on.

Spanger suddenly ran, yelping, the professor and Coco guiding him back across the recycling plant.

The cargo drones were still flitting over them as indifferently as they had been just a few hours earlier. No one stopped them or asked them to identify themselves. Their jackets with the DelEv emblem saved them from any hassle.

Coco wondered how events were unfolding in the diner. They had had brief responsibility for 4.2 million votes and decided to do nothing at all. 'What if we had ... ?' she began.

'You're wondering if we've changed the course of history by doing what we did?' Friedemann guessed. 'For my part, I have no idea. No one can say for certain whether the first courier would have escaped with the Dig-Y, or whether the Percutors would have killed him, or whether PrimeCon would have passed the changes in the law as a result of the votes.' He dragged the increasingly burdensome Spanger by his collar through the rain. 'We can't know, Madame

Fendi, so we shouldn't worry either way. What happens, happens.' He pointed to the pillar. 'Come on. We've still got to rescue Miss van Dam. That part certainly hasn't changed. Let's just hope the door won't leave us in the lurch and we'll emerge back in the same room we left.'

Coco nodded, but she didn't feel at all convinced.

A bulletin announcing breaking news appeared on a large advertising screen hanging over the lanes of traffic: a shoot-out between terrorists and an off-duty police patrol had left all participants and ten customers dead. Associates of the criminals were still on the run and citizens were advised to steer clear of the area for the time being. A Percutor unit was being despatched to seize the fugitives.

Coco did not bother drawing Friedemann's attention to the bulletin. He was running a few yards ahead of her, then he disappeared, along with the staggering Spanger, into the open passageway that led to the burnt-out generator room.

Coco followed, panting. She was not in good condition – she urgently needed a rest. She would just lie down in the little room for a few minutes, have a drink of water and take some time to recover. All this running around and excitement was consuming her powers at a rate of knots.

Gasping, Coco stepped through the maintenance door into the darkness – and was struck in the neck by a powerful blow that sent her reeling to the ground.

The last thing she heard was a shocked voice crying, 'Spanger, you drunken idiot! What the hell have you done?'

Viktor dropped to the ground and held the empty G36 out in front of him in the vain hope of protecting himself.

The beast leaped over him, its jaws snapping shut, but it missed his throat, succeeding only in biting the air with its long teeth. At the same time, shots from Dana's P99 rang out and liquid spurted out of the monster's body.

Viktor hurriedly changed the magazine and once reloaded, the assault rifle was ready again. He rolled onto his stomach and caught sight of the hellish dog-crocodile hybrid, which had come to rest against the wall. The greenish blood seeping out of the holes in its body were causing acrid smoke to ripple upwards wherever it touched the ground.

Viktor didn't dare lower his weapon; he kept his eyes trained on the beast. 'Everything all right with you?'

'So far, yes.' Dana picked up the discarded G36 and quickly checked it before aiming it at the motionless creature again and firing off four or five more shots. Only when she hit it in the head did she consider them out of danger. 'Target destroyed.'

'Back into the passage.' Viktor stood up and moved alongside her. 'There's got to be more than one of them.'

They looked at the creature more closely, but this time its outline was blurred, as if death had robbed it of its contours. A mixture of scales and fur covered its body and between its long, sharp teeth could be seen some scraps like plastic, which had presumably belonged to the Kevlar vests worn by the members of the first team.

'Whatever that thing is, it's not of this world.' Dana tried her best to avoid the corrosive gases emanating from its body, for she felt nauseous every time she breathed in.

'From an experimental lab, maybe?' Viktor let the rifle's

beam drift across the greenish-white body, which was still bleeding. 'Who knows what they've been up to in those vaults?'

Dana looked into the corridor attentively and listened. All was calm. 'I don't know what your pets are like, but my retriever certainly can't do anything like that.'

Viktor had to laugh. He lifted up the beast's lips with the barrel of his gun and displayed the fangs, then pressed against its paws, revealing its long claws.

'As you said, there could be more than one of them.' Dana pointed to the doors. 'There was something about those in the old headquarters.' She took out her phone and showed him the photos.

He scanned them quickly, but there was far too much information there to be able to draw any reasonable conclusions on the spot.

'I hope our doctor will be able to make something of it all.' She lowered her voice and covered the microphone with her hand; Viktor did likewise. 'It's all a load of shit, Troneg. This has never been a straightforward rescue mission. Van Dam is playing us for fools. He knew precisely what was down here.'

'I don't think so.'

'Because?'

'He would have sent anyone but us down.'

Dana's gaze grew hard. 'He *did* send others down. And they failed because they weren't prepared.' She privately acknowledged that *nothing* could have prepared them for a creature like that. She pointed to the doors with the G36. 'Not for *that*.' She took a step towards him. Now they were alone together, she thought it safe to solve the mystery. 'We were both in Jebel Amir. I was a mercenary and you were on an illegal Special Forces mission, am I right?'

Viktor froze. 'I *knew* it!'

'Neither of us should have been there.' Dana walked towards the line of doors. 'Do you remember?'

'Remember what? The mission?' Viktor could clearly remember the events from that period.

'The ruins near the city. And the door that was there.' She pointed to the remnants of the broken knocker. 'I could have sworn there was one there that—'

With a rumble, the door with the box lock and exclamation mark at the end of the hall flew open.

Dana and Viktor immediately swung the muzzles of their rifles into the passage that appeared in the red torch-light.

Friedemann hurried out, holding a motionless Coco in his arms. Blood was seeping from a small wound in her arm. 'Can one of you take care of the injury? I don't think it's too deep. I've administered first aid but the dressing has come undone since then.'

Spanger followed, stumbling, clutching his head. He was sweating as if he had just completed a marathon and his gaze was unfocused. His clothes were drenched and small puddles were forming around his shoes. 'At least we're back in the real world.'

Dana swung the muzzle back into the passage to secure them against any more attacks. 'I wouldn't be so sure.' She pointed at the dead beast in the corner.

Spanger swore loudly.

'It's dead.' Viktor put down the G36 and took a bandage from the rucksack Spanger had left behind before departing. 'How did this happen?'

'And where's the doctor?' Dana added from the entrance.

'He's not with you?' Friedemann laid Coco, who was just coming to, on the floor. She clenched her teeth as he cleaned her grazes and applied a fresh bandage. Then he looked at Spanger, who was rubbing his face with the triangular bandage from the first-aid kit. 'You were the last one out. Did you see him in there?'

'No, there was nothing in the chamber. I think. I thought he was examining the door from the inside and was going to join up with our Special Unit afterwards.'

Friedemann took a deep breath. 'The room was empty; we were stuck.' He briefly told Viktor and Dana what had happened to them in the future, without going into too much detail. 'In his delirious state, Mr Spanger managed to injure Madame Fendi, but it wasn't too serious.' He would have liked nothing more than to give the man a firm stab in the buttocks as payback for his stupidity. 'Last but not least, Miss van Dam was nowhere to be found, nor did we find a single clue as to her whereabouts.'

'Sorry,' Spanger said meekly. 'This Eesha is something else. It's like an E-cigarette, but better.' He tried to fish it out of his pocket but was unable to find it. He frantically patted himself down. 'Shit – I've lost it!'

Coco looked at her injury, which was gradually disappearing beneath the dressing and bandages. It burned, but she felt capable of dealing with it, despite her exhaustion. The fact that Ingo had vanished, though, that made her feel sick to her stomach. 'What about giving us some more information about these doors, Professor?' she suggested.

'What does she mean by that?' Viktor tested the bandage to make sure it would hold.

He had been listening to their tale without really considering what he thought about it all. He and Dana had killed a creature that did not exist. Then there was the suspension of gravity and the sudden-onset backwards talking. And now it appeared time travel was in fact possible, although Viktor was still not sure how much he was ready to believe their report from the year 2049.

Coco pointed at the professor. 'He's got a little book with notes in it. That's how he activated the door in the future to bring us back here, I assume. I couldn't see anything, because Mr Spanger wiped me out.'

'Yes, yes, apologies again,' Spanger called out, bringing his search for the Eesha to a halt. 'Maybe the pipe fell out of my pocket back in the chamber?' He held his head in his hands. 'Shit, I'm such a waste of space.'

'I'll explain in due course what that book's all about.' Friedemann straightened up. He was not about to tell them a single word just because they asked nicely. It was bad enough that they knew about his annotations. He'd find a way to overcome this setback at the right moment, but not until he had found what he was after. 'And now we need to get back to looking for Miss van Dam.' He adjusted his headset. 'Van Dam, can you hear me now?'

'He's off-comms, I think. We need to investigate these doors,' Viktor said. He had been wondering for some time what was written in Friedemann's notebook, and all over the portals. There appeared to be a small group of insiders who clearly knew more than they were letting on – so how did a mere geologist come across something like that?

'Why am I getting the feeling that everyone knows about this apart from me?' Dana enquired grumpily. '*What* book?'

'Take comfort from the fact that I'm just as rudderless as you,' Spanger added. 'We haven't made this trip up, but I knew that no one would believe us without some sort of souvenir.'

'Stop complaining, Spanger, and go and get Doctor Theobald out of there.'

Spanger rolled his eyes, walked to the door with the box lock and opened it. 'Out you come, Doctor,' he shouted through the doorway. 'We're waiting for you. And bring the tyrannosaurus you've found.'

Ingo emerged abruptly from his temporary prison and put his block of measuring devices on the floor. He grabbed the corpulent man by his collar. 'Did you think that was funny, you idiot?' he bellowed. 'Leaving me to stew in there?'

Spanger tried to pull the doctor's hands away, but he was still struggling from the effects of alcohol and Eesha and the parapsychologist proved too strong for him. 'Hey, calm down! We've been gone as well – and you didn't even knock, otherwise our Special Ops duo would have got you out, wouldn't they.'

'What the fuck are you talking about? I was hammering on the door like a madman,' Ingo yelled, pushing him away and flinging his helmet behind him angrily. '*Eight hours!* I thought I was going to suffocate! I banged every five minutes until I fell asleep from exhaustion. Then when I woke up, I could hear you calling for me.'

'Really? You were knocking?' Dana looked around in confusion. 'We ought to have heard that.'

Viktor had an idea. 'Check your watches.' He held his out in front of him. 'I've got it as 9:31 p.m.'

Friedemann blanched. '5:31 a.m.' Coco and Spanger looked at their own timepieces and confirmed the same. 'Doctor, what does yours say?'

Ingo stared at his wristwatch, then at the gauges, but gave no reply, instead started frantically pressing the buttons on his devices.

'What's it saying, Doctor?' Viktor asked.

Ingo raised his head. 'My watch is saying 1:31 p.m. but my devices have got it as 10:38 p.m. We're in several time paradoxes at once – or ... Hang on! The doors are ... they're creating force fields that are having an effect on our watch mechanisms,' he stammered, trying to come up with a rational justification. 'I need larger devices – better ones!' It was clear to him that once they'd found Anña-Lena, he would have to come back to investigate more closely. He ran his fingers through his shoulder-length blond hair several times. 'Wonderful – wonderful!'

'It doesn't sound wonderful to me,' Spanger remarked.

'Eight hours passing in a matter of seconds?' Ingo looked around. 'I'm not going mad here. You've seen it for yourselves.'

'We were in the future – 2049,' Friedemann said quietly. 'But unfortunately we haven't got any proof.'

Spanger cleared his throat. The effect of the Eesha might

have dwindled, but not the booze – and the accusations stung. He was shocked to find out that he had attacked the clairvoyant in his intoxicated state. He was out of control – just as he had been with Tilo, at the discount shop. He could not allow that to happen again. That's not how heroism worked. He swore to be better, immediately. 'Setting our trips aside, we were in a room in which time was running faster – have I understood that correctly? Running measurably faster?'

'In all likelihood, yes. And this is the first time it's been scientifically recorded.' Ingo looked enthusiastically at his measuring block.

'So what does that mean for Anna-Lena?' Coco asked. 'If she's missing somewhere behind one of these doors, she could be stuck in a strange world for years!'

'Or maybe only a few hours have passed for her despite being gone a week,' Viktor added.

'As I said, I need to investigate that more precisely,' Ingo rasped. 'Under better conditions and . . .'

'I know you find it fascinating, but I think it's rather terrifying. And I'm still not convinced.' Dana pointed down the corridor. 'I don't care what these miraculous doors are, and I don't care how they came to be here or how this . . . this force field works. And apart from all that, there are enemy soldiers wandering around the labyrinth that I have zero desire to encounter. Oh yes, not to mention the abandoned headquarters that looked as if it used to be the base for a unit that was dealing with these unstable doors in some way.' She looked around her. 'So let's go and find this girl and get out of here once and for all!'

'You were in a headquarters? Did you take any photos?' Ingo drew closer to her. 'Nazis?'

Dana grinned. 'No, it didn't look as though they were Nazis.' She held her phone out so everyone could see the photographs.

Spanger raised his hand as if taking part in a vote. 'Right. I want to go back and get my money – and spend it. As I've got no Eesha left.' The taste in his mouth was horrible and he looked about ready to give up. He looked at the medium guiltily.

'Agreed.' Viktor pointed at Ingo, Coco and Friedemann. 'Since you're the science and paranormal specialists, I suggest you take the other doors. And no more wandering off on your own, right?'

'Friedemann's notebook,' Coco recalled.

'Ah yes.' Viktor raised a quizzical eyebrow. 'Well, Professor?'

'When we've got a quiet moment together, I'll tell you the story, Mr Troneg.' Friedemann walked towards the doors with Coco and Ingo, hoping his bluff had worked. He wasn't about to reveal anything, even if they turned him over. 'I can assure you I'll use my knowledge in our favour. The rest falls under data protection legislation and is none of your business. Now, let's get to work!'

Coco thought better of contradicting him there and then, but she'd not be trusting the professor from now on. She held her pendulum out in front of each door; her powers were taking a little more time to work in this environment, but nothing had changed in terms of the result: the golden tip was still pointing at the passage with the X marked in red lipstick.

Ingo examined the doors with his gauges, passing them slowly over the surfaces. To his great disappointment, the energy fields remained passive.

Friedemann flipped through his notes, searching for clues, doing so slowly and carefully, so as not to damage the pages. The paper felt drier and more brittle than it had before. Their journey through time had clearly done the material no favours.

Viktor, Spanger and Dana remained where they were, keeping a close eye on the cavernous room, the doors and the passage.

'This time we'll take *my* door,' Coco insisted. 'I told you the first time around that she was behind it.'

'But we couldn't open it last time,' Ingo replied.

'Then we need to approach this scientifically,' suggested Friedemann.

'I'm working on it. But there's nothing to measure at the moment,' said Ingo regretfully.

Coco was sick to death of being ignored. 'I'm absolutely certain!' She looked at the tarnished silver ring in the mouth of the wolf that looked to be made from elaborately carved ebony. The bottom of the ring was thicker, resting on a metal plate fastened to the dark grey stone door with its black grain and inlays of white marble and onyx. 'It's the one with the X.' She reached out her hand to grab it.

'Stop!' Ingo grabbed her wrist in desperation to prevent her from touching the metal. 'Look – there's blood on the door knocker.'

Friedemann leaned forward and inspected the stain. 'No, it's lipstick. The same as the one used to make the other markings.'

Ingo let go of Coco. 'The force field was created when Spanger shot at the door.'

'Right: so kinetic energy was the trigger. In that instance, at least.' Friedemann examined the three door knockers, then glanced sceptically at the ruined bit of ring lying on the ground in front of the second door. 'Someone has made this one . . . inoperable.'

'Or it broke from frequent use.' Dana remembered the warning at the headquarters, something about a catastrophe and the past. 'Don't forget that these doors aren't working as well as they used to. They could start flying around our ears at any moment.'

Coco grabbed the knocker and lifted it up, keeping a close eye on the golden pendulum in her other hand. It trembled slightly, as if by way of announcement and warning. 'There! Can you see that? This *is* the right door!'

'Good – keep going. We're not going to make any progress otherwise.' Ingo looked at his devices. 'Actually, I can see a spike. Only a little one, but—'

Coco released the knocker.

The metallic crack it made was so loud that the six of them instinctively huddled together, clapping their hands over their ears. A brief flicker glinted across the door.

Ingo looked at his displays. 'My God – that's . . . there it is!'

Friedemann hastily pulled open the door, through which soft, silvery light was falling. A nocturnal wind was blowing and the sound of a cat could be heard through the rustle of foliage. 'You were right, Madame Fendi,' he exclaimed excitedly. 'I should have listened to you before. Please forgive me. Now, let's go and find the girl.'

Coco looked into the cool light and breathed the cool air in deeply. There was a slight aroma of forest, flowers and dew, fresh and pure, with no sign of danger. The pathway lay before her. But she was receiving some confusing vibrations. 'Anna-Lena's inside,' she told them, 'but fear is lurking there as well: fear of death!'

Ingo gave her a curt look. 'You don't need to put on a show for my sake,' he whispered to her.

But Coco's trembling was legitimate. 'It's what I can feel. In there lies . . . fear, waiting for us. I can't go in.' She took a step back. 'Never – not for all the money in the world!'

'Troneg, only you and Doctor Theobald can hear me,' came van Dam's voice suddenly in Viktor's ear. 'Don't make it obvious, please. I've muted the others. Don't answer, just listen. Place one hand on your helmet, Troneg. One tap means yes; two means no.'

Viktor casually put his hand to his helmet and pretended to adjust it and check the camera.

'Good. I received a call earlier,' van Dam explained, 'saying that unless I call you and the team back immediately, my daughter will die. I think it's a bluff – I pray to God that I'm right.'

Viktor tapped once, trying not to draw attention to himself. His eyes darted to Ingo, who casually picked up his helmet and put it on.

Suddenly Dana raised her G36. 'What was that down in the passage?'

Spanger picked up a flare from his belt, lit it and tossed it away. Only too late did he remember that it would start to smoke and spit like before. He cleared his throat in embarrassment, but this time nobody scolded him, for he had inadvertently done the right thing. Together with Dana he secured the corridor.

In the red glow the corridor looked empty, with not even shadows.

'Send Dr Theobald up to me,' Viktor could hear their client saying. 'I need him up here to help me to decode some of these inscriptions.'

Viktor tapped his helmet once.

'Thank you. I'll explain . . .'

'There – look,' shouted Spanger excitedly, 'they're coming!'

There was no doubt about it. Shadows were now making their way along the ghostly red corridor, their silhouettes suggesting they were wearing armour and carrying guns. Their opponents had tracked them down and were begin-ning their assault.

Dana aimed, then fired twice to let them know they were in for a scrap. A suppressed scream erupted from the corridor. 'Good job the door's open,' she said, without taking her eyes off the target. 'I'll secure the—'

'No,' Viktor interrupted, 'I'll do it.' Then he spoke qui-etly over the radio. 'Can't right now, Mr van Dam. We've got visitors.' He ducked and made his way to the edge of the entrance, peered into the corridor and checked his magazine was seated correctly.

Dana and Spanger ran past him towards the open door with the X marked on it.

Silvery moonlight tumbled out of it – and then a piercing howl, like that of a wild beast, sounded in their ears.

Friedemann snapped his notebook shut and hurried over the threshold into the unfamiliar terrain. 'Follow me – before its's too late.'

Spanger and Coco set off after him, with Dana right behind.

'Stop, Professor,' Ingo shouted after him, then, 'hey, wait!'

Friedemann, meanwhile, was taking the lead through the forest of ferns. He knew precisely what he was after. 'There – there are Anna-Lena's tracks through the ferns,' he announced, running after them.

Dana remained hot on his heels, to defend him if necessary. 'Friedemann, for God's sake, slow down – we've got to wait for the others.' She did not want them split into small groups again if she could help it.

A loud howl rang out, and a piercing scream could be heard from far away.

'Oh shit!' Spanger paused after a couple of paces and drew his pistol. He raised his eyes. 'Is that . . . a full moon? We're on the surface!' Friedemann had been right: the door had taken them to some forest which, for some stupid reason, was full of wolves. Somewhere in Eastern Europe?

A fear of death was suddenly flooding through Coco, a dark wave of foreboding looming over her, making her limbs seize up with fear. 'I'm not going a step further,' she whispered, backing away from Spanger.

'I'll look after you,' he promised her sincerely. 'I still need to make it up to you.' He shifted awkwardly in front of her. Never again did he want to lose control of himself like that. The fact that he had struck her mortified him; he wasn't sure he could ever forgive himself for that. 'If anything tries to attack you, it'll have to get through me first.'

'Death is lying in wait for us. All of us.' Coco couldn't stop herself trembling again. Her pendulum was pointing neatly in Anna-Lena's direction, but it made no difference now.

Dana stopped and looked at the medium and the body-guard. The idea of the team splitting up again did not appeal to her in the slightest, but the scrawny professor was obviously off on a personal hunt for the poor soul. 'Spanger, you stay here with Fendi; come and join us as soon as the others get here,' she radioed as she continued to hurtle through the ferns, on the heels of their leader. 'I'll try to take care of the professor before he runs into those wolves.'

'It's okay.' Spanger lowered his weapon and looked back into the hall through the open door they had just come through. Nothing and no one with evil intent would get near Coco. 'Troneg – Theobald? Where are you? Friedemann's found the girl's tracks.'

Viktor fired twice into the passage. He could see an adversarial figure in the reddish light, standing firm and showing no sign of retreating. 'In a minute. I need to get

rid of these attackers before they take us from behind.'
He quietly cursed the professor: in his haste he had once
again brought chaos to the group by splitting them up. It
was almost as if he were trying to weaken the team.

Ingo stopped next to him. 'I'd like to try to go back up.'
He lifted up a bundle of memory cards meaningfully. 'I'll
take the data with me and my instruments can continue
to record everything. If van Dam has got records – scientific records and maps, or any other information – I'll
actually be able to do more back on the surface. I have
to understand why the doors are creating this force field
and where they're taking us. Friedemann is acting far too
secretively for my liking.'

'You're right.' Viktor stared attentively into the passage.
He was also tired with waiting for the professor to deign
to reveal any more about his previous undertakings. 'How
fast are you?'

Ingo laughed. 'Not fast enough, I'm afraid. I'm a little
out of shape.'

'Keep right, tight to the wall, with your head down. I'll
give you cover. You'll need to go left at the fork.'

'I know.'

'Reckon you'll find your way back out without your
medium?'

Ingo gave a weak grin. 'It was a miracle we ended up
here. *With* the medium.' He ran off.

Viktor steadied himself and aimed his rifle above Ingo's
head.

'What are you doing?' came Spanger's voice, astonished.
'Where's the ghostbuster off to?' He and Coco had taken

a few steps back across the threshold and into the hall. She hadn't moved an inch from his side. 'Has Theobald scarpered?'

The lingering howl of the wolves was immediately followed by a siren that grew louder and louder until it completely drowned out the predators' cries. Spanger spun around and cast an inquisitive eye back into the dusky world on the other side of the passage. 'Oh joy. Sirens as well now. Is that the end of someone's shift, or is something else going on?'

Quivering, Coco held the silver pendulum tightly, as if it were a rescue rope to drag her out of this nightmare. 'Air-raid siren,' she said in a barely intelligible whisper.

'How can you be sure?'

'I saw a film when I was a kid about the Second World War and the Dresden bombing. I couldn't believe how dreadful it was!' Her blues eyes looked up at the sky in terror, her heart pounding ever faster and the blood rushing in her ears. At any second she expected to see glimmering cones from flak searchlights, the roar of distant engines and the silhouettes of large aeroplanes, explosions, shredded bodies, smoke and nothing but flame, ash and death all around.

Spanger too gazed suspiciously up at the clear, peaceful sky and its eerie moonlight. 'A test, maybe?' Then he looked back into the hall. 'Troneg, go ahead and kill those pricks, then come and join us. Rentski and the professor are on their own.' He drummed his fingers against the P99's grip. He would have been far happier if he'd had his G36 to hand, but he had lost the sub-machine gun in the future.

Viktor watched as Ingo hurried along the passage, concealing his whereabouts from the attackers, then the parapsychologist turned a corner and disappeared from view.

'Very good. Thank you, Mr Troneg. That went okay,' van Dam radioed with relief. 'He'll be of more use up here than down there.'

'He's still got a long way to go.' Viktor rose to his feet and slowly pulled back to the door where Spanger and Coco were waiting, right on the threshold. 'I hope he doesn't run across any of the ones who are trying to kill us.'

'I have every faith in him. Let's part ways on confident terms, before I collapse, Mr Troneg.' Van Dam took an audible sip. 'Find my daughter. Quickly, please.'

'Where's Theobald gone?' Spanger demanded.

'He wants to go and get another instrument,' Viktor lied. The truth was van Dam's responsibility, not his. 'It'll help us far more than the ones he's been using so far.' He placed his hand on Coco's trembling shoulder. 'Oh my goodness. You look like you've been through the wringer.'

'I can't go in there,' she whispered, her face drawn. She took a step back away from the doorway. 'Fear – death – we're going to die in this forest of ferns and beasts!' She tugged the pendulum on its chain towards her and tried to stuff it back in her pocket, but like a stubborn dog, it refused to cooperate. 'I . . . I'm going to follow the doctor,' she announced. 'You don't need me any more. Friedemann's found the trail of our missing woman.' If Ingo could make it to the surface, she could as well.

'But . . . how I am supposed to look after you if you do that?' Spanger was at a loss. 'Stay with us. I swear . . .'

But before Coco could push herself between the perplexed men, the four remaining doors sprang open simultaneously, a rumbling roar sounding like a distorted didgeridoo echoed around from all four corners of the room and at the same time, a shrill shriek, like a million swallows being tortured, rang out.

The deepest, most menacing blackness filled the four openings . . . then it slowly began to trickle out, carefully, exploratorily – and inexorably.

The brilliant darkness took hold of the walls. In thin braids and slender black lines it crawled its way into the red-lit hall to seize it and conquer it, erasing the messages and scribbled notes. The joints in the masonry were filling up fast.

'*Fuck!*' Viktor exclaimed, observing the spectacle before him in disbelief. 'What . . . what *is* that?'

'Run!' he could hear van Dam in his ear. 'Cross into the other world – get yourselves to safety!'

Viktor shoved a horrified Spanger across the threshold and dragged a struggling, screaming Coco with them. He reached for the handle and pulled.

But the door would not budge. It was as if it wanted to let the blackness in – and sacrificing the people in the process.

Viktor tore at the handle like a madman, but the door remained fast. He fought the urge to run away – then he felt another hand on his, helping him.

Together, Spanger and Viktor pulled the door closed, inch by inch, gasping and groaning under the strain.

Finally a sharp click sounded, followed by a crackling sound. The locking mechanism snapped into place and the force field disappeared, locking the darkness in the hall.

They realised it would be impossible to return to the surface this way.

'Madame Fendi, what can you feel?' Viktor asked breathlessly, turning around. 'Where has Miss van Dam gone?'

'Let's find the girl.' Spanger also turned to look at the blonde medium. He had protected her for the first time.

But Coco was gone.

Ice-cold fog suddenly rose from the ferns. And the sirens were still wailing.

CHAPTER VIII

BEHIND DOOR X

Dana was following Friedemann without quite catching up with him. She was gradually starting to get out of breath. His long legs gave him an unbeatable advantage in the thick undergrowth and he was surprisingly athletic for a geologist *d'un certain âge*. The howling of wolves accompanied them, which meant the animals could not be far away. 'Professor, stop!' she demanded, panting. 'We've got to wait for the others.'

'Can't you hear that? Miss van Dam is in grave danger!' He reached a clump of trees and disappeared between the trunks.

'Why did we have to come out in the middle of a wolf den? These fucking doors,' Dana swore under her breath. She had no experience with predators like these; she had always believed that wolves did not attack humans. She had had to shoot hungry hyenas, wild dogs and dingoes when they had come too close to her on certain assignments, and she had been vaccinated against rabies, but a bite could still have ugly consequences, not least infections or damage to muscle, ligament or bone.

A siren suddenly sounded among the chorus of animal noises, one Dana recognised from battles in the ruins of bombed-out cities: an air-raid siren.

'It just gets better and better.' Dana carried on walking and arrived at the forest. 'Professor?' she called and paused, listening, but she couldn't see him anywhere.

The howling of the siren was drowning out the cries of the wolves and now thick fog started rising from between the ferns, forming a swelling, milky sea; tendrils reached out and caressed her.

Fear stole into Dana's mind. She was cut off in a surreal world where at any moment a werewolf might appear in front of her. How many horror films had she seen that used that kind of siren? Did it not always signal that something awful was about to happen? Dana broke out in a cold sweat as she walked a few yards further, then switched to a stalking pose, her G36 held at an angle in front of her. She forbade herself from calling out; the radio was becoming rather an annoying presence in her ear.

Her mood was sinking to rock bottom. Not only did she still have to find Anna-Lena, but she had lost her leader as well – and only Friedemann possessed the closely guarded knowledge of how to open the doors.

A long branch suddenly flew at her from her left, but just in time, Dana managed to slam her rifle down on it, breaking the branch into several pieces. She lost her footing from the impact, only just avoiding a foot that was trying to stamp down on her. She struck the knee of the thin shadow towering over her through the fog with the shoulder support of the G36 and this time a man's voice cried out in pain.

'Stop!' Dana cried, aiming the rifle at her assailant and shining the tactical light into his face. 'Friedemann?'

The professor was brandishing a second stick in his hand, clearly about to attack her again.

'It's me, Professor,' Dana shouted. 'Stop this shit or I'll hurt you – really badly!'

'You were trying to kill me,' Friedemann whispered at her, glaring.

'Not me – I'm the one looking out for you, Professor!'

Friedemann looked around in panic. 'The people I stole the notebook from – they're here.' He put a finger to his lips, giggling. 'And they've bribed you, Rentski.' He laughed again. 'I know they've bribed you.'

'Troneg, Spanger?' Dana radioed, hoping her voice would reach them. She was still pointing her rifle at the professor. 'I could do with some help here. Friedemann's on the edge here – no idea what's got into him. It could just be this place, all the howling and the sirens.'

'We're on our way,' she heard Troneg's reply, distorted but loud enough. 'I've got the footprints in front of me. Is Madame Fendi with you?'

'What? No . . .'

'You're talking to the enemy – the *enemy*,' Friedemann suddenly screamed and started flinging himself around wildly.

'Oh shit.' Dana scrambled to her feet and tried to stop him. 'Wait, Professor – you'd better stay—'

'Get your hands off me, you fucking traitor!' Friedemann

aimed a second blow of the branch at her face as he was moving around. 'You can't have me – go and *rot in hell*—'

This time Dana failed to dodge him in time and the thick lump of wood slammed against her helmet and cheek.

With stars in her eyes, she sank to the cold, wet ground as the fog greedily devoured her.

Ingo hurtled his way through the passage, breathing hard.

He had nothing against action films where the heroes ran around shooting people and getting into dangerous situations – they were entertaining enough from the comfort of his sofa. But being the hero who had to do the running around and shooting was a far less comfortable task.

His heart was racing and he was drenched with sweat; the rucksack on his back was bouncing up and down, pressing against the Kevlar vest and making his climbing gear pinch. He could have done with a rest, not to mention a little more food in his stomach than the few hasty bites of protein bar he had been able to manage so far. He needed to calm down, get his thoughts in order and take a deep breath.

He could hear voices calling behind him, accompanied by the sound of heavy footsteps and an occasional burst of gunfire which sent bullets pinging off the rock above him. The glow of his lamp was battling to penetrate the clouds of dust.

Ingo tightened his grip on his backpack and kept his head down. This was not the sort of dangerous adventure that his experience as a parapsychologist and scientist could have prepared him for. 'Van Dam?' he tried.

'. . . hardly . . . hear you!' came the faint reply from the surface.

Ingo swore and ran on, occasionally peering behind him. The beam from his helmet lamp lit up a destroyed signal-booster on the ground.

'Oh no—' That explained the disconnections and rapidly deteriorating link to their employer.

He hesitated briefly, glancing back towards the hall, where he could see the dancing beams of light belonging to his pursuers. There was no time to examine and repair the defective device; he would be better off switching on one of the remaining ones and hiding it.

He continued his flight with his aggressors hot on his heels. His thighs were burning from the build-up of lactic acid by the time he arrived back at the rusted steel cable. He quickly removed one of the last signal-boosters from his rucksack and looked around hurriedly for a spot where he could hide the box to prevent the enemy from destroying it.

In doing so, he stumbled upon the bloody, half-naked corpse of the unknown man. And the bolt cutters.

'Van Dam! Van Dam, can you see this?' Ingo backed away from the dead man, who was lying in his own blood. Fear seized him, making him feel dizzy. 'Troneg? Anyone?' In his agitation he had forgotten to switch on the booster in his hand, meaning the only answers he received were distorted beyond comprehension.

No one can hear you, whispered a genial voice. *Only me. Don't be afraid.*

Ingo turned on his heel slowly, shining his light into

the infinitely large cave and over the ledge, without the light striking anything at all. 'Who is this?'

A friend: a nameless friend, but one who can save you from your enemies – the ones who are going to catch up with you at any moment.

Ingo wished he had his gauges with him to measure what was going on. Were these simply the hallucinations of an over-stimulated mind? Or was it a genuine supernatural event?

His eyes focused on the corroded cable. He could see a notch in it, perhaps the result of a failed attempt to sever his only connection to the outside world.

'Oh for God's sake.' He ran his finger over the weakened point where the thin, twisted fibres were gleaming more brightly, hoping it would still hold. Then he quickly tossed the bolt cutter into the abyss. He was not going to allow anyone another opportunity to cut it – the link had to be maintained.

What's to say you'll make it over, Ingo? the voice continued. *I can help you. I'll catch you if you fall.*

'Who are you?'

As I said, a friend. An invisible friend. One you could have done with before, in that back alley next to the Roscher house.

Ingo froze.

He had never mentioned the Roscher house, not since it had happened, not to his parents nor to any of his friends – not even to his wife. Or Beate.

Soft laughter penetrated his skull. *I've surprised you, haven't I?*

It was now clear to Ingo that he was in dialogue with

his own imagination, thanks to strained nerves, too much pressure, low blood sugar or whatever.

What do you think would have happened if you had had a reliable friend back then? the voice whispered. *Or how would it have been if you had proved to be a reliable friend?*

Ingo knew his pursuers were approaching, that van Dam was waiting for him, that the group was in grave danger, that the doors were begging to be investigated and that they needed to find Anna-Lena before the beasts or their enemies could reach her – and yet here he was, standing on a ledge in the darkness, feeling the cold creeping into his neck, running down his spine and spreading throughout his body. And what if this wasn't a fantasy?

They'd still be alive, Ingo. All three of them.

'It's just my imagination,' he shouted. 'This conversation isn't real!'

Arne Wilms. Thirteen years old.

'I've got to shake this off.'

Martina Klein. Fifteen years old. The Queen, as you used to call her.

'It's nothing but my imagination.' Ingo frantically hooked his climbing harness onto the rope, desperate to escape the voice that was tormenting him by trying to hurl him back into the past.

And Frieda Winters.

Ingo stopped short. 'Who's that?'

The third victim – the one without a name. Well, to you at least. The disembodied voice was clearly enjoying rubbing his nose in the names of the dead. *You didn't even know her.*

Ingo, seized by paralysis, stood there helplessly. His breathing became shallower, more staccato. His mind could create an imaginary dialogue, but it certainly could not produce knowledge he did not possess. 'You've made that up,' he croaked.

Frieda Winters. Eleven years old. And none of this is made up, insisted the voice in the darkness. *Can you still remember what happened all that time ago, in the alley next to the Roscher house? Actually, I can help you. You don't know where little Frieda was.* A sympathetic laugh sounded in his ear. *You'll see, Ingo, that I can be a true friend to you – if you experience what happened that afternoon. If you know the truth. If you grasp the full extent of your guilt, even though you never wanted that disaster to happen. Aren't those disasters often the worst?*

Ingo wanted to swing along the rope and flee from the pictures flooding his memory, escape from the new information being imposed upon him by the mysterious voice. Yet the images appeared in his mind's eye nonetheless, displacing the environment around him.

Ingo was suddenly standing in Roscher Alley with his tape recorder in his hand, the microphone plugged into it. He was wearing jeans and a checked shirt his mother had bought for him, with trainers on his feet and a thick parka draped around him. Beside him was Arne, wearing one of his big brother's old coats, and Martina, their queen and leader of the clique, clad in a military jacket. Snowflakes fluttered silently all around them. It was so cold it hurt to breathe.

'What, now? When's it kicking off?' Martina looked

around and put her hands in her pockets. She was daring and beautiful; if there was one thing she hated, it was cowardice.

Ingo wanted to be friends with her, so he could not allow himself to be a coward. 'We've got to attract their attention.'

'How are we supposed to do that?' Arne breathed onto his hands to warm them up. 'Say their name three times? Bang on the door or something?'

Ingo removed his penknife from his jacket and handed it to him. 'We all need to donate a drop of blood.' He pointed to the chopping block on the wall. 'On that.'

'I'm supposed to cut my finger?' Arne examined the blade. 'It's too blunt. It'll hurt a lot.'

'Do you want to see them or not?' Martina took the knife from him and went over to the piece of wood, which had a thick layer of snow covering it. Without hesitation she pricked her thumb and allowed several red spots to drop into the whiteness. She held the steel blade out to Arne defiantly.

He and Ingo took a step closer. 'I've seen them before,' he said, as Arne scratched his little finger and squeezed some blood out, cursing. It was a poor choice of finger – the flesh was too cold and the blood supply too poor. 'When they found the body.'

Martina licked her thumb and studied the burnt walls. 'The newspapers said they found ten bodies in the Roscher house, all dismembered and halfway through being pro-cessed. Like in a butcher's.'

'I read that as well.' Arne pressed his blood onto the

snow-covered log. The red spots formed an incomplete circle. He handed the knife back to Ingo.

He took it and ran the blade over his thumb, his eyes fixed on Martina. He didn't show any pain; he wanted to appear manly in the presence of the Queen, but she wasn't paying any attention to him. 'The killer cut them up inside,' he said, as his blood gushed out of the wound, forming lines between the droplets, 'but he beheaded each of them on the log. He thought he was an executioner, punishing them for their sins.' The red liquid showed no sign of wanting to stop spurting out of the cut. He had sliced too deep.

'And you're saying their souls are trapped in the walls?' Martina placed her hand on the brick wall.

'I swear.' Ingo was starting to fear he might bleed to death. He knew that was nonsense, rationally speaking, but the idea of losing so much blood was disconcerting. He quickly wrapped a handkerchief around his thumb and squeezed hard. 'I was taking Garfield for a walk when the police raided the house.' He pointed at the dark flecks on the wall. 'That's where the souls came out from. The officers who were supposed to be securing the window were so frightened they turned tail and ran.'

'And you?' Martina turned her blue eyes to face Ingo. 'You stayed?'

He knew his answered mattered. 'Sure,' he said casually. 'But Garfield scarpered.'

'How can you call your dog Garfield?' Arne laughed and looked down at the red-coloured snow. 'When are these ghosts showing up then? Do we have to summon them? Perform a ritual?'

Ingo put the tape recorder down and pressed record. 'They'll come. Our fresh blood has seen to that.'

Martina nodded. 'Like sharks. It's all very curious. We've tried that Ouija board, but nothing happened.'

'They'll come. You'll see.' Ingo put his index finger to his lips.

The cold wind whistled through the deserted alley, which was barely two paces wide. The mediaeval drainage channel was overflowing; it was unlit as well, so everyone avoided it. Every lightbulb installed by the local council had been destroyed within a very short period of time, as if there were a higher power present that did not want any brightness to find its way into the alley. The teenagers stood beneath the towering houses and the swirling snow-flakes, the last remnants of sunlight casting long shadows over them; it smelled of fire and mud, though the predominant scent was of blood, which Ingo found amazing. He had been present at the aftermath of a massacre in a house once before, and the very same smell had hung in the air. It could not possibly have come from their drops alone.

'Do you know what this path used to be called?' Arne whispered to Martina. The Queen shook her head. 'Hein Alley.'

'Hein?' She looked at Ingo.

'Godfather Hein. A symbol of death in German folklore,' he explained briefly. 'After executions, the hangman used to take this path to escape from the angry mobs.'

Martina laughed. 'You're such a loser. You must be joking.'

Arne grinned, 'I wanted everyone to get in the mood

a bit more. That way we'll be able to see ghosts even if they're not there.'

The girl stepped playfully towards him.

'They're coming,' Ingo insisted, staring at the wall. 'They're in there. And they're watching us.'

'What rubbish. They're all asleep.' Arne grabbed the log with the bloody snow on it. 'Tell you what – we'll wake them up.' He threw the piece of wood with all his strength. 'Hey! Wakey wakey!'

The log flew through the air, twisting in flight, and crashed six feet up against the burnt brick wall. Their bloody snow clung to the wall before the wood fell back into the alley and rolled in front of Martina's feet.

Ingo stared at the dark soot and scorch marks. They appeared to be moving abruptly, shifting rapidly and assuming different shapes. They hurriedly moved to the spot where the blood of the three teenagers had stuck to the wall. 'Can you see that?'

Arne looked at the wall. 'See what?'

'No. No ghosts.' Martina looked at Ingo, disappointed. 'I'll be off then. I've got somewhere to be. This is all too boring for me. Next time pick another girl to piss around with.'

Ingo opened his mouth to defend himself.

With a dark clacking sound, a wide crack formed over the entire side of the wall, causing dust and loose stone to trickle down onto the teenagers. Window frames burst and panes shattered, sending a shower of sharp splinters raining onto the ground.

Several pieces of glass pierced Arne's coat and embedded

themselves in his shoulder. The boy screamed like a stuck pig.

Martina reached out to pull him free from the danger area. 'Help me!' she called over to Ingo. 'We've got to get away from here!'

But Ingo was unable to move.

His eyes were fixed upon the dissolving wall across which black shadows were darting. Distorted chanting and a piercing howling sound rang out – noises that did not belong in the mortal world. 'I knew it,' he whispered, slowly lifting the microphone to record everything he could. 'I knew it—'

'Ingo!' Martina had grabbed Arne's hand and started dragging him away from the lethal hailstorm. The first bricks had started to come loose from the building itself, dropping into the alley with a harsh thud. The Roscher house was falling apart from the rage of the spirits.

'Arne provoked them.' Ingo held the microphone closer to the wall, which was now littered with cracks and fissures. The beams were creaking and the gable was starting to lean threateningly over the heads of the teenagers as it continued casting bricks down upon them.

One struck Ingo on the head; he dropped to his knees and crawled to the exit of the alley. Behind him, Martina's screams and Arne's cries for help were muffled by the rumbling thunder. He did not dare to turn around to look at the avalanche of broken joists, stones and shards of glass that had covered the two of them.

Now look back, Ingo heard the unknown voice saying. *Turn around and look back. You didn't dare to do so before.*

Ingo did as instructed.

He had been pulling the lead of the tape recorder behind him, with the recording still running. In the cloud of dust and snow he saw a young girl falling from the first floor. Her eyes were wide with terror, but the sound of her scream never reached his ears. A rucksack fell alongside her from the collapsing house as well.

That's Frieda Winters. A runaway. She had set her quarters up inside the house, remarked the unknown voice. *She is the dead girl who was never found. Because no one knew there was anyone else to look for.*

Ingo fought the nausea rising inside him. Frieda was being crushed in the air by the wall fragments. Her blood splashed against the walls and was absorbed as if by a sponge.

'Ingo,' came a soft gasp from the rubble. Martina's filthy, tattered hand stretched out through a gap. 'Pull me out. There ... there are ghosts here,' she cried out in panic. 'They're ... coming for me!'

Terrified, Ingo continued to crawl along and had just reached the end of the passage when the earth opened up and the mediaeval sewer burst forth.

The pile of rubble sagged under the force, obliterating Martina, Arne and Frieda. More dust flew up and there was a loud rattle as the fragments tumbled into the murky wastewater.

Then all was quiet. So quiet that Ingo could hear the wind whispering.

Clack, went the tape recorder. The cassette was full.

Voices were approaching the area as the local residents called out anxiously, disturbing the eerie peace.

That jolted Ingo into action. He leaped to his feet, threw the cassette player to the ground and disappeared from the alley before anyone spotted him. Later he would not be able to recall why he had done that – why he had fled. Fear of ghosts, the sense of responsibility, guilt. He had to stop to throw his guts up on the way back.

He returned home in secret, not daring to reveal his dilapidated appearance to his parents. He had a shower and put his dirty clothes in a rubbish bag that he hid temporarily in his room. Then he got into bed and closed his eyes, trying to forget everything that had just happened. The shadows. The screams. And the knowledge that he had to answer for the deaths of three people.

Because you didn't help them. Because you challenged the dead, the unknown entity's voice whispered to him.

Ingo blinked and found himself back on the ledge in the pitch-black cave.

You said afterwards that you had heard Martina and Arne had been there on a dare, said the invisible voice. *Their bodies were eventually found, deep within the sewer, crushed and broken, so unrecognisable that they had to be identified by their clothes. And they had been completely exsanguinated.*

'They lost all their blood from their wounds,' Ingo replied.

That's what everyone thinks, and perhaps that was the case. But you've got the recording on your cassette. What did you hear?

'My voice and . . .'

What else, Ingo?

He fell silent and gathered himself.

The footsteps of his pursuers echoed from the passage,

the lights on their helmets hopping up and down like bright white fireflies. They had almost caught up with him.

Ingo looked at the cable. He absolutely had to escape – just as he'd had to back at Hein Alley.

I'll tell you what you heard, said the unknown voice helpfully. *Sounds that did not come from this world. And that was what prompted you to become a ghost hunter. To pursue them with science and rationality, with gauges and explanations that you were never able to get back then. You wanted to know what it was that killed your friends after you had taken them to the presence of evil, like lambs to the slaughter.* Its laughter rang out, friendly and forgiving. *You'll find your answers down here. And I am your friend. I'll help you if you do me a favour at whatever moment I ask it of you.*

Ingo breathed deeply in and out. He quickly switched on the booster and threw it onto a protrusion from the wall, where it sat a little unsteadily. 'Troneg? Van Dam?' he radioed, hoping beyond hope that a human response would suppress the voice in his head.

I'll be here when you need me. Down here. And I'll help you to escape, the voice promised.

Ingo took a run-up in his harness and threw himself over the edge of the plateau. The cable held and he pulled himself towards the exit with all his might.

The smooth low-friction rollers purred, his arms and shoulder began to hurt almost immediately, but he refused to give up. His priority was to get away from this place, away from the past and the dead. There was no Frieda Winters. This was all in his imagination, he repeatedly told himself.

Then the cable suddenly began to swing. His pursuers had arrived at the platform and were getting down to business.

Ingo switched off his own lamp and drew his pistol. 'Go away! Go on, away with you!' He fired several times at the unknown team, who were sending off volleys of their own in his direction.

The sound of buzzing and clicking was all around him, followed by a whipping noise; the cable was starting to sag slightly. Some steel fibres had come loose but it was just about holding strong.

The swinging ended. They had abandoned their plan of cutting through the cable, instead taking cover from his bullets. Ingo quickly slid along the hawser, even faster than he had before, knowing it could tear at any moment, consigning him to what appeared to be an endless fall into the abyss.

I've scared them away – for you. You owe me your life, the voice whispered in his ear. *Me alone!*

Panting, Ingo reached the entrance of the basement and slipped into the room. He detached himself from the cable and stumbled, sweating, up the stairs. He would soon be free from the madness of these caves and he was no longer certain that he would be setting foot in these catacombs again. Not after hearing that treacherous voice that had conjured up repressed memories and demanded a favour from him.

A glistening beam of light abruptly fell upon him from above.

Ingo lifted an arm up to shield himself and blinked into the brightness, groping for his P99 with his other hand. 'Who's there?'

BEHIND DOOR X

Coco huddled trembling beneath the ferns and covered her ears.

She was breathing quickly, with her eyes screwed tight. She could not stand around for a second longer while the sirens were blaring and the distant, dark thunder of the bomber engines was booming out. The mist, which had a faint scent of grass and earth, whirled around her with cool compassion, as if trying to protect her from the unfolding terror.

Coco had never experienced this sort of fear before, terror that made it impossible to think or move. Her thoughts centred on the bombers with their lethal cargo as images of detonations swarmed through her mind, replete with fire, flames and destruction.

With Coco in the middle of it all.

She had to go – right there and then!

Coco opened her eyes and focused on the pendulum lying on the ground no more than two arm-lengths away from her, shimmering through the white cobwebby mist. It was calling to her, trying to show her the way out, away from the imminent bombing raid.

She removed one hand from her ear and reached out to grasp the pendulum, but she was still several inches short.

The whining of the sirens grew louder as the roar of the bombers caused the ferns above her to wave ominously. The aircraft had to be close, with their bomb-bay doors open, ready to release their destructive load. Everywhere would soon be a deathly inferno.

You're going to die, Beate, came a soft voice through the auditory chaos. *You are about to lose your life in this mysterious world. Unless I help you.*

'Who ... who's there?' She glanced around quickly, unable to make out anyone in the mist.

The voice laughed benevolently. *A good spirit, as you would say in one of your stage shows. Oh yes, how many people know the truth about you, Beate? About your guilt?*

Coco knew immediately what the stranger was hinting at. She hated him for addressing her using her real name. The bombers and her fear receded into the background momentarily. 'Did Ingo give me away?'

Ingo has got nothing to do with it. I know all sorts of things about each of you. You're in my world. The unknown voice was still friendly. *Do you remember, Beate? That time? When no one was able to save you?*

She remembered it all too well, although she'd rather not have. But the memory forced its way into her mind through all the fear and terror, hijacking her eyes and ears.

Beate was suddenly sitting on a chair in her dark red dress, illuminated by the harsh light of a television camera. A privately owned channel had asked her for an interview, which she was now giving on stage in front of a closed curtain, filmed a few days before the programme was due to be aired. It was her new show.

'Thank you for taking the time to talk to us. Let's get going. Jenny, start recording.' The reporter, whose name she had forgotten and whom she could not see in the glare of the light, cleared his throat and allowed a second or so before speaking. 'After a whole year you've decided to make a comeback – as Madame Coco Fendi. How are you getting on with it all? You must be incredibly excited.'

She smiled. 'I'm greatly looking forward to it – and I can promise you some unbeatable sensations,' she answered, her routine spiel.

'No concerns after last time? Are you at all worried that another accident might happen?'

'No. Next question.' She kept her smile polite. As a professional, she knew what the media could be like and had prepared herself for mean-spirited questions. She'd ensure they edited it out afterwards.

'Mrs Rasputina—'

'It's Coco Fendi. Or Madame Fendi.'

'Madame Fendi, you are considered to be an exceptional talent and you take pride in producing shows that do not, for the most part, consist of the standard, well-trodden illusions used by the stage magicians of this world. Would you explain to our viewers what you mean by that?'

'That's correct,' Beate replied, sounding superior. The best way to tell a lie was with total conviction. 'I have access to forces that are concealed from the vast majority of so-called modern humans.' She managed to feign a modicum of modesty. 'Among indigenous tribes I'd be one of many.' She pushed a cigarette into a long silver holder, lit it and took up a perfect Marlene Dietrich pose.

'Meaning? Ghosts?'

'That's just one part of the picture. But yes, I can talk to the deceased. They use ectoplasm to manifest themselves or to manipulate objects.' She formed exquisite smoke rings with her perfectly made-up mouth.

'I have to ask. Thanks to *Ghostbusters*, we've all heard of ectoplasm. Isn't it the disgusting slime that the green monster . . .'

'Slimer.'

'Yes, Slimer! Wasn't that in *Ghostbusters* when—'

'Well, people who know about these sorts of things are aware that it was not invented by Hollywood. It's a kind of spiritual energy that people have been exploring since long before 1900.' Beate was now allowing herself to slip into a form of sexy condescension, throwing back her long blonde hair and letting the black strand hang down, creating a shadow that made it look as if her face had been torn in two. 'At that time the media still dared to show these things to the public. But later they laughed at it. My aim is to show the modern world that magic really does exist.'

'That's very exciting to hear, Madame Fendi. I understand you have even voluntarily undergone a test: you will be the first person to receive something like it: a ghost certificate, so to speak.'

Beate could feel the irritation on her face showing for a second, but she nodded nevertheless. 'It's a bit unusual, but it basically serves as proof that I'm in touch with the other side. Among other things. But it takes up a lot of energy and unfortunately I can't just do it at any given moment.

'I hear Doctor Ingo Theobald from the Freiburg Parapsychological Institute has put you through your paces.'

Beate nodded again. They had moved rather too far away from advertising her new show for her liking, which was not what they had agreed in the editorial meeting. 'Can we—?'

'There are a few mischievous tongues suggesting that you and Theobald are in a relationship and that's the only reason why—'

'Next question. And we're cutting that shit out. It's none of your business,' she said coolly.

'Very well. My next question is probably more interesting anyway, as we're not dealing with rumours.' The interviewer cleared his throat again. 'Madame Fendi, a year and a half ago a serious accident occurred during one of your demonstrations as Rasputina: a little boy lost his life in a trick that went wrong. After an investigation into death due to negligence—'

'Next question. Maybe one about the show.'

'Then perhaps you could try to make me float?'

'I knew you were going to say something like that. You don't have to be a medium for that,' she said contemptuously, blowing smoke aggressively into the camera. 'But I'm not a performing monkey, you know? I prefer to provide my own types of proof.'

At the same time there was a loud cracking sound and the boom collapsed and fell into shot.

Beate avoided it easily, almost as if she had known what was about to happen. 'You should broadcast that.' She sat down, looked into the camera and flicked the end of her cigarette.

The cameraman on the other side of the bright light

gave a loud cry. 'Shit, I've just had an electric shock! The battery – it's completely discharged itself.'

Beate winked and drew on her cigarette again. 'As I said, I'll do what I want.'

The stranger's voice laughed softly and pierced its way into her memories, which began to fade before vanishing completely into the mist that was enveloping her. The bombers and sirens could be heard again in the distance. *You think it was your ability that made that happen, don't you?*

'Other people think so, and that's what matters,' she replied wearily.

But what if you require psychic assistance to escape this place? What if it turns out that you're a cheat and human lives are once again at stake? The voice continued to chatter in her ear. *Don't you remember your betrayal, Beate? Don't you remember betraying a heart, one who was in love with you? How heavily does that guilt lie on your shoulders?*

From among the cobwebs emerged a memory of the day she and Ingo sat opposite each other in a café, and once again she was forced to recall everything that had happened.

It was not any day: it was *the* day.

They held hands for a moment, then he withdrew his fingers and looked around.

Beate's smile became one of mockery. 'Afraid?'

'Afraid this is goodbye.' He looked at her seriously. 'I should never have done this.'

'I enjoyed the sex.'

'You know what I mean. Me lending my expertise to you while we were having a love affair.'

'Love? Goodness!' Beate grinned. 'Who knows? Maybe I controlled you with my mental powers and you were unable to resist?' She took a sip of her coffee, then brushed the bright strand off her face. 'I made you fall in love with me. It would be a perfectly plausible explanation if anyone were to start asking questions.'

Ingo smiled despairingly, his round glasses giving him an air of boyish shyness. 'I know it was a one-sided thing.'

'Oh, don't complain. You got some pretty decent hours out of it.'

'You know I wanted more than a few decent hours.'

'But I didn't.' Beate sighed. 'Ingo, don't act like some lovesick boy. We're both adults and we liked each other. It was never more than that.'

'Not for you, maybe.' Ingo fiddled with the spoon on his saucer. 'Fine. It is what it is. I was a sentimental idiot. And maybe you took advantage of me. But that doesn't change how I felt about you.' He looked up and became serious once again. 'Promise me that you'll never accept another job that puts others in danger – or I'll be forced to expose you for what you are.'

'What?' Beate asked irritably.

'Don't get involved with any life-threatening shows or offer to help the police to find a missing person.' He lowered his head. 'We both know you've got exorbitant levels of empathy, but nothing more. I cannot allow you to endanger others or give people false hope.'

Beate looked out the window. 'That's not how it works. I need to do it for the sake of my future.'

'Beate, promise me!'

'Or what? It would ruin your reputation as well. The university would kick you out and no one would hire you for any job worth more than a thousand euros a month,' she snapped.

Ingo leaned back in his chair. 'If you were a real clairvoyant you'd have known this was coming.'

Beate studied him closely. He looked determined, but she still recognised the softness beneath his serious demeanour. She would be the winner here, and she would always have one over on him, because she had stolen his heart and would hold a part of it for ever.

'You won't regret doing me that favour, Ingo.' Beate rose. 'I can promise you that, but no more.' She slid today's newspaper across to him. 'Page eleven.'

Ingo sighed and found the article. His feigned rebellion had collapsed.

MADAME FENDI:
Germany's first certified medium
with a licence for Ghost Talk!

Exclusive: one hour online with Coco Fendi.
Everything you've ever wanted to ask your
deceased loved ones!

That was the last time she had spoken to Ingo until their unexpected reunion at the airport. The scene from the day when everything broke between them tore apart before her eyes and melted into the mist and fluttering ferns.

The roar of the sirens cascaded over Coco and the

thunder of the aircraft engines sounded so loud she felt as if the planes were right next to her. The fear of death gripped her again with all its might and she sobbed with despair.

You are a deceiver and a traitor to love, Beate, the voice said, without a hint of scorn or contempt. *You urgently require a friend to save you from this dire situation.*

'Yes,' she croaked, 'please, I'll do anything!'

You don't have to do anything now, Beate. Just remember that one day I'll ask a favour of you.

'Yes – yes, of course—'

Good. I'll give you a clue then. Follow the pendulum. It will lead you out of here.

The first explosions from the bombs began to sound. The earth roared and shook and a hot wind blew over the ferns, pushing them down. The mist on the ground rolled away under the force of the blast, leaving her cowering on the grass without any cover, visible to everyone – trackable by anyone.

Coco screamed with panic, staring at the golden pendulum that was so close to her, and yet unattainable.

Suddenly it moved further away, sliding across the ground slowly as if attracted to something. She was supposed to follow the pendulum, the voice had told her.

'No, don't go,' Coco whispered, crawling beneath the ferns. She threw herself forwards to grab the thin silver chain. 'Not without me – you've got to take me out of here.'

A black shoe thrust itself down through the stems and leaves from above her, pressing her wrist into the soft earth. The hem of a pin-striped trouser-leg appeared in front of Coco's eyes.

And the pendulum on its chain shot off.

Coco screamed with fear and pain, 'No – the exit – I've got to get out of here! The pendulum, it's supposed to lead me away—' Her eyes remained fixed on the furrow left in the ground by the golden artefact. 'Leave me alone!'

'Madame Fendi?' Viktor was calling her from afar. 'Where are you?'

'Looking for the exit?' A hand passed into her field of vision, followed by a white shirt cuff with golden cufflinks beneath a pin-striped suit jacket. His fingers grabbed hold of her blonde hair and pulled her to her feet. 'I can help you with that.'

'Yes, please—' Coco sobbed, barely able to recognise anything through her tears and the mist engulfing her. The silhouetted man had a pleasant smell – a man who appeared to have come directly from another world where there was still beauty and safety. Was he the voice? Had he been talking to her? 'Take me away – I want to leave . . . the bombs – they'll tear me to pieces!'

The shadowy stranger moved forwards, leading her by the hair, and after a while stopped in front of another door.

Her vision was still hazy, but Coco saw him pressing a ring against it – then there was a loud crackling sound and a ghostly glow shot across the door, revealing an entrance.

'Thank you, thank you – you've saved me,' she whimpered as he pushed her through the doorway.

The mysterious figure followed Coco, closing the door behind them.

CHAPTER IX

BEHIND DOOR X

Friedemann sprinted through the forest, winding his way through the dense trees and the waist-high ferns. He had taken off his helmet and switched off his radio headset long ago.

He stopped, panting, trying to listen to what was going on around him. His lungs were burning; it felt as if the air did not contain enough oxygen. He discarded the role that he had been playing for Dana's benefit – that of the confused, hallucinating man – and threw away the branch, leaned down on his thighs and tried to slow down his breathing. After a minute or two, his breathing was back to normal and he allowed himself a good laugh.

He used this break to clean his filthy glasses, then he flicked through his notebook. 'You won't get me. I know all your little tricks,' he whispered as he turned the pages. A note professing ownership of the book was scrawled on the front, along with a name, but the decades had not been kind, rendering it all but illegible. What was certain was that it did not belong to Friedemann.

Page after page flew by underneath his fingers. The

terms 'Arkus', 'arcus' and 'Arc Project' appeared several times, but he was looking for something else. Finally he found the conclusive passage and by the light of the full moon he read the handwritten script.

TIMIDUS
— chamber of fears and horrific scenarios; some the same for everyone, some different for all
— designed as a trap to protect from intruders
— be aware that it is artificial!
— find and open passage door 2 with any Particula
— avoid prolonged visit. Can cause permanent nerve damage

'Professor?' Viktor's concerned voice sounded further away now. 'Where are you?'

'Rentski? Coco? *Anyone?*' Spanger shouted after him.

Friedemann wiped the sweat from his forehead and laughed quietly. 'You ignorant fools.' He opened a cardboard envelope stuck in the back cover of the notebook, which contained a stone as flat as a fingernail. The author had named this and other similar fragments *Particulae*. There was considerable speculation about their origin, with many suspecting some sort of undiscovered metal from within the earth, or perhaps from a meteorite. The piece resembled slate, but it shone with a smooth polish as if it were an alloy. So many people had committed murder to get their hands on this little object – and not just once.

Friedemann carefully held the wafer-thin stone disc between his thumb and forefinger, then turned it on its axis until he thought he could see a slight shimmer on it.

The *Particula* was showing him the way to the second exit, just as the author of the notebook had written.

'Excellent.' Friedemann calmly pocketed the notebook and ran in the direction specified by the *Particula*, trying to make as little noise as possible.

He ignored the howling of the beasts, the whining of the sirens, the thundering of the aircraft and the explosions from the bombs. None of this was real as long as you did not submit to the scenario at hand. The *Timidus* – the *fear* – had to bounce off you, otherwise it would manifest itself and be able to kill everything it came across. That was the effect of this room, the special feature of this place.

The notes said this chamber was used to divert and ward off enemies. Those in the know would pass through and leave via the second door, but the uninitiated would either have to return to the hall or die from whatever the *Timidus* deceived them into believing was true.

Friedemann pushed on, until he saw the flashing of a strong lamp approaching through the trees. The opposing force was moving towards him.

He ran in an arc to avoid them, and as he did so, Friedemann spotted a young woman wearing armour lying on the ground. The illuminated face with its freckles, sparkling nose piercing and red curls was clearly that of Anna-Lena van Dam. Above her rose the silhouette of an armoured man, who was pointing a rifle at her.

'Good luck, little one,' Friedemann muttered as he continued on his way. He had bigger fish to fry than saving the life of a nosey woman. He held the fragment in his outstretched hand and allowed it to lead the way.

It was not long before he arrived at the second door mentioned by the book, which was well concealed and embedded in the rock, but visible once you knew what you were looking for.

'Aha,' Friedemann exclaimed triumphantly. He took out the notebook again and after a brief search he found the passage that told him how to escape this environment: there was a particular spot on the doorframe that you had to touch with one of the special stones. Only those who knew what the marking looked like would be able to find it. Then you needed to apply pressure to initiate a reaction, either softly or by hitting it.

Friedemann got to work. 'Ah, got it.'

He gently pressed his wafer-thin sliver against the marked area. He did not dare push harder, lest the stone break. He had read something in the notes about a strong exothermic reaction that caused the *Particulae* to disintegrate. He had no intention of burning to death in an explosion.

His pressing was to no avail, however. The door remained shut.

Friedemann could hear heavy footsteps behind him, as well as some beeps from a walkie-talkie. 'We've got the girl. Eye Four has caught her. But there are still some tracks. We're following them.'

Friedemann increased the pressure on the stone. Being captured was not part of the plan. He was on the cusp of solving more riddles about the doors and the *Particulae*; after all these years his plan had finally brought him to this place. That did not deserve an ugly ending. He had sacrificed far too much in the past for that.

Cursing silently, Friedemann gave the splinter a light blow with his fist.

The door whirred and the lock released with a click.

The noise caught the attention of his pursuers. 'We've got one,' came the excited cry. 'Hey – stop!'

Stopping was the last thing on Friedemann's mind. He threw open the door, jumped over the threshold – and found himself back in the hall-like room with the five doors from which they had departed. Two flares were twitching with a final faint glow, but he didn't notice the black shadows creeping across the floor and seeping into the gap beneath the second door with the destroyed knocker.

'What—? How—?' Friedemann took a few steps back and hit the door with the question mark on it – the one he had just climbed through – in frustration. This was not where he was supposed to come out. He kept the splinter in his hand and leafed frantically through his notebook. What had he done wrong?

Just before the exit closed, the door flew open again. Two men in olive-coloured armour and closed helmets jumped out and aimed compact, futuristic-looking rifles at him.

Friedemann put his hands in the air, with the book in one hand and the *Particula* in the other. 'Don't shoot! I surrender.' He was so close to achieving his goal; something had to come up. 'I would like to talk to your leader. It's about the Arkus Project.'

'I can well imagine you'd like to surrender. Put your gun

on the ground,' the man on the right commanded with a distorted voice. 'Slowly.'

'What project is this?' whispered the other man. 'I've never heard of it.'

You're going to need a friend, a soft voice intoned suddenly in Friedemann's ear. *I can help you and see you through this mess. Because you're utterly alone now.*

His radio was switched off, so this was not somebody talking on the wrong frequency. Friedemann looked cautiously around the high room, but could not see anything conspicuous.

I'm not a figment of your imagination, the unknown voice spoke. *I can help you if you do me a favour. Quid pro quo.*

Friedemann ignored it. He had had to get himself out of trouble plenty of times before and he was perfectly capable of doing so again. Slowly, he clamped the precious booklet between his back and his belt and, with his fingers still pointing upwards, he drew the P99 semi-automatic out of its holster and laid it on the floor. 'These Arkus Project plans are a danger. To us all.'

'I don't care. I've only got one job: to capture you,' the man on the right replied. 'Looks like I've succeeded, doesn't it?'

'In any case there's far more going on down here than Ritter told us. I thought it was just supposed to be that red-haired girl and the other one from the first rescue team,' said the one on the left. 'I'd better find out what the situation is.'

'Don't you understand? We're in danger!' Friedemann shouted dramatically, trying to increase the sense of urgency. 'I can resolve it before something catastrophic happens – I know what needs to be done.' The more incomprehensible and vague he remained, the greater the likelihood they would lead him to their superior. 'I beg of you, bring me to—'

'Shut up!' The man on the right raised his gun threateningly.

Friedemann's mind was working feverishly. He clenched his hand protectively around his precious splinter. Improvisation. That's what he was good at.

'I can't get through to Ritter – too much interference. Oh well, no matter. Let's go back to the cable,' the man on the right instructed his companion. 'We can cut it off, then the rest of these fuckers are out of the game. It doesn't matter how many of them there are.'

The one on the left moved slowly away. 'What about him?' He pointed at Friedemann.

'What about him?' His finger twitched treacherously on the trigger.

Friedemann sprinted with his head down like a rugby player and ran straight at his surprised opponent. The impact hurt like hell, as the man's armour had edges to it that pressed into his thin body. But the professor refused to give up. He struck his adversary's visor with his elbow. Groaning, the man sank backwards and dropped his weapon.

'Shit!' shouted the second armoured man, firing without hesitation. 'You stupid . . .'

The bullet never even left his gun.

'*Shit! Shit! Shit!*' Panicking, the man fiddled with his rifle, which had completely jammed, slapping it several times until the defective bullet flew sideways out of the ejector.

Meanwhile, Friedemann hurried towards the door with the broken knocker, choosing this one to ensure neither his opponents nor anyone else would follow him. When he arrived at the door, he raised the hand holding the *Particula* to use the shard as a replacement ring.

The fragment struck the plate – and shattered with a loud, hideous sound. The door lit up and a shriek could be heard from the other side. Instead of the familiar rumble, a faint crack sounded from the ceiling of the cavernous chamber.

'No,' Friedemann whispered in horror, staring at the trickling pieces crumbling to the floor and losing all their lustre.

'Now you're for it,' shouted the armoured man behind him, raising his rifle once more.

Friedemann overcame his terror, opened the door and jumped into the living, hissing blackness behind it, utterly unaware of what awaited him.

Frankfurt, Lerchesberg

Walter van Dam had a fresh cup of coffee in front of him and had swapped alcohol for water. He needed a clear head if he wanted to support the team from the surface and find out more information with the assistance of Doctor Theobald.

Van Dam smoothed down his hair and his impressive sideburns and moustache. He buttoned his shirt and tied his tie without thinking as his eyes wandered over the triptych of monitors.

Most of the images revealed little more than black and white stripes; it was difficult to make out the members of the group at all. It was next to impossible to get in contact with them now. He fiddled with the controls.

NETWORK REQUIRES OPTIMISATION. WEAK TRANSMISSION. APPEARED AS PERMANENT MESSAGE. SIGNAL-BOOSTERS IMPAIRED.

He shook his head uneasily, then sipped his coffee. He quickly made other adjustments, trying to improve the transmission. 'Come on.'

Suddenly the connection improved and a new message flashed up:

SIGNAL-BOOSTERS ACTIVATED.

Van Dam's face lit up. 'That's more like it!'

He switched through the views; the video quality remained poor, but not as terrible as before. He was still getting nothing at all from Professor Friedemann and Madame Coco Fendi, neither image nor sound. Spanger, too, appeared to have switched off his helmet camera.

The remaining feeds were showing a series of still images: forest and ferns, with mangled noise sequences and distorted voices. Van Dam opened a diagnostic pro-gramme to see if the computer could investigate the cause of this error.

Curiously enough, Dana Rentski's screen remained completely white, but he could hear sirens, the howling of wolves and the roar of aircraft engines over her microphone. 'Ms Rentski? Ms Rentski, what's happening with your camera?'

'Van Dam!' Dana sounded annoyed. 'Good to hear from you. Can you see anything?'

'Just white. Is there anything stuck to your lens? Cobwebs or—?'

'That's probably all this mist.'

'Mist?' Van Dam rubbed his tired face, his stubble feeling scratchier than ever. 'Where are you? What's happening? What can you tell me?'

'It's . . . all rather chaotic. And' – she swallowed – 'and I can't see anything any more. No idea why. Friedemann attacked me and since then . . .'

'The professor attacked you?'

'He went insane – from fear, I guess.'

Van Dam took a deep breath and reached for his coffee. 'You shouldn't stay in there alone.' The bitter sweetness slid down through his mouth, reviving his mind. 'I can try to guide you out, Ms Rentski, using the camera. Your signal is coming through clearly. Yours is the only one to do so, unfortunately. Get up.'

'Okay,' Dana said. 'You've got to be my eyes, though.'

She stood up. Ferns, a forest, the full moon and her G36 suddenly became visible on the monitor.

'My God!' Are you on the surface?' Astonished, van Dam examined the environment he had just seen for the first time without distortion.

'We suspect so.' Dana clearly had no desire to tell him any more about the situation they were in. 'I'll keep turning and you can tell me what's there.'

'To the right of you is a cluster of trees. At least you'll have some cover there. Go right, slowly,' he ordered. 'The fog is thick. You wouldn't be able to see where you were going anyway.' He leaned forward to see all the details.

'I'd rather start shooting someone. Perhaps someone on the other team – you remember, don't you?' Dana walked slowly in a straight line, twisting her upper body left and right to give van Dam a complete picture of her surroundings. The howling, whining and roaring noises had still not subsided.

Then the glow of a torch could be seen between the trees.

'Take cover!' van Dam urged her.

Dana ducked immediately, the camera barely protruding out of the fog. 'I've just knelt on something hard.' The view wobbled slightly, then her dirty hand held what she had found in front of the lens. He could see a golden pendulum. It was pulling on the silver chain like a flag billowing in the wind.

'It's Madame Fendi's pendulum,' said van Dam, puzzled. 'So where is she?'

'Okay, I'll keep it with me. And at the moment I know next to nothing about what the others are doing. She should really have stayed with Spanger.'

The torch approached Dana's position. Van Dam could see an armoured man dragging a woman in combat gear behind him; she was resisting heavily.

'Who's coming?' Dana whispered tensely.

'An enemy. And he's got someone with him ...' Van Dam adjusted the depth of field. The woman had lost her helmet and long, red curls fell around her head. Was that his Anna-Lena?

The armoured man stopped. He had spotted Dana and armed his weapon. 'Hey,' he called out, 'get up slowly – I want to see you.'

Dana swung her G36 back and forth. 'Tell me where to shoot.'

Van Dam stared at the monitor, spellbound. Something had flashed on the woman's face in the moonlight. He corrected the settings, enlarged the view and turned the brightness up. His daughter's features became visible; she was cursing her tormentor and trying desperately to free herself.'

'I warned you.' The armoured man opened fire and a red and yellow flower of fire erupted from the barrel. The first shot whizzed past Dana. 'The next one is ready to go. Well?'

'Okay, now I know where he is.' Dana adjusted her G36 and went to pull the trigger.

'No! No, stop!' van Dam shouted. 'That's Anna-Lena – he's got my daughter with him!'

'Very well. You had your chance.' The armoured man had his hands full trying to keep the barrel steady because Anna-Lena was tearing at him and shaking his arm. 'Now I'll—'

Dana fired twice.

'No!' Van Dam jumped up, knocking his glass of water

over. He watched in horror as the events unfolded so far away from him.

The two bullets struck the man's armoured chest.

'Fuck!' Her opponent staggered backwards, dragging Anna-Lena with him and using her as a shield. He got her into a headlock and squeezed the air out of her, making her stop her defensive efforts. Then he steadied himself.

'He's aiming again,' van Dam warned, gripping his hair with both hands. His daughter was being used as a shield against a blind gunwoman. 'I'm begging you, Ms Rentski, don't shoot! Stay down and wait for a better opportunity. My daughter is right in front of him.'

'He won't give me a second chance, Mr van Dam.' Dana rolled over to one side, which meant the helmet camera gave van Dam a view only of the empty clearing.

'Ms Rentski? What's—? Where—?'

'Ah, now I've got you!' Dana's voice rang out angrily.

The camera swung up and to the right, as if she were suddenly on a rollercoaster and the silhouettes of two people wearing armour appeared, one standing closely behind the other.

'No – no! Anna-Lena—!' van Dam bellowed, wishing he could jump into the display to intervene. 'Anna-Lena – for the love of God—'

He heard the rattling burst of fire and saw the glare of the muzzle flash on the monitor, which turned the image white again.

Ingo stood in the cellar of the old van Dam estate, blinking into the beam of light that was keeping him fixed to the ground. He raised his arm to try to shield himself from the brightness. 'Who's there?'

Not hearing any sounds or any reply, Ingo inched forward, moving out of the glare. His other hand held the pistol hidden behind his back. 'Matthias, is that you?'

Still no response; even the mysterious whispering that had planted those cruel images of his youth in his head remained silent. His alleged 'friend', who had so cockily offered him assistance and had supposedly scared off his pursuers, did not appear to want to intervene on this occasion.

Ingo lowered his arm slowly and stepped out of the light. The beam turned out to merely be a strong reflection from above him.

Relief spread through Ingo's body. He definitely did not need any more enemies or shoot-outs.

He stumbled up the stone steps and hurried through the abandoned house.

It was pitch-black outside. The bright cold-blue xenon headlights of an expensive car piercing the windows and illuminating the steps through the open cellar door were being reflected by a mirror on the wall; he could hear an engine idling outside the door.

'Matthias?' Ingo hoped he'd find the friendly chauffeur soon so he could drive him to van Dam and then the scientific work of solving the riddles of the underground maze and the doors could begin.

Ingo left the house, but stopped dead after only one step.

Matthias was lying dead on the verandah, the handle of a kitchen knife protruding from his neck. It looked as if the blade had lodged between the vertebrae. The metal had sealed the wound, preventing any blood from leaking out, which made the sight all the more strange – surreal, almost, as if one could simply bring the chauffeur back to life with a few turns of the knife, like some oversized mechanical doll. His suit was as perfect as ever. His cap was lying next to him.

The headlights of the idling Mercedes were illuminating the front of the house and the verandah and moths were fluttering furiously through the light. The driver's door was ajar. As well as Anna-Lena's Rolls-Royce, there was an unknown BMW parked in front of the villa.

Ingo felt completely overwhelmed. The bitter realisation that he was not only dealing with opposing forces underground but also up here hit him hard. Their enemies were trying to stab them in the back. Nowhere was safe any more.

'Mr van Dam,' he radioed, 'I need to talk to you immediately!' He waited for a few seconds. 'Mr van Dam, can you hear me?'

'Not now,' the man retorted tersely. 'I'm sorry, Mr Theobald, but it's my daughter. I've got to—'

The connection broke off.

Ingo struggled to work out what had just happened. It sounded as if perhaps the team had found his daughter, but van Dam did not sound at all reassured.

He looked over at the abandoned BMW. There was no trace of the occupants; they were all missing.

Maybe they had gone down into the cave without meeting Ingo – or they were still roaming the area. Or perhaps they were somewhere else in the villa, or in the rubble of the burned-down factory.

Anxiety seized him again. Despite not having a clue how to use the P99, he drew the pistol and went over to the Mercedes sitting in the drive. At least holding the gun gave him a mild sense of security.

As he passed the Rolls-Royce, he glanced into it and received yet another nasty surprise, for the first Anna-Lena was lying on the back seat in a pool of her own blood, with her throat slit open. The attackers were evidently unconcerned about murdering a defenceless innocent.

Ingo began to feel nauseous.

The next shock did not take long to arrive. An unknown man dressed in ordinary clothes was slumped over the steering wheel of the Mercedes people carrier, blood trickling from his nose and with a gaping wound on his forehead. There was a boot print on his shirt, at chest height. Ingo looked back towards the stairs. Perhaps this was Matthias' murderer? Maybe he had been injured during the fight and had fainted in here from the pain. The wound on the back of the stranger's head looked as if it had come from a heavy fall. Beside him in the passenger seat was a tablet computer showing a screensaver of wavy lines.

Ingo started the people carrier's ignition with a flick of his wrist, breaking the silence in the forest and surrounding area. The engine under the bonnet softly ticked over.

'Hey!' Ingo gently shook the unconscious man by the shoulder while pointing the gun at him with his other hand. 'Who are you?'

The stranger slipped to one side at Ingo's touch, one arm falling from the wheel and landing on the passenger seat. The impact caused the tablet's display to spring to life. Ingo reached over and stopped the unconscious man from flipping over completely. He checked his pulse. He could not find one, but the man's skin was still warm.

His eyes fell upon the small illuminated monitor, where he saw his own likeness reflected back at him. The picture had been taken at the airport.

Alarmed, he walked around the car, picked up the device and pressed down on the screen. More windows popped up.

Ingo's eyes widened. The tablet contained information about the team members that was almost certainly not readily accessible. They even had a record of his relationship with Beate. 'What the . . . ?' He looked down at the stranger, shocked. The organisation behind this espionage appeared to have an awful lot of compromising, elucidating and terrifyingly accurate knowledge. 'Unbelievable!'

He placed the tablet on the dashboard and reflected on his current situation, deciding he had to tell van Dam everything.

Ingo did not want to take the people carrier to Lerchesberg as the car's Wi-Fi was what was maintaining contact with the team underground. Nor could he use the Rolls, not given the dead man lying in a pool of blood.

The stranger's BMW was all that was left.

Ingo turned off the ignition and found the BMW's key in the mystery man's pocket. He picked up the tablet and climbed into the BMW, where he discovered a miniature laptop too. The darkness loomed threateningly over him and the deserted landscape as he entered van Dam's address into the satnav and drove off into the night.

He turned on his radio again and announced, 'I'm on my way to see you, Mr van Dam, whether you can hear me or not. And I've got some questions. The sooner I've got my answers, the better it will be for your daughter and the team.'

He pressed down on the accelerator and the BMW shot off into the night.

BEHIND DOOR X

Spanger and Viktor ran across the clearing through the knee-high mist. The sirens were still wailing and they presumed the wolves had to be somewhere nearby. The roaring of the bombers had become more distant, but explosions were flashing on the horizon. The wind bore the stench of fire, burnt earth and phosphorous. The men were anxious; the howling and yowling and roaring were preying on their nerves.

Viktor pointed to the left. 'That way – quickly. If the planes come back and drop their bombs, we're done for.'

Spanger followed him and looked around. It was annoying him immensely that he had lost Coco, even though there had not, strictly speaking, been anything he could have done about it. This further hardened his resolve to find her again and ensure her safety. 'That can't be everything,' he wondered. 'First I'm in the future and now I'm in something like a—'

Suddenly a slim silhouette became visible a few yards ahead of him through the fog. The figure raised its arm accusingly and pointed at him. 'I'll get you, you fat pig!' he whispered menacingly.

Spanger screamed with surprise. 'Tilo? Tilo Jungsen?' He stopped dead, terrified. 'No – no, you're dead!' His body had gone ice-cold as he recalled the ominous warning of that enigmatic voice – that the dead were getting ready to come back and claim him, to pass judgement on him.

'I'm only dead because you killed me – you *murdered* me.' Black-red blood wept from the wound on Tilo's head. His face was pale and vacant.

Viktor stopped a few yards ahead, irritated. 'Who's dead? Come on, Spanger . . .' He noticed the trainee and raised his rifle. 'Holy shit! Where did he come from? Who is he?'

'Tell him who I am,' whispered the living corpse.

Spanger did not want to admit anything, not to Viktor – not to anyone. 'He . . . he's from the first team. From van Dam's first team. He must have survived.'

'Liar,' snapped the dead man. 'You're lying about what you've done. But the truth will come out and I will be the one to judge you.'

Shots rang out perilously close to them, which made Viktor swear. He ran on, his G36 locked and loaded. 'Come on – this bloke can come with us too.'

'I'll be sure to tell him.' Spanger ran after him. Apparently Viktor could see Tilo but not hear him. Hopefully that would remain the case. He focused on finding Coco. And Anna-Lena. He had to make amends for everything he had ruined.

Tilo followed him, keeping his distance. 'I'll get you. I am the end of all your lies and your dishonesty.'

Spanger ran faster and, gasping for air, panted, 'What do you want? What can I do to make you go away?'

'What do I want?' Tilo was suddenly right in his face. 'You're going to die, Fatty – you'll pay for my death,' he hissed. 'Do the others know you forged your credentials?' The undead man hit him on the head, sending Spanger reeling to the floor. 'And *that* is precisely how it felt.'

Spanger scrambled to his feet immediately and looked around. His pitiful exploits underground, his laboriously reconstructed self-esteem and the little self-confidence he had managed to forge were all about to crumble to dust. But Coco and Anna-Lena needed him. Rescuing them would be his motivation.

The living corpse was gone.

Some way off, he could see Viktor was approaching a group of people. He recognised the faces rising up out of the mist. 'It's Rentski,' he called over to Spanger, 'and she's got the girl!'

'What will happen when they find out this is your first job?' Spanger heard the spiteful voice of the apprentice taunting him once again. 'You're a nothing – a fraud.'

Spanger stumbled through the ferns, knocking the enormous leaves left and right, muttering, 'No, it's just my imagination. Jungsen is dead.' He repeated to himself, 'Jungsen is dead. He can't hurt me.'

Out of nowhere, the corpse emerged from the fern forest in front of him and struck him again with an angry growl. 'Take *that*, Piggy!'

Stars and Catherine wheels exploded before Spanger's eyes and he fell to the ground again. 'I didn't mean to – I'm *sorry* – it was an *accident*,' he bleated. His heart ached with every beat and he was hyperventilating. He started crawling on all fours until he found a tree to pull himself up with, before racing off again awkwardly. Tilo would not stop him, nor would he allow the dead trainee to distract him from his mission.

'I'll get you, you fat bastard: *I'll get you*,' came the threats from behind him, but although he could barely see where he was going, his vision still blurry from the impact of the blows, Spanger staggered on. 'It was an accident,' he insisted. 'An *accident*! I served my time – I paid my dues!' He had not noticed he was going in the wrong direction, but driven by his overwhelming desire to save Coco, he pressed on regardless.

'Spanger? Spanger—' Viktor called after him. 'What are you doing?' He and Dana were standing either side of Anna-Lena, whose stolen armour was flecked with the blood of her stricken captor; the man's body was now lying among the ferns. 'Where's the other guy?'

Spanger's outline vanished amid the trees as he shouted incomprehensibly.

'Spanger, what . . . ? Oh for fuck's sake—' Viktor turned to Anna-Lena, who picked up the rifle and tested it. 'Miss van Dam, your father has sent us to bring you back. Everything's going to be all right.' He barely believed his own words at that moment in time.

Anna-Lena tossed her red curls back, making her nose piercing flash in the light. She was glad to not be on her own any more, but that alone could not guarantee their survival.

Viktor looked at Dana in amazement, but her gaze passed through him as if he were not there. *Not a good sign at all.* 'What's up with you?'

'I can't see a thing. Friedemann attacked me and I haven't been able to see anything since. That paranoid arsehole.' She placed one hand on Anna-Lena's shoulder for support. 'What shall we do? Who's the other person you were talking about?'

'Spanger has seen someone from the first group – the ones first sent down to find Miss van Dam.'

Anna-Lena followed their conversation silently, wiping her face, not realising she was rubbing specks of blood onto her skin as she did so; in the moonlight they resembled black ink dots on her bright freckles. *The other team.* She had a vague recollection of meeting those people, but now was not the time to tell them about it.

'Bring me my daughter immediately!' Dana and Viktor suddenly heard van Dam's furious voice in their ears. 'You've already endangered her enough as it is.'

'Let's go to that copse over there, Ms Rentski. We should have some cover from our pursuers,' Viktor said, before answering their over-excited client. 'Calm down, Mr van Dam. We'll be back soon. We just need to find the others, then we can return to the surface.'

'I'm paying you for my daughter, not the others – three million, for each of you, if you bring her up now.'

Viktor ignored the offer, considering it deeply immoral. He fully understood that the businessman would gladly use all his wealth to rescue his daughter, but he had no intention of leaving anyone behind. He hadn't done that on any of his other assignments and he wasn't about to start now. 'Can you tell me where we can find our three runaways? We'll be able to find them faster that way.'

'I can help you,' offered Anna-Lena.

She did not seem at all distraught to Viktor – in fact, considering everything she must have been through, she was impressively self-composed. 'No, Miss van Dam, your father would quite rightly never forgive me if I allowed that. But you can look after Ms Rentski.' He radioed to the surface. 'What can you see on your screens?'

'No images for Madame Fendi, Friedemann and Spanger. If I'm hearing it correctly, it sounds as if Spanger's running. Doctor Theobald is on his way to me; he reported in earlier over the radio.'

Dana raised her head in surprise. 'The sirens have stopped. That's a good sign . . . isn't it?'

'Of course! No sirens – no bombers.' Viktor hurried off, following the tracks Spanger had left in the undergrowth. 'I'll look for Spanger, then we can take care of Fendi and the professor.'

'Mr Troneg, no! Troneg, that . . .' van Dam protested.

'We'll need to make sure we're in the right position then.' Dana moved Anna-Lena behind her. 'Miss van Dam, you'll need to tell me if you spot any more enemies approaching.'

'No problem,' she said, looking around attentively.

'Sorry for dragging you into all this,' Dana continued. 'We really ought to be the ones looking after you, not the other way around.'

Anna-Lena said something in response, but the words were lost amid the whispering that Dana could hear deep within her mind. *You could use a friend, Dana: a dependable friend, one who'd be of use on the battlefield. One who can save you.*

'What? Who's there?'

'Um . . . me?' said Anna-Lena, puzzled.

Only you can hear me, Dana. I would be reliable: as reliable as you are whenever you accept an assignment. Even if no one in your team has any suspicion about what you've still got left to do. The voice had the tone of an omniscient priest who was aware of everyone's sins, but did not pass judgement on them. *I know about the extra job you've accepted. Excellent acting earlier, by the way, even though you already knew about the first team that had been lost down here. And I know what's bothering you. You can trust me, Dana.*

Dana's mind wandered back to the recent past, to the moment the mysterious voice was talking about.

She was seldom seen in the sort of civilian clothing she was wearing: a mid-length green skirt, white blouse, dark grey blazer and trainers. Her backpack was next to her as she sat at a table in the little café. She was writing on a tablet, occasionally taking a sip of black coffee.

A man in an ordinary business suit sat down beside her. He adjusted his cuffs and coughed. 'Father Christmas has brought the weapons.'

'I have a machine gun now.' Dana looked up.

'Ho ho ho.'

Dana smiled at the man. 'I'm pleased to see my services are of interest to you, sir.'

'You've got a good reputation to go with your high price.'

'If you say so.' She took another sip of her drink.

The man looked around the café. 'I've been making enquiries. You used to work for Executive Outcomes, then Blackwater. Your superiors were sorry to see you leave.'

'The free market is more profitable, plus I get to choose who I shoot. At Blackwater I found myself under fire far too often. Lots of people think action films and the life of a mercenary are the same thing.' Dana retained her smile, but it became more business-like. 'But I'm sure you're not here for my memoirs, sir.'

He handed her an envelope. 'There's twenty thousand euros in there, information about my son and a USB stick with a digital version of everything. You'll get another thirty thousand if you bring my son back alive.'

Dana took the envelope and looked inside. 'An application for a rescue mission? I thought you wanted me to work for you?'

'Van Dam has already sent out a team. My son Alexander is in it and I haven't heard from him since.' He was wringing his hands nervously. 'Usually he and I go out to eat once he gets back from a job – a ritual I'd like to keep doing for many more years yet.'

Dana skimmed the pages. 'Your son trained at Levdan? Israeli training's the best. Looks like the shit must've—' She looked at him. 'My apologies, sir.'

'The shit *has* hit the fan.' He leaned back. 'That's why I'm sending you down there to find my son. I've written a few references for you about climbing and caves and so on. Reckon you can blag that?'

'Abseiling is part of the job, whether from helicopters, buildings or cliffs. I can handle it.'

'Good. I'll wait for your call then.' He stood up. 'And you should really work on your code words.'

'They're classics, sir. Lewis and Willis – and they've each got something to do with Father Christmas.' Dana smiled encouragingly. 'I'll bring your son back, sir. Feel free to book a table at the best restaurant you know.'

You see that? You've betrayed the others. You knew right from the start how dangerous it would be down here, whispered the unknown voice. *Trust me and I can protect you from your worst fears. All I ask is a small favour in return.*

Dana struggled against the memories, but it was too hard, for she had had to face her worst fear that very day, in her ophthalmologist's office.

'What do you mean by "not easy", exactly?' She adjusted her skirt. She was not used to wearing these sort of clothes; she always felt like there was more of her flesh on display than she was comfortable with.

'The largest foreign bodies were safely removed by my colleagues at the time. Your cornea has recovered.'

'I can hear a *but* coming from a mile away.'

'I'm afraid you're right.' He turned the monitor around to show her the images. 'Unfortunately, the CT scan has revealed some very fine remnants that have become embedded in the vitreous. We're talking about less than a millimetre in diameter here.' He regarded the blonde woman in some amazement. 'I hope you don't mind my asking, but how exactly did all this happen?'

'Would you believe me if I told you I survived a hand

grenade in Darfur? Sadly, the explosion had an equally disastrous effect on my eye as it did on the surrounding area.'

The doctor made no reply but turned the screen back to face him. 'You're privately insured?'

'I typically pay in cash,' Dana replied.

'I'm asking because there's a very expensive treatment available where we use a series of lasers to break up the foreign bodies. In layman's terms, it's similar to how you would remove a tattoo.'

'Another silent *but*, Doctor?'

'There is a significant risk, given how many foreign bodies there are, that too much liquid might be evaporated or the eye tissue might have too much scarring. Again, in layman's terms.

Dana gulped in an attempt to stifle the lump forming in her throat. 'Will my sight be impaired?'

'You could go blind, Ms Rentski. In all likelihood.'

'How likely?'

'Eighty-seven per cent. If we do nothing, well . . . I won't lie to you, the irritation and inflammation this has caused will have the same effect, albeit over a longer period of time. The risk will be one hundred per cent if you leave it as it is.'

There was a knock at the door and he was called out for an emergency. 'I'll be right back,' he promised. 'Excuse me.' He hurried out.

Dana breathed deeply, at first struggling to fight back the tears, then she gave way, buried her face in her hands and sobbed in true despair.

The memory felt so real that she could still taste her tears when her mind returned to the present.

I can help you. In return for a small favour that I will one day ask of you. Think about it – or you might die. Lose your sight. Let down your original client.

'Ms Rentski,' Walter van Dam wailed in her earphones, 'you'll receive three million if you—'

Dana started at the sound of his voice. She felt trapped. 'I'm already blind. How far do you think I'd make it with your daughter? You're not exactly the best guide. So just leave it, okay?'

She had to shake off the past and concentrate. She needed distraction from the images in her memory. 'Tell me, Miss van Dam, how exactly did you find your way down here?'

Anna-Lena had been examining the foreign rifle; she decided she would be able to use it if more enemies were to appear. It had already worked once. 'I've been studying my great-grandfather's records for a long time and I found them rather exciting, even though I could hardly translate any of them. He used my family's old merchant language – not exactly my specialist subject.' She looked around cautiously, checking to see whether anyone was prowling around. 'There was stuff all about entrances, transitions and passages – about the locations of the various doors and who used to use them.' Anna-Lena looked up at the moon and the clear sky. This was not the surface. They were somewhere within a sphere that had a door waiting for them. 'My father forbade me – he told me I had no business exploring the old house . . .'

'But you went looking for it.' Dana understood the young woman all too well. 'I get the impression you're wearing armour.'

'It's not mine. I stole it from one of the men who attacked me.'

'And what were you wearing before?'

'A ballgown.'

Dana laughed aloud. 'Seriously?'

'Yes. I was going to go to the opera before I started talking to my father, but I decided to drive to the old estate instead. Then I found the open door with the cable – the one my grandmother used to tell me all about.'

Dana seriously doubted Anna-Lena had been hanging from the metal cable in an evening dress and clutching a fancy handbag. 'But how did you—?'

'Not on the cable. The door in the cellar opens on two sides – it's hidden, but I followed the descriptions I found in the documents and they brought me to the chamber where the five doors are. Then I wandered around for a bit. I'll tell you what, I've been to some really weird places! Beats tripping any day. It was in this nightmare of wolves and sirens that the search party my father had sent appeared. The first squad.' She shuddered. 'I thought I'd finally make it out. But they suddenly turned around and left – and then those other armoured men arrived and started to hunt us down.' She took a long breath. 'Well, that's the abridged version.'

'Thank you.' Dana had regained her composure, shaking off the images that the voice had planted in her head. There was still one more thing left to do and this was the perfect opportunity for it. 'Oh, there's a wire loose here – just a sec.' Her feigned discovery of a technical defect allowed her to turn off the camera. Then she reached beneath her Kevlar vest and removed the photograph of the missing Alexander. He had not been one of the dead men lying in the little chamber and when Viktor had mentioned the man to Spanger, she felt rather more confident that she might be able to bring a desperate father's son back to him.

'Miss van Dam, have you seen this man down here?' Dana held out the picture.

Anna-Lena nodded. 'Yes, yes I've seen him. Him and the others. But only briefly.'

Dana's insides did a somersault. The man Viktor had been talking about could well be Alexander. 'Good. He's still alive then.'

This time Anna-Lena hesitated. 'I wouldn't be so sure about that.'

CHAPTER X

BEHIND DOOR X

Spanger stumbled through the thicket, panting and sweating. Dozens of silhouettes of the dead apprentice rose up all around him, their empty eyes pursuing him with accusatory stares. The dead had come to pass judgement on him, just as the voice of the invisible entity had prophesied.

By now it was clear he was lost. He stopped and began to search for his own tracks. Hopefully, once he found them, he would be able to make it back to Viktor, who he supposed was following him. 'It was an accident, you arsehole!' Spanger shouted, pushing his way through thorn-less vines.

Another trainee appeared in front of Spanger and struck him in the face.

Spanger collapsed for the third time, but this time he did not immediately get to his feet but breathed in the scent of the disturbed earth. If he died of a heart attack at that very moment, he would not fight it. All his suffering and humiliation would be over, once and for all.

But something had changed inside him after his attack on Coco and he had given himself a task.

'You will freeze up. You will fall to pieces. You will never survive this assignment, you fat pig,' thundered the undead man at him, 'because you haven't got what it takes to be a bodyguard. You're a fraud, nothing more.'

Spraying saliva, Spanger screamed with rage at the ground, then pulled himself together. 'No,' he said resolutely.

Brisk steps approached. 'Spanger, get up,' came Viktor's voice. 'We've got to find Fendi and the professor.'

'A fat fraud.' The undead figure vanished into the mist, whispering, 'I'll get you. The truth will get you.'

Viktor reached Spanger, who was lying pitifully in the dirt, a heap of misery, trembling like an aspen leaf. He knew the scene all too well from his previous missions. There were two types of people under fire: those who reacted and could function and those who fell apart in a state of shock.

'Come on, get up.' Viktor laid a reassuring hand on his shoulder. 'We've all got to get through this together. And we're going to make it out alive.'

Spanger could feel the warmth emanating from Viktor's fingers and it gave him confidence. Even though it cost him all he had, he put his hands to the ground and pushed himself up. Spitting dirt from his mouth, he said, 'He's gone.'

'Who? Do you mean the man from the first team?' Viktor looked around in vain.

'I wanted to strike out on my own.' Spanger brushed the dirt from his clothes. *Breathe in. Breathe out.* As long as he was alive, he had to find a way out, with all the others – and then sort his life out. 'We've got the girl – I've seen her,' he said firmly. 'Then we should get out of here.'

'No, Friedemann and Fendi are still missing.'

Viktor could see he had made a mistake, for Spanger was suddenly looking very determined.

He walked in the direction from which Viktor had just come. His legs were aching, but if he succumbed to thinking about himself now, he would become an even bigger loser. He could see it the others' eyes every time they talked about him, and he remembered the professor's words, how derisory they were, and full of disgust. Not one of them trusted him. He absolutely deserved Viktor's reproachful look. But this would be the last time.

'Bring my daughter to the surface,' Walter van Dam suddenly barked over the radio.

'Negative,' Viktor replied. 'I'm not letting anyone go back.'

'I am your employer and it is for me to decide what you do,' said the businessman over all channels. 'If anything should happen to my daughter, I will hold you responsible – all of you! No money, but three million problems instead: you can count on it.'

Viktor was not about to give up. 'Mr van Dam, I—'

'Troneg,' van Dam interrupted, 'I propose we make a deal. If you decide to go back down into this labyrinth to pick up the others, I will not stop you. You will have all the equipment you need. It'll be your own private venture. But first, my daughter: she's the reason I hired you, nothing else.'

'Oh, that's a great suggestion. Deal! We'll be on our way then,' Spanger replied hurriedly. 'We'll be up soon, Mr van Dam. We'll re-equip and come back to save the others.'

He trudged off, knowing no hero could make it far without a helmet or weapons, that was a fact.

Viktor wrestled with his conscience but van Dam was right: his orders had been clear. Cursing, he followed Spanger back to the grove where Dana Rentski and Anna-Lena were standing.

'Doctor Theobald?' he radioed as he joined the rest of the group. 'Doctor, can you hear me?' He waited for a few seconds. 'Okay, the connection's gone again.' He nodded at the others. 'Right, let's get Miss van Dam to the surface, then we can come back and look for Friedemann and Fendi.'

Dana pursed her lips. She did not approve of being patronised. 'I'll decide for myself what to do afterwards. In my current condition I'll be glad to get out of here alive. I'm no use to you blind, Troneg, not now, nor later.'

'And how exactly do we get out?' Spanger interjected. 'There's no map and without the medium—'

Anna-Lena cursed herself for losing her opponent's map during the attack; it would have been invaluable. But the piece of paper was lying somewhere in the ferns, buried by fog.

'Oh, haven't I told you I can do magic? Hocus pocus!' Dana reached into her pocket and pulled out the pendulum she had found lying on the wet grass. It was pulling gently on the chain in her hand, pointing in a specific direction. 'At least we've got our little compass back. And it appears to work independently of Madame Fendi, luckily for us. I'd lead us onwards, but at the moment I'm probably not in the best position to do that.'

'Brilliant!' Viktor took the pendulum and strode off. 'Off we go, then.'

The pendulum really did appear to be working just as well for the medium's colleagues as it had for Coco herself – or perhaps it was Coco who was showing them the way from another realm, or wherever she might be hiding.

Dana, who had put her hand on Viktor's shoulder, was followed by Anna-Lena. She handed Spanger the bulky weapon she had captured.

'I'll handle anything that tries to stop us,' he announced. After a brief examination it turned out to be a pump-action shotgun that also shot high-calibre solid bullets; the magazine was loaded to alternate between the two. His confidence now was as high as his depression had been before. He knew he could do this job, because he had dragged himself out of the dirt and had not given up.

They passed through the forest and the ferns in single file, without using a light of their own, for the full moon was still shining, illuminating the way. The wolves had fallen silent, leaving a ghostly silence. Every now and again they dodged beams from the lights of the enemy troops flashing in the distance.

Their quiet trek ended in front of a door that lay concealed within a rock wall; it was covered with leaves, hiding it from accidental discovery. The unusual pendulum compass had guided them reliably, although it was not to the exit they had expected. What was more, there appeared to be no knocker that they could use.

'Didn't we walk past here earlier?' Viktor looked at the pendulum, which was still tugging on its chain. 'How come we didn't notice this door?' He turned to the group. 'Any suggestions about how to unlock it?'

'Yes, I've got one.' Spanger pushed forwards. 'Take cover. I know how to tame this beast.' He squeezed on the trigger.

The blast rippled over the landscape like a clap of artificial thunder and in the absence of the sirens, howling and bomber engines, it could be heard for miles around. The door flickered submissively from the effect of the shotgun pellets: the force field had been built up.

'Let's get out of here!' Without waiting for an answer, Spanger opened the passage, grabbed Anna-Lena by the arm and hurried out with her.

'What a prick,' Dana remarked. 'He's just exposed our position to the search party.'

'I'm still glad it worked, though – there was no knocker, after all.' Viktor walked through with Dana and found himself back in the hall with the five doors. There was no sign of the living blackness from which they had fled earlier, but the uneasy feeling remained. 'We should get a move on.' He picked up a piece of broken stone to use as a wedge for the door. 'They won't be far away.'

'Sounds good to me.' Spanger was already on his way to the corridor. Anna-Lena, who was reluctantly following him, was looking all around her.

Viktor put the pendulum in his pocket and closed the door – and at that very moment, Dana screamed with surprise and rubbed her eyes. 'What's wrong?' he enquired, alarmed.

'I – I can see again! Out of nowhere!' Dana looked at

the closed door. 'It must have been that awful place that caused it.'

'Come on,' Spanger shouted from the corridor. He wanted to get to the surface quickly, re-equip himself and then head back down to rescue Coco. 'Before those other—'

'They'll find us,' Anna-Lena said to him, her expression calm.

Viktor and Dana came running over. 'What did she say?'

'They'll find us,' Anna-Lena repeated. 'They find *everything* – they *know* everything. They are everywhere. My great-grandparents were right: they're all-powerful.'

'What's she talking about?' Dana checked her G36 and filled the magazine so she was ready for a scrap.

'Bring me my daughter,' came van Dam's angry voice through their earpieces. 'She needs to receive treatment immediately – she's in shock.'

Viktor saw it differently. Anna-Lena certainly appeared subdued, but her green eyes were a study in determination and clarity. 'We're nearly there, Mr van Dam.' He set off with Anna-Lena and Spanger on his heels, while a deeply relieved Dana secured the rear. Her worst nightmare had vanished as quickly as it had arrived.

Viktor marched along the passage, the beams of light from his and Dana's helmets darting around them.

'Shouldn't we be at the fork soon?' Dana interjected from behind. She had just spotted one of the marks she had carved on the wall to stop her getting lost on her way to the headquarters. 'I think we might be going around in circles – at the end of this corridor we'll be back in the hall.'

'That's what I thought as well.' Viktor picked up the

pendulum, which was now hanging limply from its chain. Their compass was on strike.

'No – don't tell me the corridors have moved around!' Spanger simply could not allow that to stop him. He had managed to pull himself together and he was going to return to the surface, no matter what – along with the girl, as befits a proper heroic story. And there was still a second girl needing to be saved.

'Who's to say these were the same doors and same room we started from?' Dana replied. 'I feel like anything could be happening down here.'

The familiar entrance to the hall from which they had set out appeared before them.

'Oh for fuck's sake!' Spanger kicked the rock wall in frustration.

Dana was about to try to calm him down when the rumble of a heavy door opening sounded. It swung towards them and struck the walls with a clatter. She released the safety of her automatic rifle. 'Sounds to me like they've let the dogs loose.'

Frankfurt, Lerchesberg

Walter van Dam finished his hundredth cup of coffee and placed it absent-mindedly on the saucer sitting in front of his triptych of monitors alongside piles of books and maps.

His daughter was getting closer to the surface.

He suppressed his euphoria, along with the desire to talk to his beloved only child over the radio. First she had to be brought to safety. There would be time for discussion later. Van Dam instead contented himself by staring at her every time her face appeared on one of the two cameras.

Seeing her in her borrowed armour was odd: this was not the Anna-Lena he knew. She looked like a real warrior now: his daughter the Amazon, who was having to fight for her life in the labyrinth.

Ingo swept into the office without knocking, his bad temper apparent. 'Tell me right now what sort of hell you sent us into!' He threw down the harness, pulled his frayed, dirty clothing straight and marched towards the desk. He spotted the maps immediately and his anger grew. 'So you did know exactly what to expect down there?' For a moment he wanted to hit van Dam, but he thought better of it.

'No, I didn't know.' Van Dam met his stare. 'Otherwise I'd have torn all this up long ago and razed the place to the ground, just as my mother had wanted.'

Ingo let out a deep breath. He flopped into a chair and studied the maps. 'But you've clearly been hoarding so much information about this labyrinth and the doors – how can you possibly say you don't know anything about it?'

'I'd never looked at any of this stuff – not until recently. It belonged to my grandfather and I didn't believe the stories. Unfortunately, my daughter was interested in them, until I forbade her from carrying on. Her grandmother and her mother were constantly telling her all these fanciful tales; naturally, I dismissed them as nothing more than fantastical horror stories.' Van Dam stroked his moustache, then straightened his tie. 'I've always lived my life in the present, Doctor Theobald. I've got an empire to run – I have no time to waste thinking about such matters.'

'Well, I'd say that's no longer an option.' Ingo briefly told him about the doors and the three dead men outside. The mini laptop and tablet were still in the BMW – he'd go back for them later. 'I don't think it was your daughter in the Rolls,' he concluded.

'No, it's not. Troneg's found Anna-Lena. They're on their way up now.'

Hearing Matthias' death confirmed hit him hard. The man had been an honest soul and a reliable employee. He had not deserved such a demise. 'I have no idea who the unknown murderer could be working for,' he admitted.

'For the same people who were hunting us.' Ingo took one of the sets of blueprints from the desk and peering through his round glasses, examined them. 'This is an excerpt from the cadastral record of the responsible authority. That area of the forest is designated as being built up, but . . . there aren't any further entries.'

'The house was a sawmill long before 1900. My grandfather bought the whole thing and attached a joinery and antiques shop to it. Not long after the First World War, the workshop was shut down. It stood empty and alone among the splendour of the estate. My grandfather and grandmother lived in the house for a while, but she was terrified of it – it drove her slowly mad. But she often used to talk about the past, about doors and about beings from other worlds, conspirators and sacrifices and dead children, and dozens of slaughtered prisoners. My father always dismissed her ramblings as symptoms of the disease.'

Ingo picked up a clean coffee cup from the trolley beside the desk and poured himself a cup from the almost-empty Thermos. He sniffed deeply; the aroma was enough to revive him a little. 'I'm afraid it's all true.' He picked up van Dam's grandfather's book and opened it at random. 'We'll need all the knowledge we can get if we're to get our team safely to the surface.'

The book revealed doors, side by side, made from wood, iron, sandstone, every material possible, and ranging from the simple to the magnificent. Some were as small as a stable door while others were triumphal arches, located in the most diverse places on the planet and from every culture imaginable.

Most of the handwritten notes looked as if they were encoded; they were incomprehensible to Ingo. There was occasionally something unencrypted scrawled alongside, a correction or hasty addendum. Something called *Particulae* were mentioned several times.

Faced with this treasure trove of information, Ingo feared they would have to spend weeks translating the pages, sifting through them and making decisions about what on earth they could possibly do with all this knowledge.

'I can read a lot of it,' van Dam interjected. 'It's our family's old merchant code – we used to write all our correspondence in this way to prevent competitors from understanding it. But I won't be able to decipher everything. At the end there are other statements relating to complex matters of chemistry and physics and those go completely over my head.'

With each turn of the page, Ingo's eyes widened even further. He took out his smartphone and swiped his thumb over the screen. 'Keep talking,' he muttered. 'I'm capable of multi-tasking.'

'My daughter has been listening to the stories since she was a little girl,' van Dam repeated, then added, 'She became more involved as a teenager and eventually found the old books. She was all set on going into the cellar of the abandoned mansion to find out whether my grandfather was a lunatic or a genius. But I forbade her – the house is unstable.'

'So why did she go in anyway, then?'

'Daughters don't always listen to their fathers, Doctor Theobald. She made her preparations, I found out about them and we argued. I told her I'd have the villa burned to the ground, just as my mother requested in her will – that's what drove her out there, on the night she had been intending to go to the opera. Anna-Lena is very impulsive.'

Ingo looked at the records, his fascination increasing. He picked up a loose page for which Van Dam had provided a rudimentary translation. 'It's a mixture of physical and chemical calculations.' His eyes focused on the signs and symbols that had been beyond the businessman's ken. 'And that there? That is alchemy.'

'No hocus pocus?'

'No – this explains why the effects on the doors and the force fields can be measured. What's happening is real. Unfortunately, it's still inexplicable, at least for now. I've got to change that, fast, otherwise Beate will be lost down there for ever.'

'Beate?' Van Dam frowned.

'Coco Fendi is just her stage name.'

'Ah yes, right – it fitted her so naturally that I quite forgot, Doctor Theobald.' Van Dam looked at the screens, where the resolution had once again deteriorated. 'The outages are increasing again. Maybe it's the doors themselves that trigger them.' The images on the triptych became undefined, then clearer; sometimes the sound quivered. 'Mr Troneg, hurry up,' he ordered. 'I won't be able to stay connected to you for long.'

Ingo held up a sheet written in plain text. 'There's something here about people and animals disappearing in and around the house: dogs and cats, and staff – sawmill employees. The cellar appears to be some sort of a black hole.' He flipped through the pages. 'And here are reports of mysterious creatures – and a ragged exorcist?'

The displays on the monitors suddenly went blank. The screen started blinking.

NO CONNECTION POSSIBLE

'I really didn't want to hear what you've just read out,' Spanger suddenly complained over the radio, his crackling voice barely reaching them at all. 'Creatures and the like – like the beast that Troneg and Rentski shot. And you're saying all this comes from Hell?'

'No, I don't think there's anything supernatural going on,' Ingo replied. 'Who knows what these doors can do?'

'Something like genetic manipulation, then? A cat enters one of those force fields and comes out as . . . a monster?' van Dam mused. Or the energy created almost perfect copies, like the duplicate of his daughter.

'Can we limit radio communication to just the exchange of useful information, otherwise Spanger's going to start driving us mad,' Dana requested. 'His nerves are already shot to pieces.'

There came a knock at the office door and a woman entered the room. Ingo remembered her; she was the one who had received them at the door of the mansion. She was wearing a trouser suit, her make-up perfect and not a hair out of place, almost as if she were an android with no need for sleep. 'Excuse me, gentlemen.'

'This is Ms Roth, my peerless executive assistant,' van Dam informed him briefly, still trying to concentrate on the sounds emanating from the speakers. 'Thank you, we don't need anything for the time being.'

'Ah, bollocks! I can see some armed men ahead,' came Viktor's muffled voice. 'Change of plan. We— Miss van Dam, stop!' he exclaimed suddenly. 'Don't go in there!'

Ingo and van Dam stared at each other, terrified that something had just gone badly wrong.

'Follow her!' Dana ordered. 'If the door shuts behind her, she could end up anywhere—'

'Excuse me, Mr van Dam,' Ms Roth tried again from the doorway.

'I can't keep up,' Spanger was panting through the speaker.

'I . . .'

'Not now!' van Dam snapped at his employee. 'Anna-Lena – *Anna-Lena!*' he shouted over the radio, despite being fully aware that his daughter couldn't hear him. 'Stay with the others – come out of the chamber, *immediately!*'

There was a droning rumble, followed by a clank and then a crackle. The speaker fell silent.

Ingo and van Dam looked at the three blank monitors: *complete loss of signal.*

'Mr van Dam.' The woman at the door was not giving up. 'This is really important.'

'What is it?' he barked, wiping the sweat from his forehead. 'For heaven's sake, Ms Roth, what is it?'

'There is a Professor Friedemann at the door for you.' She was looking baffled. 'But he looks rather different from when I last saw him.'

'I totally forgot about him.' Van Dam slumped in his chair. 'Please excuse my tone, Ms Roth.'

She smiled. 'Not to worry, Mr van Dam.'

'What did you forget?' Ingo frowned.

'The email.'

'Talk in full sentences, please,' Ingo pleaded. '*What* email?'

'From Professor Friedemann, asking me to pick him up from the airport – but after you had already gone underground. I thought there had been some sort of technical error.' Van Dam waved over to Ms Roth, who bowed slightly and ushered the visitor into the office.

Ingo groaned. 'Not this as well.'

The man who entered was just as thin as the man they knew as Professor Friedemann, and his clothes and glasses were identical, but otherwise he bore no resemblance whatsoever to the professor who had gone missing on their expedition. His eyes were kinder and his demeanour was strikingly less arrogant.

'Good day.' Friedemann opened his brown leather briefcase and removed some documents from it. 'I hear there's been a mix-up?' He handed the papers to van Dam. 'That should be proof enough that I'm the one with whom you've been corresponding, Mr van Dam. And here's my passport.'

Van Dam and Ingo glanced through the papers presented to them. There was no doubt about the man's identity.

'As I had been asked during our email correspondence not to contact Mr van Dam in advance, for reasons of security,' Friedemann continued, 'I adhered to that condition. It wasn't until there was no one at the airport to pick me up, despite it having been otherwise agreed, that I decided I needed to send an email. The telephone number I had been given was incorrect.'

'Unbelievable: you're the real Professor Friedhelm Rüdiger Friedemann.' Van Dam looked at his passport, concern etched on his face.

'Correct.' The professor removed his glasses and cleaned them with his handkerchief. 'Given how shocked you both are, I suppose someone else has turned up pretending to be me?'

'Yes. But he's missing now,' said van Dam curtly.

Ingo let out a breath. 'Just be glad you weren't part of the expedition, Professor. It's been quite the ordeal.'

'Oh.' Friedemann put his glasses back on his head and

looked at Ingo in his dirty, torn gear. 'Can I help? Now I'm here?'

'No. Thank you, though.' Van Dam reached into his desk drawer. He did not need any more confidants. He pulled out an old-fashioned chequebook and filled in the first page, which he tore off and handed over the geologist. 'For your trouble, Professor. Please, find yourself a nice hotel at my expense and forget all about this. And once again, please accept my apologies for the confusion.'

'That's very generous of you, Mr van Dam.' Friedemann looked at the cheque. 'That's more than sufficient. Thank you very much. If you do need my opinion about anything, please feel free to contact me. And I wish you every success,' he said courteously, and followed Ms Roth from the room.

Van Dam sank deeper in his chair, holding his head in his hands. 'A swindler.'

Ingo looked at the black screens. Who was the fake Friedemann, what did he know – and why had he gone down there voluntarily? What secrets lay beyond those doors? And then there was the small matter of that notebook. 'How did the imposter find out about this? The expedition and the chambers?' he wondered aloud.

'We will find out,' whispered van Dam, 'as soon as my daughter is safe.'

Coco was curled up in a ball, her face resting on her knees, in the corner of a cell that was barely illuminated by an ancient-looking lamp. She was shivering with cold and fear.

After they'd left the chamber, the man in the suit had

put a sack over her head, then thrown her into this room. He must have thought he could fool her by doing that, but once she'd removed the sack, Coco knew precisely where she was. The walls and the inscriptions gave that away. This was the abandoned headquarters Dana had investigated and photographed; it was a good thing she'd shown everyone the pictures.

The voice in her head had not returned. She had surely imagined the whole thing, triggered by the sirens and the roaring engines and this suffocating fear of death which had overwhelmed her.

In her desperation, Coco resorted to silently repeating one of her old stage incantations to calm herself down. It was to no avail, however, and a miracle failed to materialise.

There were no such things as miracles or magic. Her powers had abandoned her.

Coco ran her hands slowly over her blonde hair, stopping at the base of her neck. *Ingo.* Ingo would come for her. She rocked gently back and forth.

But if he didn't, then . . .

The latch of her cell door began to hum and clicked as it unlocked itself.

Did I do that? Coco thought, raising her head with joy. Light from the passage outside flooded into the room. She had stormed the castle with her magic: *anything* was possible in this place! Coco rose quickly and crept towards the exit. Her escape was to begin here.

'Now, now, Ms Schüpfer.' The outline of the man in the pin-striped suit slid gracefully into the doorway. 'Surely you don't want to leave us? Not when I'm bringing you a cellmate who's also a little lost?'

Coco hated the man for making her *Beate Schüpfer* again. She had always loathed that name.

The man in the pin-striped suit gestured to one side and two armoured soldiers appeared, pushing Professor Friedemann into the prison. 'Well, what do you think, Ms Schüpfer? Isn't it nice to see a familiar face again?' He smiled and placed a hand on each of his men's shoulders. 'Allow me to introduce myself. My name is Ritter. I've been sent here to clean up the filthy corridors. Mainly to clean up blood, it would appear.'

'We're not filth.' Friedemann stopped in the middle of the room and looked around. This had not been part of his plan.

'No, you're not. But you've got nothing to lose by staying here in our old headquarters.' Ritter's ring blazed in the light. 'We abandoned it after realising the doors had become uncontrollable and were suddenly leading to all the wrong places. And then you and the irrepressible Miss van Dam turned up and blew the cobwebs off those memories. And you're still messing with my plans.'

So Coco had not been mistaken about her whereabouts. 'What do you intend to do with us?' she asked.

'Keep you here while we capture the rest of you. And then we've got all the time in the world to talk – about everything, Ms Schüpfer.'

'What about the Arkus Project?' Friedemann walked slowly towards Ritter. This was his trump card – his pass to freedom or, even better, into this organisation. 'They might—'

'I know, I know. You've been telling my people about that often enough,' Ritter interrupted. 'But I still haven't the faintest idea what you're talking about, Professor.'

'My notebook – it's all in there!'

'Aha. And where is this infamous book of yours?'

'I . . . lost it. When your lackeys picked me up.'

'Ah!' Ritter's expression darkened. 'What a pity. I would have liked to read it.'

Coco looked at Friedemann, irritated that the geologist was trying to curry favour with the enemy. 'Do you know who Ritter's working for?'

'No, he doesn't,' Ritter replied. 'No one knows, apart from those of our number.' He motioned to his goons to shut the door. 'Please excuse me. We're still missing Mr Spanger, Ms Rentski, Mr von Troneg and young Miss van Dam. And this other chap. Not that they're about to end up in the claws of a beast like they did last time.'

'The one in the corridor?' Friedemann asked. 'What was that?'

Ritter shrugged. 'It probably came through one of the doors. But you managed to kill it. Fortunately.'

'And then?' Coco frowned at his answer. 'What's going to happen once you've caught us all?'

'We'll be going to a much nicer place. And I'll introduce you to an archangel.' Ritter laughed and the door closed behind him. 'See you later. It won't take long.'

The bolts locked with a clink. Their footsteps died away.

Friedemann turned to Coco. 'It would be great if you could put your reservations to one side and use your gift to get us out of here, Madame Fendi.'

'It won't work. There's a shield around the cells,' she lied. 'I've tried everything and I can't seem to penetrate the barrier mentally.'

Friedemann grimaced. 'Ritter and his organisation will have thought of all such eventualities, of course.' He sat down in a corner and stretched out his long, skinny legs. 'Looks like we're just going to have to wait, then.'

Coco stood over him and looked down. There was no way the professor could evade her now. 'What's in your notebook?'

'I've lost it, Madame Fendi. It won't be of any use to us,' he replied tiredly.

'It didn't belong to you.'

'No. I acquired it. In fact, it originally belonged to a Nicola something-or-other. I couldn't quite decipher it. Something French. From the nineteenth century. The woman had it on her.' He hoped his tone was sufficiently final.

He was wrong. 'Where—?'

'Madame Fendi, are you using Ritter as a way of interrogating me?' he interrupted. 'If you're able to read my thoughts, you'll be able to learn everything you want.' When Coco blushed, he laughed. 'I thought so. You're no clairvoyant. You and Theobald had an affair and because of that he gave you a certificate.'

'You think you've got the right to interrogate me now?' she retorted angrily. Lately it seemed like the whole world knew about her and Ingo. 'That's completely unreasonable.'

'I learned it from Ritter – he mentioned it on our way back. He appeared to find it rather amusing that someone had sent down a fraud who was suddenly supposed to fix everything with a magic pendulum.' Friedemann sighed. 'It looks like we've all got our secrets, and these people know them all.'

'What? *All* of us?' Coco's ears had pricked up. 'So what's yours, Professor?'

Friedemann gave her a meaningful look. 'Who says I've only got one?' His gaunt face produced a grin that suddenly turned into a booming laugh; but his eyes remained cold, emotionless and cruel.

Coco was suddenly very afraid.

CHAPTER XI

Ritter emerged on the ledge at the entrance to the corridor system. He looked entirely out of place in his pin-striped suit. A group of armoured men followed him some distance behind with their weapons locked and loaded: his bodyguards.

Ritter stepped out into the glow of their lights, a stylish leather rucksack slung over his shoulder. 'They're not here either. Go back to the hall with the doors. I'll be there shortly.'

The lights moved off without so much as a comment or word of enquiry from the men.

Ritter quickly pulled his own lamp out of his jacket pocket and placed the rucksack at his feet. 'What could have happened to them?' He shone his light into the darkness, where no light at all reflected back, then along the ledge and down the vertical stone wall.

'I know you're here.' His voice wafted through the air like an echo. 'And I am very, very disappointed in you. We had an agreement that you would handle everything at this end and in return I would bring you back one day. That's the only reason why you're still alive.'

No reply.

Ritter looked around the passage to confirm his men had all gone. He could not afford any witnesses. 'I'm in trouble because of you. A lot of trouble. You have done nothing in response to these intruders.'

A faint, dark laugh rang out from the darkness, hinting at all manner of wickedness and evil. 'Intruders? I haven't noticed any.'

'Oh, you knew about them. You know everything.' Ritter laughed. 'You've almost certainly been playing your little psychological games with them, whispering things in their ears and their minds. Telling them you want to be their friend and that you can save them if they do you a favour.'

'You know me so well. I just wanted to have a bit of fun before I—'

'You let them escape.' Ritter clicked his tongue. 'We're shutting everything down here – for good. It's become too dangerous for the Organisation.' Ritter took an envelope from his rucksack and threw it over the edge into the depths below. 'These are the instructions for your door, telling you what you have to do. Go back to your own world. I'm not angry with you.'

The paper fell silently into the gloom and was caught with a rustling sound.

Ritter smiled and retrieved three hand grenades from his rucksack, which he had tied together into a bundle.

A rattling announced the opening of the envelope with anticipation and a greedy sense of haste. After two seconds a furious exclamation could be heard. 'Empty? Where are the instructions you promised me?'

Ritter removed the circlips from the hand grenades,

waited for a brief moment, then threw the bundle over the edge, before pushing the now-empty rucksack over as well. Turning on his heel, he said, 'I'm really not angry with you.'

He stepped into the corridor. Half a second later, a muffled explosion could be heard from beyond the ledge. A red ball of flame rolled into the darkness and the floor beneath his expensive handmade shoes vibrated, causing the boulders around him to shake up and down.

'Just frightfully disappointed.' Ritter walked happily down the corridor, followed by a fine cloud of dust. He hummed a tune to himself. *The British Grenadiers*. After all, he had just snuffed out a faithful foot soldier – his *secret* soldier, known to neither Archangel nor the Organisation.

Meanwhile, his men were hunting down the intruders, who first of all knew far too much and secondly were protecting a petty thief who had stolen a very valuable splinter from him. He could not accept either of these matters.

He certainly could not allow it to be revealed that one of the most powerful *Particulae* had been lost while he was in custody of it. He would have to come up with something plausible to deceive Archangel, otherwise there would be no chance of her letting him off.

Ritter's preliminary assessment made him cautiously optimistic. They had caught Schüpfer and the fake Friedemann. Troneg, Spanger, Rentski and van Dam, meanwhile, had fled into the chamber where time had gone mad since the ancient *Particulae* had become wholly unpredictable.

He would take care of old van Dam and Theobald later, but right now, his people were waiting in the hall for him to decide what to do next.

Suddenly Ritter thought he could hear his footsteps in duplicate. He stopped.

The second set of footsteps also fell silent.

He slowly carried on walking; the echoing steps returned.

Ritter stopped again and spun around. He raised his hand holding the lamp and shone it back down the corridor leading to the ledge, but the bright light illuminated nothing but bare rock, concrete structures and brick.

'What's going on?' Ritter continued walking, this time, facing backwards. The sound of extra steps was missing this time, but as soon as he turned to face forwards and resume walking normally, the sound of the duplicate footsteps reappeared.

The soft laugh he had heard earlier in the darkness suddenly rang out, evil, dangerous and full of loathing. 'You tried to kill me.'

Ritter swore quietly and increased his pace. He would be safe when he reached his people.

His invisible pursuer remained close by. 'You're unbelievable. First you kidnap me, then you banish me to this wretched place and now you're throwing ... were they *hand grenades* ... at me?'

Ritter broke into a run.

'Now I'm wondering whether I should treat *you* like an intruder and do the job you requested of me.'

'Get back!' Ritter shouted over his shoulder into the darkness behind him. 'You should be grateful that—'

'Back? Back *where*? How am I supposed to go back without the information I need? You're demanding gratitude for making me live my life in this hole, for trying to murder me and for betraying me?'

Ritter reached the end of the corridor. He could see the lights of his heavily armed companions still a way off. He picked up his pace once more.

His pursuer stopped. 'How do I get back?'

Ritter ran as fast as he could back into the hall.

'How do I get back, Intruder?' the voice called after him. '*How?*'

BEHIND DOOR !

Spanger, Viktor, Dana and Anna-Lena stood in the empty chamber into which they had withdrawn to escape the approaching enemies. It was better than standing in the hall without any cover and engaging in a fight they had no chance of winning.

The ammunition shells from the sub-machine gun that Spanger had fired during their first stay here lay all around them.

'Any suggestions?' Viktor collected everyone's knives and wedged them beneath the entrance door in an attempt to make it as difficult as possible for their opponents to open to the door. 'Let's just hope they haven't got any explosives.'

'Quite,' said Dana contemplatively.

'What does she mean by "quite"?' Spanger pointed the

barrel of the shotgun at the entrance. He felt comfortable with the gun, but of course, the other lot had precisely the same weapons.

'Quite. We're stuck,' Dana explained. 'We've exhausted all our options.'

'Anything's better than being shot.' Spanger fiddled with his shotgun, slowly beginning to understand how it worked.

Viktor looked at Anna-Lena. 'Have you got any ideas? You must have used the doors a fair amount.'

'A little. I suppose there's something I could try.' She walked past him and placed her hand against the wood, then her ear, closing her eyes and listening carefully. Slowly she raised her arm and rapped it with her knuckles – once loudly, then twice quickly, then three times with a short pause between each one, and finally she stroked them tenderly over the door panel.

'She's gone mad,' Spanger intoned.

'I believe there's . . . power on it. Some kind of passive force field.' Anna-Lena ran her hand once more over the wood. 'I can feel it as a sort of tingling. As if . . . something's building up on the other side.' She took a step back.

A second later the door flew open and a blond man hurtled over the threshold, covered with blood and with wounds all over his body. His clothes were tattered and he wore a broken harness and badly scuffed elbow and shin pads. He ran over Anna-Lena, knocking her to the ground, but luckily, her armour cushioned the fall.

Spanger, Viktor and Dana raised their weapons.

The newcomer was holding two long antique daggers

in his battered hands, both of which had blood dripping from them. He looked around the chamber slowly, his teeth bared, breathing deeply.

'I'll blow the fucker to—'

'Nobody shoot!' Dana shouted. She had recognised the man immediately. 'He's part of the first search party van Dam sent out.'

'How do you know that?' Viktor was still nervous. The expression on the man's face – a mixture of confusion and aggression – lent itself to unpredictability.

'I'll explain later.' Dana lowered her rifle. 'Hello, Alexander. Calm down – do you hear me? We're friends. *Friends.* Don't worry, we'll bring you back to the surface with us. Back to your father.' She pulled his photograph out from underneath her Kevlar vest. 'He gave this to me, do you understand? We're your friends.'

Alexander shook his head, snorting and waving his daggers around. The blood was obviously fresh, for it ran in small rivulets onto the floor of the chamber.

'Alexander, you have to trust me,' Dana continued imploringly. 'Your father's worried. He's booked a table for you – to eat at – at the restaurant. As you always do after—'

The addled man threw a dagger at Dana, which she deftly dodged, then he rushed her.

Dana remained calm, avoided the first fierce thrust, then rammed the barrel of her G36 into Alexander's stomach, causing him to collapse, gasping for air. He dropped the other dagger, which she quickly knocked out of his reach. 'Quiet, my lad. You're all confused. This world—'

Alexander straightened up with a jerk, grabbed her pistol from its holster and as he pulled his arm back, he shot her. The bullet struck Dana in the arm, decorating the wall with red speckles.

Screaming in agony, Dana took a step away from him and swung the shoulder holster into his face, but with an animalistic grunt he managed to dodge away.

'Get down!' Viktor yelled; neither he nor Spanger could fire as long as Dana was standing in front of the young assailant. She'd become his unwilling shield. 'Rentski, get down!'

Alexander put the barrel of the P99 to her temple. 'You're all phantoms – *phantoms!*'

Without hesitation, Anna-Lena jumped up from behind him, clutching one of the curved daggers in her right hand, and quick as a flash, she stabbed Alexander twice, once in the neck and once in his torso. Her green eyes, fixed directly ahead, were disturbingly vacant, as if her body were being controlled remotely.

The young man collapsed, panting, Dana's P99 clattering to the stone tiles.

Anna-Lena winked, then her eyes jerked sideways, towards the injured Dana, and regained their focus.

'Miss van Dam – put the dagger away,' Viktor pleaded.

Anna-Lena looked down at the bloody weapon in her hand and cried, 'Oh my God!' Her fingers released the handle and the dagger fell to the floor beside the man she had stabbed. 'My God – what . . . what have I done?'

Dana checked Alexander's pulse and shook her head. 'Nothing more to be done.'

Meanwhile, the door swung shut slowly.

'Fuck, no!' Spanger tried to run, but slipped in the pool of blood and fell to the floor.

The lock clicked shut, this time making a crackling sound. The force field that Alexander had created from the other side had been erased.

'For Christ's sake!' Spanger raised his rifle. 'Let's open it again, then.'

'No, stop,' Viktor ordered. 'I really don't fancy going where that poor bloke has just come from.'

Dana looked at the wound on her arm, which had blood pouring out of it. 'Spanger, help me to put on a compression bandage, will you? That would be a far better use of your time. And then we can think about what to do next.'

Anna-Lena pointed at the motionless Alexander. 'I don't know why I did that. It just came over me. A kind of ... instinct.'

Dana gritted her teeth as Spanger began to apply the bandage. 'You saved my life, Miss van Dam. Thank you.'

'But your extra income is gone. How much was he going to give you, Rentski?' Spanger studied her. 'His father, if I understand correctly.' He tied a knot and checked the bandage was sitting correctly. 'You're no free-climber, are you? That was just your cover.'

Dana made no reply but took a step towards the corpse and patted it down. She removed his watch and wallet, then closed his lifeless eyes. She also pocketed his daggers. The stab wounds that Anna-Lena had made in his heart and neck could not have been more precise. Such exactitude betrayed years of practise, not instinct. 'Poor chap.'

'I don't understand.' Anna-Lena studied the blood on her hands. *Blood. Finger. Fists. An argument.* She had been through something like this before – recently.

Memories rose in her mind, devouring her thoughts.

She was standing in a very modern meeting room containing a large table and several screens on which some films were playing. She had just stumbled into it after having passed through a door. She was dressed in her dirty, tattered ball gown.

'Shit! Shit, how can this be?' Anna-Lena muttered, looking around her.

More doors were embedded in the walls all around the room. In the middle of the table was a tray containing some small metal splinters and chips, arranged neatly on a bed of velvet and each was inscribed with a location, date and some words. Anna-Lena took a step forwards and examined them closely. She touched one fragment after another, without taking any.

Then she glanced around at the screens and realised her mistake. These were no films. They were live recordings of important international politicians. She knew some of the men and women from the news, but the scenes before her were not public: these were of people moving around in their private abodes, some sitting down for supper with their families, or in their underwear, even in the lavatory.

Anna-Lena continued to look around.

There was a list of what looked like assassination targets and operations in prevailing global conflicts written in flowing handwriting on a whiteboard. A large block of monitors under a cover showed stock prices – for the day after tomorrow and in a year's time, if she was reading the dates correctly.

'No one will believe me.' Anna-Lena rummaged through her handbag and pulled out her smartphone to take photographs. She suddenly stopped, for the man in the pin-striped suit had entered the room.

'What the hell?' he called out, hurrying over to her.

Anna-Lena backed away from him and rattled each door in turn, but none of them opened.

'You will behave yourself – and you will explain how you got in here.' The man reached out to grab her.

Anna-Lena pushed his hands away and kicked him in the shin. With a cry, he tried to seize her red curls but she deftly wriggled out of his grasp and jumped onto the table. She leaped, trying to escape on the other side, and her lovely dress acquired another tear.

'Oh no you don't!' He pulled her legs out from under her.

Anna-Lena stumbled and crashed onto the tray of splinters. Something fine drove through the silk and pierced her skin, but the slight stinging sensation quickly vanished amid the pain of her impact on the table.

'Stop – don't you dare!' shouted the man, sliding across the table towards her.

Anna-Lena fell to the floor on the other side and jumped to her feet. She staggered forwards and rammed her shoulder against one of the doors. If it was not going to open voluntarily, she would have to try it the hard way. She might not weigh very much, but she was deceptively strong.

No sooner had Anna-Lena touched the wood than a

glimmering flicker washed over it, a loud crackle erupted and it sprang open. With a gasp, she threw herself head-long out of the office and slammed the door shut behind her.

'You were in a meeting room, Miss van Dam?' she could hear Viktor saying.

Her memories of the hereafter slipped away.

Anna-Lena returned to the present and realised she had been telling her story aloud. 'Yes I was. And the man in the pin-striped suit was there as well. Later he locked me in the chamber with the sirens, to have a bit of fun with me, I suppose. He's an arsehole and a sadist. I think his name's Ritter.

'These doors must have come from Satan himself,' Dana grumbled. 'Ritter. Yes, I heard the men looking for us in the passage calling that name.'

'Ah, damn – I forgot about this in all the excitement.' Anna-Lena fumbled in her armour for a moment. 'This will give us something useful, I hope.' She pulled out a very familiar-looking notebook.

The trio looked at her in wonder. 'That's it,' Viktor exclaimed, 'Friedemann's notebook!'

'It was lying in front of the door we came through ear-lier. I thought I'd better take it with me.'

'Show it to me.' Spanger tried to grab it, but Anna-Lena held it at arm's length away from him.

'No, we'll look for clues together. I'm more familiar with the material than you are anyway.'

As they huddled around her, she started, 'It says Nicola . . . I can't decipher her last name, but it's definitely not Friedemann.' She leafed through the pages. 'We've got notes, sketches of doors, information about certain places, then a few crossings-out and ... here!' She pointed to a picture. 'Isn't this the chamber with the five doors?'

Dana nodded. 'I bet Friedemann attacked me on purpose. The more I think about it, the more plausible it seems. And his real reason for joining the team was certainly not to save you, Miss van Dam, but to discover the secrets of this place.'

'You're right, Ms Rentski. Friedemann is definitely not a speleologist.' Viktor grew annoyed. 'It was the first time he had used a climbing harness. I saw that – I really should have caught on much sooner.'

A prolonged round of applause suddenly erupted from the door.

The quartet whirled around in alarm. Deep in concentration, they had not noticed that the door to the hall had been silently opened.

Spanger readied himself, noting Viktor had already raised his rifle.

At the threshold stood Ritter in his pin-striped suit, clapping nonchalantly. He was lit up from behind by several lamps and covered by his armoured bodyguards.

'That's the man from the office,' Anna-Lena whispered.

'Con-gra-tu-la-tions. Finally, our team of heroes emerges!' He doffed an imaginary hat. 'Although you've caused me rather a lot of trouble. You managed to last longer than the other unit, at any rate. Allow me to introduce myself: my name is Ritter.'

'Who are you, and who are all these men in armour?'

Viktor had no intention of lowering his weapon. 'What kind of organisation is this?'

'You know my name now; everything else is immaterial – but I can send you Madame Fendi and Professor Friedemann's regards. They're in my care – for their own safety.'

'What the fuck's going on?' Spanger raged. 'Let us go and . . . nothing bad will happen to you.' Another sentence from his mouth that just fell out. He really had to stop doing this, as a matter of some urgency, be less a showman, more a hero.

'Of course you may leave.'

'Fendi as well?' Dana interjected. 'And Friedemann?' She wanted to distract him, because something was definitely going on behind Ritter.

'That's not what we're talking about here. I confess it all went a little bleak earlier.' Ritter looked down at the corpse of the young mercenary. 'That is why I'm suggesting' – his eyes were now fixed on Anna-Lena – 'that I simply take back my property and refrain from killing you.' Ritter held out his hand, revealing a ring with a series of flat, shimmering splinters on it. 'If you would be so kind? I'm in rather a hurry.'

'What do you mean?' Viktor showed him the notebook. 'Did Friedemann take this from you?'

'Ask your little thief here,' Ritter said, not taking his eyes off Anna-Lena.

'Me? I haven't taken anything,' she replied hotly.

'I know you've got it – come on, hand it over!' Ritter demanded.

Anna-Lena looked at him in irritation. 'But ...'

'Right, I'm going to shoot the suit,' announced Spanger. It was time for him to do something heroically stupid. They were in a situation where there was nothing else for it.

Ritter stepped quickly to one side behind the door frame. 'I'd better be off then.' He closed the door of the chamber slowly. 'I'll be back every day to ask about my property. Let's see how long you hold out for. Oh, and by the way, just so you don't get your hopes up, you won't be able to escape from the chamber because I—'

'Fuck you!' Spanger sprang up with astonishing speed and wedged the barrel of the automatic weapon into the closing door: his act of heroism. Anna-Lena had to get out – they all had to get out. Alive. 'Eat this!' He pulled the trigger.

The chunky shotgun emptied its mixed load shot and bullets mercilessly into the hall until the magazine was completely empty. Shrill cries and swearing erupted outside, interspersed with moans and the thud of falling bodies.

'Bet you didn't expect that!' Spanger tossed the now-useless shotgun aside and drew his P99. He rammed the door with all his weight. 'Let's go – I'll cover our retreat.' Then he was out and the semi-automatic buckled immediately under the weight.

'Come on,' Viktor ordered Dana and Anna-Lena, and together, they ran out of the chamber, following Spanger, who had truly surprised them all.

Frankfurt, Lerchesberg

Ingo cast his eyes over the translated documents van Dam had provided and as he did so, he reviewed the recordings from his own gauges and compared them with the notes. Shaking his head in fascination, he added his own remarks. This was the first time in his long career as a parapsychologist and scientist that alchemical formulae actually matched empirical data.

It was getting light outside: a new day was dawning, but there was no knowing whether it would end with more puzzles or bring about the much-desired return of those who were missing.

Van Dam restlessly paced back and forth on the carpet, his headset on, occasionally taking a sip from his endless coffee. 'Troneg? Can you hear me?' he tried for the umpteenth time.

'Just leave it. Troneg's enough of a professional to report back as soon as he's back in range.'

Van Dam stopped and appeared to be wrestling with himself. Then he picked up the pot and topped up Ingo's cup. Ms Roth had provided them with fresh coffee and some eatables to keep them going. 'If only it were that easy, Doctor.'

'What do you mean?' Ingo deliberately kept his eyes down. 'Was that not the case with the first team?'

He bit his lip for a moment, then admitted, 'Yes. They went off-comms once they had found Anna-Lena – which is why I'm so worried.'

'Would have been nice if you'd told us that earlier.' Ingo looked up from the papers. 'Who were these people?'

'Mercenaries. Men with bucket-loads of experience and nerves of steel.' Van Dam looked inside his cup. 'I didn't tell you because I was afraid you'd turn down the job if I had. The make-up of your team, with your unique talents, looked far better to me this time. I felt I needed more than just firepower to save my daughter.'

Ingo asked, 'How did you find us?'

'In part through a short-notice application process and in part by asking friends to make enquiries with some . . . some very specific people. I invited you and Madame Fendi. Ms Rentski and Mr Troneg applied via an exchange for special operations. Friedemann . . . well the real one I contacted is really a luminary in the fields of geology and speleology; I hired him to provide expert help to assess the precise situation down there. But I have no idea how this fake professor found out about it, or what his motivation was.' He drank the rest of his coffee.

'The puzzles to be solved span the whole earth.' Ingo leaned back and pulled up various photos he had taken of the doors, displaying them on one of the monitors. 'Anyway, there are clear matches here between these images and the recordings your mother made.'

'My mother?'

'Yes. This is a woman's handwriting.' Ingo pointed to the lines of text. 'She obviously tried to find out the secrets. I'm already in a position to say that the markings on the door frames and knockers come from all manner of different cultures: Celtic, Babylonian, Roman, and there are some that I would have to attribute to the Far East. The same goes for the scribbles and messages on the walls.'

'Can you work out how old they are?'

'The materials, frame and door leaves don't look antique, if that's what you mean, not as a whole. It could be the case that the individual elements are from different centuries and someone just came along and put them all together.'

'Which could lead us to conclude that these sorts of . . . passages . . . have been used for thousands of years?'

'Indeed.' Ingo pointed to one of the symbols. 'That's probably a scorching sun. I've seen this one most commonly on the walls and door knockers.'

'Or an eye . . . no, an exploding star.' Van Dam moved closer and studied the sign. 'Its rays are burning everything.'

Ingo shook his head thoughtfully. 'Possibly.' He circled various sections of the photographs with his finger. 'There's a pebble here in the centre of the doors with knockers; they're referred to as *Particulae* in the records we've got. Using the knocker triggers a reaction that builds up the force field. But everything that happens afterwards' – he shrugged – 'I will need to examine more closely, and with far more precise devices than my instruments are.'

'You really want to go back down there? Apart from the doors and the dangers they present, there's also the small matter of a team of gunmen sneaking around who know far more about the place than we do.'

'Beate – I mean, Madame Fendi – is still in there, and without my expertise she wouldn't be here.' Ingo turned back to his work. 'It's my fault she's stuck down there, Mr van Dam. I won't simply abandon her.'

Suddenly van Dam reached for his headset. 'Troneg?' He strained to listen through a mass of background noise. 'I can't hear you! Is that ... *gunfire*?'

Ingo sprang up from his chair and switched the audio over to the speaker so he could listen in too.

The rattling and roaring of various automatic weapons blared through the office, interspersed with shouts, screams and gasps.

'We're on our way back,' Viktor reported. 'Spanger's securing the rear; we've got your daughter with us.'

'Good – excellent,' cried van Dam, both excited and worried.

The roaring became quieter, to be replaced by the hasty footsteps of several people running over the stone floor.

'Another one!' Spanger shouted, then, 'Oi, wanker! Who's the fraud now?' He loosed a volley. 'You won't get past me – see that, Jungsen? I'm more dangerous than you could have possibly imagined!' He sounded exuberant.

'Spanger, come on,' Viktor commanded. 'You've done your job.'

Ingo and van Dam listened with strained expressions; the video feed was still down.

'I'm a fucking good bodyguard, you know. I've always said so.' Spanger giggled like a little boy, hysterical from the euphoria of his own success. 'I've always said so: a true fucking hero—'

Then came a dull moan, followed by a rumbling sound.

'Spanger? Spanger, report,' Viktor called out. 'Rentski, go and look for him.'

Van Dam and Ingo exchanged bewildered looks.

'He's dead,' Dana reported a few seconds later.

'You sure?' asked Viktor.

'Shot in the head. I'll take up the rear,' she added tersely. 'You two go on.' She fired off a long burst. 'The enemy's on the move. We haven't got much time left.'

'What about Friedemann and Beate . . . I mean, Madame Fendi?' Ingo waited for their answer, his heart pounding.

'They're not with us. We believe they've been captured by a man calling himself Ritter,' Viktor replied curtly. 'I'll tell you all about it once we've escaped.'

Ingo stared at the displays, the indistinct flickering of their remaining images. Beate was still in the cave, with their unknown enemies. 'I've got to find her – otherwise she'll never get out.' He leaped to his feet and had hurried off before van Dam could try to stop him.

Viktor and Anna-Lena arrived at the ledge, breathing heavily and deeply relieved that their worst fear had not come to pass: thankfully, the rusty old steel cable was still stretching assiduously through the darkness to the cellar door of van Dam's mansion.

Several fibres were broken and had unravelled, judging by what they could see in the glow of Viktor's helmet lamp. The bolt cutter really had done some damage to the corroded wires.

'Come on.' Viktor clicked himself on and allowed Anna-Lena to wrap herself around him, then secured her to his armour with two more carabiners. 'Ready?'

'Yes.'

Viktor pushed off carefully and he and Anna-Lena

slipped through the cave. They reached out for the cable, grabbed it and under their combined strength, sped off briskly towards the exit.

Dana appeared on the platform and threw away her G36 – the magazine was empty, so the weapon was just unnecessary weight. She drew her pistol and briefly looked back to check the passage. 'All clear,' she announced. 'No one's following us.'

Viktor and Anna-Lena were already beyond her cone of light, but the cable was bouncing around alarmingly and making noises like a guitar string being slowly but steadily overwound. 'Come on, Rentski – who knows how much longer the cable will hold!'

It was only then that Dana noticed the damaged end; she swore loudly, then added, 'Well, hopefully long enough for us to get to the other side.' She stretched, then began to latch herself into the carabiners and rollers. The compression bandage was evidently still holding, as there were no specks of red on her injured arm. 'Let's hope we get lucky,' she muttered. 'If it breaks when we're on the last few yards, that'd be—'

Ritter, emerging out of the dark corridor, pelted towards Dana, shouting, 'Not so fast!'

She fired as he dodged her dancing beam of light, but couldn't hit him, for he was moving too fast.

Then Ritter was on her, grabbing her by the throat and slamming the pistol out of her hand with his other hand. 'Out of my way!' He grabbed her harness in order to fling her into the abyss. 'I've still got work to do.'

'I think you'll find your work is done,' hissed Dana, and

pulling one of the antique daggers from her belt clip, she plunged it into him.

The blade sliced through the thin fabric of his suit and lodged a couple of inches deep in his sternum. With a cry, he released Dana and grabbed the protruding handle of the dagger. He doubled over in pain.

Dana landed on her back, but she gave him a hard kick to the hip, which sent Ritter reeling. He stumbled past her towards the edge of the plateau, grabbing her arm at the last moment and gasping, 'At least I'll take one of you with me!'

'No, you won't.' Dana tore the dagger from his chest and Ritter screamed in agony. She plunged the blade into his forearm, sliced through his suit and broke his grip on her. 'Just you.'

Roaring with anger, the man plunged into the blackness below.

Dana staggered to her feet, groaning. 'I'm coming,' she called to Viktor and Anna-Lena as she latched herself onto the cable, swung herself off and slid back along it.

Another rusty strand gave an audible crack. The ailing cable was breaking apart.

Ritter landed hard on a rocky ledge and at the last moment managed to grab hold of a jutting piece of the porous stone with his uninjured hand. Groaning, he sat up and shone his torch on the wounds on his chest and arm; he could see his shirt and jacket were drenched in his blood.

'Shit.' Then, in the bright light, he noticed his *Particula* ring was missing – he must have lost it in the fight with the mercenary, so perhaps it was still on the plateau. That could mean his salvation.

Despite his wounds, which were making things much more difficult, Ritter tried to find grips on the rock wall to begin his ascent. Warm blood bubbled from both the hole in his chest and the cut in his arm. When he had to stop to cough, he realised that damned woman might have damaged his lungs. In that case, every second would count before one or both of them collapsed or filled up with blood.

'I haven't taken my eyes off you, *Intruder*,' said the familiar, spiteful voice, followed by a venomous laugh.

Ritter winced.

A shadow became visible in the light: a human outline. 'I can smell your blood. So someone got the better of you . . . and now you've fallen at my feet like the envelope you used as bait so you could kill me.' There came a gleeful chuckle. 'Are you trying to finish the job yourself this time? Or are you going to blow yourself up along with me as a grand sacrifice for Archangel and the Organisation?'

Ritter suddenly had a glimmer of hope. 'Help me back to the top,' he said with feigned self-assurance, 'and I'll help you in return.'

The laughter became nasty. 'You want to go back this time?'

'I swear to you—'

'You can go back no more than I can,' the voice interrupted coldly. 'Only once the Arkus Project has achieved its full strength is there any hope for me.'

'Its true strength? What . . . what do you mean?' Ritter stammered, flabbergasted. 'Then *you* know something about it?' He had not expected this, but he suddenly felt a little more confident. If he could deliver the creature he had successfully hidden from the Organisation for all these years, then he might be able to persuade Archangel to forgive his failings.

The three escapees slid along the cable above them, their helmet lights shining all around. They were well on their way to safety in van Dam's cellar.

Ritter knew this would only be a temporary sort of safety. No one could win against them. *No one.* He would like to personally take care of their elimination. The Organisation knew their names and where they lived; the fact that they had escaped now counted for nothing – that is, as long as he made it back to the plateau, found his ring and revealed his long-held secret to Archangel.

'Of course I'm familiar with the Arkus Project. At least, that's your name for it. But until that day comes, there are other things I could do,' the voice mused. 'I could escape from my prison, travel the world and see things for myself. There must be thousands of beautiful locations out there. Maybe I'm curious.'

'No! No, that would be far too dangerous,' Ritter replied hastily, trying not to groan in pain, but he was feeling dizzy now, which meant his circulatory system was beginning to fail him thanks to the blood loss. He had to get back to his team – they'd make sure he got the treatment he needed. 'I left you down here so you'd be safe.'

'So the world would be safe from me, you mean,' whispered the voice. 'The time for waiting is over. I am revoking our agreement.'

'You can't do that,' Ritter murmured, pressing his hand against the hole in his chest. He felt energy seeping out of him with every heartbeat. 'If you go up there, you'll die. Do you understand? The sun will kill you – it's not like the ones you know.'

The laughter rang out again. 'You broke the rules once and I am the consequence of your actions. I'm sure I'll like your world and you know perfectly well I'm not fussy.' Then the shadow clicked its tongue. 'Your suit will serve until I find something better.'

Ritter was about to respond when a shadowy arm jerked forward and a loud crack sounded as the creature broke the man's neck with ease.

Ritter flopped over to one side, already dead. His body lay inert on the outcrop, his eyes wide open and facing the swirling beams of light overhead. The torch fell from his hand and came to rest at an angle, illuminating the wall and the narrow ledge.

The indirect beam of light lit up the humanoid shape that had started manhandling the corpse. Ritter was quickly stripped bare and a moment or two later, his clothes were now dressing the shadow. The suit fitted its new owner perfectly; the blood, holes and slit in the arm did not bother him in the slightest. It was a temporary solution, after all.

Then the prisoner swung himself up the stone face, relishing the prospect of his imminent freedom.

Viktor and Anna-Lena gripped the cable tightly. It was making increasingly alarming noises and sagging noticeably as they made their way through the cave. The cable's tension had diminished perceptibly, which was making it harder to pull themselves forward.

Finally, the glow of Viktor's helmet lamp struck the far doorframe, which, like the cliff-face, had now become visible. 'Nearly there,' he announced. His shoulders ached from the constant strain; the last few hours had tested his body and mental toughness to the extreme.

Anna-Lena, sweating just as much as he from the exertion, looked at him and kissed him lightly on the cheek. 'Thank you.'

Viktor smiled weakly. 'You're most welcome.' He was looking forward to a few moments of rest, some food and drink and perhaps even a little bit of sleep before returning to the labyrinth with renewed vigour. Coco and Friedemann must not be allowed to stay in the hands of their unknown captives, no matter what. Who knew what Ritter and his ilk were capable of.

There were still a million unanswered questions – about the doors, the dead ends, the headquarters, the way the enemy controlled powerful people, the share prices in the future – the list went on. Friedemann's lost notebook might contain some of the answers, or he might find them himself on his next visit, which Viktor sincerely hoped he would not be undertaking alone. Dana had been shot but she still seemed fit for service. Ingo, however, probably wouldn't be much good if it came to a fight.

'It's me.' Light fell on them from behind. Dana joined them and the cable sagged even further. 'Quickly – it's about to snap!' She gave Viktor a hard shove with her foot, sending the pair unceremoniously across the threshold and into the cellar. 'It won't last much longer and—'

With a bang, the last of the fibres cracked and the cable jerked abruptly downwards.

Anna-Lena and Viktor landed safely in a tangle of limbs on the ground.

Dana reacted instantly, activating the freewheel lock on her climbing equipment to prevent her from shooting down the loose cable. She crashed against the rock face and began to swing two yards beneath the entrance. 'I'm all right,' she called out, feeling her wounded arm tearing open.

Without having the cable to block it, the door began to swing shut.

'Quickly!' Anna-Lena unfastened the hooks connecting her to Viktor, crawled over him and tried to wedge her knife between the door and the frame, but she got tangled up in the steel cable and her outstretched arm failed to reach as far as the door. 'No—!'

The door that was closing in front of Dana suddenly stopped, evidently of its own accord, a few inches before shutting completely.

The light of a torch shone upon the faces of Viktor and Anna-Lena. 'You're safe,' said Ingo from behind the light. His hand was what had prevented the door from closing.

Anna-Lena stood up. 'That was too close.'

'Where . . . where's Beate?' Ingo helped Viktor up while Anna-Lena opened the door wider. 'She wasn't up here – is she . . . ?'

'Let's get Rentski up first. She's hanging from the rope.'

Viktor gave the parapsychologist an encouraging nod. 'Madame Fendi is still in there. This Ritter chap said he had her and Friedemann, that he had spoken to them.'

Ingo hid his disappointment, but nausea was rising in his stomach as he grabbed the cable and gave it a tug. 'It wasn't the real Friedemann,' he said. He had failed to rescue Beate from the clutches of these mysterious enemies and now she was completely stuck down there – and all because of him. She had only been hired because he had faked that certificate for her.

Dana's helmet appeared and Anna-Lena jumped to her aid, supporting her weight as she climbed up. The two smiled at each other and shook hands.

Ingo wedged the door open with a small piece of wood to stop it from closing again. He needed access to the labyrinth. 'The real professor turned up at van Dam's.'

'What?' exclaimed Dana. 'We had an *imposter* with us? But—'

'Let's get out of here first. We'll bring our client his daughter, then I'll go back in,' Viktor announced firmly. 'Come on.'

They hurried up the stairs.

'I'm in too,' said Ingo – and Anna-Lena nodded as well, to the surprise of the men.

But Dana remained silent. She had every reason to find Ritter and beat the shit out of him, especially knowing he would be alone. But the armoured men would be waiting for her and she had not forgotten the horror of being blind. There didn't appear to be any good reason for her to return to the old headquarters. She silently handed Coco's pendulum to the parapsychologist. 'I think you should pay close attention to whatever this tells you until you can give it back to her.'

Ingo, fighting back tears, pocketed the pendulum with a grateful look.

Since none of them turned around at any point, they failed to notice a dark silhouette in a battered, pin-striped suit pushing its way through the door they had left wedged open.

A short-haired, platinum-blonde woman stood on the ledge at the edge of the precipice, seething. The headset in her ear was a model that was not available in any shops and could only be purchased in the not-too-distant future. She was wearing a very expensive linen suit, white, with fine black pin-stripes. Only two people in the entire world knew her real name now. She was entirely without documentation – if there were any records extant, the information would be false.

Ever since the time someone had said aloud that she bore a certain resemblance to Tilda Swinton's Gabriel in the film *Constantine*, her friends – and enemies – had called her *Archangel*. Her age was difficult to estimate – she was maybe somewhere around fifty – but then, angels were not bound by time.

She looked at the ragged remains of the rusty old cable, then at the deactivated signal-booster she had found. Using the battery-powered searchlight in her left hand, she illuminated the surrounding area. The steel cable should never have been tolerated – and she should not have tolerated

Ritter's solo ventures either, certainly not for such a long time. And now the consequences had to be borne: the *final* consequences.

Archangel carelessly tossed the transmitter over the edge. The white of her suit gleamed in the light, making her look even more like a supernatural figure.

The headset beeped; she answered the call.

'Yes?' Archangel listened. 'I still need to confirm that. It looks like Ritter has failed. I've issued *Code World Destruction*.' She turned and walked briskly down the corridor. 'I know, we should have done this earlier. Ritter told me he was searching the passages for forgotten knowledge.' She was interrupted by the caller and forced to respond to their question. 'No, he's got to be down here somewhere. I don't care. I'm going to have the doors destroyed as well. We can't take any more chances.'

A first, silent explosion lit up behind her, filling the cavern with spectacular colours. The spectra would have made the real Friedemann weep with excitement.

Archangel was unimpressed. She knew what the effects of the bombs she had dropped would be. She strode down the corridor calmly, still talking.

'Two prisoners? They're not important. I'm sure Ritter captured them for his own personal enjoyment rather than just killing them at once.' She took a second to consider her options. 'We'll leave them here. Then it's done.'

Behind her came another flash of light and a hiss signalling an impending storm.

Archangel turned into the hall and stopped in front of the middle door.

She looked at the question marks on the first three doors, drawn in lipstick by the curious young woman, before she placed one hand on the knocker. It was a risk to trust the damaged *Particula*, but it was the only quick way of entering and leaving the old headquarters.

Bright light flared through the passages and a hot, pungent wind pushed its way into the hall. When the bombs exploded, the second stage released a wave of energy that left no trace of the corridors, the halls and the caves – or the doors. For those living in the area, it would feel like an earthquake: one that would cause large parts of the forest to collapse.

'Tell me, have you ever heard of the Arkus Project?' she asked the person on the other end of the call. 'One of the men from the search party mentioned it. I've got a feeling this is something we need to pursue so we're not surprised by something that might thwart our plans.'

The answer had a dramatic effect on Archangel's expression, which suddenly changed from annoyed to alarmed. She used the knocker ring, pressing down hard on the *Particula*. The door *whirred* and the roaring and thundering stopped suddenly, almost as if the portal could sense it was being used for the last time and was mourning that fact.

Archangel opened the passage. 'In Old Irish script? From the fourth century BC? With Basque origins?' She looked behind her and saw the bright white light racing towards her. Everything was going according to plan. 'No, I had no idea that Basque culture had no links to other European cultures or that it was linguistically isolated.'

Archangel waited for a reply, then responded, 'So what's

that got to do with the Arkus Project?' She took a step across the threshold into the darkness beyond. 'We'll discuss this later. I'll be losing reception any minute now.'

The door closed behind her.

The gleaming light reached the hall, accompanied by an explosion that melted the rock.

Frankfurt, Lerchesberg

Walter van Dam sat at his desk and slowly raised his head as he heard loud voices and running footsteps outside his office. His throat tightened and his heart ached with anticipation.

The door flew open, Anna-Lena came running in and van Dam leaped out of his chair and rushed over to greet her. She threw her arms around his neck. Father and daughter were embracing each other, silent tears pouring down their cheeks, as Ingo, Dana and Viktor entered the room, dirty, sweaty and utterly exhausted. Ms Roth stood smiling in the doorway, basking in the vicarious glow of paternal love.

Ingo was hanging on to the pendulum in his pocket as if it were the most precious thing on earth. He clenched his teeth at the sight of van Dam and his daughter being reunited. Those two had been granted a happy ending, but he had not yet been afforded such luck. Beate was waiting for him to rescue her from a situation for which he was entirely responsible.

Dana briefly ran her hand over her trouser pocket, checking that she was still carrying the watch belonging to the young mercenary. She gave a resigned sigh at the thought of having to deliver the tragic news to his father.

Viktor was glad that the matter had come to a satisfactory conclusion for both father and daughter. They had driven back from the old house in the Mercedes, leaving behind the Rolls. It wasn't their job to dispose of the bodies, but they had put the dead strangers in the limousine. Anna-Lena had at least been spared the ordeal of seeing her murdered clone. No one wanted to see themselves dead.

Van Dam released his daughter and looked at her happily, then, still incapable of speech, he pulled her back towards him and kissed her on the forehead.

After that, he shook hands with each of the team, his fingers still damp with the tears he'd had to wipe away. 'Thank you! Thank you all – I don't know how—'

'I know how. I need equipment, preferably the same as we were given at the start,' Viktor interrupted. He would insist on this at least. 'Doctor Theobald and I will go back to look for Miss Schüpfer once we've rested up a bit.'

'Don't you know?' Van Dam gazed at him in astonishment. 'I heard it over the radio. I'm not sure whether the passage still exists.'

'Why not?' Ingo practically yelled. 'What's happened?'

'An earthquake, followed by an explosion. The house has been destroyed.' Van Dam switched on the television and searched for a news channel. Helicopter images showed an enormous rupture in the surface: the forest had sunk into the ground and was on fire.

'My God,' Ingo groaned, staggering into a chair. He felt cold and nauseous. 'Beate – she was still down there . . .'

'Whatever blew up must have been pretty spectacular,' Dana remarked. 'I think Ritter and his organisation didn't want us – or anyone else – taking a closer look.' She laid a hand on Ingo's shoulder. 'They'll have definitely moved their prisoners out beforehand. Don't lose hope.'

Ingo was grateful for Dana's words. He immediately began thinking how best to find and free Beate. He started picking through the records for the grounds and the doors spread out over his client's desk.

'This is the way – we can do it using the information here,' he announced after a few minutes.

'The old headquarters has been destroyed anyway.' Anna-Lena looked at the drawings. 'Now you have to believe me, Papa.'

Ms Roth brought in mineral water, coffee and tea and sandwiches, and at the sight of the food, the returning team realised they were all ravenously hungry. This might not be a real victory, but they had survived the ordeal and that counted for something.

'I know this is asking a lot, but … Mr van Dam,' Ingo insisted, 'you have to help us – you've got the means to do so. The means *and* the knowledge. We really do need your help to find out where they've taken Beate.'

Anna-Lena put a hand on her father's shoulder. 'Of course he'll help us. After all, my family has an obligation now.'

The businessman looked at his daughter in astonishment. 'Anna-Lena, surely you don't intend to—?'

'Great-grandfather had something to do with the doors and the strange people down there, Papa. No one can deny that. There are clues everywhere in these records. And what I saw in that headquarters – that modern headquarters – was unbelievable. We've got to stop them. Who knows for how long they've been deciding the fate of humanity?' Anna-Lena picked up the notebook belonging to someone called Nicola that the fake Friedemann had lost. 'This is incredibly valuable and I'm sure it'll be able to help us. Let's piece together the puzzle.'

'I've got to find Beate,' Ingo insisted.

Van Dam looked at his daughter with disbelief. 'Darling, I've just got you back and now you want to go and put yourself in danger all over again? In such great danger?'

She nodded. They were all looking determined, as if they had formed an unbreakable covenant down in the cave. Even Dana had changed her mind and decided to stay with the others.

'Spanger would have come with us as well, I'm sure.' Viktor had never thought he'd be talking up the man's bravery, but in his time underground, he'd somehow transformed from an action-film caricature to some sort of real hero.

'To Spanger.' Dana raised her glass and her gesture was echoed by the others.

Viktor took a sip. 'There's plenty for us to find out, such as who on earth the Friedemann imposter was.'

'Aside from that,' Ingo interjected, 'they know where you live, Mr van Dam, and they certainly know far more about your parents and grandparents than you do. I think Ritter's people won't wait long to ensure their secrets remain safe, even if they have blown up the old headquarters and the villa in the woods. That's going to affect you, your daughter . . .'

'. . . and us,' Dana added, holding her injured arm. 'Count me in. Even if it's just for my own interest.'

Van Dam looked at the quartet from his desk, perturbed, then he banged the tray with his fist. 'You're right, all of you! We shall have to pre-empt them.'

Ingo breathed a sigh of relief. 'Then let's go. The doors are portals, passages; and they're easy to open if you know how. We need to work out how to get to their headquarters as soon as possible – their new headquarters – and disrupt their plans.'

'Plus, Nicola's book has got a list of other doors that might help us to find the headquarters.' Anna-Lena rubbed an itchy spot on her back, not knowing it was where the *Particula* splinter had pierced her skin.

'I'll arrange for financial support.' Van Dam looked at his daughter, who smiled back at him and squeezed his hand gratefully. 'I promised you this, Mr Troneg, as long as you returned my daughter safely to me. And you've upheld your side of the bargain.'

Viktor smiled. 'You are an honourable man.'

'Hopefully we can make up for the actions of my great-grandfather and his friends.' Anna-Lena flipped through the notebook. 'There's something else here, about "the Arkus Project". It appears to relate only partially to the doors. It's probably another site – a larger one, by the looks of it.'

Ingo clapped his hands. After food and coffee, filled with new energy, he had started to dare to hope. 'Quick shower, fresh clothes and then we'll be off – we've got a lot to discover.' He hung Beate's pendulum around his neck and pointed to the notebook. 'May I see it?'

Anna-Lena handed it over to him.

'I've got to make a call,' said Dana with a sigh. 'And a doctor would be a good idea, before my arm drops off. A discreet one, mind. I can't have them reporting these gunshot wounds.'

'A capable surgeon is waiting for you in the guest wing, Ms Rentski.' Van Dam picked up the phone and gave his secretary some instructions. 'I had arranged for one to be here ready as a precaution. You'll be patched up without a fuss.'

'Who are you calling,' Viktor asked curiously. 'Cancelling a date?'

'Alexander's father. He won't have to make any more restaurant bookings. Although I'd have rather given him different news.'

As Dana walked out, Viktor rose. 'I need a shower and a few hours' sleep, otherwise I won't be able to function.'

'And you shall. Tell Ms Roth what you need. The guest rooms are at your disposal,' van Dam offered.

'Thanks. See you later.' Viktor left the office.

Meanwhile, Ingo spotted a list in their recently acquired notebook. 'Ah, see here? These are the doors we need to look at. The author has marked them separately.' He showed the page to van Dam and his daughter. 'With their locations as well. We'll just have to visit each one and have a look around.' He was eager to leave: Beate's well-being was his priority now.

'Which one do you want to start with?' Anna-Lena leaned forward and looked at the page. 'Looks like they're scattered all over the world.'

'We can decide that together. Later.' With a long sigh, Ingo touched the pendulum around his neck. They would set off tomorrow; he would make sure of that.

'I'm going to carry on translating the records my grandfather left behind,' van Dam announced, suppressing a yawn himself. 'There might still be some important clues hidden in them.'

Ingo tiredly rubbed his ears. He knew he had to try to get some sleep, no matter how difficult it would be, for they would not get far without clear heads. Body and soul definitely needed a little respite.

The telephone on van Dam's desk rang.

After a brief pause, he lifted the receiver. He was not in the mood for a business discussion. 'Walter van Dam.'

He listened, his features blanching, then, frowning, he activated the loudspeaker and hit the *record* button so he could play the discussion back to Viktor and Dana later. 'Would you please repeat that? I've turned on the speakerphone.'

A woman's voice laughed softly. 'Certainly, Mr van Dam. You do not know me, but your daughter and her new friends recently made our acquaintance. I am the late Mr Ritter's superior.'

Anna-Lena and Ingo held their breath. They had expected to encounter resistance at some stage, now they'd aroused the interest of what Ritter had called 'the Organisation', but it came as a nasty shock that the other side had got in touch quite so quickly.

'What have you done with Beate?' Ingo shouted.

'You should know that my contacting you is a once-in-a-lifetime matter and is owed to your collective bravery. You should also know it would be easy for us to remove you from the equation in a matter of minutes,' Archangel continued. 'You did an excellent job down there, and that is why we are granting you your lives. But consider yourselves, if you will, as a bomb with an immense radius. Should you mention your experiences to *anyone*, that bomb will blow up and end with your deaths, the deaths of your family, of your friends and of your friends' friends.' The woman took a breath. 'Should you undertake any further research, you will blow up. If we spot any of you in the vicinity of any of our special doors, you will blow up.'

'You've got some nerve!' whispered van Dam with barely suppressed rage.

'It's the truth. And you know we're not making empty threats, Mr van Dam,' said Archangel, her voice suddenly harsh. 'If you behave yourselves, in one year's time we will release Professor Friedemann and Ms Schüpfer. You are being watched, ladies and gentlemen. Do anything that displeases us and from that day on, you will be the death of anyone of value to you, anything you have ever looked at or touched.' She cleared her throat and sounding curiously satisfied, added, 'We will be sending a messenger during the day to pick up your documents, plus the notebook and everything the van Dam family owns concerning the doors. I would also like to have the splinter back. Tell your daughter.'

At least she now knew what it was Ritter had wanted back from her. 'Ritter took it from me!' Anna-Lena shouted, thinking on her feet. 'He said he wanted to use it for his own purposes. Because of something he called the Arkus Project.'

'Then he did know more than I'm comfortable with. That little bastard. Oh well, he's received his punishment now,' Archangel murmured, almost to herself, and, apparently swallowing Anna-Lena's lie without question, finished, 'I wish you all a pleasant life. Use it wisely.'

Click.

Ingo was overwhelmed with anger, helplessness and a deep hatred for the kidnappers, but on the outside he remained unmoved and unaffected. His eyes were fixed on the scattered documents and the notebook in Anna-Lena's hand, then he glanced up at van Dam and his daughter.

Slowly, the trio came to the cruel recognition that the plans they had been making so enthusiastically had been crushed. The Organisation would obliterate everyone around them – because they could. Because they had the means.

'We have no answer to that,' whispered Ingo helplessly, pushing himself up out of the chair like an old man. 'I'll go and tell Rentski and Troneg. They need to listen to the message. They'll come to the same conclusion.'

'Doctor Theobald, I ...' Anna-Lena started, looking shocked.

'Leave him,' said van Dam, placing one hand on hers.

'He's right. They've got the better of us. In every way possible.'

Ingo staggered through the office towards the door. In the adjoining room, Dana was just delivering her tragic news over the phone and Viktor was retrieving a dressing gown and some towels from a servant.

His face told them immediately that something terrible had happened.

'It's over,' Ingo stuttered, before bursting into tears.

ECHOES

Germany, Spessart

Nine-year-old Ina was running through the forest playing hide-and-seek, but this time she had to take a different path from the one she generally used on the walks with her mother because of the earthquake. Even Ina's solidly built family home had quivered from the impact and the small collection of elf figurines in her bedroom had fallen over.

After the quake, there had been an enormous explosion that had destroyed the empty villa Ina and her friends used to walk past to scare each other. They called it Ghost Castle.

The forest surrounding the old sawmill was still burning, just as the news on their car radio had reported. The reporter's voice on the radio had told her that experts suspected an underground methane bubble had been released during the tremor and had gone up in a tremendous burst. Ina did not know what methane was, but whatever it was, was nasty and it reeked.

'. . . nine, ten!' Her mother's good-natured voice rang out. 'Ina? Are you hiding?' Ready or not, here I come!'

Ina squeezed her way through the green bushes and saw a man sitting on the ground behind her, leaning against an apple tree. His pin-striped suit was scorched and shredded. His features were almost unrecognisable as a result of the soot and blood all over him. His breathing was quick and rasping; he gasped and moaned as if he had just finished running a marathon.

She stopped in shock, then shouted, 'Mummy! There's a man over here – he looks hurt!'

'It's all right. I've just got to . . . get something to eat,' breathed the man in a scratchy voice. 'This sun – it *hurts*. It's burning me worse than the fire I've just escaped from.'

'Ina, where are you?'

'Here, Mummy – I'm over here!'

The injured man in the suit cleared his throat. 'Have you got any food on you?'

Ina nodded. Even though she was afraid, she knew she was supposed to help people who were in difficulty. 'A choc'late bar.' She took it out of her pocket. 'Would you like it?'

'Ina? Don't approach him,' her mother shouted. 'Do you understand me, Ina?'

'Chocolate. Chocolate is good. Do you know, little Ina, I think I'm dying in this sun. At least I'll have something sweet on my tongue before I go.'

Ina looked up at the sun, which was obscured by the dark smoke from the fire. 'Like Superman, but the other way around?'

'Superman?'

'You don't know Superman?'

'No.'

'Oh. Well, he's a superhero from another planet who

gets special powers from our sun.' Ina gave him a pitying look. 'But our sun is killing you.'

'Yes, I'm afraid that's exactly what it's like.'

'Oh. That's a shame.' Ina's doubts had evaporated. The man did not look nasty – only injured and weak, like her grandma in hospital.

'I agree.' The man smiled beneath the layer of dirt and soot. 'Would you bring me the chocolate, please?'

Ina raised the hand holding the chocolate bar.

At the same time the man stretched out his own bloody, battered hand in the tattered suit jacket sleeve. His burnt, soot-covered fingers drew closer to her, trembling, then he grabbed the chocolate bar slowly. 'Thank you, little Ina.'

'You're welcome.' She looked around and thought about what she could do. 'If we put you in the shade, would that be better?'

'I don't think so. But we can try it. Under the earth – that would do the trick. But I haven't got much time left. Let's get your mother to hurry up a bit.' His injured fingers suddenly dropped the chocolate bar and grabbed the child's wrist with lightning speed.

Ina screamed loudly with shock.

'Ina?' her mother called out in alarm, cracking branches and twigs as she rushed over to where she thought her daughter was. 'Ina, where are you?'

Would you like to know what would have happened to our team of rescuers if you had opened the door marked with a question mark or the door with an exclamation mark?

Pick up *DOORS ? COLONY* or *DOORS ! FIELD OF BLOOD* and discover a whole new adventure!

ABOUT THE AUTHOR

Markus Heitz studied history and German language and literature before writing his debut novel, *Schatten über Ulldart* (*Shadows over Ulldart*, the first in a series of epic fantasy novels), which won the Deutscher Phantastik Preis, Germany's premier literary award for fantasy. Since then he has frequently topped the bestseller charts, and his Number One-bestselling *Dwarves* and *Älfar* series have earned him his place among Germany's most successful fantasy authors. Markus has become a byword for intriguing combinations: as well as taking fantasy in different directions, he has mixed mystery, history, action and adventure, and always with at least a pinch of darkness. Millions of readers across the world have been entranced by the endless scope and breadth of his novels. Whether twisting fairy-tale characters or inventing living shadows, mysterious mirror images or terrifying creatures, he has it all – and much more besides.

DOORS is a work of new opportunities and endless possibilities, with each book following our team of adventurers as they choose a different door. Do you dare to cross the threshold and explore the unknown worlds beyond?

WHICH DOOR WILL YOU CHOOSE NEXT?

When his beloved only daughter goes missing, millionaire entrepreneur Walter van Dam calls in a team of experts – including free-climbers, a geologist, a parapsychologist, even a medium – to find her . . . for Anna-Lena has disappeared somewhere within a mysterious cave system under the old house the family abandoned years ago. But the rescuers are not the only people on her trail – and there are dangers in the underground labyrinth that no one could ever have foreseen.

In a gigantic cavern the team come across a number of strange doors, three of them marked with enigmatic symbols. Anna-Lena must be behind one of them – but time is running out and they need to choose, quickly. Anna-Lena is no longer the only person at risk.

They little expect door ? to take them back to the 1940s – but this is not the 1940s they know. In this timeline, Nazi Germany capitulated early, the US has taken control of Europe and is threatening the Russian-led Resistance with a nuclear strike. If the team is to rescue Anna-Lena – and survive themselves – they will have to stop this madness – at all costs!

DOORS: THREE DOORS, THREE DIFFERENT ADVENTURES. WHICH DOOR WILL YOU CHOOSE?

Available in paperback and eBook

Jo Fletcher
BOOKS

WHICH DOOR WILL YOU CHOOSE NEXT?

When his beloved only daughter goes missing, millionaire entrepreneur Walter van Dam calls in a team of experts – including free-climbers, a geologist, a parapsychologist, even a medium – to find her . . . for Anna-Lena has disappeared somewhere within a mysterious cave system under the old house the family abandoned years ago. But the rescuers are not the only people on her trail – and there are dangers in the underground labyrinth that no one could ever have foreseen.

In a gigantic cavern the team come across a number of strange doors, three of them marked with enigmatic symbols. Anna-Lena must be behind one of them – but time is running out and they need to choose, quickly. Anna-Lena is no longer the only person at risk.

Who could have imagined that the portal marked with ! would take the rescuers into a different time completely: it is now the early Middle Ages – and they are about to find themselves in the middle of a world-changing battle . . .

DOORS: THREE DOORS, THREE DIFFERENT ADVENTURES. WHICH DOOR WILL YOU CHOOSE?

Available in paperback and eBook

Jo Fletcher
BOOKS